DRIVEN TO CONQUEST—
IN A WORLD RULED BY HATE

Sam Palmer—He knew all about hate and killing, but he had to be taught to love.

Caroline Potter—She was proud and passionate, but just a girl—until Sam stirred up her unquenched womanly longings.

Atticus Perry—The fiery black sergeant was determined to prove himself a soldier as well as a man.

Bokhari—He was ruthless, fearless and would stop at nothing to avenge his people with a river of white man's blood.

Jack Hoffenberg
Anvil of Passion

AVON
PUBLISHERS OF BARD, CAMELOT AND DISCUS BOOKS

ANVIL OF PASSION is an original publication of Avon
Books.

AVON BOOKS
A division of
The Hearst Corporation
959 Eighth Avenue
New York, New York 10019

First Avon Printing, February, 1971
Sixth Printing

BOOK I

CHAPTER 1

THE SOLID BLACKNESS OF ARIZONA NIGHT, BROKEN ONLY by scattered pinpoints of tiny jeweled stars, enveloped the desert like a blanket. From the northeast, the brisk cold wind moved down across the ragged peaks and rims of the Maricopa and Sauceda mountains chilling the floor that had by day blazed under relentless heat. Now, that wind, icy-tinged, washed loose dirt and debris through steep canyon passes, sweeping it over the rolling slopes of Monte de Lágrimas.

On the desert floor, sand swirled before the gusting wind, driving tumbleweed, broken sticks and straw erratically in all directions; adding another layer of dust on isolated ranch houses and barns, stinging into the hides of range cattle and corraled horses, sifting through the skeleton rafters and uprights of other ranches that had been burned out and left to mark attacks by Apache raiders from the south in Sonora, Mexico.

Nine miles southeast of the Sauceda foothills, the wind roiled on, lashing with unrestrained fury at Fort Bandolier, whipping the tall multiarmed saguaro sentinels standing guard over a vast parched garden of low-growing brush; cholla, prickly pear, gnarled juniper and snapping ocotillo branches. Out there, hidden in burrows and beneath rocks, desert families of lizards, snakes, gila monsters, rodents and birds slept, waiting for the wind to abate and the warmth that would come with the morning.

On the ten-foot-high platform that ran around the entire inside wall of logs that enclosed Fort Bandolier, sentries stood with carbines ready, huddling inside their greatcoats, peering out into the nothingness of black night, unable to distinguish saguaro from mountains from sky; yet the watchers were alert, always aware that the Apache was somewhere out there waiting for his opportunity to strike at the Fort, his prime target west of Tucson and south of the Gila River; at least, keep it under watch to count the comings and goings of its patrols, knowing to the man how many soldiers remained to defend against attack; keeping it under surveillance while their brother Apaches roamed about almost at will attacking isolated ranches, killing, burning, running off cattle, horses and mules, destroying precious wells by dropping dead animal—and not infrequently human—carcasses into them to render them unfit for water consumption.

On the rampart above the Main Gate, which was Post Number One, the sentry heard the soft clatter of boots, the clink of a sword chain as the Officer of the Day, First Lieutenant Lewis Carpenter, stepped out of the guardhouse. There was a pause for a brief moment and the sentry heard the spin of Carpenter's Colt .44 as he checked its load before making his four o'clock rounds. Then the guardhouse door opened and the Sergeant of the Watch, Art Petrie, came out onto the porch, carrying his pistol belt over one arm while his cold fingers worked feverishly to button his outer coat. Carpenter looked at Petrie with amused tolerance and said, "Trouble sleeping, Sergeant?"

Petrie was a well-liked, rawboned man of about twenty-six who, in garrison, on patrol or in battle, had often shown superior qualities, but seldom talked of his military background. Now, in the lantern light that spilled through the doorway, he flushed and replied, "Sorry, Lieutenant. With all the excitement last night, I didn't get to sleep until half an hour ago. I—"

Carpenter said, "It's all right, Petrie. I don't imagine anyone in the Fort is getting too much sleep tonight." He hesitated while Petrie completed buckling his gunbelt around his waist, then added, "God, I could use a cup of hot coffee."

"There should be some in the cook shack, sir. I can get a pot of it and—"

"Do that, will you, while I make rounds. Keep it hot on the guardhouse stove."

"Yes, sir. I'll catch up."

"Don't bother. I'll handle it myself. While you're at it, make sure the stable sergeant is on his toes, then wake Sergeant Major Riley. Palmer is bunking in with him and is due to leave before dawn."

"Yes, sir."

"And Lieutenant Zimmerman's patrol is due out."

"Yes, sir. At first light. The lieutenant, Scout Logan, Sergeant Tyler, Corporal Zentz and eight men."

Carpenter smiled. "Do you always commit the O.D.'s order list to memory, Petrie?"

"Yes, sir. I think it's best for two to know. A system of checks and balances."

"I'm glad you think the way you do. Where did you get that 'checks and balances' thing?"

"My father, sir, may he rest in peace. He was head accountant in a Richmond bank. 'Checks and balances' was a favorite expression with him."

"He sounds like he was a man with a very orderly mind."

"He was that, sir. He believed that for every action there must be a reaction, for every force, a counterforce, and for every credit, a debit. In people, nature and in figures."

"A very intellectual point of view."

"Yes, sir. He was an educated man, but timid. He died poor."

It was a curious statement, almost an indictment, and took Carpenter by surprise. "Petrie—" he began, and paused.

"Yes, sir?"

"Ah—never mind. Except that it is quite possible he may not have died as poor as you may think." Before Petrie could, if he had intended to, reply, Carpenter walked toward the rampart ladder beside the Main Gate, then paused and turned back. "Did you say Richmond, Petrie? Virginia?"

Without hesitating, Petrie replied, "Yes, sir. I fought on the other side."

"Rank?"

"First Lieutenant, sir, but according to the surrender terms, former Confederate Army officers were not allowed to hold officer rank in the Federal Army."

"Yes. Of course. Well—I'll look for that coffee when I get back."

As his foot hit the first rung of the ladder, the sentry's voice boomed out. "Halt! Who goes there?"

"Officer of the Day."

"Advance, Officer of the Day, and be recognized!"

Lieutenant Carpenter's day had begun.

In the stables, Sergeant Brigham Quitt put a match to the wick of his lantern and at the same moment called out, "Rise an' shine, you sleepin' beauties! Let's start movin'! Up on your flat feet, you horsemaids! We got a patrol to

11

move out. Ingram! Get that mule packed for Sergeant Palmer an' his horse fed an' saddled. Put an extra grain bag on the mule an' get a second canteen filled. Peters! Zeno! Best! On your feet!"

The four men began the motions of rising, groaning and creaking in the early morning chill, pulling fatigue overalls up over long underwear, lacing up work boots.

"Oh, Jeez!" ex-corporal-now-Private Ingram moaned.

Private Zeno said to no one in particular, "Join the cavalry an' ride, they tellen me when I signed on. What they meant was, get ridden by a flea-bitten sergeant with the heart an' brains of a goddamn ornery mule."

"Take it easy," Private Best enjoined. "That bastard hears you, we'll be cleanin' out latrines as well as stables."

Sergeant Quitt parted the burlap sacking that separated his private quarters from the double stall which had been rebuilt to hold four wooden double-decked bunks, his hairless cannonball head gleaming with dampness from a quick dip in his washbasin. His walnut-tanned face cracked into a malevolent grin. "You got me all cussed out yet, Ingram?"

Zack Ingram, sitting on the edge of his cot, drawing on the second boot, looked up with sleepy-eyed innocence. "Who, me, Sarge?"

"Who the hell else but you is named Ingram in here?" Quitt snapped.

"Dunno, Sarge. You the on'iest man knows ever'thing aroun' here, ain't you? 'Swhy you wearin' them three stripes, ain't it?"

"Ah, smart boy. Leastways, I know enough not to go brawlin' over a Mexican whore in Malhado an' losin' my stripes, three months' pay an' windin' up on stable detail."

"How come you're on it, Sarge?" Ingram asked slyly.

"Because I *like* horses, that's why, Private. An' mules. A damn sight more'n I like most people. Now get movin' on the double or all of you goin'a miss breakfast." Quitt allowed the burlap shield to drop into place and backed out.

Best said warningly, "You foul us up again, Ingram—"

"Ah-h, shut up—"

Zeno laughed. "Is that you talkin' or the two stripes you lost, Zach?"

"I had 'em before, I'll have 'em again. An' when I do, Zeno, you'll be laughin' outta your tailside."

"Yeah. Like they say, Private Ingram, rank do have its

privileges. Onliest thing is, you ain't got no more stripes than the rest of us right now, so save it for the Resurrection."

They were dressed and their day, too, had begun.

Sergeant Major Peter Riley, despite only two hours in bed, needed only the light touch of Sergeant Petrie's hand on his shoulder to bring him awake from a deep sleep. Only since Matt Donnelley had been killed in Chancla Canyon the week before had he become the top-ranked noncommissioned officer in the Fort, falling heir not only to Donnelley's extra stripes, but his private quarters: a one-room affair that stood on two-foot stilts between D and E barracks. Only four hours ago, he had had another cot placed in it for Sergeant Sam Palmer in which to spend his last night in the Army.

"Wh—?"

"It's Art Petrie, Sergeant Major."

"Oh." Riley sank back on his pillow for a moment. "I'm up, Art. You can go ahead."

"Uh-uh, Sarge. Two feet on the floor. Orders."

Matt Donnelley's orders, Riley recalled. In waking a relief man, or any sleeping man, he could not be considered awake unless he had two feet on the floor, which would necessitate sitting up. "Sure," Riley said compliantly. He swung around and placed both feet on the cold, raw boards of the floor, shivering slightly.

"Want your lamp lit, Sarge?" Petrie asked in a low whisper.

"No. I'll get dressed first, then wake Palmer."

"I'm heading past the cook shack. Send some coffee over?"

"Yeah. Thanks, Art."

Petrie left quietly and the night fell silent again. Riley found his boots and woolen socks and drew them on over his long underwear. From the chair beside his bed he picked up a pair of blue woolen trousers, slipped them on quickly, then his shirt. As he pulled on his cavalry boots, Sam Palmer stirred in the other cot. "Pete?" he called out.

"Just gettin' dressed, Sam."

"How long to first light?"

"About an hour."

"I want to be on my way—"

13

"Sam, what's all the rush? Whyn't you wait a couple days an' go in to Tucson with the mail escort?"

"I've got to get to Tubac as soon as possible, Pete."

"You're takin' a risk, man—"

"I've traveled alone before."

"Listen to the man!" Riley said exasperatedly. "Before ain't the same as now. After you brought in Anaka's head last night, every benighted heathen in Arizona Territory'll be lookin' for your head. Cochise'll put one hell of a price on you, man. Some two-bit *bandolero* or bushwacker could become a rich man if he brings you in alive."

"Pete, I've lived through four years of a bloody war and two years out here fighting Apaches. I think I can make it to Tucson and Tubac on my own." Palmer sat up and began pulling his clothes on. "God, I'm stiff from head to foot."

"Petrie's sendin' some coffee over. The stable detail's gettin' your horse an' a pack mule ready. Soon's you finish, we'll eat an'—"

A Mexican boy, the son of one of the kitchen help, knocked on the door and entered, carrying a canister of steaming coffee and two thick mess-hall mugs. Riley, lighting his oil lamp, turned and indicated the small pine table. "Put it there, *muchacho*."

"*Sí*, Señor Pete."

They drank the hot coffee gratefully while Palmer continued to dress, his new civilian buckskins contrasting with Riley's Army blue. He pulled on his own cavalry boots and tried on the soft felt hat with a wide brim, planter's style. Riley grinned and said, "How's it feel, bein' a civilian?"

"It'll take some getting used to. Where'd it all come from?"

"The sutler's store."

"I mean, who ordered it?"

"The old man. Colonel Hatfield himself. Man, takin' Anaka out of circulation, like the colonel says, it lifts a lot of pressure off the Fort. I heard him tell Captain Greene it was worth a whole regiment, gettin' rid of Anaka. At least for a while. The clothes are his present to you. There's another outfit on the pack mule, a week's supply of grub, water, feed an' ammunition—"

"It won't last for long, Pete. I mean the raids. Ask Willy Logan. Cochise will send somebody in to take Anaka's place, you can bet on it. He's got to keep this

14

Fort bottled up and shorthanded, else he'll lose everything he holds west of Tucson and south of the Gila River. On my way in late yesterday, I saw the smoke signals starting already. I'll bet a month's pay Cochise knew about Anaka before I brought the news in last night."

"I won't be arguin' the point, Sam. An' speakin' of a month's pay, the old man gave me an envelope with four-hundred-eighty-seven dollars to put in your saddlebag, the money you had ridin' on the books. It's over there at the foot of your cot."

"Thanks, Pete. It'll come in handy now."

"You made any plans?"

"None beyond getting to Tubac and try to explain to Ruth's father and sister how I happened to leave her and the baby out there on the ranch all alone—"

"There were the Grays, McLenahans and Hamiltons—"

"And all of them wiped out together. It's not much of a comfort, Pete. Not to me, Max or Caroline—"

"Sam, it wasn't your fault an' you shouldn't take it that way. She wouldn't come in to the Fort when you begged her to, said with the McLenahans, Grays an' Hamiltons around her, an' bein' an expert rifle shot—"

"*I* know, Pete, and *you* know, but it doesn't make it any easier to bear. And how do I explain to Max Potter and Caroline that I wasn't man enough to insist, demand, bring her and the baby in by force if need be?"

When Riley did not reply, "Pete, do me a favor?"

"Sure, boy. Anything."

"You get a chance, ride out to the ranch there to see that the coyotes and wolves don't get to the grave. Soon as I can arrange it, I want to bring them back to Tubac so Ruth can be buried at Tres Flechas, beside her mother."

"Sure, Sam. Count on it."

"You ready? Let's go by the stables first."

"Come on."

Outside, they could see the lights of the guardhouse, in the kitchen that stood between the officers' mess and the enlisted men's mess hall, the stables. Instinctively, both men looked toward the east, but there was no trace of light in the sky as yet. The wind was abating, but the air remained chilly and brought tears to their eyes as they hunched forward against the wind and walked briskly toward the stables. Lights began coming on in Troop E barracks, the men for Lieutenant Zimmerman's patrol being wakened by

15

Sergeant Petrie. There was a single light in the bachelor officers' quarters and one in the private quarters occupied by the two civilian scouts, Ira Gorton and Willy Logan. A few men assigned to orderly and mess-hall duties moved about in the darkness, carrying lanterns and throwing vague shadows. Riley and Palmer drew pure air into their lungs, expelling gray vapor, not talking as they crossed the drill field.

They knew that for the time being there would be no bugle calls heard within the walls of the Fort. Trumpeter Trueman had been killed in the massacre in Chancla Canyon two weeks earlier and Trumpeter Harrison had died in the more recent Monte de Lágrimas battle. Until replacements for them—as well as the many other men needed—were sent in from elsewhere, first call, reveille, morning colors, chow call, assembly, recall, retreat and taps would be announced by verbal commands.

At the stables, Riley and Palmer found the men busily engaged in preparing the horses for their morning's work. Riley spoke a few words to Sergeant Quitt while Palmer checked his horse and the pack mule, then together they crossed a corner of the parade ground and entered the enlisted men's mess hall. They sat at the Sergeant Major's private table, set for four as a privilege of his rank, which permitted him to invite other noncoms to eat with him; but none dared sit there without his express invitation. All the other tables in the room were long planks on sawhorses, benches for seats, the wood bare. Riley's table, like those in the officers' mess, rated a checkered cloth and napkins, chairs, china and silverware.

Riley called to a Mexican mess attendant and ordered his own and Palmer's breakfasts. Fried mush with molasses, eggs, thick slices of bacon, biscuits and coffee. It came to them hot, still sputtering in the usual overdose of grease, and somehow managing to carry with it an aroma of Mexican influence—spicy condiments with which the civilian cooks flavored their own meals.

Outside, the men due for patrol were beginning to form up, waiting for Lieutenant Zimmerman's inspection before Sergeant Mike Tyler ordered them inside to eat their last mess-hall meal for a week. They clumped into the huge room, Tyler's voice calling for service the moment he came through the door, leading nine others. Two mess-men came on the run carrying large coffee pots and platters of hot food. The ten men were fully dressed for the field except

16

for rifles, sidearms, and bandoliers of ammunition they would carry on their persons.

In the room on the north side of the kitchen, the officers' mess, Lieutenant Zimmerman was breakfasting with chief scout Willy Logan, discussing details of the upcoming patrol—destination, routes, location of water holes, its purpose.

The contrast in the two men was somewhat remarkable; Zimmerman about twenty-nine, slender and urbane, his voice tinged with a New England accent even after nearly seven years in the Army, a student at Harvard College when the Civil War erupted. Willy Logan was in his early fifties, a farm boy in his youth, turned hunter, trailbreaker and guide for wagon trains heading west, soldier and scout. Logan had lost his left hand, now replaced by a double-pronged hook made of spring steel set into a short wooden cuff that was lashed to his wrist and arm by leather thongs. He was a tall, heavy man with inordinate strength and a sober face that seemed to have been carved out of granite, from which a pair of bright, alert eyes peered; eyes that had seen almost everything worth seeing, good and evil.

In his capacity as a five-dollar-a-day civilian scout, he was usually taciturn and dour, but in the case of a likable young officer, Logan took a fatherly interest in passing on the fruits of his wisdom and knowledge in an area where ignorance and indecision could cost a man his life as well as the lives of the men under his command.

"Should be a breeze, Willy," Zimmerman was saying. "With the licking Major Boyden and you gave 'em up in Monte de Lágrimas and later in Mesa Plata, they'll probably be holing up to lick their wounds for some time to come. Now with Anaka dead—"

"Don't count too hard on it, Lieutenant," Logan replied soberly. "These ain't Cheyennes or Arapahoes you dealin' with. Onliest time an Apache quits is when he's dead. You seen 'em in action before, I don't need to tell you. They taken a beatin', that's for sure, but don't ever let the colonel hear you playin' down an Apache."

"Ah, Willy—"

"Zim, son, I been fightin' an' scoutin' red men since I was eighteen years old, an' I'm goin' on fifty-three now. I seen 'em in California, Oregon, across the whole middle country, over in Texas an' New Mexico, down in Sonora an' Chihuahua, an' there ain't nothin' I ever seen could stand up to an Apache. You know what that name means?"

"Apache? No, what?"

"It means *Enemy*. What their original name was, *Hiuhah*, means Men of the Rising Sun. That was along about the year 1200, I been told, when they first drifted down from the far North. The aborigines here we only know as *Hohokam*, means Ancient Ones. Then these poison-mean fiends come down, murderin', stealin', burnin'. Wasn't no Spaniards here 'til aroun' 1500-an'-somethin', but there were Papagos an' Pimas, peaceful enough people who built aqueducts, farmed the land an' lived like decent people. It was them gave the Apaches their name *Enemy*. Tell you, Zim, you get a good Pima scout like Quana on your side, you got yourself a real Apache-hater you c'n trust anytime aroun' the clock."

"What about Cochise, Willy?"

"Well, he's somethin' else again. He was the same as any other Apache, kill, plunder an' burn. Back in '60, he must of been somewheres between forty-five an' fifty an' gettin' tired. Also, he could see more whites comin' in an' less Apaches bein' born. Give him this much, he tried to turn peaceful an' make a treaty. Then, along come this Lieutenant Bascom. Somebody accused Cochise's Apaches of runnin' off with a rancher's stepson an' some of his cattle, fella name of Ward. Bascom was sent after Cochise to get the boy back, even though we know now Cochise's people never had nothin' to do with stealin' the boy or Ward's cattle. So this Bascom went lookin' for Cochise an' found he was up in Apache Pass. He sent word he wanted to parley, an' when Cochise come in with a few of his people under a white flag, Bascom double-crossed him an' taken him prisoner.

"Well, Cochise got away, but others died because of it, Apaches an' whites alike, an' Cochise been on the warpath ever since."

"I've heard about the Bascom affair. I think everybody in Arizona has by now. Tell me, what do you think personally, as a professional Indian fighter and scout?"

"About what?"

"About Indians, Apache and any other tribes, our moving in, always pushing them back, killing off their buffalo, deer and elk for hides, shoving them off the reservations we told him he could have to live on and hunt on, just because gold or silver was later discovered on his land, cutting his timber for profit—"

"Look Zim, I don't make the laws or no treaties,"

Logan replied. "I give my word, I keep it. I don't fight the Apaches for political reasons, but mostly because he's rampagin' an' ruckusin', killin' for the love of it. Like I'd kill a rattler without askin' him first what his intentions are. I ain't no political animal, just a five-dollar-day civilian scout, but—"

"Well, Willy, I've heard other stories, too. That white men have killed Indians for bounty scalps, raped their women, poisoned them with strychnine—"

"Zim, I don't know what to answer you. Neither side is right when it comes to things like that, an' I'd just as soon kill a white scalp hunter lookin' for bounty money or a white civilian or soldier I caught rapin' an Indian or white woman. I don't know how it got started or by who, but I can't live an' know it's goin' on. Bein' white, I fight on the white man's side. Like you do."

Zimmerman drank the last of his coffee. "First light. Time to go, Willy." He pointed out of the window. "I see the old man heading for his office. He'll want a final word with us before we pull out."

Zimmerman stood up and Logan pushed away from the table, using the double-pronged hook that served as his left hand to lever himself up. As Logan stood and scratched at his unshaven cheek with the metal hook, Zimmerman said with a wry smile, "Tell you one thing, Willy. I'm sure glad you're on our side. You'd make one hell of an Apache."

Sam Palmer stood at the Main Gate with Sergeant Major Riley, exchanging last words. In his saddle scabbard was his personal Winchester repeating rifle, a poignant reminder of Ruth. Around his waist was a cartridge-studded belt with a Colt .44 nested in its holster. On the pack mule was a week's supply of bacon, dried beef, beans, flour, some canned peaches, grain for the animals to supplement what grazing they would find. Shoved into the blanket roll was a double-barreled shotgun and in a haversack, along with a frying pan, coffee pot, tin plate and eating utensils, were six boxes of shotgun shells. There were two large field canteens filled with fresh water in addition to the smaller one that hung from his saddle pommel. Four hundred dollars of his $487 was in his saddlebag along with his honorable discharge, a letter of commendation from Colonel Hatfield, and other personal items.

The sun had not yet risen above the rim of distant

19

mountains to the east, but the sky was lightening and the desert mist had begun to rise, floating almost invisibly in a long flat layer against the paling sky. It would be another hot day, and Palmer felt he had lost more time than he could afford to spare.

"Pete," he said, "take care of yourself."

"I'll do me best to look out for Mrs. Riley's son. You look out for your scalp, Sam. We'll see you, won't we?"

"Sure. I'll be back one day to take Ruth and Sam, Jr. home to Tubac."

"I mean, you wouldn't be goin' East or out to the Coast, would you? We c'd use another civilian scout here, you know."

"I've got nobody in the East, Pete. My mother died back in '61, just before the war. She's buried outside of St. Louis. My father died soon after and I signed up the same year." He paused and sighed deeply. "California sounds interesting, but I can't decide on that right now. I'll have to think on it."

"Well, luck, trooper."

"Thanks, trooper, and luck to you."

"Open up!" Riley snapped the order crisply and two sentries raised the locking bar that rested in its cradle across the Main Gate. Sam Palmer heeled his mount and rode eastward without looking back.

Ten minutes later, Lieutenant Zimmerman and Scout Willy Logan stood on the veranda of Colonel Hatfield's headquarters. Zimmerman was ready and fully prepared for what lay ahead of him during the next seven days. He and Logan had been fully briefed the night before and both were acutely aware that this would be the only military patrol abroad and must be ready for a surprise attack—or nothing.

Late on the afternoon before, the Pima scout, Quana, had returned to the Fort to report that he had cut across fresh Apache sign in the area of Dos Viudas—the Two Widows—Mountains which lay a good two days' ride to the south. Because of the rocky terrain, Quana had been unable to get an accurate reading or establish whether this was a raiding or hunting party. No matter which, there were a number of rancher families scattered about this fertile area who were vulnerable to attack and might suffer a serious loss of cattle, horses, mules, even their homes and lives, depending upon the Apache strength.

Hatfield had given Zimmerman his best civilian scout, but could spare no more than ten seasoned troopers. The lieutenant had seen to the issue of ammunition and rations personally, then checked carbines and revolvers, condition of horses; hoofs, bits, bridles and saddle girths. He had briefed the men by lantern light before breakfast, noting that they were in good spirits, even eager to move out of the Fort, since they had taken no part in the recent actions in Monte de Lágrimas or Mesa Plata.

Waiting for Colonel Hatfield, the men heard the sergeant major's voice order the opening of the Main Gate and turned to watch as Sam Palmer rode out, no longer a sergeant, but a civilian, and not without envy of many of those who remained behind. Still watching as the gates were closed and the locking bar lifted into place, they heard the voice of the adjutant, Captain Marcus Greene, call out, "Atten-*tion!*" and saw the tall, rangy figure of Colonel Dion Hatfield emerge from the headquarters building onto the veranda. The men snapped to attention beside their horses. Zimmerman braced himself and saluted the commanding officer of Fort Bandolier.

Hatfield returned Zimmerman's salute and looked the crisply dressed lieutenant over, then turned to the more comfortably clad scout. "Good morning, gentlemen," Hatfield greeted.

"Good morning, sir," Zimmerman responded.

Logan stopped chewing on a wad of tobacco long enough to reply, "Mornin', Colonel."

Hatfield stepped off the veranda and inspected the ten troopers briefly, missing no detail. He nodded his approval and returned to the veranda to address himself to Zimmerman.

"Lieutenant, you have been briefed and have your orders. I will only reemphasize that if it is at all possible, I want you to avoid contact with hostiles in greater force than your own patrol. I doubt, after the battle in Monte and Mesa Plata, you will encounter a war party in force, but I suspect that with Anaka's death and heavy losses, there may be a shortage of food in his Sonora camp, which would be sufficient reason to send a hunting party north to search for cattle, horses and mules. I know that whatever you run into, you and your men will give a good account of yourselves, but keep firmly in mind that we cannot afford to sustain any further losses at this time. I shall expect you back one week from today. Good luck."

21

Zimmerman saluted and said, "Thank you, sir." He turned and signaled to Sergeant Tyler, who ordered the men to mount. Zimmerman and Logan then mounted their own horses and rode toward the Main Gate where Sergeant Art Petrie ordered it opened and the Officer of the Day noted the time of their departure in his Day Book.

An hour and forty minutes later, the guard was changed, the colors run up and the Orders of the Day announced. At the conclusion of this brief ceremony, the officers and men of the Fort turned to their normal operations and work duties—quartermaster, ordnance, hospital, repair and construction, stable duty, guard, drills, cooking and baking. In the laundry washroom, four Mexican laundresses attacked huge piles of clothing and linens. The blacksmith-farrier's hammer rang out on his anvil and a carpenter's detail began shoring up a section of logs in the west wall where they were sagging.

A detail of six troopers from Troop K fell out for inspection by Sergeant Major Riley, and the buggy to carry Mrs. Holly Martin west to Mesa Plata was rolled out, a fine black mare nudged between its shafts and harnessed. A hospital orderly strapped two boxes of medical supplies onto the small baggage platform at its rear and covered them with canvas, lashing the tarpaulin down tightly. While Riley went off to notify Mrs. Martin that her escort was ready, Major Kane Boyden sat in Colonel Hatfield's office in conference over coffee and cigars.

"Your report on the Monte de Lágrimas and Mesa Plata affair pleases me very much, Major," Hatfield said while holding the report in his hand.

"Thank you, sir," Boyden replied.

"On your return from Mesa Plata day after tomorrow, I shall have added my endorsement for General Litchfield's consideration and Governor Mitchell's approval. I intend that when you deliver these to Tucson, there will be a copy for Governor Mitchell's eyes only, in case General Litchfield does not see fit to forward the original document to the governor."

"I understand, Colonel," Boyden said. "In either case, I intend to use my full persuasive powers on the governor to bring Fort Bandolier up to strength, and approve my request for relief as his military aide and permanent transfer to your command. I can't suggest how long this may take, sir—"

"As long as is needed, Major. The situation here, while not desperate at the moment, could become perilous. I have no doubt that Cochise will send in a replacement for Anaka with sufficient braves to constitute a serious threat to this Fort, to Mesa Plata, the rancher families in this entire area, as well as the peaceful Chiricahuas up in the Monte de Lágrimas reservation."

"I certainly intend to make that clear to the governor, sir."

"Good." Hatfield dropped the report on his desk and sipped at his coffee. "Apart from the official, Major, may I ask about your personal plans?"

"Of course. Once I have delivered Holly—Mrs. Martin—to her parents in Mesa Plata, I will see to the distribution of the medical supplies among the civilians. I will leave Medical Sergeant Schurz in charge of hospital facilities and see to lifting the martial law order. I will look into the needs of the ranchers in the Carancho Valley who were burned out during Anaka's retreat and see what can be done to supply them with the lumber and supplies they will need to rebuild.

"The following evening, I will return here with Mrs. Martin and proceed to Tucson under escort and report in fullest detail to Governor Mitchell and stress the need for full replacements here—"

Hatfield's head was shaking from side to side in an expression of doubt. "I still don't see where they will come from."

"If I may, Colonel?"

"Go on, Major."

"I have been giving that part of it some thought, and I have an idea that might work. I would prefer not to enlarge on that at the moment, but wait until I get to Tucson and speak with the governor in private."

Hatfield stared at Boyden, checked his reply, then said, "Very well, Major. I have been locked within these walls for too long to question your judgment, therefore I will leave the problem in your hands. Let me add that I am tremendously pleased with the leadership you have displayed during your brief and temporary assignment here and will commend you to Governor Mitchell in my endorsement of your report. Now, what about Mrs. Martin?"

"Holly will return here with me after her overnight visit with her parents, Mr. and Mrs. Atwill. I intend to take her on to Tucson where she will be the guest of

Governor and Mrs. Mitchell. They are old friends from Baltimore, you may remember. As soon as possible, I will return here, hopefully with a permanent assignment. Within a short time after that, Holly and I will be married."

Hatfield's face split into a rare smile. "My congratulations, Major. Mrs. Martin is a very fine person and will make a happy addition to our Fort families."

"Sir, are you—"

"As soon as we are brought up to full organizational strength, one of my first orders will concern the return of the wives and children who were sent to Tucson and to their homes in the East for safety. We will require a construction force to build new quarters and recreational facilities, a school and chapel—. Well, that lies in the future and we'll discuss those details at a later date." Hatfield swiveled around and faced the closed door, calling, "Sergeant Major!"

Riley knocked and entered.

"Is the Mesa Plata detail ready, Riley?" Hatfield asked.

"Ready an' waitin', sir."

As the detail escorting Boyden and Holly Martin rode through the Main Gate, Colonel Hatfield watched from the veranda. And watching, he mourned the loss of his old and dear friend and comrade in arms, Major Owen Travis, caught in the Chancla Canyon massacre; and thought of Travis's widow, Ellen, waiting with her children in St. Louis for word that would bring them back to a reunion at Fort Bandolier; but instead, would receive a letter soon reading:

> DEAR ELLEN: *I deeply regret to inform you that on the morning of . . .*

And thought of his own wife, Clara, waiting back in Ohio with her parents; of their daughter, Annamarie, who was now seventeen, and whom he had not seen since they were sent away almost eighteen months ago. And of his son, Christopher, now twenty-one, soon to be graduated from the Academy at West Point, wondering if someone, somehow close to the workings of fate, would send Chris westward to a camp or fort in New Mexico, Texas, or even California—anywhere that would permit a delay en route and give leave to visit him before too many more years flew by.

Hatfield saw the gates close and returned to his office; he

24

picked up Boyden's report and began to scratch a few notations on a pad. Then he heard a familiar signal rapping on his door and called out, "Come!"

Captain Marcus Greene, his adjutant, entered. "Good morning, sir," he said stiffly.

" 'Morning, Marc. Well, we've got a lot of paperwork ahead of us. Have the clerk make me a copy of Major Boyden's report while I draft my endorsement. Then bring me the daily report—"

Colonel Hatfield's day had also begun.

SAM PALMER MADE HIS WAY EASTWARD WITH THE GREAT-est caution, keeping off the main route wherever possible, irked by the need for the pack mule that slowed his pace. He was fully conscious of Pete Riley's warning that he was a marked man, now the one man in the entire territory most wanted by Cochise, preferably alive in order to exact as yet unheard of atrocities upon him in revenge for his slaying of Anaka, one of Cochise's most able war leaders.

The desert, to one who knows and understands it, can be friend as well as enemy. Here, a man might easily die of thirst or starvation while within reach of certain plant life that could provide food and water. For two full years, the desert had been Palmer's school, under the expert tuition of guides like Willy Logan, Ira Gorton, the now dead Pima scout, D'jiia, and others. Blessed with intelligence and an inquisitive mind toward the strange and curious, Palmer found his instructors more than willing to impart their knowledge to him and in time, had been frequently chosen to act as scout when there was a shortage. His ability to pick up the harsh, awkward tongue of the Apache was another mark in his favor and had won for him special assignments that gave him certain personal privileges seldom accorded enlisted men—such as permission to live off post on the ranch Max Potter had given him and Ruth when they were married, located just nine miles north of the Fort in the foothills of the Sauceda Mountains.

The desert, Palmer had learned from the start, was a school in which he must pass every rigorous test if he was to remain alive. To fail was to die. Now, as he rode along, his eyes automatically scanned the earth seeking signs: animal tracks, their droppings, the hastily covered ashes of a recent or old campfire; tiny, scattered bits of food that would indicate whether the campers had been Anglos, Mexicans or Apaches; the print of a saddle in the sand where someone had used it to rest against; the way in which a plant had been cropped by a horse's teeth; the manner in which underbrush had been trampled or mashed or marked by a horse shod in rawhide (Apache) or iron (Anglo or Mexican); a cigar butt dropped in passing, a few grains of pipe tobacco left behind, a wad of chewing tobacco spat into the sand.

He was careful to avoid direct glare from the sun above and the sand below so that his vision would not be affected. When dust appeared in the distance ahead he studied its drift carefully to determine whether it was caused by the wind or by riders. His ears were keenly attuned, sensitive to every sound he heard, peering out of the corners of his eyes, identifying the elf owl, no more than six inches long, which nested inside a giant cactus; the gurgling of a mourning dove, the piercing scream of a sage grouse being attacked by a vicious horned owl.

There were reptiles to watch for; deadly diamondback rattlers, king, and other snakes whose colors blended into the desert background and made them virtually invisible; horned toads, whiptail and collared lizards, the banded gecko, skink, chuckwalla, gila monster; dangers in spooking horses and mules as well as inflicting serious bites to a careless man on the road; but first and foremost, the greatest danger of all was from the human hunter, the Apache.

Palmer made cold camps and rested a safe distance from where he placed his saddle and blanket, rifle on one side of him, revolver on the other. He slept for no longer than an hour or two at a time and only when he could do so among rocks off the trail. Malhado Pass, through which he must travel, was a particularly dangerous point: a high-walled canyon whose rims could hide a hundred men on either side, similar to Chancla Canyon where he, Corporal Belden and Scout Ira Gorton had safely passed through in advance of Major Owen Travis and the escort patrol en route to the Fort from Pradero, only to find them cut down minutes later by arrows and bullets of a strong force of Apaches hiding in the upper reaches on the west side of the canyon.

Viewing Malhado Pass from a distance, Palmer knew he could climb into those rims to make certain, but by doing so, would have to go far out of his way and lose almost a full day of travel. Therefore, he elected to gamble and, approaching the pass, dismounted and walked his horse for the last few miles, resting for an hour before

27

entering its mouth. He reached the entrance at dusk as he had planned, in order to go through while the shadows were deep, yet provided sufficient visibility to avoid the deep crevices in the road and the fanged rocks that jutted out sharply from both sides. He made the dash through the canyon without incident, then found a burned-out ranch on the other side where he could bring horse and mule under cover of a section of an adobe barn that still stood.

He skirted the town of Malhado—its population heavily Mexican—known as a haven for cattle and horse rustlers, road agents, and those more sympathetic to Apaches (in exchange for information and protection) than to passing immigrants, freight wagons, or the military; except when the soldiers came after a payday at the Fort to spend their money and let off their pent-up steam.

Swinging north of Malhado during the early morning hours, Palmer was well past it by noon and veered southward in a wide curve to bypass Encantado and, in need of rest and sleep for himself and his animals, spent the night deep inside a grove of cottonwoods where he could wipe out his tracks. On the following day, he rode boldly through Celeste, now only eighteen miles from Tucson and with enough traffic on the road to forestall an Apache attack. On the morning of the fourth day he could see the outskirts of Tucson; it was like riding into Eden after traveling through Hell, although Tucson was a rough and ugly town in itself.

If he had not been so weary, Palmer would have skirted Tucson and taken the cutoff road into San Xavier del Bac, which would put him on the principal road south to Tubac, but the events of the last ten days had taken too much out of him. At least, Tucson would provide a hot bath and shave, a change into clean clothes, a much-needed meal and a bed.

He came into the lower end of Calle Principale, then shunted off on a side street, and still another, until he came to Ainsworth's Livery Stable, a short block from the Congress Hotel. Turning his animals over to a Mexican attendant, he carried his rifle, shotgun and saddlebags through a back alley and entered the hotel by way of the rear entrance. He saw no one he knew among the four men who were seated in the lobby staring out the window at the passing scene.

There was no clerk behind the desk. Palmer tapped the

bell lightly, his back to the lobby loungers. A door behind the counter opened and the Mexican clerk emerged, startled by the grime-covered, bearded apparition who faced him.

"Madre mío! Señor Sam—"

"It's me, Carlos. Have you got a room for me?"

"Por supuesto!" Still staring, Carlos swung the register book around and offered Palmer a pen. He wrote his name in the book and because he no longer had a permanent address, added that of his father-in-law, Rancho Tres Flechas, Tubac.

Carlos Azuela said, "Three days ago, *señor,* the newspaper, the whole front page, it tells of the battle in Monte de Lágrimas, that you kill Anaka and bring his head in to Fort Bandolier in a sack."

So it was known in Tucson. And if in Tucson, everywhere else in the Territory. He knew now he would never be allowed to forget it, for this was the manner in which, right or wrong, legends of the frontiers were created, repeated, exaggerated and sustained until long after a man was dead and buried.

"Carlos, I am very tired. I want a tub of hot water brought to my room. Also a barber to cut my hair and shave me. And a hot meal—"

"At once, *señor*—"

"Then I want to sleep the rest of the day. And I don't want anyone to know I'm here. *Tu comprendes?"*

"Sí, señor. They say *el diablo,* Cochise, he looks for you—"

"Gracias. If he comes calling, ask him to wait here in the lobby until I wake up, eh? Send up some hot coffee, eggs, bacon, anything."

"Pronto, señor. Jose! Pablo! *Vengaquí!"*

He stripped and lay on the bed while the two boys filled the tin tub with hot water. A third boy brought a platter of eggs, beefsteak and tortillas, which he washed down with three mugs of coffee, then lighted a cigar and lay soaking in the tub. He scrubbed away the crusted sand and dirt accumulation of four days, then allowed the barber to shave him while he was in the tub; and later, he sat upon a hard chair while his hair was trimmed. Finally, he sent the man away, locked and barred the door with a chair beneath its knob and fell into bed as though it were a grave.

When he awoke, it was dark, but he could hear the street sounds and music from below and knew that the hour was earlier than midnight. He lay on the bed and allowed himself to waken slowly, without feeling the sense of urgency he had known for six long years in the Army. He was now a civilian, a free man. With a sad task to perform. To ride to Tubac and see his father-in-law, Max Potter, and his sister-in-law, Caroline. To try, somehow, to explain how it had all happened, this collapse of his entire world, the loss of everything he had ever wanted in life.

He got up and dressed in the other suit of clean underwear, trousers, shirt and vest, pulled on his boots, strapped the gun belt around his waist, locked his door and went downstairs. It was nearing nine o'clock and Carlos Azuela was again on duty.

"Señor Sam," Carlos announced, "it is known you are in Tucson. The boys, Jose and Pablo, and Pablo, the barber, all have told it, *el héroe de* Monte de Lágrimas. The people await you at the Congress Saloon next door to honor you—"

"I'm leaving for Tubac at once, Carlos. My bill—"

He felt the gentle slap on his back and turned, looked into the smiling face of Marcos Espuela. "Hello, Sam. We've been reading about you. The Tucson *Star*—"

"Hello, Marcos. Forget what you read. They're making a mountain out of a molehill."

"Anaka was a molehill, *amigo?* Then the Chiricahua Mountains are a rathole in the sand. Tucson waits to honor you—"

"I haven't got the time, Marcos. I want to get out of here and on to Tubac. I'm in a hurry."

"If you walk outside, the people will carry you on their shoulders. Sam. I—Ruth and the little boy. I am sorry for what happened—"

"It's all done, Marcos. I'm anxious to get to Tres Flechas and I don't want to be held up here."

"Listen. Go out the back way. I will go ahead and get your horse ready. Ainsworth's?"

"Yes. There's a mule, too. Leave him there. I'll get him when I come back. I'll pay Carlos, get my gear and meet you at Ainsworth's. And thank you, Marcos."

"*De nada.* Fifteen minutes."

For most of his twenty-two years, Marcos Espuela had lived with a strong spirit of competition. From his father he had inherited strength of body, height and litheness of movement. From his mother had come a certain easy, graceful manner, good looks and a beguiling smile that was disarming. In his few years as an adult he had already acquired a reputation that, in any frontier community, merited respect, even envy; and in some, produced a quiet fear. Marcos had killed three men for varying reasons.

One, an Anglo gunslinger, had called him a "Mexican bastard and son of a whore." Another had tried to rob him of his horse, Mano, only two days after his mother had given him the horse with a silver-mounted saddle on his twenty-first birthday. The third had been one of Casimiro Lizardi's gunmen who doubted that Marcos was as fast with a gun as he was reputed to be. After this last episode, Marcos waited calmly for Lizardi to send another *pistolero* to exact revenge, but none came; instead, Casimiro invited Marcos to become a member of his band of hired guns, rustlers and killers who would work at anything to make a dishonest dollar. To his credit, Marcos politely refused without offending Lizardi, and thereafter, no one made any effort to test Marcos's ability to draw swiftly and shoot accurately.

It is also possible that Lizardi passed the word that Marcos was not to be challenged, and the reason was that Lizardi's *vagos* used the Cantina Espuela de Oro—The Golden Spur—as an informal headquarters in Tucson, and the cantina was owned by Inez Espuela.

Yet, there was a half truth in the blunt charge of the first man Marcos had killed. The attractive Inez Espuela was Marcos's mother, and this fact was well known to all. But his father, a few knew and some suspected, was Martin Van Allen, married to a vinegary woman who had lived on his ranch some six miles north of Tucson on the Santa Cruz River. Van Allen's wife had long ago returned to Boston with their son and daughter who were attending school in that city of their mother's birth.

Martin Van Allen was a man of considerable wealth. The Congress Hotel and Congress Saloon, which stood side by side, were owned by him. Various parcels of Tucson real estate were in his name and he had made numerous investments in local businesses, some known, some unknown. And although the Cantina Espuela de Oro was in Inez Espuela's name, it was generally suspected that it had been bought for her by Van Allen during those earlier years when she had been his mistress.

Marcos had been schooled at the San Xavier del Bac Mission until he was seventeen, and the brothers had singled him out as one of their most intelligent and promising students. However, Marcos became bored with study and left when Judge Aubrey Tennant offered him a job in Tucson as a clerk. Judge Tennant also recognized a certain latent academic ability in Marcos and urged him to read the law; whereupon Marcos abruptly quit to become a deputy to Town Marshal Russ Yarborough.

Three months later, he left Yarborough because the marshal restricted his activities to the Mexican quarter with a "hands off white men" policy. For a year Marcos worked as an interpreter at Fort Lowell, where he met Sam Palmer, and from him Sam learned to speak Spanish fluently. After Marcos left his job because it was too confining, they still remained close friends.

It was shortly after Marcos had killed his third man that Martin Van Allen, for the first time, became dramatically aware that the son of Inez knew who his father was. Late one cold winter night, Van Allen left a poker game in the Congress Saloon, a little less than sober and a winner with over $800 in his pockets. As he untied the horse and prepared to get into his buggy for the trip back to his ranch, a man stepped out of the shadows and jammed the muzzle of a rifle into Van Allen's back, warning him, "Don't turn around, mister. Just hand over the money inside your coat pocket."

At that moment, Marcos Espuela turned into Calle Principale from Calle Guadelupe, coming from a visit to the home of a girl. From a distance of fifty yards he saw the attempted holdup and ran swiftly, gun drawn, to where the two men stood beside the buggy, their backs to him. At the last moment, the holdup man, preoccupied with the business at hand, heard the clink of Marcos's spurs and half turned, but Marcos called, "If you so much as make a move, it will be your last one, *hombre*. Let your rifle fall to the ground."

Trapped, the man did as he was ordered. Marcos stepped in and kicked the gun to one side. "You want him killed, Señor Van Allen?" Marcos asked calmly.

"No," Van Allen replied somewhat shakily. "No, Marcos. The marshal—"

Someone came out of the Congress Saloon, saw what was happening and called to the others. Soon a crowd formed, among them Marshal Yarborough, who took the

32

man into custody and led him off to jail. When the crowd finally dispersed, Van Allen said, "Come see me at the hotel tomorrow, Marcos. I owe you—"

In a low voice, Marcos replied coldly, "You owe me nothing, *padre mio*. You gave me my life, now I give you your life. We are even." He turned, but Van Allen's voice stopped him.

"Wait a minute, Marcos."

"There is nothing to wait for, *señor*. Everything that can be said now, has been said. What should have been said and done long ago, it is now too late to say or do. *Adiós*."

Marcos walked away, head held high, until he reached his room at El Aguila, on the edge of the Mexican quarter.

Martin Van Allen changed his mind about going home to his ranch. Instead, he drove to Espuela de Oro. When Inez saw him enter, she went to her private room at the back of the cantina. Van Allen followed a few minutes later.

"What is it, Martin?" Inez asked.

"A man tried to hold me up. Marcos saw him and saved me. I could have been killed."

"Then it was good that he was there, no?"

"Inez, he knows. He called me *'padre mio'* and said he was returning my life for the one I gave him."

With some pride, Inez said, "He is not *atontado*, a fool, our son, Martin. He has Spanish and Mexican blood in him, as good as yours. He is a proud one."

"He has death in his eyes."

"And in his fingers. He is swift."

"Yes. I have seen it." After a moment's pause, "What can I do for him, Inez?"

"Nothing. He has what he needs. What he wants, he takes. I give him money. Girls go to him freely. He wants nothing from you. *Acaso*—"

"Perhaps what?"

"Something you never gave him. Your name."

"No, Inez. Anything else—"

Inez shrugged. "He may one day take it."

"How?"

"Maybe by the law, in court—"

"I'll kill him."

Inez laughed, but without humor. "Not you, Martin.

33

You have grown old and he has eyes in the back of his head, in the tips of his fingers."

"Inez, I warn you—"

"Do not warn me, Martin. His blood is young and runs hot. Yours has become cooled with age. He was a child of love, your blood and mine. Warn him yourself if you can look into his eyes and deny him."

"I will give him money and send him away. A ranch of his own somewhere—"

Inez laughed again. "From here, the only home he has ever known? Your words are foolish, Martin."

At Ainsworth's, Palmer's horse was rested and ready. Sam tied on his saddlebag, thrust the Winchester into the saddle scabbard, the shotgun into his blanket roll. He paid the attendant and arranged for the pack mule's care until he returned. Ready to mount up, he saw Marcos leading his own horse from a nearby stall.

"We are ready, *amigo?*" Marcos asked with laughing eyes at Palmer's questioning look.

"We?"

"I go with you, Sam."

"Marcos, I don't need a bodyguard."

Marcos shrugged. "I'm not going as your bodyguard. I go to Tubac to visit cousins I have not seen for many months. At Tres Flechas."

"What cousins?"

He knew Marcos was laughing at him, but the younger man's charm was irrepressible. "*Amigo,* in the presence of an Anglo like yourself, all Mexicans become cousins, even a *mestizo* like me. Your wife, Ruth, was half-Spanish. Her sister Caroline, also. Thus, Caroline is my cousin. Not her Anglo papa. Not my own papa—"

"Marcos, forget Van Allen. He is a powerful man."

"No man who is clumsy with a gun is powerful, *amigo,* only those he hires to do his killing for him. And I am faster than all of them, even Casimiro Lizardi."

"Nobody can be faster than all of them together, Marcos. Only one at a time. And every man's time runs out sooner or later."

"Maybe two at a time?" Again there was laughter in his words if not on his face.

"Only if you're lucky. Damned lucky."

"*Amigo,* I was born under a lucky star. I am one lucky *bastardo.* With women, with cards. And I am tired of

34

talk. Let us ride together in the quiet night, away from the stink of Tucson, eh?"

"All right, Marcos. Let's not rush it and get there before anybody's awake. Max's guards can get mighty trigger happy in the dark."

They reached Tubac an hour before dawn, the horses not overly tired, having been watered at a creek while Sam and Marcos rested and smoked cigars. Marcos was an ideal riding companion, eager to be on the move, respecting Palmer's desire to keep conversation at a minimum.

The village of Tubac was still deep in sleep. They cut off the main road and headed west and south, conscious that they were already on Tres Flechas land, but still a considerable distance from the four-acre caliche-walled compound behind which stood the main *hacienda,* barns, horse corrals, blacksmith shop, *vaqueros's* barracks, servant quarters and perhaps another dozen miscellaneous buildings. Like the fortress it had been in ancient times, the wall was pierced chest-high for riflemen, with a four-foot-wide parapet that ran around the inside wall at the six-foot level, manned by hard-faced *vaqueros* by night; men who were keenly aware of the dangers and penalties of carelessness. Outside the walls there were over 150,000 acres, the original grant to the de Dorantes y Ruiz family of Sonora whose daughter, Ysabel, had married Lomax Potter back in 1847, at the close of the Mexican-American War.

Tres Flechas—Three Arrows—had been Ysabel's dowry, along with the responsibility of caring for 150 *vaqueros* and their families living on the land; also a starting herd of 2,000 head of cattle, many horses, pigs, sheep and turkeys. Through the Civil War, when Tubac was practically a ghost town, Tres Flechas was well-manned and well-armed to fight off Apaches, the white men who came hunting for silver and gold, and the horse and cattle rustlers. Children had been born on Tres Flechas, grown, married and died without ever having left the land or traveled farther than the village of Tubac. Only those skilled with arms were permitted to drive cattle to Army posts where they were needed.

"We are close, no, *amigo?*" Marcos asked suddenly.

"A few miles ahead. By first light we'll see the compound walls," Palmer replied.

35

The wind had come up stronger during the night and so close to dawn, with little to stop its knifelike thrusts across the flatlands, it felt much colder. Far to the east, they would soon see the first lightening of the sky over the Dragoon Mountains. As always before the dawn, the sky seemed blacker than at midnight, a velvet backdrop to make the stars shine more brilliantly before giving way to daylight. There were no lights showing in the main house where four women household servants and the daughter of *el patrón*, Señorita Caroline Potter, slept. Nor were there any lights in the other buildings. The wind brought with it the sounds of neighing, nickering horses, the occasional barks or yelps of dogs responding to the howls of coyotes in the distance, the whipping of tree branches, balls of wind-blown tumbleweed scraping against a corral. To those who were awake this night, each sound was heard and carefully catalogued for exactly what it was.

El patrón himself, Lomax Potter, the *vaquero* guards knew, was there among his men as a leader should be. On the walls and on the ground, the men of Tres Flechas waited.

Shortly after dark, Andreas Icaza, foreman of the south range, had sent word by a fast-riding messenger, Rufino Flores. Apaches had been observed coming stealthily from the southeast, heading in the direction of the main *hacienda*. Icaza had counted forty, a more than respectable raiding party, evidently determined to attack the *jefetura*.

Max Potter had sent Rufino back to Icaza with word to keep the men with the herds to prevent their stampeding or scattering. The day crews, about thirty able *vaqueros*, would handle the invaders from inside the compound walls. Almost eight hours had passed and still they had heard nothing, seen nothing, smelled nothing; and thus, Potter reasoned, they would be hidden in the woods at the base of the gently sloping hill, a few hundred yards to the east, until time for the attack, which could come at the first crack of light in the sky.

At his post on the ramparts facing due east, Venustiano Carras stirred, drew his blanket coat closer to his throat, leaned his rifle against the wall and rubbed warmth into his hands, then picked up the rifle again. Lying asleep on the wooden decking of the parapet, his eldest son, Tomas, who was fifteen, turned in his blanket and whimpered. Venustiano leaned down over him, rifle gripped between his knees, then placed one hand upon the boy's mouth and shook him gently with the other.

"Wake up, *jovenito*," he whispered.

"Eh—*qué pasó, padre?*" the boy mumbled.

"The light comes soon. Get up. Do not raise your voice."

Tomas threw the blanket to one side and stood up quickly. "They come, *padre?*"

"They will come."

"When?"

"Do not be so eager, *joven. Al amanecer.* When the first light rises above the mountain top. Stay awake. Warm your hands and keep your rifle near. Remember, do not be too quick to shoot at shadows. Aim carefully and lead your target."

"I know, *padre*. I have killed birds and coyotes—"

"Birds and coyotes do not shoot back with guns or arrows."

"I will do well, *padre*."

Venustiano grunted softly. "Four hours on watch after a long day in the saddle. Ai-ee, I am weary. I grow old at this game I have played all my life. My bones shake with cold, my belly shrivels and grumbles for hot food and tequila. I could sleep—."

"Watch it up there!"

It was the quiet, crisp voice of *el patrón*, noting the nearness of dawn. Soon they would come. "*Madre de Cristo*," Carras said to himself, "be with me today."

Tomas reached for his rifle which was leaning against the wall. His fingers were numbed with cold and the rifle slipped, its butt clattering against the wooden decking.

"Careful, Tomas!" Venustiano's whisper was sharp. "The sound carries long distances in the wind."

"*Lo siento, padre*."

"It is not enough to be sorry. Rub your hands together and give them life."

"*Sí*—"

"Quiet!" Venustiano peered over the wall, head cocked to one side. The sound he heard was like the whine of a dog, the wail of a child. He caught it on the edge of a gust of wind and when it had passed, heard the sound again. He leaned downward toward the ground inside the compound and called in a sharp whisper, "*Hist! Hist! Patrón!*"

37

Max Potter was there in an instant. *"Qué pasó,* Venustiano?"

"Up here, *patrón.* Come, listen."

Max Potter mounted the steps to the platform, a dark shadow in the blackness. He peered in the direction of Venustiano's hand, seeing nothing, straining to hear over the gusting wind.

"I heard it two times, *patrón—*"

"Coyote?"

"No. A cry—"

Then the wind shifted and the three of them, Potter, Venustiano and Tomas heard it. A cry, yes, but a cry for help; faintly, a whisper riding on the wind. *"Madre— Madre de Cristo! Patrón—ayuda—ayuda—"*

Potter uttered a curse under his breath. Venustiano crossed himself and Tomas exclaimed, "Rufino! It is Rufino Flores! I know his voice!"

"They have taken him," Potter said needlessly.

"Sí, patrón," Venustiano agreed. "They have him. *El tormento—"*

Tomas cried out, "We must do something—"

"Quiet, *joven,"* his father cautioned. "We can do nothing until we can see."

Others, attracted by their voices, came along the platform to join them. Alvaro Calles, Emilio Pluma, Cesar Carillo and Felipe Prieto. All had heard the cry, the plea for help. Rufino was but sixteen, the son of Diego Flores, head man of the home ranch, being trained by Andreas Icaza on the south range. A moment later, Diego Flores himself appeared, a serape over his shoulder, a rifle in hand.

"Patrón, I will go out—"

"You will not go out, Diego," Potter replied firmly. "There is nothing anyone can do now."

"Patrón, I can do nothing here. He is my son. Out there, I will find a way—"

"Diego, I grieve with you, but you know it is an Apache ruse. Rufino is staked out there within our hearing. In a little while, we will be able to see him. When we try to release him, they will shoot the rescuers from the woods, then put an arrow into Rufino's back."

"This I know well, *patrón,* but I cannot stand and wait."

"It is suicide if you go."

"It is the same if I do not go."

"You have a wife, other children to think about."

"That, *señor*," Diego replied with dignity, "does not make Rufino any less my son. I must go to him."

"Then go with God, *amigo*."

Diego turned and ran down the steps. The two men at the gate removed the iron bar, opened the gate a crack and one muttered, *"Vaya con Dios,* Diego," as he slipped out, just as the first break came in the black sky, a thin streak of brass-gold light; then another. Moments later, the sky paled to the east. Below the walls, halfway between the compound and the woods at the bottom of the hill, the men on the ramparts could make out the irregular lines that formed the thicket of trees in which they knew the Apaches were hiding, waiting.

"They caught him on the way back to the south range," Max Potter replied to Cesar Carillo's question. "He was told to make a wide circle westward, then go south—"

"Patrón!" It was Venustiano Carras, keeping watch while the others discussed the situation. Now, all seven men present leaned forward over the rim of the wall.

Halfway between the compound and the copse of trees, it stood like a monument, a sacrifice to the morning sun. Four long lances had been tied about a foot apart, their sharp points thrust into the earth. Strips of rawhide crisscrossed the four lances vertically and horizontally and lashed to them, raised three feet off the ground, the boy, Rufino Flores, had been spread-eagled and bound to the rawhide strips by other strips, at waist and throat, across his chest, around his thighs and ankles and wrists. Crouched over, less than sixty yards from his son, Diego Flores crept, rifle in left hand, a large knife in the other. On the rampart, rifles were raised, resting upon the wall, ready to fire at the first sign of movement from the woods; yet there was none amid the dark shadows of the trees. Quickly now, as it is common in the southwest, the sky grew brighter. Time was of the essence, and Diego ran more swiftly, arms reaching forward, crouched over. He was at the torture rack now and had reached up with the knife high to slash through the rawhide bindings, then saw that they had been braided and soaked with water. He laid his rifle on the grass to give him freedom to use both hands.

From the thicket of trees below, a volley of shots rang out. Diego fell and lay motionless on the ground. Rufino cried out, although no bullet had touched him. The men on the wall understood that Rufino's body had been battered and slashed only enough to keep him alive to cry out; bait to lure the *vaqueros* out from behind the safety of the caliche walls of Tres Flechas and to inevitable death.

Sam and Marcos heard the volley of shots as they came over the small rise that gave them their first sight of the walls of the familiar *hacienda* across the valley on the next rise. Between them, at the valley bottom, lay the grove of trees that sheltered the Apaches.

Marcos pointed to the grove. "From there."

Palmer nodded. In both minds were certain facts not necessary to discuss. The attackers, they were certain, were Apaches, in greater strength than the six or eight shots represented. The question they asked themselves silently was, How many?

Now they heard other shots, fainter, so that they must be coming from the *hacienda*. If they could create a diversion on this side—.

"Let's go, *compadre*," Palmer shouted, heeling his mount. Marcos, without hesitation, followed at once. At a point no more than thirty yards from the grove, Palmer pulled up, leaped off his horse and let it run, dropping prone into a small depression in the ground. At once, he began firing, random shots, spacing them about three feet apart, keeping them low. Marcos dropped in beside him and began pumping away. They were rewarded with a howl, another, the shriek of a horse in pain, high-pitched neighing of fright.

Several Apaches came to the edge of the woods, facing them, crouched low, peering out and jabbering excitedly. Marcos got the first one, Sam the second. More came, dropping flat, firing. A bullet ripped a tear through the shoulder of Sam's outer coat, but did not touch his flesh. The jarring made him more cautious, seeking definite targets, using the rifle flashes from the woods to guide his aim.

On the *hacienda* side, there was an awareness that help of some kind had come. Twenty armed *vaqueros* lined up at the gate and as it opened only wide enough to permit one man to leave at a time, they crouched low to the ground and ran a wide pattern, alternating to right and left, zigzagging down the slope. Max Potter was the first man out, signaling dispersal orders to the others as they followed. From the wall, the remaining *vaqueros* watched for rifle flashes and poured return fire into the woods.

Inside the thicket of trees, a single signal cry went up. There was a temporary lull in the firing as horses were cut loose from their picket lines. The Apaches mounted and broke out of their cover, heading southward, bent low and close along their horses's necks. From the east, Sam Palmer and Marcos Espuela poured rifle fire into the fleeing Indians, dropping four horses and then the Apaches who were left afoot. Some were racing toward the south end of the woods, firing and shouting. Close to a dozen bodies lay strewn on the grassy valley, and while the furious *vaqueros* knelt to finish off the wounded, others scoured the woods to make certain that none left behind remained alive.

Emiliano Pinedo, slowed down by a bullet in his left thigh, leaned against Rufino Diego's rawhide gallows. As predicted, Rufino had been killed with a final shot in his back. His father, Diego, lay sprawled on the ground, face upward to the new sun, mouth and eyes opened, cut down by two bullets. Emiliano shouted the news to the others, then sat on the ground to bind his thigh with a strip of shirting.

The enraged *vaqueros* returned to the scalping, cursing with every cut of the knife, with each tug at the gory hair. Max Potter made no effort to stop them. They would return to their quarters in some minor triumph, with a total of nineteen scalps to dry out and treasure in memory of Diego and Rufino Flores.

Potter then walked into the woods in order to escape witness to the barbarous custom he had seen many times before in his life, but had never gotten used to. Coming out on the east side, he saw the two strange men who had obviously been helping them, one man mounted and riding toward the horse of the other.

He walked toward the man on foot, recognizing the Winchester rifle in his hand before he recognized the man himself, then put one hand to the side of his mouth and shouted, "Sam!"

Max Potter's son-in-law had returned home.

CHAPTER III

IN HIS STRONGHOLD IN THE DRAGOON MOUNTAINS, Cochise sat alone in his private wickiup, the one set aside for solemn and undisturbed meditation. Outside, four vedettes stood within call should the Great One desire food, water or tizwin, and until he called out or made an appearance, no one must approach him. Braves, old men, women, children and animals must be kept away from the area of isolation under pain of punishment.

Camp routine went on as usual, but under the tension of restrained quiet. Before the sun went down, the second of two expeditions was expected to return. Smoke signals had been relayed from watchers on the slopes, a simple message without elaboration. *Tan-hay returns*. No word of how many were returning with him, and this in itself was an ominous note.

The first raiding party had returned in mid-morning, led by Bokhari, coming northward from Mexico and bringing with them sixteen captured horses, eight mules, eleven guns, sacks of pinole and maize, cloth and blankets. Bokhari and his forty men had swept into the Mexican village of Meridiano just as dawn was breaking on the day before, killed twenty-three men and women, whose scalps had been taken and which they carried as evidence, those of four Mexican *rurales* among them, and this without a single loss. In a quiet ceremony, Cochise had praised Bokhari and rewarded him with his choice of the stolen goods.

Now he waited for Tan-hay.

Three days earlier, Cochise had been faced with a difficult decision, a painful one to make since it was a constant reminder of the death of his most favored of all subleaders, Anaka. When the tragic word was received by smoke signal, confirmed two days later by an exhausted runner who had been in Monte de Lágrimas with Anaka, a great sadness had fallen upon the entire camp. Anaka's head, it was told, had been removed and carried away to the fort of the Pinda Lick-o-yi, Bandolier, which stood like a malignant cancer in the desert between Tucson and Yuma, with its blue-clad soldiers defending not only the white ranchers and travelers moving from east to west and west to east, but preventing Cochise's couriers from persuading or forcing Chamuscada's Chiricahua Apaches out of Monte di Lágrimas to return to their brothers and wage the common war against the white soldiers.

Chamuscada, aging, had signed the Pinda Lick-o-yi treaty and gone into the reservation with his people, yet Cochise had had word that all was not well. The White Eyes miners and ranchers of Mesa Plata had repeatedly broken the treaty by hunting in Monte de Lágrimas, driving the elk and deer out of reach of Chamuscada's braves; forcing them higher and higher into the mountains. And yet the old warrior had stubbornly insisted that it was better to live in peace on little than at war with more; including death.

Anaka, brave and totally loyal to Cochise, had gone with a strong force into Monte de Lágrimas to convince Chamuscada that no treaty made by the White Eyes was lasting, but he had encountered a force of soldiers from Fort Bandolier, led by Major Boyden. Anaka had fought well, the runner said, but had been overwhelmed by cannon, which the Indians had never learned to use. Anaka had lost one hundred and forty-three men; more than a hundred and fifty horses, an uncounted number of rifles, adding up to well over half his tribe.

Therefore, the celebration for the victorious Bokhari, coming after the news of Anaka's defeat and death, had been restrained, without the customary singing and speeches of praise.

We will see, Cochise thought, what news Tan-hay brings. If he has destroyed Tres Flechas, the decision will be less difficult than before. If he was driven off with losses, then Bokhari will succeed Anaka. Bokhari is younger and bolder, but Tan-hay was Anaka's closest friend, the husband of Anaka's sister, although she was his third wife. We will see.

So it was that when dusk fell and Tan-hay came up the long, narrow, rock-lined canyon that guarded the opening into the stronghold, word had been passed from crest to crest into the principal camp: Tan-hay and only twenty-one of his original party of forty were returning, some on foot, some riding double. No one wanted to carry the news to Cochise in advance. He would know soon enough that nineteen braves had died, creating more widows, lessening the overall members of the tribe while the White Eyes continued to flourish in numbers and strength.

Cochise, faced with the dilemma of choice, had narrowed the selection down to two—Bokhari and Tan-hay. Both eager rivals for the honor of replacing Anaka in the west desert to raid, kill and destroy the white intruders, then launch unrestricted war upon the Mexicans who had placed a bounty on Indian scalps; one hundred dollars for that of a brave, fifty dollars for a woman's, twenty-five dollars for that of a child.

So who, Cochise asked, were the savages? The Indians who had been robbed of their lands and sources of food, or the white and Mexican scalp hunters who preyed upon his diminishing tribes for money—paper, round coins and yellow iron which could not be eaten, worn, provide warmth or made into weapons?

On receiving word of Anaka's death and the loss of one hundred and forty-three braves, he had gathered together one hundred and sixty braves and their families and sent them to Anaka's camp in Sonora with Vicenzo to guide and command them until a new subleader could be decided upon.

It was nearing full darkness when Cochise heard the stirring outside his wickiup, the first wailings of those who had become widows. He sighed, already knowing he must face the survivors, order a mourning period for the dead, somehow find husbands to take another wife from among the widows and become fathers to their orphaned children.

As usual, Cochise acted swiftly. He heard from Tan-hay's own lips the story of the attack on Tres Flechas, his defeat and losses. And as usual, Cochise was generous to the defeated as he had been to Bokhari and his victorious braves. There was little use or benefit in humiliating a man who had done his best. To punish him would be fruitless. To accept loss graciously was to make him strive harder next time. But Cochise's choice for Anaka's replacement had been irrevocably settled by events.

To the gathered assembly, he named Bokhari to follow Vicenzo and take command of the Sonora camp, taking with him his choice of ten braves. In a small firelight ceremony, Cochise placed a necklace of yellow iron with a

44

large, polished turquoise in its center around Bokhari's neck. Bokhari would leave sometime before the sun would rise again; quickly, so that the pain of his presence would not be felt by Tan-hay. Bokhari preened with pride during the short ceremony. Over the roasted meat, mescal, cakes and fruit, with tizwin to follow, he boasted of the deeds of his men, careful not to include himself in a clear show of modesty, knowing all were well aware that as their leader, his was the reflected glory in the overall victory.

Bokhari was born in the late 1830's, the only son of Heah-Lik, a ranking member of Cochise's Council, and an elder who had served under Juan Jose until the death of that Chief of Chiefs of all Apache tribes in the entire Southwest. When Cochise became supreme leader of the Chiricahua Apaches, Heah-Lik chose to serve him, although Mangas Coloradas had offered him far greater rewards to live with his Mimbres Apaches. Cochise, in turn, rewarded Heah-Lik by elevating him to head a band of information gatherers, not unlike an intelligence corps, to keep the Great One informed on the movement of soldiers, immigrants, freight and cattle; of new and undefended ranches, of sparsely protected villages ripe for raiding.

Thus, besides knowing where and when to attack, Heah-Lik became a clever war strategist, suggesting tactics and subterfuge as well as the number of men to send on a specific raid, weighing the possibilities and probabilities of their success. But Heah-Lik himself was not a warrior, and this he regretted deeply. Although he begged to be allowed to go out on raiding expeditions, Cochise persuaded him that he was more valuable alive on the Council than dead in the field. And in 1836, in his fifty-sixth year, Heah-Lik's wife died without having given him a child.

Soon after her funeral, Cochise sent to Heah-Lik's tent Es-Quiel, the widow of a young brave, to cook, sew, clean and look after his chief counselor. She herself was no more than seventeen. Heah-Lik paid her little attention beyond accepting her as a servant; but one day some months later, he felt a need growing within him and took her to his blanket, discovering in her a warmth and comfort beyond his belief. Within a short time he married Es-Quiel in a full tribal ceremony, this to the dismay of the clan of older widows. Nor would he take more than one wife as his status permitted.

Bokhari was born to Es-Quiel during the year that followed and Heah-Lik was determined that his son would achieve the status of War Leader in his own right. Thus, Bokhari, from his sixth year, was seldom far from his father's side. The boy was sturdy and strong. He was bathed in icy spring waters almost from birth, stripped naked and rubbed with snow during winters in the high mountains, fed the choicest meats obtainable. Bokhari was turned over to the most eminent among the tribe's instructors in mountain and desert fighting and survival. He learned from these experts to track, hunt down and kill animals many times his own size, using the "silent death"— a bow and arrow carved and strung by his own hands. Where there was no water, he was taught to quench his thirst with a variety of cacti that gave off moisture, to find shelter beneath the sand, among rocks, in mountain forests. From the very start, he was taught to ride and shoot.

Heah-Lik undertook his son's education in other matters. Thus, Bokhari learned the almost forgotten history of his own people, their sacred laws, rites and taboos; of the creation of the Sun and Moon, the Stars which were the souls of departed Apache war leaders. Heah-Lik recited the valorous deeds of ancestral heroes, chronicles of ancient times, prophecies for the future.

Meanwhile, with others of his age, he participated in games designed to build strength and endurance; wrestling and running that added muscle and physical energy; seeking game animals on foot, berries and roots to stave off hunger when meat and grain were scarce. And later, reaching from youth into manhood, he accompanied raiding parties, learning to steal horses, mules, sheep, cows; to kill white men, capture young women for use as servants, children who would soon forget they were white and become members of the Apache tribe.

And learned always, that to kill an enemy was the greatest and most honorable achievement of all. In particular, a soldier enemy.

Bokhari, there was little doubt, attained many accomplishments. Heah-Lik and Es-Quiel expected a superior performance in all things, even demanded it, and were seldom disappointed. Bokhari won every contest of skill and performance he entered, carried off prize after prize so that his father's tent was crowded with blankets, bows, arrows, and other awards for excellence. And so deeply ingrained in him was the spirit of competition that he could accept nothing less than total victory.

46

But although he was praised for his ability and intelligence by his elders, Bokhari had few friends among those of his own age. He was Bokhari, who lived only to win. By tribal custom, he could not be shunned, but he was never warmly accepted by his contemporaries and secretly excluded when the serious work of the day was over and games were played purely for pleasure.

When he was eighteen and his aloneness began to prey upon him, he asked Heah-Lik, "What is it? Why do they not want me?"

Heah-Lik replied, "Because there is envy in them. They know that the destiny of the son of Heah-Lik lies in greatness."

It was an acceptable answer, one in which Bokhari could take pride, but it did little to assuage his loneliness.

To these same questions, Es-Quiel told him, "Walk with your head high. You are Bokhari, son of Heah-Lik, upon whom the Great One smiles."

"But no one else smiles upon me as they do on others."

"Be patient. I will find you a wife who will smile upon you and bear you children."

He began to visit the widows of slain warriors and found some physical comfort in their wickiups, but they were older women, as lonely for companionship as he was, and he wanted a girl of his own age, or younger. Es-Quiel talked with other mothers, but these gave her many evasive answers and sent their daughters off with young men who, unlike Bokhari, knew the meaning of laughter and pure enjoyment.

Then Heah-Lik died of a coughing disease and Es-Quiel, too, was alone; yet, because she was the widow of Cochise's chief counselor, she was sought out by men who yearned for Cochise's favor, and soon she was remarried. It was then that Bokhari, unable to see a coarse man of lesser stature than his father together with his mother, moved into a wickiup of a widow with whom he had whiled away many hours, now declaring his intention to marry her.

He did, and in time he became a father of two sons, born a year apart, whom he named Malha and Tanzay, who gave him much joy. But his wife, in delivering Tanzay, became sickly thereafter and for the past eight years gave Bokhari no physical comfort or pleasure, and became a servant to him and his two sons.

So it was that on this day of his greatest victory and

47

selection to take the place of a warrior he had long admired, Bokhari's delight knew no bounds. And in a moment of self-gratification, he chose from among the newest widows the youngest of the lot, Lo-Kim, who was no more than fifteen years old, married less than a year and without children of her own. So there was another ceremony as Lo-Kim became Bokhari's second wife, made brief by order of Cochise, who was tiring of these empty celebrations. When it was over, Bokhari personally selected the ten braves who would accompany him and ordered them to make themselves and their families and possessions ready to leave late that night.

Two hours before departure time, Cochise sent for Bokhari. In his meditation wickiup, the Great One motioned his newest war leader to a pallet opposite him. Cochise sat erectly, proud of his height that gave him a certain psychological advantage when dealing with his braves, able to stand or sit and still look down upon them. Bokhari, elated with tribal praise, a little drunk on tizwin, and perhaps eager with the thought of the new young bride who awaited him, sat cross-legged, facing the Great One. Now, Cochise removed an amulet from his own arm, one that had been carved from a shell and was studded with turquoise symbols of the Sun and Moon. He handed it to Bokhari and said solemnly, "Brother, let this guard you by day and night, on the hunt and in battle."

Bokhari slipped the amulet on his arm and responded, "As it has guarded my Great Leader in the past, it will guard me in the future, that his work will be done."

"*Enju*," Cochise replied. (The Apache word meaning, It is well, or, So be it.)

Cochise then spoke of that which lay closest to his heart. "Brother, listen. You have been given the place of a great war leader, Anaka. He and his braves have killed many Pinda Lik-o-yi, Anglo and Mexican. He died with honor in battle and I mourn him. Thus, the honor to avenge his death and the deaths of one hundred and forty-three of your brothers lies in your hands.

"I have sent Vicenzo with more in number than those Anaka lost to his camp in the Sonora Mountains that was his stronghold. Vicenzo is a good lieutenant. He will remain and obey your orders. Now, brother, these are mine.

"Listen. As long as I remain on this side of the Santa Cruz and San Pedro rivers, the white general in Tucson will keep most of his soldiers scattered and spread thin across these deserts and mountains, searching for me. To the west of Tucson and as far as Yuma, from the Gila south to the Mexican border, there is only one fort, the one known as Bandolier, to protect a vast land. They, too, have lost men. It becomes harder for them to protect the ranches that keep growing as well as the White Eyes who move from east to west and from west to east.

"To the west and north of Fort Bandolier lies Monte de Lágrimas. Years ago, our brother Chamuscada broke away from his Chiricahuan brethren and went there with his people to live on the white man's reservation. This was wrong and I said so, yet he would not yield, which by tribal custom was his right. But I know the White Eyes have broken the treaty they signed with Chamuscada. White men from Mesa Plata hunt on that reservation killing deer and elk for pleasure and skins, allowing needed meat to rot in the sun, or for the buzzards to feast over. Thus, Anaka and his men were killed while trying to find Chamuscada and persuade him to return to the Chiricahua way of life, to join Anaka and destroy Fort Bandolier.

"In two years, Anaka's braves have taken many Mexican and Anglo scalps, burned Mexican and Anglo villages and ranches, taken women and children prisoners, their food, horses and cattle. They have poisoned wells and burned what they could not take. This, until his last battle, has been done well.

"Listen, brother. As time passes, more White Eyes cross the desert from Tucson to Yuma and to the great ocean beyond. Others come from the great ocean eastward. If we do not kill them, they will grow in numbers until they will sweep us aside as the wind sweeps sand before it. They must not be allowed to spread and grow. This is your task.

"You will have more braves now than did your brother Anaka. With this force, you will form small bands to attack their stages and wagons, their ranches. You will run off their cattle and horses, take their rifles and ammunition. Send those horses and rifles you do not need to me. Be careful when you attack the soldier patrols to do so in force, for they are trained fighters.

"Hear me, brother. You will send emissaries to Chamuscada, to his son, Jarana, and urge him to join you. With your power and his together, you will be able to attack and destroy the Fort, then go west and do likewise to the largest village between the Fort and Yuma, Mesa Plata, where the silver miners are. Near it lies the Carancho Valley with many large ranches and many cattle and horses, enough to feed every living Chiricahua for many moons.

"By striking hard and often, you will create turmoil. If more soldiers are sent from Tucson and other forts, then I will strike where they are weakest. And one more thing, brother.

"From the renegades who sell us rifles in exchange for our yellow iron, I have learned the name of the man who killed Anaka and cut his head off to take to his chief at the Fort. His name is Pom-mer. Sam Pom-mer. He was married to the daughter of *el patrón* of Tres Flechas in Tubac, where I sent Tan-hay and forty braves to find him.

"Listen, brother. I want that White Eyes for my very own. I want him alive, but if he is killed, I want his head in payment of our Brother Anaka's head. I have sent word to every Apache tribe that the reward for this Pom-mer will be the richest ever paid. I have caused this word to be spread among renegade Mexicans and Anglos, that much yellow iron will be paid for him alive, less if he is dead. But I would wish to pay that reward to a brother than to a renegade.

"Brother, I have spoken what has lain in my heart and thoughts for many days and nights. I can say no more."

It was a long, emotion-packed and passionate speech and the effect on Bokhari was sobering. For a full minute the two men sat in silence, staring at each other. Then Bokhari spoke.

"Great Leader, I am honored to be chosen to replace my brother, Anaka, whom I have known and admired for a long time. Though I am younger, we have hunted together, raided together. Anaka taught me many of his ways, none of which I have forgotten, ways that have raised me in your esteem.

"I have listened well and will remember what I have heard. I will reach the Sonora camp in three days. I will organize my braves in small bands, join them together when we strike at the Fort and at Mesa Plata.

"Hear me, Great Leader. I will do those things I have been told to do. And more. I will send you rifles, ammunition, animals, food and those prisoners that survive and can be useful. For every brave slain, I will slay twenty White Eyes. And I swear upon Anaka's soul that I will find the White Eyes Pom-mer, and send him to you, alive as you wish, his head if it is not to be otherwise. Now I will sleep for one hour and be ready to leave. I have spoken what is in my heart and on my mind. This I promise. This I pledge myself to do."

"*Enju*, brother. Go and sleep now. Leave with your people in an hour," Cochise replied simply.

Bokhari rose and left the wickiup. Cochise remained alone to spend the night. In the morning, he would speak to Tan-hay, whom he favored over Bokhari, and allow the others to see them in open conversation so that Tan-hay's tarnished pride would be somewhat restored.

By mid-morning, the bodies of Diego and Rufino Flores had been prayed over in the chapel on Tres Flechas. Max and Caroline Potter sat in the first row with the widow and her three remaining children. All those who could be excused from their work, which meant all but a small guard lookout, were present. Sam Palmer and Marcos Espuela, as visitors, sat at the rear. After Father Ramon Paz had properly commended the souls of father and son to God and spoken his words of comfort to the widow and children, Diego and Rufino were buried side by side in the old family cemetery whose first occupant dated back to 1749.

Later, workmen dug a common grave beyond the grove of trees where the Apaches had hidden to make their fight and nineteen corpses were thrown into it without ceremony, minus their scalps, which their takers had hung up to dry in the brilliant sun.

The night range crews, relieved after daybreak, had attended the earlier services, eaten, heard the story of the attack, and were now asleep. Marcos, with less need for sleep, had mounted up and ridden off to visit his "cousins" at one of the four Tres Flechas range communities scattered over the 150,000-acre ranch.

After the funeral, Max Potter took his noonday meal with his *vaqueros* in the public dining hall which could accommodate a hundred men. Caroline had hers in her room. Sam Palmer, restless, and dreading the emptiness of the formal family dining room, had wandered out to the cookhouse and helped himself to some meat, beans, tortillas and coffee. Sooner or later, he knew, he would have to sit down with Max for a sober talk. To bring it to its conclusion without further delay, Sam went to Max's study-office to await him there. At two o'clock, he heard Max coming down the hallway, heard him say something to

51

Caroline and her indistinct reply. A moment later, they entered the room together.

"Sam," Max said, "I'm beholden to you. You couldn't've come along at a better time. You an' Marcos hittin' 'em from the east gave us a chance to break out an' go after 'em while they were confused."

"I'm glad we were of some help, sir," Sam replied.

"That you were, believe me, son." Potter sat in a handmade rawhide-covered chair behind his ancient carved desk and indicated the chair beside it for Sam. He turned to Caroline and said, "You goin'a ride today, Caro? Be sure you stay close—"

"Not today, Papa," Caroline replied. "I think I'll stay here with you for a while, then take a nap. I was up on the wall most of last night." She sat in the chair opposite Palmer, eyes on the tips of her polished riding boots.

Sam Palmer refused the cigar Max offered him and simply sat waiting for some way to introduce the sad subject he must talk about, less willing to discuss the matter in the presence of Caroline. Then Max said, "Well, Sam, I guess we got some things to talk about."

"I—yes, sir. I came as soon as I could."

"Quicker'n I expected."

Again there was an awkward pause and Sam felt Caroline's and Max's eyes on him, waiting. Ruth had been his wife, little Sam his son; then whose loss had been the greatest? Max's for his daughter and grandson? Caroline's for her sister and nephew? Or his own? It hardly mattered which. They had all suffered a great loss.

He began speaking slowly, as though each word must be incised in their minds and so expiate his guilt in some way. Throughout the solemn recitation, Caroline sat stiffly erect in her chair, hands tightly clasped on her knees so that even though they were well-bronzed by the sun, as her neck and arms were, her knuckles showed white beneath the tightened skin. At twenty, she was tall and lithe, wearing a tan riding skirt that was split to give her more freedom, and without the usual feminine fuss or frills. The shirt was tight across her matured bosom, the skirt firm around her slender waist, flowing outward from her hips down over the tops of her riding boots. Her hair was light brown, drawn back tightly in traditional Spanish-Mexican style, differing only in that the two long, braided plaits were drawn over her head into a crown instead of a bun at the back of her neck. Her eyes were large and dark and

52

her cheekbones were high enough to give her eyes a slightly slanted effect; somehow different from Ruth, Palmer thought, and yet so much alike.

Lomax Potter leaned back in his oversized chair as he listened, the cigar between his teeth gone dead. He was in his fifty-sixth year, but had worn those years well despite some slight thickening at the waist and a sprinkling of gray in his hair. Max was a tall, robust man, deeply browned, his neck and face furrowed with shallow lines, toll of the years spent in the outdoor world of active men. In Mexico during the War of 1846 where, the following year, then a lieutenant of cavalry, he and his patrol of eighteen men had fought off forty or more guerrillas bent on sacking the de Dorantes y Ruiz estate in San Antonio de la Huerta, in Sonora, the family *hacienda* of Don Estevan in his absence.

In that engagement, Max had taken a lance thrust that barely missed his right lung, yet it was a serious wound. Cared for by the elder daughter, Ysabel, he fell in love with her and by the time he was able to travel, had received Don Estevan's permission to return to call upon them. Max went back to Fort de Fronteras and when the war came to an end in 1848, came back to San Antonio de la Huerta to claim Ysabel, this to the great surprise, if not dismay, of Don Estevan. Yet, he had extended the invitation and received Max politely.

Ysabel and Max were married six months later and following the ceremony and festivities, Don Estevan signed over the original land grant to Tres Flechas at Tubac to the happy couple.

So now, as they sat in Max Potter's thick-walled study, its walls hung with memorabilia of his military life, hunting trophies, a case of rifles, shotguns and revolvers, Apache lances, and the symbol of Tres Flechas (three crossed arrows against a varnished placque), there was something ominous in the late afternoon dimness and solemn attention as Palmer amplified the brief message they had received by Army courier three days after Ruth and Sam, Jr. died at the hands of one of Anaka's band of raiders; omitting the grisly details, yet knowing that Max and Caroline were fully familiar with the savage methods of Apache torture.

" . . . so that night before I was due to leave for Pradero with Major Travis and the escort patrol, knowing we'd be gone for four or five days, I begged Ruth to let me take her and little Sam to the Fort, but she insisted they'd be safe with the Grays, Hamiltons and McLenahans nearby, that the Apaches had never come that far north or close to Fort Bandolier since before we moved there, but—"

Max's large graying head nodded, eyes sad and dull, mouth drawn into a grim, tight line; and yet, Sam could feel a sense of understanding and compassion in his father-in-law, overriding his grief for the loss of his elder daughter and grandson. Caroline, however, sat like a carved statue, eyes staring past Sam through the window and across the family corral to the caliche wall that surrounded the ranch headquarters.

" . . . and as soon as I can do it, sir," Sam concluded, "I intend to drive a wagon back to the ranch and bring them home to be buried in the family cemetery here at Tres Flechas."

Max nodded and found it necessary to clear his throat as the words he wanted to speak were choked back with deep emotion.

"And I brought the deed to the ranch back with me." Sam reached down and picked up his saddlebag from beside the chair, placed it on his lap and began to undo the straps.

"Why?" Max asked.

"Because I don't want it. You gave it to Ruth and me. Without Ruth, I couldn't live there or work it—"

"You could sell it, Sam. Some day it'll be worth—"

"No. It was yours before, it's yours now." He withdrew the deed and placed it on the desk and slid it toward Max, who made no move to touch it.

"I gave Ruth to you with my blessing, son, and what was hers then, is yours now. Keep the deed. Later on—"

Palmer shook his head from side to side. "As of the day I left the Fort, sir, I'm no longer in the Army. My time was up and I've been discharged. I don't think I'll be staying on in this part of the country."

He saw a shadow fall across Max's face. "Where do you think you'll go?"

"I don't know yet. I haven't had time to think about it."

"Then don't decide until you have. You'll stay here with us—"

In the brief moment of silence that ensued, Caroline spoke for the first time and her voice came with shocking force, startling both men with its harshness.

"Let him go if he wants to, Papa!"

Unaccountably, tears sprang into Palmer's eyes as he

realized then that Caroline's underlying anger and resentment toward him had reached the point of overflowing. He looked at her quickly, saw the glistening path of tears coursing down her cheeks.

"Caro," Max began, but without looking at either of them, she rose and ran out of the room. It was a moment of painful anguish for both men. Max got up and came to where Sam sat slumped back in his chair and placed a roughly gnarled hand on the younger man's shoulder. "Sam," he said softly, "don't hold it against her. When the word came, I guess it hit her even harder than it did me. She's been holdin' it inside her and this is the first time she's cried. It'll come out now and pass over."

Sam listened and was torn by Max's fatherly words. Almost compulsively, Max continued. "Special as Ruth was to me, she was more special to Caro. When their mother was killed back in '57, Caro was just about ten or eleven years old. I was damn well broken up an' had to be away a lot, so Ruth kind of took Caro over. Until Ruth married you an' moved away, they were inseparable."

"I didn't realize how strongly she felt. I'd always thought Caroline and I were good friends. She didn't seem to mind me taking Ruth away."

"She minded. Many a night Caro cried herself to sleep or just wandered around half the night, but if it made Ruth happy to be with you, she was willin' to give in to it. Right now, she blames you—"

"I tried, believe me. I argued, but—"

Max smiled grimly. "Sam, Ruth was her mother's daughter. Beautiful, headstrong and willful. Like Caro. Both of 'em had a will like Ysabel's. You couldn't make either of 'em do somethin' they didn't want to do any more'n I could convince Ysabel she should take half a dozen *vaqueros* the time she went to visit her family in Sonora back in '57, when the Apaches got her, the driver and her maid. Ruth and Caro both got that same streak of stiff Spanish spine.

"I did what I could for 'em, taught 'em to shoot, ride, hunt, dress a deer, ever'thing I'd of taught a son if we'd had one. Maybe their mother would've done a better job, but I did the best I knew how. 'Til you come along that time, I even got to believe they were boys, 'stead of girls. Hell, from twenty yards off, the way they dressed, nobody could tell they weren't boys."

55

"I—well, sir," Sam said, "maybe I ought to get along up to Tucson, get my thoughts lined up in a row—"

"No, Sam. I want you to stay here 'til you make up your mind what you want to do, where you want to go. Caro'll get over it—"

Sam's head shook from side to side. "Not the way she looked and sounded. Every time she sees me, she'll remind herself that—"

"Son, listen. Give me credit for knowin' my own daughter, good points and faults. Once she's cried it out, she'll come around." When Sam hesitated, Max added, "Do an old man a favor. Losin' Ruth, I lost a lot. I don't want to lose the only son I ever had on top of that."

There was the need and the plea in Max's voice, this man who in the brief period in which their lives had touched, had been more of a father than Lucas Palmer had been to his son in the first twenty years of Sam's life; an unpredictable gypsy without roots, without a destination or future.

"I'll stay the night," Sam conceded, "and think about it."

Max Potter did not push the issue further. He clamped Sam's shoulder with one hand and went out. Tomorrows always had a way of changing things, sometimes for better, sometimes for worse; and he left Sam with the unsettled feeling of being out of place and time at Tres Flechas, one that was disturbing to him.

Everything he had ever thought he would ever want was here, now with the exception of Ruth; but this was something separate and apart from Ruth. She was gone and there was nothing he could do to bring her back.

Almost as unsettling to him, he now suspected, was Caroline. Something in the way she walked, sat a horse, wore her flat planter's hat with its chin strap hanging loosely. Something in her voice, her choice of words and expressions; never replying to a question quickly, but taking a brief moment, as though thinking out her answer, before she spoke it. Something in her manner toward the *vaquero* children, a smile that showed deep warmth shown to almost no one else, not even Max.

She was two years younger than Ruth, so that now she was as old as Ruth had been when Ruth and Sam were married; and when this thought came to him, it was as though he were living in the past again, his first meeting with Ruth. Except for Caroline's coloring, darker than Ruth's, her hair with no trace of Ruth's blondeness; yet the shape of her face, her nose and mouth, height and figure duplicated Ruth's.

He found it impossible to look at Caroline without making comparisons. Her early shyness, in Ruth's presence, was gone. Caroline was as self-assured now as her older sister had been two years ago. She gave orders to the servants with Ruth's crispness, intelligence and firmness, and they obeyed her as they had once obeyed Ruth.

And he wanted, more than anything else, not to have this living, breathing reminder of the woman he had loved, married and lost, as a constant reminder of his own guilt.

Despite the fact that he had never enjoyed formal schooling, in fact, had never spent a single day of his life inside a schoolroom, Sam Palmer possessed a better than average education. He had been born in 1841, in a wagon, to Elisabeth Edison Palmer when she was twenty-seven, a former school teacher from Beaufort, South Carolina. She had married Lucas Palmer, an itinerant preacher, after a whirlwind courtship that had lasted the entire week he had held a ten-day revival meeting midway between Beaufort and Port Royal.

Years later, after having traveled many miles without ever a home to call her own, asking herself, "Why?" she could come up with only three reasons: 1) Lucas Palmer was a glib and persuasive talker, even though he was ten years older than Elisabeth; 2) she had never traveled outside a ten-mile circle of Beaufort, while Lucas had been "just about everywhere"; and 3) she was an orphan, living with an elderly farm couple, and Lucas Palmer had been the first man who had asked her to marry him.

Sam's own recollection of his life before the Civil War was a confusing conglomeration of hundreds of small towns visited and revisited in Mississippi, Alabama, Georgia, the Carolinas, Virginia, Maryland and Pennsylvania, later Ohio and Missouri, where Lucas preached and eked out a most meager living. There were many times when there was so little money that Lucas was forced to take temporary harvesting jobs in order to feed his family and two horses. Often, Elisabeth worked beside him and when he became old enough, Sam joined them in the fields.

He remembered best those days when, while traveling, Elisabeth brought new worlds to him from her small store of books. He became engrossed with history and geography long before she taught him to spell, read, write and calculate. More than anything else, Elisabeth dreamed that Sam would one day go to college and set about preparing him for the necessary entrance examinations; but as time passed, her hopes dwindled, knowing there would never be enough money.

By the time Sam was sixteen, Elisabeth was forty-three, grown weary of incessant travel among strange faces, without roots or having made a single lasting friendship. Lucas Palmer became a morose, stern, taciturn man who came alive only when they reached a new temporary stopping place. People came more out of curiosity than spiritual need, for Lucas preached himself into a frenzied state of near exhaustion in his belief that all men and women were sinners who must heed him and be saved, else be doomed to an afterlife of hell-fire and damnation; all of which left him hoarse and virtually speechless until they reached the next town.

Lucas turned a deaf ear to what he called Elisabeth's "rantings and ravings" about Sam's future. He fully expected his son to follow in his footsteps and later support his parents in the same manner in which Lucas had supported his wife and son, not a very pleasing prospect to Elisabeth or Sam.

As time passed, Elisabeth's hopes died and she no longer spoke of college for Sam, a permanent home somewhere, a normal life instead of this gypsy existence that pointed in many directions and led nowhere. Sam drew closer to Elisabeth and farther from Lucas, assisting him with the wagon and team, setting up and striking the tent, but never attending the "service" he knew by heart and in which he held no belief. He began reading Elisabeth's Bible and the more contradictions he discovered in Lucas's preachings, the more he leaned toward becoming a true minister of the Gospel. Elisabeth encouraged him secretly and from somewhere among the hoard of books on the subject of theology that were Lucas's, and to which he hadn't referred in many years, she began to guide his studies seriously.

At eighteen, Sam was far more learned than Lucas and discovered that the more he learned, the less he had in common with his father. He had long ago discovered that Lucas was not only an ecclesiastical fraud but a philanderer as well. More frequently now, his father returned to their wagon with the heavy fumes of cheap whiskey on his breath, with cheap perfume on his clothes. Several times, ne had been beaten severely, by atheists, he claimed. On one occasion he was herded back by a sheriff at the point of a gun, ordered to "pack up an' git outa town afore that gal's daddy comes a-lookin' fer yore hide."

Shortly before Sam reached his twentieth birthday in January of 1861, they were on the outskirts of St. Louis, an entirely new and strange part of the country to them, this to satisfy Lucas's needs for fresher fields. It was here that Elisabeth contracted typhoid fever and died in the same wagon in which she had spent her honeymoon, labored to bring her son into the world, lived the entire twenty-one years of her married life. On that last night, in a rare lucid moment, she whispered to Sam, "Don't leave me—"

"I've got to go find Pa, Mama."

"No, Sam, please. I don't want to see him. Darling, listen to me, carefully. Now, you won't have me to think about. Leave him. Please. Leave him and make a life for yourself, Sam—" Her voice fell to a whisper and she lapsed into silence.

And died.

Lucas returned the next morning and found Sam sitting beside Elisabeth's body, her hand held between his own as though trying to bring warmth to it. When Lucas climbed into the wagon bed unsteadily, Sam looked up at him and said, "Go back to town. She's dead."

Lucas blinked. He began mouthing a prayer for the dead, but Sam stood up and said, "I've already said what needed to be said. If you want to stay, get the shovel and start digging a resting place while I make a coffin."

"Don't you be tellin' me what to do, boy," Lucas snarled.

Then Sam struck him across his unshaven face. "You're not fit to be in her presence. Now get out of this wagon and do as you're told or go back to town and spend your last cent swilling more whiskey. We don't need you."

Sam was crying and Lucas, for once, was without words. He climbed over the tailgate of the wagon and went back into town. Sam got some planks from a sympathetic farmer nearby and built his mother's coffin. The farmer's wife and daughter prepared Elisabeth for burial and the farmer and his two sons helped Sam bury her in this strange place, in strange earth, with strangers as the only witnesses of her departure while Sam prayed and eulogized the mother he had loved so deeply.

He returned to the wagon that night, but Lucas had not

come back. He waited for a week, working for the farmer for his meals only, driving himself from early morning until late at night in order to lessen his grief. Later, he would make plans for his future without Lucas.

Then, late on the following Saturday night, the marshal came, waking Sam from a deep sleep. "Your name Palmer?" he asked.

"Yes. Sam Palmer."

"You know a Lucas Palmer?"

"He is my father."

" 'Fraid I got some bad news for you, son."

"What is it, Marshal?"

"Well, seems like he got caught comin' out of Connelley's General Store long after Andy'd closed down for the night. One of my constables seen him comin' out the back door, the lock busted off, him loaded down with two sacks of food, some clothes an' other stuff. Called to him to stop, but instead, he ran, still holdin' on to them two sacks. Well, the constable fired a warnin' shot, but he didn' pay him no mind, so he shot him."

"How bad is it, Marshal?"

"He's dead, son. We taken him to Doc Hardy's. You c'n come with me an' see him. We're right sorry, knowin' you lost your mother jus' las' week, but—"

Sam went with the marshal, identified Lucas and signed a required form of release. Because there was no money, the city offered to bury Lucas in the town cemetery, and Sam accepted the offer despite the farmer's suggestion that he would permit Lucas to be buried beside Elisabeth; an offer which Sam deliberated briefly, then declined with polite thanks.

Next morning, he sold the wagon, team, tools and odds and ends to the farmer for a hundred and twenty dollars, moved into town and accepted a job with Abel Wormser, who ran a wagon outfitting and supply operation for immigrants heading West. He acquired a horse and saddle, a rifle and revolver, and learned to ride and shoot from a fur trapper who had given up his trade because of a deep scalp wound received during an Indian attack and which, from time to time, rendered him somewhat addled in his thinking and movements. The trapper now worked, when able, for Mr. Wormser, doing odd jobs and helping the hostlers. Listening to the old trapper, learning from him, Sam began exploring the idea of joining a wagon train as hunter or scout, but wagonmasters turned him down for lack of experience, despite his offer to work without pay.

So it was that in mid-April, when word reached him of the firing on Fort Sumter and President Lincoln's call for volunteers, Sam drew his wages, said goodbye to Mr. Wormser and the old fur trapper and enlisted in the United States Cavalry. Next morning, he sold his horse, saddle, rifle and revolver to Wormser and headed for Jefferson Barracks with a contingent of other enlistees, to find the first real home with four walls he had known in all his lifetime.

Sam Palmer became a good cavalryman. He had a natural love for horses and once out of training, was not bothered by moving from place to place, something he had done all his life. A good student, his mind retained what he learned. He made friends easily, out of hunger for friendship denied him previously. He became hardened in body as well as in his dedication to the belief, unlike that held by Lucas, that slavery imposed upon any human being was against God's will and man's true nature. He carried Elisabeth's Bible with him and took comfort from reading it whenever the opportunity presented itself, often quoting from it, enjoying the nickname given him by his new friends. Preacher.

In Virginia, he saw his first combat. Dismayed and horrified by the sight of wholesale death of man by man, he learned quickly to hate war, yet he fought well and won his corporal's stripes for meritorious conduct under fire after six months. Later, he drew a third stripe for exemplary conduct and leadership when his platoon leader and sergeant were both killed in a patrol action, and Sam assumed command and successfully accomplished the mission. Still later, he was offered a field commission, which he refused, feeling that while he was dutybound to fight for what he believed was right, he could not conscientiously lead others to kill when they might feel otherwise.

As the long hard war drew to a close, Sergeant Palmer again considered the ministry as a career, but in April of '65, when it finally came to an end, he decided to remain in the cavalry and help rebuild a new world from the carnage and ashes left by four years of bitter conflict. In a way, he saw it as the work of a missionary, this healing of the rupture between brothers, and recognized that with peace, brotherly love did not come automatically. He stayed on to complete his six-year enlistment and was sent to Arizona

Territory to help make passage safe for the thousands of immigrants who were eagerly moving west in search of new land, a new life with new hope.

Late in 1865 at Fort Lowell in Tucson, which had been established in '62 as a supply depot for Southern Arizona and was now a base of operations against Apache hostiles as well as a center for military escorts, word was received that some sixty Apaches had the large Tres Flechas ranch at Tubac under attack. A patrol of thirty men was somewhere in that area, its exact location not known. Rather than draw off more men from the already shorthanded garrison, Major Linus Dutton suggested sending a scout to find the patrol and deliver orders to its commander, Lieutenant Nicholas Patricola, to proceed at once to Tres Flechas and give aid and relief to its owner, Lomax Potter.

Major Dutton won approval of his suggestion and chose Sergeant Sam Palmer, one of his most reliable military scouts, who had returned the day before from a patrol in the Dragoon Mountains and knew the Tubac area. Palmer, with a fresh mount beneath him, set out at once. By mid-afternoon he had cut across several signs of unshod Apache horses, then circled wide to the west and found what he was seeking—the imprints of Army-shod mounts. Long before dusk, he caught up with Lieutenant Patricola eight miles west of Tubac, proceeding in a leisurely southwesterly direction. The message delivered, Patricola gave the order to change direction and began a swift ride toward the Tres Flechas Rancho.

On arrival, they barreled up the long slope toward the walled compound, a veritable fortress from which Potter's *vaqueros* were giving a good account of themselves. Its one disadvantage was that when such a defensive battle was fought, Tres Flechas cattle and horses must be left vulnerable to slaughter and theft.

The Apaches, expecting no resistance from outside, had corraled a considerable number of steers and horses to take back to their camp and, flushed with success, were now trying to crack the defenses of the main ranch headquarters. At first sight of the hated bluecoats, they withdrew, then charged in and were beaten back. They charged once more and were hurled back for a second time, taking heavy losses. Now, in a wild dash, they attempted to stampede the horses and cattle they had rounded up, but the cavalrymen cut into their lines, wedged themselves between the attackers and the animals, driving off the Apaches empty-handed just before night fell. On the green slopes before the walls of Tres Flechas, more than thirty Apaches lay dead. The bluecoats has taken one casualty, a lance thrust in Corporal O'Hara's leg. Then out from behind the walls rode a score of *vaqueros* to round up the animals under guard of the cavalrymen. When darkness finally came, all was safe once more. Tres Flechas counted no men dead, five wounded, half a dozen head of cattle and two horses killed.

As they rode toward the compound, *vaqueros* rose upon the thick walls and waved their *sombreros* and rifles in thanks to the troopers, while others opened the thick bronze-studded oak gates to admit them. Lomax Potter, an unlit cigar clamped between his teeth, leaped down off the wall to greet them, his rifle still warm.

"Welcome to Tres Flechas, Lieutenant. My house is yours. We've got hot food for your men, feed and water for your horses."

"Thank you, sir," Patricola replied. "We came as fast as we could once Sergeant Palmer here brought us the word. Any casualties to report, sir?"

"Only some minor wounds and a few animals, Lieutenant. My *vaqueros* will bring in the dead steers and butcher 'em. The few horses are our only real loss. I'd guess we gave 'em another lesson. I make it about half the damn rascals dead."

"We'll go in pursuit—"

Potter said, "Waste of time, Lieutenant. They're ridin' light and'll be well inside the mountains before you can even get close to 'em. Dismount your men an' let's get 'em fed."

A slight figure, wearing a large *sombrero* and soft buck-skins that showed many washings and wearings, came across the compound carrying a late model Winchester repeating rifle, one exactly like that carried by Lomax Potter. The *sombrero* pulled off, Palmer saw it was a blonde-haired girl with dark, flashing eyes, the beauty of which he hadn't seen in years. Max Potter curled an arm around her shoulders affectionately, his voice filled with paternal pride. "My daughter Ruth, gentlemen."

Patricola saluted and Sam Palmer removed his forage cap. "Ma'am," both said simultaneously.

"Lieutenant—?" Potter hinted.

"Patricola, sir. Nicholas Patricola."

"And Sergeant—?" Ruth Potter said.

"Palmer, Miss Potter. Sam Palmer."

"Thank you, Lieutenant, Sergeant," Ruth said. "They'd have run off a good sixty head of cattle and two dozen fine horses if you hadn't come along. And no telling what other casualties we might have taken."

"Very expensive beef an' horseflesh," Potter added.

"I guess they lost about thirty or more of their braves, didn't they, Papa?" Ruth asked.

"About. Where's Caro?"

"Still up on the wall. She did fine, Papa."

"My youngest," Max Potter explained. "Caroline, I mean. She's sixteen. Ruth here's eighteen."

"Almost nineteen," Ruth chimed in. "Are we going to jaw the Army to death or feed them, Papa?"

"Shuh. You run tell Emelita to set a table for these troopers and the Lieutenant—"

"I sent word already. There's plenty of food. Sergeant, you can show the men to the shed behind the kitchen. There's water for washing and I'll send some fresh towels out."

The Army men ate outside in the warm night, seated around a long table, served by Mexican women and men servants. In a long barracks-type adobe building, the *vaqueros* gathered for their own meal, drinking with gusto, each relating incidents of the recent engagement. Already, there were new Apache lances, bows and arrows to add to the many other relics hanging on the walls.

Max Potter sat between Patricola and Palmer, giving his account of the attack, chuckling happily over their success in driving the Apaches off without a single fatality sustained by his own, and the Army men.

"Must be new in this area," he said, "else they'd know they'd lose more'n they could gain. Hell, this rancho's been standin' since 1744, when Don Miguel de Dorantes y Ruiz built it for his northernmost outpost."

"You hold out against the Apaches when the Army pulled back to Tucson in '61?" Patricola asked.

"Hell, we held out against Apaches, rustlers, drunken miners, cutthroats an' every damned thing else, before the War an' since. I got nigh onto two hundred *vaqueros* here I trained myself. From the top of that wall, we could stand off five hundred men. 'Course, it's tough on my stock, but they can't get it all. I've always got it spread out over 150,000 acres of range an' four camps, plus open rangeland. Take every Apache in Arizona an' New Mexico to round up all my cattle an' horses at one time."

Palmer had finished his meal, excused himself, and walked toward the cookhouse in back of the main house, where he found Ruth supervising the servants. With her, he saw her younger sister, Caroline, who appeared shy and went toward the main house as he approached.

"Something I can get for you, Sergeant?" Ruth asked.

"No, miss, thanks. Except maybe—"

"Except maybe what?"

"I—uh—that rifle you were carrying. Never saw one like it before."

Her eyes brightened. "Isn't it a beauty? The newest model Winchester repeater, still in the experimental stage. Wait here, I'll get it."

She went into the house and returned with it. Palmer hefted it for weight, found its center of balance, operated the lever, pumping out shells as Ruth caught them. He sighted along its barrel, caressing it as a man would caress a woman or horse he loved, then took the cartridges from the palm of her hand and reinserted them. When he held it toward her, she seemed almost reluctant to take it, then did so and gave it to a boy she called Miguel and told him to take it into the house.

"You're right," Palmer said. "It's a real beauty. Is it accurate?"

"Allowing for windage and distance, you can hardly miss. Papa's cousin at Fort Leavenworth sent him four of them with a shipment of goods that came through a couple of months ago."

"Fort Leavenworth. I was there once, taking some goods there from St. Louis. Back along in early '61."

"Maybe you know them. Olmstead—"

"And Son," Sam finished. "Sure. The big trading post and wagon outfitters."

"That's the one. Aaron, Libby and a son and daughter. Loren and Laurie. They would be about my and Caroline's ages right now."

"When did you see them last?"

Ruth laughed musically. "Never. Well, Papa saw Aaron and Libby years ago. Papa's father and Aaron's father were right close, one living in St. Louis, the other in Fort Leavenworth. It's a long story. Aaron inherited the business from his father and Papa has been trying to convince Cousin Aaron to sell out and come here to live."

"Be nice for you-all, having family to live with. I never had any, just my mother and father."

"Well, there's miles of room out here. Maybe in a few years they'll be able to make up their minds. Excuse me, please, Sergeant Palmer? I've got to keep behind the servants—"

"Uh—sure." He turned to leave, turned back and said, "You ever come to Tucson, Miss Ruth?"

Her eyes twinkled as brightly as her smile. "Sometimes with Papa, to order supplies, or when a big shipment comes through. Or when we're invited to a *baile*."

Sam said, "I wish I could see you again."

"You can always come to Tubac."

"Not always."

"Don't you ever get time off, a furlough?"

"Only when there's a good enough reason. We're short-handed."

Her next question was slyly put and surprised him with its frankness. "Would the Army consider me a good enough reason, Sergeant?"

He caught his breath and a slow grin broke over his face. "Miss Potter," he said, "the Army would be awfully stupid if it didn't." Then he turned and went back to the tables where the lieutenant and other troopers were smoking Max Potter's cigars and drinking a refined version of mescal.

The troop spent the night at Tres Flechas. In the morning, they breakfasted on hot corn cakes with honey made from a type of desert cactus fruit, steak, eggs, biscuits and strong coffee, then resumed their patrol to the southwest, leaving Palmer to return to Fort Lowell to report back to Major Dutton. The troop left first and when Palmer saddled up, Ruth had not made her appearance. Max Potter rode up to the corral and dismounted.

"Well, Sergeant, all set?"

"Yes, sir, and thank you for your hospitality. It was the most enjoyable assignment I've had in my entire Army experience."

"Thanks are on the other side, son. If you hadn't come along to bring the others here, I could have lost those cattle and horses to them damned redskins. I figure you-all saved me a good two-three thousand dollars, countin' the breedin' stock. I'm grateful."

"It's our job, Mr. Potter."

"Your name is Palmer, I recollect."

"Yes, sir. Sam Palmer."

"You're a mighty polite-mannered man, Sam."

"Thank you, sir."

Potter mounted his horse, turned toward Sam and said, "My Ruth, she tells me you taken a fancy to her new rifle."

"Not a fancy, sir. I was only admiring it."

Potter reached for the one in his saddle scabbard, withdrew it and threw it to Palmer, who caught it with both hands. "Beauty, ain't it?"

"Yes, sir. I examined Miss Ruth's last evening. I wish the Army had them as good as this."

"They'll be gettin' 'em some day soon. These were the first. Always takes the Army longer to make up its mind. Well, maybe we'll run across you in Tucson some day. Tres Flechas does some business with your Quartermaster Supply Officer, Colonel Scott. You know him?"

"I know of him, sir. We're somewhat far apart in rank."

"Yeah. I guess that's so." Potter reined the sorrel in and turned him. "Well, good luck, son. You get a chance to come visit, you'll be welcome here."

Palmer handed the Winchester back to him. "Thank you, sir."

Potter backed the sorrel off a few steps. "It's yours, Sergeant, compliments of Tres Flechas."

"I can't accept payment, sir—"

"Payment, hell. I've given blooded horses to men I liked in my time, son. I'm givin' you the Winchester because you appreciate a good weapon when you see one. *Hasta luego, amigo.*" He pulled the sorrel around again and went galloping through the open gateway, leaving Palmer with the rifle in his hand and his mouth open, thoroughly dazed.

He hoped he would see Ruth before he rode out, but neither she nor Caroline made an appearance, and the sun was rising. He needed to be on the road north if he wanted to get to Fort Lowell before dusk. He mounted up reluctantly and left, holding the rifle close to him, thinking of Ruth's warm smile.

He saw her next in Tucson about five weeks later. She had come up with Lomax and a crew of his *vaqueros* to deliver some horses and lay in supplies for the ranch. During the day, Potter stopped by Troop D barracks to ask for Lieutenant Patricola, who was out on a mission, then for Sergeant Palmer, who had just returned from a paymaster escort patrol to Fort Bandolier. They greeted each other warmly and Potter invited Sam to dine with him at the Congress Hotel, which Sam accepted with great delight.

Ruth's name had not been mentioned, so his surprise at seeing her was as great as it was genuine, struggling hard to restrain his rising excitement. The meal was plentiful, if lacking in quality, but no one seemed to mind. The conversation was limited to weather, rumors of Apache hostiles in this area or that, Palmer's uneventful escort trip to Fort Bandolier, a bit of news quoted from an Olmstead letter from Fort Leavenworth.

The meal over, Max Potter asked to be excused. "Got to see a man at the saloon, next door, a cattle deal."

"Don't try to fill any inside straights, Papa," Ruth said impishly.

"Godderned women," Max replied with feigned annoyance. "You teach 'em all they know, all's they do is use it against you. I'll be back here by midnight."

"I'll see that bet and raise you fifty," Ruth chided.

"All right, missy. I come in before midnight, it'll cost you fifty."

"I'll risk it," Ruth said with a laugh as Max left them.

"He's quite a man," Sam said.

"Quite a man," Ruth agreed. "How do you like your new rifle?"

"I've got you to thank for that, haven't I?"

"Papa said you saved us—"

"I didn't do it for a reward, Miss Ruth."

"If I thought you had, you'd never gotten within a hundred yards of that Winchester."

"It's the finest weapon I've ever seen, let alone owned. The whole camp is green with envy. And you should have seen the boys at Fort Bandolier. I could have gotten a whole year's pay for it."

"I knew you'd love it. I hope it takes as good care of you as you take of it."

"It will. Oh, it will. Shall we leave now?"

"Yes. I'd like to walk around and see Tucson at night. I've never done that before."

"I should hope not."

It was a beginning. Palmer received a note from Ruth later in the month. He asked for and received a weekend

68

pass to visit Tres Flechas. Ruth came into town on several occasions to buy dress materials, to attend a wedding, to go to a *baile,* once when Max drove two hundred head of cattle to deliver to the Army Quartermaster. They managed to see each other on most of those occasions and a few months later, Sam got another weekend pass and rode south to Tubac.

On Saturday, when supper was finished, they sat on the porch beneath the *ramada* and listened to the guitars and songs from the *vaquero* quarters, the click of dancing heels and spurs, the happy laughter. Caroline, after an active day riding, grew sleepy and went to bed. Then Ruth excused herself and went inside, giving no reason, but none was needed.

Max waited, drawing contentedly on his cigar, a glass of tequila on the table beside his armchair. Sam was tongue-tied, trying to think of some way to introduce a revolutionary new thought. And it was Max who finally did it for him.

"You got something to say, Sam, cough it up before it chokes you."

"Sir, I—"

"When you ever goin'a stop callin' me 'sir' an' call me Max, like everybody else does?"

"I—well, sir, I can't be that informal to the man whose, uh, daughter I want very much to marry."

Max laughed quietly. "Goddern it, you finally said it, didn't you? Hell, I could see it on the tip of your tongue long ago. Now, all I got to do to get me a son-in-law is say, 'Sure an' God bless you,' hey?"

"It would be a great relief to me, sir."

"Then, sure an' God bless you both." Max stood up and went to Sam, a large bearpaw extended. "I'm mighty glad, son. I want for Ruth what she wants for herself, and if it's you, that makes it fine an' right with me."

Sam felt his hand in a rock-crushing grip. "Thank you, sir. It's what I've wanted ever since the first time I saw Ruth pull that floppy *sombrero* off her head. There's one problem I've got to mention."

"The Army? That's no problem. How long you signed up for?"

"I've got fifteen months left of my six-year enlistment. And the Army *is* my—our—problem at the moment."

"How so?"

69

"I'm due for transfer to Fort Bandolier, halfway between Tucson and Yuma."

"I know where it is an' I know Colonel Hatfield, the C.O. there. Well, it ain't the end of the world an' fifteen months'll pass. I'll miss Ruth, of course. So will Caroline."

"I was thinking more of Caroline. They're so close. I wouldn't want her to hate me for taking Ruth away from her."

"Caroline don't hate anybody. She's shy an' she'll miss her sister, that's for sure, but she'll get used to it. She's got to learn to rely on herself. She can't have Ruth to lean on all her life."

"Yes, sir, I understand—"

"Tell me, do married people get to live off post these days, Sam?"

"In Tucson, yes, and wherever there's a sizable town nearby. Nearest to Fort Bandolier is Mesa Plata, too far away."

"How about if you an' Ruth had, say, a ranch out there, close by to the Fort?"

"There are some ranches out there, but I can't afford a ranch on—"

"Ruth can. Matter of fact, I own some land out there I was thinkin' of givin' Ruth some day—"

"Sir, that's not really true, is it?"

"Son, I'm a reasonable fellow, anybody'll tell you that, so don't tell me what's true or ain't true. Them enlisted men's quarters on an Army post ain't fit to live in, so I'm goin'a give Ruth a ranch an' a house as near as I can put it to the Fort. I'll give her a couple of Mexican families to help out. When the Fort can spare you, you can be with her. Ain't been no trouble that close to the Fort since they reactivated it in '64, has there?"

"None I've ever heard about."

"All right, then, it's settled. I'll go in now. You stay here. I got an idea Ruth's waitin' to hear me go past her room to my own." He shook Sam's hand again. "Just remember, Sam. She's Lomax Potter's daughter, but she's got Spanish blood in her that goes back to the Conquistadores. She's a good girl, but she's got a will of her own an' I never lied to her but what she didn't know it."

"There won't be any need for her to exercise that quality, sir," Sam replied.

They were married in the chapel on Tres Flechas and

70

after a week in Buenavista, Sonora, returned to Tucson. Meanwhile, Max Potter bought the ranch of Milo and Eleanor Gilman, who hadn't the money to stock and work a small ranch and wanted to move back to Yuma. It was located somewhat less than nine miles north of Fort Bandolier, with the McLenahan, Gray and Hamilton ranches for neighbors.

When Sam was transferred to Fort Bandolier two months later, the ranch had been refurnished completely, stocked with a small herd of cattle, half a dozen horses, a new well brought in, and Mexican help from Tres Flechas to put in a vegetable garden and care for the pigs, turkeys, chickens, cattle and horses. Every off-duty day and night when Sam was free, he spent at the Poca Flecha, or Little Arrow Ranch.

Ten months later, Sam, Jr. was born. Strong, healthy, and happy. Max and Caroline came to stay a month, bringing gifts and more servants from Tres Flechas. Sam was relieved of patrol duty during this period and was free to share the company and the ranch rang with song, laughter and the music of guitars, with little to interfere.

But to the south of the Fort, Apache movement was increasing. Anaka, anxious to show his strength to Chamuscada and thus convince him to return to traditional Apache life, sent his bands of braves ranging through the area on a program of destruction. More ranches were burned out, more rancher families were wiped out and those who had been fortunate enough to escape with their lives were returning to Tucson or Yuma to seek a haven of refuge.

When Max, Caroline and the extra Tres Flechas help left, Poca Flecha fell into an unnatural silence. There was apprehension among Palmer's neighbors, but none of this seemed to rub off on Ruth, who had experienced Apache attacks at Tres Flechas and had fullest confidence in her accuracy with rifle and revolver. So it was that when Sam was called upon to leave for Pradero with Major Owen Travis and two squads and scout to make a diplomatic call on Jesus dePeñas, the new governor appointed by General Benito Juarez after Juarez had overthrown Emperor Maximilian on June 28, 1867, he pleaded with Ruth to take Sam, Jr. and her servants to Fort Bandolier until his return. Ruth scoffed at the idea of leaving her home and possessions for any stray Apaches to loot and burn.

"I won't do it, Sam. I've stood up against Apaches be-

71

fore and they don't scare me one bit. Besides, if I go, I'll be running out on the Hamiltons, Grays and McLenahans. That's why we're here, isn't it, for mutual protection?"

Sam's arguments were lost on Ruth and he began to more fully understand Max's statement about the depth and strength of his daughter's will.

And why she and Sam, Jr. were now dead.

The patrol to Pradero had been gone for three days and had no way of knowing that on information brought to Fort Bandolier by the Pima scout, D'jiia, a relief column, led by Lieutenant Douglas Kennard, was on its way to find them and escort them back to the Fort.

The purpose of Major Travis's patrol was to make contact with Governor dePeñas and seek permission for United States Cavalry troops to cross the border into Mexico in pursuit of Apaches who used Mexico as a safe haven. The French had never permitted this "foreign invasion of our territory," but with Maximilian deposed, there was a chance that Benito Juarez would give his consent, and Colonel Hatfield wanted that chance badly.

On their second day out of Bandolier, Lieutenant Kennard's patrol had run across strong Apache sign heading in a direction that would very likely intercept Major Travis on his return. Kennard at once sent D'jiia back to the Fort for instructions, and Hatfield had sent word back ordering Kennard to split his column in half and take one platoon west and south to try to reach Travis as quickly as possible. On the morning of that fourth and last day, Kennard was still searching for some sign of the patrol, but instead of heading north and east for Fort Bandolier, Travis was actually heading north and west for Mesa Plata, sending Kennard farther west than he thought would be necessary.

On that fourth morning, Major Travis was in a depressed frame of mind. The meeting with Governor Jesus dePeñas, despite overtones of cordial affability and courtesy, had not gone well.

All Pradero was in a mood for continuing the long celebration in honor of the Juarista victory over the French. There was a riotous carnival spirit in the air. *Señoras* and *señoritas* danced nightly in the streets in brilliantly hued skirts, low-cut blouses and embroidered *rebozos,* their fervor heightened by much mescal, wine and food from the French commander's stores that had been found in his headquarters. The American troopers coming upon this joyous scene, even young Trumpeter Trueman, had succumbed to the celebration and fell happily into the arms and beds of girls and women eager to share their new freedom with the Americanos, even though they had had no part in the liberation.

DePeñas had welcomed Travis as a brother in arms, "my so-good friend and brother ally to the north." He listened, nodded with approval, drank more wine, set forth a repast truly worthy of an important ambassador of good will, and offered the major his choice of several lovely young companions to warm his bed: which Travis politely refused.

After considering Hatfield's proposal, dePeñas finally agreed—with one condition.

The situation among the hard-laboring Mexican nationals in Mesa Plata must first be corrected. DePeñas had received numerous complaints of ill treatment among the families who lived and worked under the iron rein of Señor Jeter (which he pronounced "Hay-ter") Kilrain, owner of the silver mine. He enumerated the complaints, expounded on them. Therefore, dePeñas concluded, the proposal to allow United States Cavalry troops to cross the border into Sonora must hinge on a new working agreement with Kilrain; an agreement which must be put into writing and lived up to. A small thing to ask, no, for what the great Governor of the Arizona Territory wished?

Also, dePeñas would send his cousin, Manuel Pedro Ortega, with Travis to help lay the Mexican case before Señor Kilrain and remain in Mesa Plata as *alcalde,* or chief of the mission, to see that the terms and conditions of the agreement were obeyed. Let no one say that Jesus dePeñas was unwilling to cooperate with his great and strong neighbor to the north.

Mesa Plata lay in the foothills of Monte de Lágrimas, the last of the high mountains south of the Gila River. South of Mesa Plata the land sloped sharply downward into the desert flatland, leveling off as it reached toward Pradero, fifty-one miles away; fifty-one miles of dry, flat country, broken occasionally by huge buttes, treacherous malpais, steep canyons, arroyos and barrancas. Across its vast emptiness, giant saguaro rose startlingly among prickly pear, cholla, Spanish bayonet and other members of the prolific cacti family in a desert of rodents and reptiles; heat by day, cold by night. And sudden death.

There was no road or trail as such between Pradero and Mesa Plata. The few scattered ranches and farms were spaced far apart, and their owners generally picked their way through the open desert when it became necessary to come into Mesa Plata to order supplies, often grouping together in convoy for protection.

Travis rode like a man carrying a weighty burden, only half listening to the constant chatter of Manuel Pedro Ortega who rode beside him. Travis's dog, Old Blue, having celebrated as never before in his life with his Mexican counterparts in Pradero, lay dozing happily across the saddle in front of his master, the sand and sharp malpais too hot for his feet, and with a tendency to romp off to investigate snakes, scorpions and small desert animals. Behind Travis and Ortega rode the sixteen troopers in a column of twos, suffering intensely from the spoils of overly indulgent hosts and hostesses, the heat of a blazing sun stimulating fierce thirst, and trying to evade the dust kicked up by the horses in front of them. The air was hot and dry. Breathing became a form of torture. Man and horse alike showed the effects of its enervating influence and were near exhaustion from the effort to keep pace. Sergeant Major Matt Donnelly brought up the rear, keeping the column closed up as best he could.

Up ahead, perhaps a mile and a half on point, Ira Gorton was approaching Chancla Canyon, known ribaldly by the troopers as *Chancre* Canyon, with Sergeant Sam Palmer and Corporal Henry Belden some two hundred yards behind him as flankers, now drawing together to enter the narrow corridor. Gorton rode up the steep trail to inspect the east rim. He studied the ground for signs and found none. He looked across the canyon to the opposite rim, scanned it for several minutes, then turned and rode down again, waving his arm in signal to Palmer and Belden that he was going through.

Far behind them, Ortega was saying, ". . . so we do not fear the Apache as the United States Cavalry does, Señor Major—"

No, Travis thought, of course you don't. And why should you when Anaka and his cutthroats can attack ranchers and our wagon trains and stages and scurry across the border for asylum in Sonora, where we're not allowed to follow them? And how much does your life- and liberty-loving Governor dePeñas take for his cut of Anaka's loot, the way the French did? How many captured rifles, rounds of ammunition, horses, how much food—?

". . . but is of most necessity that our people working in the mines are paid a better wage, their living condition improved, no? As I have said to El Gobernador in your presence, the work in the mines grows more difficult. The tunnels are deep and narrow. The heat in the shafts rises to 125 and 140 degrees. There are cave-ins and our people die. After a flash flood they sometimes work in water over their bellies. For this, they must be better paid—"

With measured patience, Travis said, "I have heard your complaints, Señor Ortega, and the demands of the governor. When we reach Mesa Plata, I shall go with you to Señor Kilrain and put them before him, but I cannot promise you he will accept them. However, I have the word of the governor that even if he should not, there will be some measure of cooperation which will allow our troops to cross the border and pursue—"

"Por supuesto! It is for this reason that El Gobernador, my cousin, asks me to accompany you, to hear for myself what is Señor Kilrain's answer. Señor Kilrain, he is what you call—*terco, obstinado*—he will not listen to me, Manuel Pedro Ortega, the one appointed *alcalde* of my people in Mesa Plata to protect—how you say—the rights—"

Why the hell don't you shut up, Travis thought with sudden savagery. Bad enough that dePeñas had exacted the promise from him to confront Kilrain without having to drag Ortega along to witness his defeat and humiliation. Kilrain would listen and laugh at the demands with his usual sneering arrogance. And why not? Where could the Mexican laborers and their families go? Back to Pradero, Castillo, Lamorros and wherever else they had come from, to starve? And when Kilrain refused, what could dePeñas do about it apart from refusing to cooperate with the Army?

Why, groaned Travis, can't our damn-fool government let us do what we're sent here to do—protect American life and property from the Apaches, and send civilian authorities to settle civilian disputes and complaints. Damn it all to—

He swung his somewhat thickening body around in the saddle to check the troopers behind him. No need. They were sagging in the heat, but properly shaped up under the eyes of Donnelly, whose head bobbed up as he caught the major's eye, nodding to indicate all was well. Travis turned back, thinking the scout and two flankers up ahead were perhaps too far out in front, wondering if he should send Trumpeter Trueman ahead to draw them back; but Gorton, Palmer and Belden, he saw then, had begun to disappear into the mouth of Chancla Canyon.

Ah, well. The men would be glad enough to spend the night resting quietly in Mesa Plata after their carousing in Pradero. In the morning, he would see Kilrain, already anticipating and dreading the strong rejection he would meet. Ortega would then report back to dePeñas, and Travis would make the last leg of his journey back to the Fort to report his failure to Colonel Hatfield and prepare an unsatisfactory statement to forward to Tucson.

They came into the canyon, the shade of its towering walls falling upon them with a sense of relief to be out of the sun that had been bearing heavily down upon them for over three hours. Travis looked back before he turned the bend. The column was well closed up. Ahead and above them, Travis's eyes searched the ridges, knowing that Gorton, Palmer and Belden had taken this precautionary measure in passing through ahead of them. He lifted the dozing Old Blue, cradled him in the palm of one hand, bent over as far as he could and let him drop to the ground. Old Blue came awake, barked happily and ran toward a small bush and began relieving himself.

They wound through the canyon bed carefully, eyes on the small boulders and sharply edged stones the horses were trying to avoid. And then lightning struck.

It came from the west rim in a hail of twanging bows and singing arrows, followed seconds later by an intense volley of rifle fire. Travis sat up straight in his saddle, his face registering shock beyond belief. His right arm shot up instinctively, moving forward as he shouted, "Trumpeter! Forward, gallop, ho!"

Before young Trueman could find the mouthpiece of his trumpet, or sufficient saliva to wet his lips, he was dead with an arrow through his heart. Donnelly came thundering up, repeating Travis's command. Bullets and arrows from the west rim of the canyon were hailing down on them as they tried to control their rearing mounts. Two horses fell, spurting fountains of blood. Manuel Pedro Ortega had reined his horse to a full stop, frozen with fear as the shouting cavalrymen rushed past or milled on either side of him in turmoil, pulling carbines

76

from saddle scabbards, leaning forward over their mounts to compress themselves into smaller targets.

From the west ridge overhead, rifle fire and arrows rained down upon them like hail. From every notch in the irregular skyline, empty only moments before, rifle barrels were thrust out, spitting flame and death. Matt Donnelly was the second man to die, shot through the chest as he wheeled around to fire upward at an enemy he could not see. A second later, Ortega fell to the ground, an arrow imbedded deep in his back.

Up forward, Travis turned in his saddle to look back. A bullet tore through his cheek, another struck his neck and a third entered his back. He fell to the ground, trampled under the thrashing heels of his terrified horse. As the life drained out of him, he saw his troopers caught in a hopeless trap, in a gully where there were no boulders sufficiently large to furnish cover. Horses and men were falling about him. The unearthly screams of the animals drowned out those of the men. Seasoned troopers fell from saddles as horses reared and pawed the air and lay on the rocky ground, attempting to sight in on an enemy that offered no target, trying in some unfathomable way to dodge the unerring arrows, lances and bullets that sought them out.

Concentrated in the narrow gap, they had no chance. Within minutes, not a single man remained alive. Six horses escaped, two to the north, four to the south. Old Blue had been caught up in the excitement and confusion, scurried among the fallen men, escaped the lashing and thrashing hooves of wounded horses until he found Owen Travis. He licked his master's face and whimpered, then looked upward with a furious growl and began barking shrilly. From above came the howls of joyous victory; then, almost as an afterthought, a single arrow found Old Blue with such force that it pinned him to the ground beside Travis. With one last painful growl, he was dead.

A dozen Apaches came swiftly down a steep narrow trail to loot the fallen of their rifles, ammunition belts and the Indians' favorite prize of all: the blue cavalry forage caps which they almost preferred to scalps. They were so engaged when a hooting signal came from above to warn them that the three White Eyes they had permitted to pass through unharmed were now returning. Reluctantly, the looters grabbed up their spoils and began climbing the trail upward. The last man snatched up Major Travis's ornamented forage cap, then raised his knife and cut off Old Blue's short gray-and-white speckled tail. Then they were gone.

Sergeant Palmer and Corporal Belden were a little over a mile north of the canyon when they heard the first volley of rifle fire. Palmer pulled the revolver from his holster and fired a shot to attract Scout Gorton's attention, but Gorton had already heard, wheeled his horse around and was galloping back toward them. The three men tore across sand and through chaparral, leaning forward in their saddles, allowing their horses to pick their way, meanwhile unlimbering carbines from their scabbards. Palmer was in the lead, his mouth open, screaming meaninglessly at his horse.

To no avail. They came into the canyon at breakneck speed. The horses, touching the stony bed, slowed and skidded into its mouth. Gorton pulled up short at the entrance and turned his horse west to find a trail that would lead him to the top of the rim, but there was none from the north side. He followed Palmer and Belden into the canyon. The narrow slot the Apaches had used to climb down into the canyon was for moccasined feet and not cavalry boots. Palmer was kneeling, holding Major Travis's head against his thigh. Belden ran from one man to the other like a madman, trying to find some sign of life in the others. He found no one alive.

Gorton stopped at the first crumpled body he saw. He turned it over. It was young Trumpeter Trueman, his face reposed as in sleep, an arrow through his heart. How much younger he looked, Gorton thought. How much at peace. Dead even before he had begun to truly taste life. Gorton picked up the shiny trumpet and laid it on the boy's chest, put one dead hand over it to hold it in place. Flies rose in angry humming clouds from their bloody feasts. Columns of ants had begun moving in, coming through sand, over stones. Gorton stood up and looked away, muttering curses under his breath. There were three wounded horses, screaming, struggling, blood running from bullet and arrow wounds, one horse streaming from his nostrils. The scout shot the three animals, using his revolver.

Palmer was crying openly. Belden's face was contorted with mute rage. Gorton, holstering his pistol, looked gaunt and drawn. "I don' know how it could of happened," he muttered dully. "I clumb the east rim an' there wasn' no

78

sign nowheres. I looked acrost th' west rim. Wasn' no sign. Nothin'. God Almighty, Sam, I—"

Palmer looked up through tear-dimmed eyes, hating the civilian scout while knowing he couldn't be blamed alone. I should have taken the west rim, he thought guiltily. I'm as much to blame as Ira. God forgive us all.

He went to his horse who was neighing and pawing the ground nervously. "You two wait here until I come back. I'm going to ride south to see where they've gone. We'll bury them when I get back. Keep an eye open. They may have left one or two behind somewhere to bushwhack us."

And high above the canyon, as though the word had been telegraphed ahead somehow, a lone *buitre* had begun to circle. Soon there would be other of his brother vultures to join the feast.

D'jiia rode ahead of Lieutenant Kennard's column, making circles as he cast about for some sign. Since he had returned from the Fort, Company K had been split into two platoons, Zimmerman taking his platoon south and east, Kennard heading south and west to link up with Major Travis's party, which should be returning from Pradero. Kennard had no way of knowing that Travis would be heading north and west toward Mesa Plata instead of north and east toward Fort Bandolier. And then D'jiia was racing back toward the column.

Painstakingly, because his knowledge of the Pima dialect was weak, Kennard asked D'jiia to repeat what he had found. Three shod horses north of Chancla Canyon. Army shod. Kennard shook his head in disbelief that Travis would be so far west. And why only three horses? D'jiia saw the look of doubt on the lieutenant's face, the puzzled eyes and furrowed brow, and began repeating his words, using his hands to make more elaborate signs, pointing repeatedly in the direction of the ridges that formed the canyon. Kennard decided it was worth the chance, since they had found no other sign, and ordered the platoon to move ahead.

At the point where Gorton, Palmer and Belden had joined up and turned back toward the canyon, D'jiia stopped and pointed out the sign, reading it for them as Kennard would read a cartographer's map. Kennard motioned him southward toward the canyon, ordering the platoon into a gallop. They approached the entrance

79

from the north. D'jiia had pulled up for a momentary halt and pointed toward and into the canyon mouth. Kennard raised one hand to his forehead and peered across the shimmering sand, then made out the figure of a man, a rifle raised upward in one hand.

He signaled the column on, spurred his own mount ahead and finally recognized the man as Ira Gorton. Within moments, he led the platoon inside where Corporal Belden stood beside the bodies of the dead that he and Gorton had laid side by side, Major Travis lying a few feet apart from the others. And Kennard thought, even in death, protocol dictates that the officer remain apart from the enlisted men. The body of the Mexican, Manuel Pedro Ortega, lay to one side on the opposite end of the row, evidently to indicate that he was a civilian and no part of the military.

The blood on blue fabric had already turned to the color of rust. The air was filled with fine-powdered grit, sour sweat, the nitrogenous stench of the horses and damp leather, but mostly, it was the suffocating heat that enveloped them all, the dead, the living. Kennard could hardly keep his eyes off Old Blue, split through the middle by the arrow, one paw reaching out toward his master, and his tail, for some mysterious reason, missing.

While Gorton and Belden were telling the tragic story, they heard hoofbeats approaching from the south. One horse. They waited in silence until they saw Sam Palmer come slowly through the bend in the canyon toward them. He dismounted, saluted and reported to Kennard.

"They're headed for the border into Mexico, sir. It was a good-sized war party. I'd estimate there were close to sixty of them."

Kennard said, "Sergeant, I want a full report. I want to know how this could have happened with Gorton riding point and you and Belden as flankers." He looked up and said to Sergeant Duncan, "The entire platoon. Burial detail. Get those shovels working and gather plenty of rocks to cover them with."

Palmer and Kennard went to one side and Palmer corroborated Gorton's and Belden's version of what had happened. When he finished, Palmer added, "It wouldn't have been nearly so bad if we were among them, sir."

Kennard said sternly, "Let's not have any more of that, Sergeant. We'll take care of things here first, then get back to the Fort and report to Colonel Hatfield." He turned to see that most of the men were already working with their field shovels, the rest gathering rocks with which to cover the graves. "I hate to be the one to bring this back to the colonel. He and Major Travis have been together since long before the war." He kicked at a loose stone, then looked overhead to where a dozen vultures were circling lazily, waiting. "They'll feast well on the horses, but I'll be damned if they get Old Blue. See that he's buried beside the major, will you, Palmer? Let's start collecting personal effects."

At both ends of the canyon, two troopers stood on guard. Before he turned back to the gruesome job, Palmer thought of the old saying about locking the barn after the horses had run off.

When the grisly task was over and the dead covered in their single common grave, Lieutenant Kennard placed a cross, made of two ocotillo branches, at its head. He turned to Palmer and said, "You've had some experience with this part of it, haven't you, Sergeant?"

Palmer looked away. "I never got that far, sir," he replied.

Lieutenant Kennard doffed his cap and stood behind the cross. The others bared and lowered their heads. Kennard said simply, "The Lord giveth and the Lord taketh away. Blessed be the name of the Heavenly Father and may he attend thee, our brethren. Amen."

And so were put away fourteen enlisted ranks, one officer, one Mexican civilian, and Old Blue. The dead horses would serve as food for the circling carrion.

On the following morning, the seven Apaches had come before dawn, advancing first on the McLenahan ranch, carrying out their murderous mission with extraordinary quiet and skill. The McLenahans had no dog to warn them, having run off the week before. And so they died, four in all. Next, the Grays, whose dog was killed with an arrow through him as the first bark began to rise from his throat into his mouth. Three victims. At the Hamilton ranch, Miles and Annie and their Pima were swiftly butchered.

All attention now turned to Poca Flecha, largest of the four ranches. The Apaches crept in quietly, but the Irish setter, Big Red, wakened, sniffed, and bounded toward the corral. They had split into two parties, one of four, the other of three. With the wind coming from the south,

Big Red headed in that direction where the three Apaches waited, racing as fast as his legs could carry him, growling ominously. Then he found them, and with a low growl leaped for the throat of one, but the other two caught him in mid-air and one sank a knife into him before his teeth could find his target's jugular vein.

At the first sound Big Red uttered, Ruth Palmer leaped out of her bed and grabbed the rifle standing next to the bed, loaded and ready to fire. She killed the first Apache who burst through the door and wounded the second, but the third ran his lance through her. The four other Apaches took care of the servants and Sam, Jr.

It was all over within minutes and they moved quickly, first setting fire to each of the ranch buildings.

On that morning, the Fort was nervous and it showed in the faces of the troopers, on and off duty, in the civilians quartered for protection, the officers, the Mexican workers and their laundress wives, even in the stockade prisoners. The word brought in by D'jiia had spread and the concern varied with the individual. But it was universal.

The officers and men speculated separately on whether the news of Anaka's raids would move Chamuscada to bolt the reservation in Monte to join forces with Anaka in a massive attack on the Fort. If this happened, they were of the general opinion that the Fort would fall and its occupants wiped out.

Some of the civilians, whose ranches had not yet suffered attack, wondered if Anaka's bands had reached their vacated homes and destroyed them. The stockade prisoners were worried over their own plight. In case of attack, would Colonel Hatfield turn them loose and arm them so they could aid in the defense of the Fort, or would he be afraid to arm them lest they turn on the defenders and shoot them down in a move to escape?

Hatfield seemed to take no notice of the nervousness that prevailed. At dawn the following morning, he walked from his quarters to his office as erect as always, sat at his desk and drank the coffee Riley had brought him. As Riley turned to go, the colonel said, "Sergeant."

Riley turned and stiffened to attention. "Yes, sir!"

Hatfield hesitated, then said, "Riley, I'm more than a little concerned about those four ranches to the north, between us and the mountain."

Riley said, "The Apaches never been in that close to us on the north before, Colonel, sir."

"No. And they've never been as close to us from the south before, either. Sergeant Palmer's wife and son are out there, and Palmer is on escort patrol with Major Travis."

"Yes, sir."

"Riley, I want you to take six men and get out to Palmer's ranch. Bring Mrs. Palmer and young Sam into the Fort, even if you have to use force. She's refused to come in before this."

"Yes, sir. Ruth, she was raised in Tubac. Max Potter taught her to shoot a rifle when she learned to ride, an' that wasn't hardly more than the time she began to walk, sir."

"Riley, I don't want any arguments from her *or* you. I want her and young Sam brought in by any means you've got to take. Then circle around to the other three ranches and give them a good shaking up. Warn them and try to get them to come in."

"Iffen they don't come, sir?"

"You won't be able to do anything about it if they refuse. They're civilians. But Ruth Palmer is one of our people and I want her and that boy here in the Fort if you have to tie her on her horse."

"Yes, sir!"

"Move out at once. Take any six off-duty men you can find and get out there as quickly as you can."

"Yes, sir!"

"On second thought, it might be well to have an officer along. Send the orderly over to the officers's quarters and tell Mr. Mason-Field I want to see him."

Within thirty minutes, the party of eight, led by Lieutenant Mason-Field, wheeled out of the gate and turned northward. This, Mason-Field thought, would be a moment to record in his personal ledger; it was the first time as an officer that he was in sole command of a body of troopers, leading his own men without the aid of a guide or scout. As he rode on ahead in a gallop, he could easily imagine that behind him stretched a long column of troops, platoons and platoons of seasoned, hardened cavalrymen, being led into action against superior forces of Apaches who were somewhere out there—.

First Sergeant Riley pulled up beside him, interrupting

83

his dream of power and glory. Mason-Field tossed him an annoyed look. Riley inched in closer.

"Drop back, Sergeant!" Mason-Field called out.

"Sir! Beggin' the lieutenant's pardon, sir."

"What is it, Sergeant?"

"Sir, by the lieutenant's leave, request permission to ride ahead on point."

"Permission denied," Mason-Field replied curtly.

"Sir, we're only eight of us. If we run into trouble an' lose even one man, Colonel Hatfield—"

At the mention of the colonel's name, the bubble of Mason-Field's dream burst and he returned to reality. "Permission granted. Move up on point, Sergeant."

Riley saluted, grinned and spurred his mount on.

The distance from the Fort to the Palmer ranch was a little less than nine miles. It was the ranch closest to the Fort, flanked on either side by the Gray and Hamilton places, with the McLenahan place lying just north. Riley had visited Ruth and young Sam with Sam on occasional weekends for a meal other than the usual Fort mess, and Ruth, in Riley's own words, was "a broth of a lass an' one hell of a fine cook."

Riding well ahead, Riley peered out from beneath the short brim of his forage cap through the shimmering haze, allowing his eyes to range from side to side to catch any sign of movement. The land was flat, broken only by desert growth; saguaro, cholla, mesquite, paloverde, ocotillo, and unnamed brush. He thought he had caught something up ahead and raised himself in the saddle for a better look, suddenly alarmed.

He turned quickly in his saddle and looked back. Mason-Field and the six troopers were about two hundred yards behind him, galloping along easily, spread out in a skirmish line to avoid the plumes of sand kicked up by their horses' hooves.

Riley shouted, knowing his voice would not carry, then raised his right arm high aloft and waggled it forward. Without waiting to see if they had caught his signal, he spurred his mount on, leaning low along its neck. He seemed not to mind at all that his cap had blown off in his need to reach his destination; and as he came closer and the smoke became clearer and denser, he began muttering long-forgotten prayers under his breath, mingling them with the foulest curses he could remember. Now he could make out small, bright tongues of flame, licking hungrily through the black smoke that hovered over everything.

When the others reached him at full gallop, Riley was kneeling on the ground beside the scalped body of Ruth Palmer. He had covered her naked, mutilated body with pieces of clothing that had been dragged out of the house and were flung around the clearing. Near the well lay the broken, almost unidentifiable body of Sam, Jr. One of the Mexicans who worked for the Palmers was hanging from the well rope, choked to death. The naked body of his wife and daughter had arrows driven into them, apart from other mutilations that had been expertly performed at closer range.

The house had been emptied of its furniture, piled into a large heap and set afire. The roof of the house and barn had been set afire by flaming arrows and were partially caved in. The breeding cattle Sam had prized so highly as the nucleus for his beef ranch now lay about in an enclosure with their throats cut, hearts and livers removed to be eaten raw, as delicacies. A calf had been gutted and thrown into the well.

Mason-Field dismounted and stood weaving unsteadily beside Riley, speechless at his first sight of the horror of Apache handiwork. His face blanched white, his mouth slightly open, the burn and sting of vomit rising in his throat. He turned to one side and retched, threw up a semi-liquefied mass, wiped his mouth with the back of his gloved hand. "Oh, my God! My God!" he muttered over and over again.

Riley crossed himself and stood up. The six troopers looked on helplessly, angrily, staring away from the dead, unwilling witnesses to the atrocities, the unspeakable cruel slaughter. Mason-Field was leaning against the adobe wall around the well, gripping its rim as though fearful of falling.

Riley called out, "Silbert, Downey, Sorensen! Burial party. Norris, Rouse, Linderman! Mount up an' check the other ranches. Move, damn it! Make a list of the dead in each place, then bury 'em. We'll come along soon's we're finished here. Move! Move out, damn you, or I'll blister the hides off'n every wan of ye!"

In all, they counted and buried seventeen men, women and children. Reading the signs, the Apaches had attacked at dawn, doing their work with expert thoroughness. One, perhaps two, Apaches had been killed or wounded, but

Riley could not do more than guess at the numbers since they had been very quietly removed, leaving only several trails of blood behind.

And this, coming on the heels of the massacre in Chancla Canyon, was what Sam Palmer learned on his return to Fort Bandolier.

Sam Palmer spent a wakeful, restless night. Even after he had finally fallen asleep in the early hours of the morning, he awoke when he heard the first soft chatter of the women cooks in the kitchen behind the main house, Emelita's voice overriding the others, briskly assigning each a task to perform. In the low barracks-like buildings where the *vaqueros* slept, lamp lights began to show as the men prepared to dress and eat their first meal of the day. Most of them would ride out just before dawn to relieve the night riders whose duty it was to guard the "family herds" of cattle and horses on the home range within a few miles of the ranch headquarters.

Outside, youngsters clattered about in the stables, tack house and corral while others roped and saddled the mounts to be used by the day riders. Palmer pulled on his shirt and pants, slipped into his comfortable boots and left the room. Beside the community dining hall, he poured a basin of water, washed and dried his face and hands. The *vacqueros*, wearing tooled leather chaps, spurs clinking musically, were moving toward the dining hall. Servants rushed platters of frijoles, meat, tortillas and huge pots of scalding coffee across the fifteen yards that separated the hall from the cookhouse. The men, coming alert at the sight of the food, began calling to Tereza, Consuela, Pepita and the other serving girls, mocking, laughing, teasing.

Perhaps because he unconsciously wanted to avoid an encounter with Caroline, Sam went to the cookhouse and entered. At once, Emelita greeted him. *"Señor,"* she asked in swift Spanish, "I can get something for you?"

In her own tongue and almost as fluently, he replied, "Only some coffee, *por favor,* Emelita."

"Ah. You wish nothing to eat?"

"No, *gracias.* Only the coffee. I will eat later with *el patrón.*"

Emelita poured a thick mug of freshly made coffee and handed it to him. He sipped it slowly, gratefully, savoring its flavor and warmth, and when he had finished, he poured

86

another cup for himself and returned to the house. Outside, the sky was still black velvet, the stars brilliant diamonds in the clean, clear atmosphere, perhaps a half hour to the first crack of dawn light. He passed Caroline's room, then the one Ruth had occupied for most of her life, tempted to enter, knowing it was kept in the same good order as when she had left it to marry him.

He decided against it and sipped more of the coffee, then walked along slowly; here was a storeroom for linens, opposite, a room for cleaning supplies, then Max Potter's room. As he came to it, the door opened and Max, fully dressed, even to the wide-brimmed, flat-topped planter's hat and Mexican-engraved leather gun belt, emerged.

" 'Mornin', son," he greeted.

"Good morning, sir."

"You up early."

"I—yes. I was restless and the coffee smelled good."

"Had your breakfast yet?"

"No, sir."

"I'm goin'a have to eat with the men an' ride out to check the south herd. You want to come along?"

"Not this morning, thanks. I've got some planning to do."

"Sure. You do that. You'll be company for Caro while I'm gone."

Sam almost smiled at the thought. Max said, "Forget what she said yesterday, Sam. That wasn't Caro talkin'. She'll be up soon an' I'll bet you five dollars she apologizes first thing."

"I don't like to win money on a sure thing," Sam replied.

"All right then, it's a bet. See you when I get back." Max turned toward the rear of the house, then stopped and turned again. "Sam?"

"Yes, sir?"

"Give her a chance to make her peace with you. We'll need that if we're goin'a be together."

Sam had an impulse to remind Max of his intention to leave for Tucson as soon as he could, but didn't feel like starting another long, drawn-out discussion. He had left the deed to the ranch on the table in Max's study yesterday and would take nothing but his own personal belongings, including the Winchester repeater which had been a gift from Max and Ruth that predated his marriage.

"See you aroun' sundown," Max said, and Sam nodded.

Another day couldn't matter too much in a life in which he had formulated no definite plans for his now direction-less future.

He went into the dining room and sat at the massive, handcarved table, its top a magnificently polished single piece that had been cut from the base of a tremendous oak tree and around which a dozen people could be seated without crowding. Marguerita, a young serving girl, entered the room softly.

"*Señor*, you wish to eat now?"

He ordered a breakfast far different from that which the *vaqueros* normally ate. Eggs, bacon, flapjacks and coffee. As Marguerita's head bobbed up and down in acknowledgment, he heard Caroline's bootheels on the tiled hallway floor. She came in, ordered a lighter breakfast, then turned to Sam as Marguerita went out, bare feet pattering out of hearing.

"Good morning, Caroline," Sam said probingly.

"Good morning, Sam." Her voice was normal and sweet, but no smile accompanied the words. "Did you sleep well?"

"Afraid not. Strange bed, I guess."

"I'm sorry. You'll get used to it. Did Papa ride out? I knocked on his door—"

"He said he would as soon as he's had breakfast with the men. South range. Be home by sundown."

For a moment, neither spoke, then Caroline said in a low voice with evident contriteness, "Sam, I'm sorry for yesterday, what I said. I didn't really mean it. Seeing you again upset me, thinking of—"

"Don't apologize, Caroline. It doesn't make things easier for either of us to talk about it."

"I'm sorry," she said again.

His voice took on a note of annoyance. "Don't keep saying you're sorry. It sounds as though you don't really mean it and are trying to make yourself believe it. If it makes you feel any better, I'm carrying a heavy load of guilt on my own shoulders."

"Sam, please." One of her hands reached out toward him, but the table was too wide at that point for her to touch his own outstretched hand. "I mean it. I know it wasn't your fault. I'll get over it, but it takes time."

"All right, Caroline." He eased back in his chair. "Let it stand. I'll be leaving soon. Staying here can only make all of us miserable and I don't want that. Max has been more father to me than my own. I love you the way I would my own sister, if I'd had one—"

Caroline drew her hand back and stood up. "I'll go see what's holding our breakfast up."

"There's nothing holding it up. Sit down."

She sat down. Sam reached into his shirt pocket and withdrew a small gold bowknot. He held it up for her to see. "There wasn't much left at Poca Flecha, but Ruth thought the world of this pin. She wore it in her hair. Colonel Hatfield gave it to her when little Sam was born, and she acted like it was the Medal of Honor. I want you to have it, Caro. She loved you very much and she loved this pin, so I figure you two ought to go together."

Caroline reached out and took the pin, stared at it through moist eyes, and when she tried to thank him, the words wouldn't come. "Keep it, Caro," he said. "Wear it."

"What about you, Sam?"

"I don't need anything to remember Ruth. She'll always be a part of me, too big to ever forget."

Marguerita returned with two platters of food, Emelita behind her with the silver coffee service on a tray. Caroline put the gold bowknot in her shirt pocket and tried to concentrate on the food over Emelita's constant chattering at Marguerita.

Later, he sat on the porch in the shade of the ramada and watched as Caroline walked to the family corral to get her favorite horse. She was tall, like Ruth. Beautiful, like Ruth. Dark-haired and sun-tanned, unlike Ruth. Again like Ruth, she wore a split skirt of soft doeskin that came to mid-calf, just below the tops of her hand-tooled riding boots, graceful as she mounted and swung her right leg over the saddle, seated herself firmly and rode toward the gates slowly as two guards hastened to unbar and open the thick wooden doors. As she passed through them, she heeled her horse into a gallop and her hat blew back from her glistening hair, but its chin strap caught at her throat and held it.

He wondered then if there would ever come a time when he would not compare Caroline with Ruth. Because he had never had a sister or brother, Sam may have felt an exaggerated sympathy for Caroline's loss of her only sister, even greater, perhaps, than his own, which seemed unbearably impossible. To see Caroline so enveloped in grief accentuated his own painful loss. How curious, he thought, this difference between Max and Caroline; Max's complete understanding, her lack of it. And with so much activity going on around him, he felt incredibly out of everything and alone. He wondered where Marcos was at this moment.

CHAPTER IV

DURING THE FIRST FOUR DAYS OF THE WEEK-LONG PA-
trol, they had come upon nothing to excite the interest of
Scout Logan or Lieutenant Zimmerman. The ten men
riding behind them were in the restless stage generally
resulting from lack of action. They had cut across old
signs, the ashes of cold fires, the skeleton of a steer that
had probably been killed for food, its bones now picked
clean by buzzards and desert rodents. There were no tracks,
for it had rained heavily on the third night out of Fort
Bandolier, and most of the desert had become pockmarked
with tiny craters caused by large raindrops.

From the first morning, it was believed the patrol would
be a dull one, coming so soon after the total rout of
Anaka's band, with heavy losses; and only three days
after the remnants of the marauders had made their
vengeful attack on Mesa Plata while in retreat, inflicting
little more damage, but losing more men.

On the night before the patrol, Colonel Hatfield, in his
briefing to Zimmerman and Scout Logan, had said, "Remember that even the most minor loss, until we are reinforced, diminishes our striking ability to a dangerous
minimum, yet we must continue to make some show of
strength. We cannot allow the Apache to suspect that we
cannot afford to exercise military control in the area of our
responsibility. Your patrol of ten men, Mr. Zimmerman,
is the largest we can afford to mount at the moment.
Take good care of it."

"Yes, sir," Zimmerman replied at once.

Logan chewed on his cud of tobacco, still imprinting the
colonel's words on his mind. "Mr. Logan?" the colonel
said.

Logan nodded. "You callin' the shots, Colonel," he
replied simply.

So now, on the fifth morning, the men were grumbling,
as expected, over their diet of dried jerky, beans and
wormy hardtack. Luckily, they had trapped enough rain-

water to refill their canteens after finding two known waterholes dried out and the wells of two burned-out ranches poisoned by dead animal carcasses.

Mounted by sunup, they were skirting the foothills of Dos Viudas, Logan about a hundred yards ahead and in clear view, Sergeant Tyler and Corporal Zentz about sixty yards ahead and to left and right, as flankers. Behind Zimmerman, the remaining eight men rode in a column of twos, saddle-weary, sand-crusted, unshaven and uncomfortable, looking forward to mid-afternoon when, if they made no contact, they would turn due north and head directly back to the Fort.

They heard the lieutenant's brisk, *"Look alert!"* and sat up erectly in their saddles. Zimmerman's gloved hand was raised, calling them to a halt. Up ahead, Mike Tyler and Mannie Zentz had pulled their horses up and waited for Willy Logan, who was riding back toward the column. When he reached Tyler and Zentz, they wheeled their horses and fell in behind him.

They gathered in a small knot, Logan, Zentz, Tyler and Zimmerman, out of hearing of the other eight men who were now staring with some apprehension in every direction, particularly upward among the ridges of Dos Viudas. When and if it came, they knew it would come from those barren, rocky ridges.

"What is it, Willy?" Zimmerman asked.

"Fresh sign, comin' out of one of them finger canyons, Lieutenant. Hide-shod hoofs, ridin' north an' a little east. Some horse droppin's, no more'n an hour or two old. My guess is it's a meat-huntin' party."

"How many, Willy?"

"Say maybe ten or twelve. If they're huntin' they'll be gone most of the day. There ain't nothin' less'n half a day's ride from here in that direction."

"What about following them?"

Willy shook his head negatively and scratched his five-day old beard with the double-pronged hook that replaced his missing left hand. "Wal, thinkin' on it, Lieutenant, I'd say no. First off, they got a good head start on us. Ridin' light, they're a lot faster'n we are. North an' east of here, you got the Willis spread with about ten pairs of hands to defend it. Then there's the Scott spread, six men. Also, the Rainey place with four men an' two women, been there a long time. Them women, Sarah an' Rebecca Rainey, they're good as any man with a rifle."

92

Logan shifted the wad from one cheek to the other and spat into the sand. "Best them Apaches can do is maybe run off a couple head of strays off'n open range. They'll kill 'em, do a fast butcherin' job, then pack the meat back here with 'em. Up inside that finger canyon, I'd say is their temporary camp, prob'ly got half a dozen women an' old men to do the final butcherin' an' packin' to haul back to their camp in Sonora. That's how I read it, Zim."

It was as far as Logan, as a scout, would go. Read the signs and interpret them. He had already vetoed Zimmerman's first suggestion to pursue the hunters and now he would wait for the lieutenant's decision.

Zimmerman was young in years, with fourteen months in Arizona after four years of field action during the Civil War, a brevet first lieutenant at the age of twenty-seven, no Academy training, but with two citations for bravery under fire. He came to his decision quickly.

"We'll move in, Willy. You'll scout that canyon carefully. If possible, we'll go in and take the camp party prisoners, then wait for the others to return and take them by surprise."

Logan nodded his immediate approval.

"Give us an accurate reading, Willy. We can't take the horses in without rousing the camp. See if there's some place where we can picket the horses out of sight and hearing. When we're ready, we'll go in fast. If there are only women and old men, I want no unnecessary killing. Once we've taken them, we'll bind and gag them against giving an alarm, then wait for the rest to come back for our surprise party."

Logan nodded and began to move out. As he turned, Sergeant Tyler said, "Lieutenant?"

"What is it, Tyler?"

"Sir, permission requested to accompany Scout Logan."

Crisply and with full assurance, yet without arrogance, Zimmerman replied, "Permission denied, Sergeant. If Scout Logan requires help, he will signal us."

"Yes, sir."

Logan, who had paused during this brief exchange, completed his turn and rode eastward. Zimmerman turned back to the rest of the column, Tyler and Zentz beside him. He ordered the men to dismount, then detailed the plan of action to them. Gone now was the lassitude they had shown during the past four days of monotony. Eyes became brighter with eagerness to make contact, to make a victorious return to the Fort, bringing prisoners and captured horses, the beef the hunters would return with. Up ahead, Logan had already disappeared from view, lost in one of the many entrance canyons into the Dos Viudas.

They waited, always a difficult period, under orders not to talk above a bare whisper, not permitted to smoke.

Waiting, as Logan had earlier related a conversation between Major Boyden and Lieutenant Mason-Field up in Monte de Lágrimas, was the most enervating part of any military action. "A lesson, Mr. Mason-Field, if I may," was how Boyden had put it. "The game of war is a game of waiting. You wait for hours, days, even weeks and months to place yourself in the most advantageous position possible. And when it comes, finally, you fight for seconds, perhaps minutes. But mostly, you wait."

And Scout Logan's added comment, "Long's you goin' up ag'in Apaches, Lieutenant, waitin's one thing you don't have to worry about too much. They'll come."

How true. Zimmerman had not been with them in the mountains or in Mesa Plata and had suffered from envy to have missed the action. And wondered how it happened that the eighth son of Avrum Zimmerman, an immigrant from Bavaria who had become a fairly wealthy manfactur-er of shoes in Boston, had felt a compelling need to leave his studies at Harvard and family to enlist in a war Avrum had insisted was none of his affair. It was the commission he had received in '62 and the battlefield promotion won at Gettysburg a year later that had made up his mind to continue a military career, to the dismay of his family and his own personal joy at finding himself in a position of command over other men.

Three-quarters of an hour passed and the men were beginning to fidget. Without ordering them to do so, Zimmerman wet his neckerchief from his canteen and brushed it across his horse's muzzle, allowed it to nuzzle the cloth between its lips to suck up what moisture remained. The others did likewise and it pleased Zimmer-man to note that they approved of him and the small things he did as well as follow his orders without question.

Tyler's low-pitched voice, close to his ear, startled him. "Lieutenant!"

"Yes. What is it?"

"Up ahead. Scout Logan returning, sir."

Logan's wiry horse, once the pride of an Apache sub-leader, loped across the desert floor easily. Pulling up

94

beside Zimmerman, Logan dismounted and waved his iron claw in an informal salute.

"Anything, Willy?"

"I'd say so. I tied up a little ways inside an' went up the canyon trail on foot. Sign everywhere. About three hundred yards up, there's a level floor, pretty much a box canyon. I bypassed it on another trail that taken me up higher, so's I c'd look down on that floor from a narrow ledge."

"What's in there?"

"Wal, like we talked about. It's a hole-up camp for about twenny, maybe twenny-five people. Five wickiups, small corral, the carcass of a mule the women were butcherin'. I'd guess about a dozen in the huntin' party. I seen four old men an' women, probally left behind to do the final butcherin' an' packin'. Four mules in the corral, no horses."

"That's it?"

"That's the way I read it, Lieutenant."

"All right, Willy. We'll go in, picket our horses, move up on foot and take over. We'll take them, keep them in the wickiups out of sight. Six men will remain there. The other six will take cover above the trail leading in and we'll catch them from front and rear."

Logan nodded, visualizing the trail, the rocks above it that would provide adequate protection. "We can do it, Zim," he agreed. "Three men on each side of the trail close to the entrance into the box. The six men inside open fire if need be, an' we cut off any retreat."

"Fine. Let's line it out for the men and go in."

"Right. 'Fore we go in, I'd have the men gather up some brush to wipe out our tracks as far as we go, then strip down gear to rifles, revolvers, ammunition an' one canteen a man to reduce the noise."

Zimmerman nodded and turned back to the men.

They worked well under Tyler's orders. At a little past two o'clock, they had worked themselves into position and were ready. They had climbed over boulders and dropped into the canyon trail less than fifty yards from the narrow entrance into the box canyon, then formed up on Lieutenant Zimmerman. On signal, they burst into the open area with carbines at the ready. At the first sound of cavalry boots, the terrified Apache women and old men found no place to run except to their wickiups, but the bluecoats followed and drove them outside again, lest there

95

be arms hidden inside. Resignedly, the Apaches stood in the center of the clearing, stolid in the face of what they surely knew would be death for the men, rape for the women. This was the way of the White Eyes, they had been taught from early childhood, and now they anticipated the very worst.

"Willy, tell them——." While Zimmerman spoke, the four women huddled together in fear, chattering swiftly in alarm. The old men simply waited with philosophical calm to be shot down.

Logan began speaking in the gutteral Athapascan tongue of the Apaches, enunciating meticulously, using his right hand in sign language so that each word and gesture would be understood.

"Hear me, *Hiuhah*," he began, using the ancient name of the Apache which meant Men of the Rising Sun. "We do not wish to harm you or your men who are away hunting, yet we cannot leave you here to kill white ranchers, drive off their animals, burn their homes and poison their water. It is the order of the white leader who commands the Fort that all Apaches return to the government reservations to live in peace with us. If your hunters agree, you will be taken by us to the Fort, then sent to the reservation. If they refuse and fight us, they will be killed. Do you understand me?"

One Apache who seemed older than the others nodded, speaking for all. "You are too many and too strong for us, therefore we will obey you, we old ones who remain behind while the others hunt. I cannot speak for them."

"This we know," Willy replied. "We will deal with them when they return. Until then, we must bind your hands and feet so that you cannot escape, tie your mouths so that you cannot give the alarm. What happens to the hunters will rest with them."

The old man nodded. "They will fight you, kill you, then release us."

"That will be for the gods to decide, old one."

Tyler, Zentz, Gregoris and Hall bound and gagged the women while O'Shea, Dean, Phillips and Collison did likewise to the men. When this was completed, the women were carried into one wickiup and the men into another. There were three wickiups remaining, and while Zimmerman and Logan discussed the situation and placement of the men for the upcoming encounter, Gross and Shuster checked out those three wickiups. The first two were empty except for sleeping pallets and the bare necessities for cooking. Tyler walked to the last of the wickiups, smaller than the others, and threw the flap aside, crouched over to enter it, then drew back quickly.

"Lieutenant!"

"What is it, Sergeant?"

Standing at the entrance to the wickiup, holding the flap to one side, Tyler said, "Lieutenant, you'd better see this for yourself."

Following Zimmerman and Logan, the other men began crowding toward the small wickiup. Zimmerman called out, "You men keep back. Zentz, see to it."

Logan, meanwhile, had reached Tyler. He bent over low and entered the wickiup on hands and knees. From the entrance, Zimmerman and Tyler heard him exclaim, "Holy mother!"

"What is it, Willy?" Zimmerman asked, but Logan was busy tugging at something, dragging it toward the entrance. Tyler and Zimmerman saw a pair of badly worn scuffed leather boots tied at the ankles with a rawhide thong.

"Give me a hand with this, Mike," Logan called to Tyler, who bent over to assist him. Grasping the ankles, they tugged hard and eventually the body of the man emerged into the open, his hands tied behind his back at the wrists, a gag in his mouth knotted at the back of his neck. Behind them, the men whom Zentz was restraining caught their first glimpse and muttered with surprise, "What the hell!" and other startled expressions of disbelief.

Logan whipped out his hunting knife and cut the bindings, helped the man to his feet. When he finally stood erect, rubbing his chafed wrists, the man displayed two rows of large white teeth in a grin that seemed to split his face in half.

"Thank you kindly, gentlemen," were his first words. "I'm sure happy to see some white faces for a change."

Logan stared at the man who easily equaled the tall scout in height and width, and said, "Well, I'll be good an' goddamned!"

The man was black, with predominantly Negroid features and a thin matting of nappy hair. He was naked to the waist, and from that point downward, wore a pair of tattered cavalry pants of regulation blue, although ragged and faded, and boots that had seen much wear. They were ripped along the sides, the soles almost completely worn through, with numerous cracks across the uppers. Now

97

he addressed himself to Lieutenant Zimmerman's astonished face, raising his right hand to the side of his forehead in a formal military salute. "Thank you very much, sir."

"Wh—who the—devil are you, man?" Zimmerman asked. "What are you doing here?"

"Sir, could I have some water? I've been bound and gagged since before dawn. Those damn Apache rascals—"

Logan unscrewed the cap of his canteen and handed it to the large Negro. He took a mouthful, rinsed his mouth and spat it out, then drank more. When he finished, he handed the canteen back to Logan, who pushed it back and said, "Keep it, boy. You need it a sight more 'n I do."

"Who-ee! That was sure good. Mighty good. Thank you, mister."

Zimmerman had recovered his wits, conscious that time was running close. "All right, man, speak up. Who are you and what are you doing here? Let's get to it, we don't have much time to waste."

"Sir," the Negro asked, "may I ask where we are?"

"You're in Arizona Territory, about twenty miles north of the Mexican border and about forty-five miles south of Fort Bandolier, which is between Tucson and Yuma."

"Whew! I'm sure a long way from Texas."

"Texas?" Zimmerman's voice was incredulous.

"Sir," the large man said, "I'm Sergeant Atticus Perry of the 10th Cavalry out of Fort Bliss. I was—"

"The *United States Cavalry* at Fort Bliss?" Zimmerman asked.

"Yes, sir. The United States 10th Colored Cavalry, Fort Bliss, Texas, authorized by the United States Congress in July of 1866. That would be last year, I guess. I had no way of keeping a record of the weeks and months since I was captured by Comanches in August of '66, sir."

Logan said, "I've heard of the 10th, Lieutenant—"

"So have I. Also the 9th Colored, but I never expected to run into it here in Arizona."

"Sir, I can explain. We were out on a patrol when we caught up with a dozen Comanches who'd crossed the Red River to do some raiding. We chased them back across the Red when suddenly we found ourselves trapped in an ambush by about a hundred more Comanches. We tried to break out, but there were only eight of us and they had us surrounded. I was wounded early and was unconscious. When I came to, the others were dead and scalped. Seems like I didn't have too much of a scalp to take—" Perry rubbed one hand over his woolly mat— "and they'd never seen Nigras before, at least, no Nigra soldiers, so they kept me for a slave. Worked hell out of me for about five months, then traded me off to some Navajos for some rustled cattle. About eight or nine months ago, I can't remember exactly now, these Navajos ran into some Apaches down around Mesilla. There was some parleys and trading and after it was all done, I found I'd been traded to the Apaches for two horses. Then I was taken to Cochise's stronghold in the Dragoons and became a Chiricahua slave. Later on, I got moved down here in Mexico to Anaka's tribe because he was running short-handed."

"You know that Anaka is dead?"

"Yes, sir. The word came over by smoke signal when it happened, then the rest of what was left of his braves came back. Looks like they'd run into the whole Army somewhere. The camp down in Sonora is short of meat and that's the reason for this hunting party. There are two other parties out doing the same."

"How many are there in this party out hunting?"

"Ten, sir."

"And why are you with them?"

"Just to do the mule labor, sir, helping pack the meat back to Sonora. They go out in the morning, they tie me up. When they come back, they untie me and I help the women and old men with the butchering and all. Not much luck this trip, though. We been out for five days and they're due to pull out and go back to Sonora in the morning. The mule they butchered over there is their own."

"Time's running out, Lieutenant," Logan warned.

"Yes. All right, Perry—that is your name, Perry?"

"Yes, sir. Atticus Perry."

"All right, Sergeant, we'll give you a revolver and some ammunition and you can come with us." To Logan, "Let's split the men up and get them set." And to the men, "All right, you've heard enough to know how this man happens to be here. Keep in mind that he is a part of the same Army we belong to. He is a sergeant, but for the time being will have no command function. Now move in closer and listen carefully. We're going to set our trap—"

Dusk had lengthened the shadows of Dos Viudas by the time the hunting party returned. They came up the narrow canyon trail on their blanket-covered ponies and the six white men who peered down on them from the rim of rocks above could see no evidence that they had had any luck in their search for meat. As the Apaches entered the small, hidden box canyon, the leader called out, surprised that there were none to greet them. At that moment, Zimmerman, Logan and four troopers broke from behind the wickiups, carbines leveled at the ten Apache hunters.

The reaction came swiftly. The Apaches raised their rifles, the troopers opened fire, cutting down two of the Indians on the first volley. The Apaches fired back and killed Private Harry Shuster and wounded Private Thomas Collison. Then the bluecoats in the rocks above the canyon opened fire and four more Apaches fell from their milling horses. The remaining four hunters, unable to draw a bead on any target because of the thrashing of the horses, saw reason in surrendering and dropped their carbines and raised their hands high. It was over in less than a minute.

Of them all, Sergeant Atticus Perry, late of the 10th Colored Cavalry of Fort Bliss, Texas, and with the most to gain, was the happiest.

Collison's wound was in his upper shoulder and, between Tyler and Logan, he was made fairly comfortable, although the bullet still remained and would stay until they could get him back to Dr. Breed at Fort Bandolier. It was decided to cook a hot meal on the fire that was still going, then mount the prisoners on the captured horses and leave for the Fort as quickly as possible.

While they ate, the men listened to Atticus Perry's story in detail.

He was, he told them, "a free Nigra," manumitted by his master, Dr. Lyle Sumner Perry back in 1861 so that he could accompany the doctor's son, Walter, when Walter joined a volunteer troop raised in Columbia, South Carolina, and was commissioned a lieutenant. Atticus had been Walter Perry's body servant since he was fourteen and Walter only a year younger. Atticus's parents and grandparents had been house slaves to the Perrys, and Atticus selected to take care of Walter. Therefore, when Walter was being schooled by a private tutor, Atticus had been ordered to be present and thus had learned to read, write, do sums, speak correctly and even had a smattering of a premedical education, since Walter had expected, until the war broke out, to follow in his father's footsteps.

On the eve of Walter's departure, Dr. Perry called Atticus into his library and presented him with a handwritten certificate of freedom, on his solemn oath to look out for Walter. So, he had followed Walter into the service of the Confederacy and remained with him until '62, when Walter took a bullet in his chest and shortly thereafter died of the complication of pneumonia in a Union prison hospital. Atticus was then given his choice of remaining free to wander about or swear allegiance to the Union and join a Negro Infantry unit—which he did. At war's end, knowing he could not return to face Dr. Perry, he remained in the Union Infantry, rising to the rank of corporal. In '66, when the Negro Cavalry units were authorized, he requested a transfer and was sent to Texas to join the 10th. Shortly thereafter, because of his military background and ability to write and read, he was promoted to the rank of sergeant; and within two weeks, he had been captured by the Comanches.

When he finished his story, Zimmerman asked, "Then there will be records to substantiate your story, Perry?"

"Yes, sir. If there's still a 10th Cavalry, the records will be with them at Fort Bliss, or wherever they are now."

"That will probably take a little time, I suppose, but in the meantime, we'll take care of you at Fort Bandolier. When your records come through, you will probably be sent back to Fort Bliss, or wherever the Army decides to send you. We'll be back at the Fort by tomorrow night and turn you over to Colonel Hatfield for disposition."

"Well, sir," Atticus Perry said with a broad grin, "I sure hope he's got a good one."

Perry asked permission to look at Collison's wound and thought he could, with a heated knife blade, remove the bullet that was lodged there. The choice was left to Collison, who agreed. While four troopers held Collison, Perry probed with the knife, felt the bullet not too deeply beneath the surface. Efficiently, quickly, he incised the opening and removed the slug. From the medical kit, Perry applied necessary unguents and bandaged the wound expertly, thus preventing gangrene from setting in.

When darkness fell, they moved out, the Apache men and women boxed in by the troopers, their wrists bound behind their backs, ankles tied together under the bellies of their horses. Shuster had been buried in a single grave, the dead Apaches in a common grave. Collison rode beside John O'Shea, bearing up under the painful wound.

And throughout the night journey, over the soughing of the wind which had risen, came the mourning whine of the Apache women for their dead.

Zimmerman could not estimate the problems of introducing a Negro sergeant into the all-white Fort Bandolier command, although he reasoned they would most certainly be present. As they rode along, he took careful note that none of the men would ride close to Perry, avoiding him almost as they would avoid a hated Apache.

On his third morning at Tres Flechas, Sam Palmer was awakened by a soft rapping at his window. He raised up on one elbow, heard the rapping repeated and called out, *"Qué pasó?"*

"Put away the gun, *amigo.* It is Marcos."

"Where've you been, *muchacho?"*

"Where? This is one damn big *rancho.* It took me two days to visit only the north range."

"How were all your cousins?"

Marcos laughed. "Who could see them all? Only the girls. The pretty ones. Ah, *amigo,* if I lived here, I would die an old man in six months."

"Climb in. I'm glad you woke me. I want to get back to Tucson."

"I am ready. You get dressed while I go see Emelita and get something to eat."

"Leave some for me. I'll be there in ten minutes."

He washed quickly in the basin on his nightstand, then dressed, belted on his gun, found his hat and went out. As he passed the dining room, Max Potter called out, "Sam, that you?"

"Good morning, sir."

"Come in an' have somethin' to eat. Caro's sleepin' in this morning' an' I can't stand my own company this early."

"I was on my way to the cookhouse to eat with Marcos. We're leaving for Tucson as soon as we're finished."

"We'll send word to him to sleep it off today. From what I hear about our young friend Marcos, he won't have the strength to lift a tortilla without help. Besides, you and me got some talkin' to do."

For two days, Sam had waited for Max to give him a few moments to explain why he must leave, but Max had ridden off "to check the herds," obviously a tactic to avoid him yet keep him on Tres Flechas.

"All right, I'll tell him."

"Sit down. Marguerita will be back in a minute. You can order your breakfast an' give her the message. Marcos won't mind the delay. He'll either find another cousin or catch up on the sleep he's missed."

Marguerita brought Max's breakfast of beefsteak, eggs, tortillas and coffee. She took Sam's order and left with the message for Marcos.

"All right, Sam," Max said when they were alone, "I guess if I don't talk to you now, you'll ride off."

"I was planning to. Incidentally—" Sam took five dollars from his pocket and shoved them across the table toward Max. "I owe you this."

Max's forehead crinkled into deeper furrows. "What for?"

"We made a bet the other morning. Caroline. She apologized the way you said she would."

Max chortled and pocketed the money. "One bet I'm happy to win. Told you I knew my own daughter."

"Well, I still don't think she's really over it."

"Which of us is, Sam?" Max asked soberly.

"I didn't mean it that way. I mean Caroline blaming me for what happened."

"And I tell you, it'll pass. Give her a chance, Sam, just a little time. She's still young."

"Well—" Marguerita returned with Sam's steak, eggs and a stack of tortillas. Max cut into his beefsteak with serious industry. As Sam began rolling a tortilla, Max said, "What about Tucson?"

"I don't know about Tucson or any place else. I'm going back to decide what I want to do with the rest of my life."

"Runnin' away ain't goin'a make it less easy to come to a decision, son. Face up to it. You got no family of your own. Caro an' me are the only family you got left." Max rested his hands on the table so that knife and fork stood upright, his eyes directly on Sam's. "Son, do me a favor, will you, a real personal favor?"

"What, sir?"

"Will you for God's sake stop sayin' 'Sir' to me like I was a godderned second lieutenant? I'm 'Max' to a lot of people I'm a hell of a lot less fonder of than you. Can you remember Max instead of sir?"

Sam was forced into a grin. "All right, Max."

"Well," Max mumbled, "I finally accomplished somethin'! Now let me ask you this: you made any plans at all since—you know?"

"No, none at all. My mind's been too full of other things."

"Then why do you think you'll be able to decide your future any better in a dingy room in a noisy, dirty place like Tucson than here. Or is it Caro that's still botherin' you?"

"No, sir—Max. Not exactly, except that being here doesn't help clear my mind up any. Besides, in Tucson, I can talk to people, maybe get some ideas."

"Like what?"

"Well, I might try my hand at some mining—"

Max rocked his head from side to side. "Odds are all against you, Sam. Prospectors been over most of the land in these parts with a fine currycomb. I know because I've grubstaked more'n fifty of 'em from time to time."

"I could go back to the Fort and scout for Colonel Hatfield."

"For three dollars a day to start an' five dollars after a whole year? Then maybe you could take up carpenterin' or clerkin' in a general store or somethin' else big. Sam, listen to a man who's lived in this part of the country since '46. For those twenty-one years, you got to respect my judgment even if you don't want any part of Tres Flechas—"

"I don't want anything I didn't work for, Max. I had a hell of a time with Ruth over that ranch you gave us, outfitting and stocking it the way you did—"

"Son, you got a funny sense of values. Everything I got here, or any place else, don't just belong to me. It belongs to me an' Caro. It belonged to Ruth, too, an' that meant her share of it belonged to her husband an' son. Also, some of it belongs to the people livin' on it an' workin' it. Man, I didn't give you that ranch as a bribe to marry my daughter. If I hadn't wanted you for her, you'd never got within a mile of her.

"But I won't argue that point no more. I've got somethin' better to talk about, somethin' been in the back of my head waitin' for the right man. Waitin' for your time to be up in the Army, for you an' Ruth an' little Sam to come back. Not here," Max added quickly. "Tucson. Somethin' big enough for you to build, big enough so we could be partners in it. Me put up the money, you run it. Sam, it didn't work out the way I planned, Lord knows, but

104

you an' me, we can still do it an' you won't be beholden to nobody on this man's earth. I know you better'n you think, an' I know this is somethin' you can handle an' like doin', a man's job." He indicated Sam's half-finished meal with his fork. "You through?"

"Except for the coffee."

"Then pour yourself a fresh cup an' come to my office. Let's make it businesslike."

Settled in Max's office-study over coffee and cigars, Max brought out a large roll of parchment and spread it out across his desk. From where he sat, Sam could see it was a map of the lower portion of Arizona and New Mexico, from the Gila River south to Sonora, from the Colorado River east to include most of New Mexico and part of Texas.

"Pull your chair up closer, son." Sam did so and Max continued. "This country is just beginnin' to open up. Since '48, when they found gold in California, an' exceptin' the years from '61 to '65, tens of thousands of immigrants been pourin' West, a lot of 'em across New Mexico an' Arizona to avoid the snow an' ice an' sleet up North. A lot of 'em stopped in Arizona an' settled. A lot who didn't find what they were lookin' for in California came back to settle here. Not as many as stayed in California, I'll grant you, but we're growin' an' you can see signs of it more'n more every day that passes. Biggest problem here is gettin' 'em through from, say, Santa Fe to San Diego an' Los Angeles or up to San Francisco, but one of the worst parts, once they come through the Chiricahuas an' Dragoons, is from Tucson to Yuma." Max's spatulate finger drew an imaginary line across the map.

Sam said, "Max, are you talking about what I think you are?"

"Right, Sam. A new freight an' stage line, Tucson to Yuma right now. Later on, east to Lordsburg, west to the California Coast."

"The old Butterfield Line—" Sam began, but Max cut across his words quickly.

"Butterfield ran for three years, '58 to '61, then quit an' moved North to the shorter route when the damn war broke out. But people are still comin' through from Santa Fe an' El Paso, preferrin' the Southern route. They come in alone, in small wagon trains, any way they can. If we can get 'em through from Tucson to Yuma safely, they'll ride with us, ship their goods by our freight wagons. The word'll spread an' more'll come in. Merchants an' ranchers all along the route need supplies, need 'em bad. We'll do their freightin' for 'em. We'll carry the mail, haul Army supplies—"

"Hold on, Max. You can't carry mail without a government franchise, nor Army contracts to haul Army freight."

"Don't let that worry you one little bit. I been fiddlin' with this thing ever since before you an' Ruth got married. This ain't no overnight idea I got. I'll take care of that end of it."

"But, Max—"

"What?"

"I—I'm thinking."

"That's what I want you to do, son. Think on it. But not in Tucson. Right here, where we can both think an' talk about it."

"Max, I don't know—"

" 'Course you don't know, because you ain't given it enough thinkin' time. Tell you, Sam, you put your mind to it for a couple more days. That'll bring us to Friday night. If you can't see anything in it by then, I'll stop pesterin' you to stay. You can leave at daybreak Saturday mornin', you an' Marcos. Caro an' me are goin' up to Tucson an' you can ride shotgun for us."

"I didn't know you were planning to go in to Tucson."

"I didn't tell you. Caro an' me been invited to the governor's mansion. A wedding. Major Boyden an' Mrs. Martin from Mesa Plata."

"Oh. I remember now."

"Sam, think about it. Get on your horse an' ride out over Tres Flechas. Pure clean air never hurt a man's thinkin' none. We'll talk again on Friday night, after supper."

"All right, Max. I'll give it my best thinking."

"I hope you will, son. This is right for you. For us."

Marcos was no problem. He was delighted to stay, dally among his "cousins," to play the guitar and sing to the girls who adored him, pampered him, loved him, and would dream of him long after he had left. The miracle of his charm was that some jealous young *vaquero* hadn't slipped a sharp knife blade between his ribs.

Sam chose a blooded stallion in need of exercise and rode the range, avoiding contact with Tres Flechas *va-*

queros, sleeping out under a blanket with his saddle for a pillow, preparing meals over his own fire. The only luxury he permitted himself was a supply of Max's cigars.

During those two days and nights, he thought of the overall plan for a Tucson-to-Yuma stage and freight line, then addressed himself to the details of establishing a *safe* operation. Among the many obstacles, the greatest of all was the need for protection from Apaches, renegades, bushwhackers and gunslingers in search of profitable enterprise with the least effort. There was the matter of considerable rolling stock to acquire, stages and wagons, mules and horses, station stops to build and man at reasonable intervals, extra animals for the relay stations, food for passengers and feed for animals to store. For how long, he wondered, could the line operate at a loss until it could prove its ability to deliver passengers, freight and mail safely in order to win Army contracts and a United States mail franchise?

It was impossible to evaluate the cost factors involved, the rates that must be charged. That Max Potter was wealthy there was no doubt, but wealth held in land, cattle and horses was one thing; cash or bank credit to buy equipment and meet payrolls was another; but those were Max's problems, not Sam's.

And having delved deeply into possibilities, probabilities, imponderables, odds for and against, he examined the personal side of the project. If he rejected the idea, what would he do? Move on to California, already crowded with thousands seeking opportunities?

From all accounts, there were a thousand or more failures for each modest success, fifty thousand against striking it rich. Go east into the chaos and unsettled state of affairs brought on by the war, even after two years had passed? The thought of the ministry lay dead and buried, too deep to revive. The Army had been too vital a part of his life to entertain the thought of working indoors as a clerk in an office, for which he was woefully unprepared, or in a store selling merchandise.

And above all, there was his rapport with Max Potter, a mutual feeling of admiration and respect, even love, if that word could have meaning in the relationship between two men of action.

Sam returned to Tres Flechas late on Friday afternoon with no clearly defined answers. Marcos met him as he rode up to the family corral and turned the black stallion over to a boy to unsaddle and rub down.

"Welcome back, *amigo*. You have had a pleasant time with your thoughts?"

"If not pleasant, I have been kept busy with them. All is well here?"

"All is *excelente, compadre*. We leave for Tucson soon?"

"In the morning at daybreak."

"Good. We will arrive in time for a big Saturday night. I feel happy, lucky. I will drink, gamble, win, and find myself a willing girl to spend my money on."

"Your life in a nutshell, eh, Marcos? A philosophy for the young."

"What could be better, *amigo?*"

"Depends on your outlook. Tell me, have you ever once considered that you might lose?"

"Marcos Espuela is not a loser, *amigo*. Contemplating losing is for old men. I do not lose because I was born under a lucky star. I have never lost."

Walking toward the house, Sam smiled and said, "Tell me, Marcos, what have you ever won that has meant anything?"

"Ah, Sam, those are things yet to come. I do not worry about them now. Meanwhile, I win memories to cherish and keep me warm in my old age."

Sam stared at Marcos for a moment. "Hold on to them, *amigo*. They will have great value. But be sure you live to enjoy them."

"Señor Max waits to see you. He sent me to tell you."

"I know. First I will bathe and shave, then I will see him. Tell him that for me, eh?"

"Por supuesto, amigo."

He took longer than usual in the bath house, luxuriating in the tub. He shaved, dressed in clean clothes and, in order to avoid a discussion that would include Caroline, ate in the cookhouse, then found Max in his study, bent over the large map and sheets of paper filled with figures and notations. Their initial meeting, as always, was cordial and warm, and after a glass of tequila and a cigar, began discussing the "imponderables" that had crossed Sam's mind.

Financing, he learned, was the least of their problems. Max's wealth ran far beyond land and cattle and horses. "But," Max added shrewdly, "for practical reasons, I intend to bring in some outside investors, merchants now runnin' freight at a loss whose equipment we can buy, merge with ours an' use to ship their freight all along the line. Problem is to establish relay stations an' operate regular an' safe schedules. That'll be your second big job, Sam."

"What about the stages and wagons?" Sam asked.

"That'll be first on your list of chores, but I've got an ace in the hole I haven't turned over yet. I've talked to Jeff Lennon, used to be a Butterfield driver, then became the Tucson agent until the line quit in '61. Jeff tells me the Butterfield people stored half a dozen stages in Lordsburg, along with about a dozen freight wagons. Here's a letter from the Butterfield office in Tipton, Missouri, no more'n eight months old, sayin' they'd be interested in sellin' out since they've got no need for the stuff. That's providin' we don't plan to come North to compete with 'em on the overland route."

"Then the last big problem will be manpower."

"I figure on movin' some of my *vaqueros* to Tucson an' Yuma to help us get started. They won't like bein' away from home much, but we can use 'em until we get well under way."

"And protection?"

"Well, that'll be your department, son. I figure you learned enough about that end of it with six years in the Army under your belt. If that's all the questions you've got for now, let me tell you how I see it. We'll open our headquarters in Tucson. Next, we'll—"

In the foothills of Monte Babiacora, Casimiro Lizardi rode in the lead with Hector Moreno, Orlando Vega and Julio Campos on his heels. All four knew they were being watched every yard of the way by Apaches who made no effort to conceal themselves. They were behind every rim, every rock, it seemed, passing the word along by visual arm signals, that four lone riders were approaching.

Where the main trail crossed a ridge and entered a level area, Lizardi turned and said to his men, "Wait here and do not move until I return. Lay down your rifles and remove your gun belts. Leave them on the ground in the open where they can be seen. Do not start a fire. Smoke, eat and drink, but remain together. Do not go into the *bosque* to relieve yourselves or you will draw their fire.

What you do must be done in the open where they can see everything."

Lizardi placed his own rifle and gun belt with the others. From his pocket he removed a square of white cloth, which he tied to a stick, then remounted, holding his flag of truce up for all to see. Without further word, he spurred his horse upward on the trail. For over an hour he rode over dirt and grassy trails, crossing one crest, dipping into a valley, rising over malpais to the next crest, moving through a steep gorge. Occasionally he looked upward to his left or right and saw that he was still under the eyes, rifles, lances and arrows of the silent watchers.

He came through a very narrow canyon and began his descent into a grassy valley, and where it opened into a broad and wide meadow, he was met by twelve Apache warriors who showed neither friendliness nor hostility; only suspicion and awareness that told Lizardi he was, no matter what else, an alien.

There were no words exchanged. The leader of the band simply indicated by hand signals that Lizardi was to accompany them. Six rode ahead, six behind him, and all were armed with rifles. Thus they came across the open valley and disappeared into a canyon on the far side and began climbing again until they reached an open level plateau.

This was the base camp Anaka had established in Sonora, safe from pursuit by the United States Cavalry, subject only to infrequent harassment from Mexican *rurales* who were seldom effective. Six miles south of the foothills of Monte Babiacora lay the village of Cienguilla, its population of 250 so cowed by the near presence of Apache strength that in exchange for occasional gifts of maize, they were permitted to live without fear of attack. Not infrequently, Anaka had been known to give the villagers a few head of stolen cattle and horses as a gesture of goodwill.

Now the camp in Babiacora belonged to Bokhari. To his disgust, it was overpopulated with the mourning widows and children of those braves slain in Monte de Lágrimas, weeping women whose wailing placed a blanket of gloom over the entire camp, affecting even the new braves who had preceded him from Cochise's stronghold under Vicenzo. More mouths to feed with little enough work to keep them busy. A troublesome thing.

Only that morning, Bokhari had decreed that all braves

110

who had but one wife should consider taking another; that all unmarried braves consider choosing a wife from among the widows. He could not issue a direct order, for this was against Apache tradition, but he indicated that this would greatly please him; and there were few who would wish to displease the new war leader. It was his intention to eliminate much of the surreptitious night movement of the younger braves among the tents of the widows, also the petty jealousies among them; and give the women a new, legitimate interest in life. A man to work for and, in time, forget those who had died.

Now there was a more important matter of business to occupy his mind.

Lizardi was brought into the base camp under many curious eyes and he marveled that so many could have come so quickly to replace the former leader and the slain. He estimated the number of braves visible at perhaps 150, besides those who guarded the trail all the way from the foothills, a total of about 250 in all, ignoring the women, since they were not fighters and thus were unimportant to him.

The escort leader dismounted and motioned Lizardi to get off his horse and follow him to a wickiup where a wave of an arm indicated that the Mexican was to enter. When Lizardi did so, he saw that Bokhari was alone. He waited silently until Bokhari spoke.

"Sit." Bokhari spoke in gutteral Spanish and pointed to a woven straw pallet of distinctive Indian make. Lizardi sat as the chief did, cross-legged.

"The great chief sent word he wished to parley," Lizardi said.

"You were told to come alone," Bokhari replied sternly.

"My men are over an hour's ride from here. They have been told to wait for my return."

"It does not please me when my orders are disobeyed."

"It will not happen again."

"Enju." There was a pause for a few minutes while both men studied each other, then Bokhari said, "It has been told that you sold guns to my brother Anaka."

"Yes."

"For the yellow iron."

"Yes."

"I will deal with you as my brother did."

"Great chief, it grows difficult to get the guns. The Anglo soldiers watch more closely."

"I need the guns. There is enough yellow iron to make the risk worthwhile."

Inwardly pleased, Lizardi said, "I will see what can be done. I have fifty or sixty now——"

"I do not wish old, worn guns whose bullets do not fly straight."

"These are new guns, never used before. But the price is higher than before."

"Bring them. And the bullets. I will pay. And for all others you can find."

"*Enju*, Great One." Lizardi began to get up, but Bokhari reached out a hand to stay him. "Sit. I am not finished."

Lizardi waited.

"Tell me, *señor*," Bokhari said finally, "how much yellow iron can one horse carry?"

Lizardi at once suspected the purpose of the question but gave no sign of his awareness. "That," he replied, "would depend on the size and strength of——"

"The largest, strongest horse you own."

"Eh? I do not know. I would say, all any man would ever want for the rest of his life."

"Then hear me, *señor*. I say this to you: if you will do one thing for me, that much yellow iron will be yours."

Lizardi exhaled slowly. "What is this thing, Great One?"

"A man I want. Whom our Great Leader, Cochise, wants. He is a White Eyes who is called Pom-mer."

"Ah. The man who killed Anaka."

"Yes. I want him alive to take to Cochise. If he is dead, there will be only half as much yellow iron, but I want him either way."

"It is not an easy thing you ask, taking this man. He is a soldier, well-armed, the son of *el patrón* of Tres Flechas, which is well-guarded by many *vaqueros*."

"No man can be forever guarded, *señor,* and I know it is not an easy matter. Thus, Cochise will pay much for him."

The silence between them deepened, then Bokhari added, "He is a White Eyes among other White Eyes and this is why I seek your help and offer a great reward. There must be no trickery, I warn you, or all in the village of Cienguilla will die for it."

Lizardi nodded. "It will take some time. I will think about it, make a plan."

"*Enju*. When will you bring the new guns?"

"In fourteen days."

"You will have a plan by then?"

"I will do my best."

Bokhari grunted, then clapped his hands. Two braves threw aside the flap and waited. Lizardi rose. The interview was over.

Marcos and Sam Palmer rode on either side of the handsome carriage drawn by a splendid pair of matched bays. As well as Sam and Marcos, Max and Caroline were armed with rifles too. Caroline had delayed them by almost an hour, trying on various dresses and seeking reassurance, since she was so accustomed to range attire that was much more practical and comfortable on Tres Flechas. Slippers, hair, dress length and tightness of undergarments had driven her to the brink of desperation, but in the end she was a delight to the eyes of the women who fussed over her, to Max, to Marcos; and Sam, who saw an even more amazing and disconcerting resemblance to Ruth.

A maid had been squeezed into the back seat among the baggage and parcels Caroline would require, food to be eaten en route, presents for relatives of some of the ranch people who lived in Tucson. Still, they made good time and arrived at the Congress Hotel by late evening. Marcos disappeared at once, carrying gifts to their recipients in the Mexican quarter and to visit his mother at Espuela de Oro.

Caroline had a bath in her room and went to bed immediately after supper. The maid went calling on friends and Max left for a poker game with the men he hoped to interest in his new project, leaving Sam, who had refused Max's invitation to join him, to himself. He went to his room and decided to ride out to Fort Lowell to visit with old friends. He changed his shirt, tied a fresh neckerchief in place and was ready to leave when he heard a tap on the door, a hand trying the knob. "Who is it?"

"Marcos. Open up."

Sam unlocked the door and Marcos entered quickly, locked the door and went to the window that faced out on Calle Principale and pulled the blinds down.

"What the devil's going on, Marcos?"

"You." Marcos turned to face him. "You are in trouble, *amigo*. Big trouble."

113

"Trouble? With whom? What are you talking about?"

"Sam, listen and believe me. I come from Espuela de Oro, my mother's *cantina*. There is much talk about you."

"What kind of talk?"

"The price on your head."

During his stay at Tres Flechas, the thought had been driven from his mind, but now there was no doubt about the depth of Marcos's sincerity. "Here in Tucson? That's crazy."

"Not so crazy, *amigo*. Cochise has sent word to every tribe in Arizona and New Mexico territories that he will pay much in horses, blankets and guns to the one who delivers you to him alive. Dead, if necessary, but double the reward if you are alive. Also, the word has been spread to every renegade and bushwhacker that he who brings you in will not only leave in safety, but with as much gold as his horse can carry."

"And for this, *amigo*, you leave your pretty cousins panting for you?"

"Don't laugh, Sam. Any flea-bitten gunslinger with wrinkles in his belly would—"

"Marcos, thanks. I'll keep my eyes open, but I'm not going to leave the country—"

"For a little while, eh? I will go with you—"

"Forget it, *amigo*. I've just made a deal with Max and I can't go back on my word."

"Is your word worth dying for?"

"Marcos, I'm far from dead and I'm not going to let some tinhorn bushwhacker carry me off to Cochise, dead *or* alive."

"All the gold a horse can carry is more than most men will ever see in a whole lifetime, in ten lifetimes. Many could be tempted, Sam."

"That may be, but the man who gets it will have to earn it. What else did you hear at the *cantina*, any names?"

"No, but one would not have to look far."

"How far?"

"Casimiro Lizardi, the hungry one."

"Lizardi. Was he at the *cantina*?"

"With three of his favorite *bandoleros*. Campos, Vega and Moreno. It is known that you are in Tucson. That's what caused the talk."

"Word travels fast."

"Swifter than the wind when there is a big reward."

"If I wanted to find Lizardi alone, where would I go?"

114

"Ah. A good question. Let me think." Marcos crossed the room and peered through a small opening in the cracked window blind. After a moment, he turned and said, "Later, when the *cantina* grows quiet, he will go to the *casa* of his woman, Alma Arboleya."

"You know where she lives?"

"The street, but not the house. I can find out at the *cantina.*"

"Find out for me, eh? And remember, this is between Lizardi and me, Marcos."

Marcos grinned. "But without me, you cannot find the *casa*, eh, *amigo?*"

"I don't want to involve you."

"I am already involved. Everybody knows I am your friend."

"My friend and my brother, Marcos."

Marcos laughed. "Hey! That is much better than a cousin, no?"

Through a smile, Sam replied, "Much better, Marcos."

Shortly past midnight, Sam Palmer stood in the narrow opening between two small, decrepit houses on Calle Carroza near the corner of Calle Maricopa. It was a filthy, littered barrio of disreputable wooden shacks occupied by Mexican field hands, laborers, servants who worked in the homes of Anglos, shop, hotel, saloon and stable employees, water haulers, prostitutes and unemployed. Here and there the dim light of an oil lamp or candles flickered from an open window or through a sleazy curtain, but the street itself was empty at this hour. Sam waited.

Twenty minutes later, he heard the sound of bootsteps in the dirt of Maricopa, turning into Carroza, stopping. *"Amigo?"*

"Here, Marcos." Sam stepped out from between the two houses, a shadow among other night shadows.

"Follow me and walk softly. He left the *cantina* fifteen minutes before I did. The woman was with him."

They walked along Carroza, crossing Esmerelda, Lucero, Quiroz. Without speaking, Marcos touched Sam's arm, then pointed to the third house from the corner of Quiroz. Between it and the near house was a narrow alley, down which Marcos led the way, stepping lightly over the general litter. In a house nearby, a dog growled in his sleep. Another barked shrilly in response, and a thick voice shouted for quiet. From bedroom windows came snores

115

and other human sounds. At the rear of each house was a small unfenced yard that faced other unfenced yards across the alley. Marcos turned to his right and halted.

"This is the *casa* of Alma Arboleya," he whispered. "Let me try the door." He lifted the latch and pushed the door open. Sam followed him inside. "This is the kitchen," Marcos whispered into Sam's ear. "Next will be two sleeping rooms. They will be in the front bedroom. It is larger and will be cooler there."

They tiptoed into the back bedroom, feeling their way through the darkness. At the far side of the room they heard low voices beyond the closed door, inched their way forward to listen.

"You will stay long, Casimiro?" Alma asked.

"Until I am ready to leave," Lizardi replied.

"When?"

"You are anxious to have me gone so you can entertain others, *muchacha?*"

"No, Casimiro, you know that is not true."

"Then be satisfied. I will leave when I am ready. And when I return I will bring you more presents. Pour me a drink."

They heard the shuffling of bare feet across the wooden floor, the sound of a bottle clinking against a glass, the gurgling of liquid, again the bare feet as they crossed the room once more. There was the rustling of feminine garments as Alma said, "You have been gone—"

"Two weeks. Too long. Don't put out the light, *querida*. I have not seen you so—"

"You like what you see, Casimiro?"

"Almost as much as what I feel. Come to bed now and stop chattering."

Sam put a hand on Marcos's shoulder and Marcos moved to one side. Sam raised his right foot, drew it back and slammed it against the flimsy wooden door, shattering it, leaped through it in a single move, revolver in his right hand. Lizardi jerked himself upright in bed, the tequila spilling on his bare chest as he dropped the glass and slid across the bed toward where his gun belt lay on the chair.

"Hold it, Lizardi!"

Lizardi, fingertips within a few inches of the silver-inlaid revolver, froze in movement. Alma, naked, grabbed for her recently removed undergarment and covered herself, standing speechless, pure fear in her eyes.

116

Lizardi, his back still turned to Sam, said, "What fool is it who disturbs Casimiro Lizardi, eh?"

"Turn around slowly, Lizardi, hands over your head. Easy—"

Lizardi turned back slowly and stared into the muzzle of Palmer's .44. Marcos had stepped into the room, revolver in hand. To the terrified Alma he said, "Turn up the lamp more, *muchacha*, so Señor Lizardi may see better."

"Ah, Marcos." The words escaped Lizardi's mouth in a sibilant hiss.

"And the man whose head is worth all the gold a horse can carry, Casimiro."

"Ah, Señor Palmer. You do me honor."

"You are a careless man, Lizardi," Sam said. "I could put an end to your greed with one bullet, but instead, I will let this stand as a warning. Make one move against me, or Marcos here, and you will become the target for every *vaquero* on Tres Flechas and those in Tucson who would wish to earn a reward. If any harm comes to either of us, in any way and no matter by whom, you will pay for it with your life. You understand, *vago?*"

"You speak my language very well, *señor.*"

Marcos, with Lizardi's eyes on him, had emptied Lizardi's revolver, then threw it, together with the gun belt, under the bed.

"And you, *joven*, have become my enemy as well?"

"Casimiro, I have never been your friend, nor you mine. If we have become enemies, it is your own doing," Marcos replied.

"Eh, *bueno*. Then we know where we stand."

"Next time, Lizardi, there will be no second chance," Sam said.

"It is so understood, *señor*. Now if you will leave us—"

With Willy Logan on point, Zentz and Gross as flankers, and Sergeant Tyler bringing up the rear, Zimmerman did his best to keep the column moving, using Atticus Perry to transmit orders to the captives in the Apache tongue, in which he was fluent. The twelve prisoners, however, had no intention of bringing their internment, possibly worse, to a swift conclusion and did everything possible to slow their progress, no doubt hoping another party of Apaches would cut across their trail and rescue them. But no such phenomenon occurred. During the next day they stopped briefly for meals and to rest their horses. For periods of short duration, the troopers dismounted and walked their horses to preserve their strength in case they ran into hostiles.

Thus they reached Fort Bandolier shortly after the last rays of the sun had disappeared behind Monte de Lágrimas. From a distance, and because it was a larger party than Lieutenant Zimmerman's original patrol, the sentry at Post Number One hailed the Sergeant of the Guard with the warning of an approaching party of "unknowns," thus alerting the Officer of the Day. Lieutenant Douglas Kennard at once mounted the rampart platform above the Main Gate and stood beside the sentry, watching the column through a telescope, dim in the distance as nightfall came on.

"It's Lieutenant Zimmerman's patrol," Kennard informed the sentry finally, then called below, "Stand by to open the gates! Patrol coming in with prisoners."

The sergeant of the guard motioned the two gate tenders to be ready, but the words, "with prisoners," drew at least two dozen off-duty troopers, including Sergeant Major Riley and Captain Breed, the Fort surgeon. As the column came within fifty yards of the gate, the sentry, despite Kennard's recognition, bawled out a loud, "Halt! Who goes there?"

"Lieutenant Zimmerman, patrol and prisoners," Zimmerman's shout came back.

"Below there! Open the gates!" Kennard came swiftly down the steps to ground level. The gates were thrown open and the column trooped inside. Zimmerman, with an audience that now included Colonel Hatfield, formally reported his mission returned, the death of Private Harry Shuster, killed in action, Private Thomas Collison wounded, twelve Apache men and women prisoners, four mules and twelve Apache ponies.

Lieutenant Kennard received the verbal report, returned Zimmerman's salute and said, "Log 'em in, Sergeant of the Guard. A detail to carry Private Collison to the hospital. A guard detail for the prisoners, separate quarters for men and women. Notify the stable sergeant—"

"Lieutenant!"

Both Zimmerman and Kennard turned to face Colonel Hatfield, both replying, "Yes, sir!" simultaneously.

"Lieutenant Zimmerman has not given a full report

118

and Lieutenant Kennard has accepted it. Not satisfactory, gentlemen!"

Zimmerman and Kennard flushed, grateful for the oncoming darkness to cover their humiliation. Zimmerman recovered first.

"Sir, I regret the omission. In the Apache camp, we found this man, trussed up, a slave-prisoner, whom we released."

"Bring him front and center. Lieutenant Kennard, have him logged by name, then send him and Lieutenant Zimmerman to my office. I will want to see Mr. Logan, too. That is all."

Hatfield returned their salutes and marched off toward the headquarters building. A litter was brought to carry Collison to the small hospital, Captain Breed walking beside him, speaking reassuring words.

The group of curious enlisted men formed a tight knot around Sergeant Tyler as Willy Logan, Zimmerman and Atticus Perry followed the colonel across the parade ground.

"Mike, where the hell did the nigger come from?"

"He a Nigra or a black Apache?"

"Big bastard, ain't he?"

Mike Tyler grinned. "Tell you one thing—" he began, but Sergeant Major Riley stepped in and said, "Ye'll be tellin' nothin', Tyler, 'til the lieutenant makes his official report, unless ye want to go on report yerself. All right, you men, break it up an' get back to whatever you were doin', even if it was nothin'."

"That's it," Tyler added to the disappointed group. As he led his mount toward the stables, Riley fell in beside him. "Who's the booger, Ty?"

Slyly, "Sorry, Pete. Orders. Can't open my mouth 'til—"

"Now, now, Ty, that's for the men. This is the Sergeant Major talkin' now."

"Seems to me it was the Sergeant Major told me to button my lip up."

"Ty, me boy, ye got a lot to learn about your Sergeant Major. F'r one thing, he c'n recommend a sergeant for promotion to First Sergeant, seein' as how there's a vacancy. F'r another, he's got a list of dirty details waitin' for sergeants who don't know up from down—"

"Okay, Pete, I get the signal. Let me tell you one thing first. This Fort is in for one hell of a surprise when they find out who Atticus Perry is."

119

"Well, start tellin' me now so it won't be that big a surprise when I get it official."

"Okay, Pete, it's like this—"

Colonel Hatfield listened first to Lieutenant Zimmerman's account of the patrol, then to a brief acknowledgment from his top civilian scout. All the while, Atticus Perry stood at ease until Zimmerman introduced him into the report and felt Hatfield's eyes upon him, which caused him to stand at attention.

"Sit down, Sergeant," Hatfield said finally. To his adjutant, Captain Marcus Greene, "Give the sergeant a cigar, Captain."

Greene did so and handed Perry a match. When it had been lighted, Hatfield began questioning him at length, taking note of points of reference he would require for verification; time, dates, places. Atticus was very definitely aware of the colonel's more than casual questions and answered in meticulous detail, giving the names of the commanding general at Fort Bliss, other high-ranking officers he could remember, his battalion and company commanders, and the last known date in his mind, that of his capture by the Comanches, and where.

"Very well, Sergeant," Hatfield said. "You will wait in the outside office. Thank you, Mr. Logan, you are dismissed. Lieutenant Zimmerman, when you have eaten and otherwise refreshed yourself, I will have your written report. On your way out, have an orderly tell Sergeant Major Riley I wish to see him at once."

When they had left, Hatfield turned his gaze on Captain Greene. "What do you make of that, Marc?"

"I don't know what to make of it, sir. I've never encountered a similar situation," Greene replied.

"He's a United States Cavalry sergeant, 10th Cavalry, out of Fort Bliss."

"Yes, sir."

"I want a dispatch sent to the Commanding General of Fort Bliss as soon as possible. Use Lieutenant Zimmerman's report for reference as soon as it has been written and approved, ask for verification and disposition of Sergeant Atticus Perry. Also, we'll need his pay data. As I figure it, he's got seventeen months of back pay coming to him, and I'm sure he can use it."

"Yes, sir."

"Meantime, we'll issue clothing, feed and quarter him—"

120

"With the other men, sir?"

Hatfield's face turned stern, his voice again formal. "Captain, I said that Atticus Perry is a sergeant in the United States Cavalry, didn't I?"

"W-we have only his word for that, sir."

"Which we will accept until it is confirmed from Fort Bliss or we learn otherwise. Turn him over to Sergeant Major Riley. He is to be treated no differently than any other man of his rank. I will not tolerate any show of military disrespect or discourtesy to his rank. Understood?"

"Yes, sir. And, uh, duties, sir?"

"Put him on rotation as Sergeant of the Guard for the time being. Later, he will be used on patrol. Since it was Zimmerman's group that rescued him, assign him to Troop E. That is all for now."

"Yes, sir. Ah, what about his present pay status, sir?"

"Until we receive his records, authorize him to draw a sergeant's pay. If he is returned to Fort Bliss, we will provide transportation and make claim on Bliss for what he has drawn here."

"Yes, sir."

Fort Bandolier's normal strength complement of 240 men and twenty officers was at a critical low of just under one hundred men and seven officers, including twelve enlisted men and one officer in the hospital. Of those fit for duty, approximately twenty men were assigned to maintenance, clerking, stable, quartermaster and other noncombat duties. Two of the officers, medical and quartermaster, fell into that latter category, and two others, Colonel Hatfield and his adjutant, were concerned with administrative duties; which left Lieutenants Carpenter, Kennard, Zimmerman and Mason-Field for strictly military operations, the latter in the hospital recovering from a lance wound received in the battle at Monte de Lágrimas.

Colonel Hatfield's strongest hopes rested on Major Kane Boyden, for two years an aide to former General Brett Mitchell, now Territorial Governor, who must act on Boyden's request for transfer to Fort Bandolier as Hatfield's executive officer. Boyden's influence with Governor Mitchell was considerable, and Hatfield hoped not only to gain Boyden as his second-in-command to replace the late Major Owen Travis, but to exercise his influence to have General Litchfield, Territorial Military Commander

121

in Tucson, fill out those missing, and desperately needed ranks.

Every operating unit at the Fort was shorthanded, with noncoms doubling for officers in many departments. Certain purely traditional customs and regulations had been relaxed for lack of proper supervision. The number and rigidity of inspections had been reduced, drilling periods practically abandoned, the men given longer rest periods in order to be fresh for the two most urgent military necessities—guard duty and outside patrols. It was regarded as somewhat of a blessing that they had been able to hire and retain Mexican men and boys for mess and other menial duties, their wives serving as laundresses. Some of the work load had diminished now that the civilians who had been brought to the Fort for protection prior to Anaka's defeat had left to return to their ranches.

Like Colonel Hatfield, the ranking officer, Sergeant Major Riley, the ranking noncommissioned officer, had his problems. Without a single first sergeant in the Fort since he had stepped up to Matt Donnelly's rank, and with the easing of military pressures on the post, the men had grown sloppy in appearance, restive and quarrelsome. Barracks fights broke out over the most minor, previously ignored, causes. Sergeants and corporals with more power in the face of reduced officer supervision, did not care to exercise that power and refused to administer company punishment for infractions; but Riley's prime concern, made known forcefully to every man, was that the command would be alert and ready for guard duty and ordered patrols.

Troop E was down to twenty-six men, including Sergeant Mike Tyler and Corporal Mannie Zentz, now the smallest of all functioning military units. The addition of Sergeant Atticus Perry to Troop E did little to increase its morale.

"Goddamn it, Pete," Tyler protested when he was informed of the assignment, "I don't want him. I don't care how big or good he is, or says he is, all he spells to me is trouble, and I sure as hell don't need any more'n I got."

"Well, that's just fine, Ty, me boy," Riley replied unperturbed. "You want to come with me an' tell that to the colonel? I want to be standin' right alongside you whilst you tell him what you want an' don't want, since himself told me to my face to put him in wid Troop E."

"Pete," Tyler pleaded, "I've got twenty-five men in that

122

barracks and at least twenty of 'em are dyed-in-the-wool Southerners—"

"Ye're tellin' me some of your men are *prejudiced,* Ty, after President Abe, may the good Lord rest his soul, freed all black men? Ye're sayin' your men are that shriveled in their brains—"

"Don't lay that malarkey on me, Pete. You know damn well what's going to happen to what's left of Troop E if I bunk him in with us."

"Maybe, Ty, maybe, but I also know what's goin'a happen if y'don't. I'd hate to see the faded part of y'r shirt sleeves when them stripes get peeled off."

"How the hell am I—"

"Ty, a man of your intelligence an' fine way of speaking, *an'* with fourteen years in the Army, *an'* a fair chance to make first sergeant as soon as things open up here, don't need no ignorant Irishman with no schoolin' at all t'tell y'how to run y'r troop. It's only until the word comes back from Fort Bliss an' we ship the booger home to Texas. Six weeks, two months at the most."

The hint that he might lose his three hard-earned stripes and the opportunity to add a diamond and three rockers below those three stripes, had the necessary effect. "Where's he now?" Tyler asked morosely.

"Captain Breed is lookin' his handsome physic over, then he goes to the Quartermaster to get outfitted from head to foot, if they c'n find boots big enough to fit him. Then he'll be ready for you. With three yellow stripes on his sleeve, remember."

Tyler groaned. "Zentz—"

"Before he reports to you, I'll have a quiet little talk with Corporal Zentz over a drink or two at the sutler's store. At me own expense, mind you, an act of me personal friendship for you."

"Thanks, friend," Tyler snorted with mild contempt. "As the good colonel would say, 'That is all, Sergeant.'"

"I'd like, by God, to believe that," Tyler replied.

Three hours later, when Sergeant Atticus Perry entered the Troop E barracks laden down with extra clothing and military gear, he walked into a solid wall of silent hostility. All twenty-six men were present, a surprising thing in itself, some lounging on their cots in various stages of undress. Six men were engaged in a poker game for matches, two over a game of cribbage for the same

123

stakes. Some were reading old, worn letters, two were polishing their boots. Those who had returned from the patrol that had rescued Perry were still talking about the event while cleaning their carbines.

As he came into the long narrow room, it seemed as though the world had come to a halt. All conversation and motion stopped, even the hands of Emory Pedersen, he in the act of dealing a new poker hand. Twenty-six pairs of eyes locked on the big man, now dressed in cavalry blues, who stared about him as he waited just inside the doorway. From the far end of the room, Tyler broke the silence.

"Sergeant Perry!"

"That's right, Sergeant," Atticus replied with a slow smile. Grudgingly, Tyler added, "Down here. Take the bunk opposite mine."

Perry walked erectly down the center aisle to the farthest corner to where Tyler waited for him, then put his carbine, extra clothes and gear on the indicated cot. Zentz sat on the cot next to Tyler's and Atticus took note that there was a wide space next to his own, from which two cots had been removed. He assumed that the lack of vocal expressions, or dismay, or objections, no doubt stemmed from a lecture the men had been given by Tyler. Or by Sergeant Major Riley. The one thing about which he was really sure was that Colonel Hatfield was the man responsible, for such an order could only filter down to this level from the very top, not merely from Lieutenant Zimmerman.

Atticus arranged his clothing in his locker box, cap and hat on the shelf, pack over the foot of the cot, carbine slung at its right side, belt, canteen and first-aid packet suspended from a nail in the wall. There was no doubt that the man knew what he was about. No one but a soldier with ample experience would know how to properly dispose of all that clothing and gear without much repeated practice. Tyler stood by watching, seeking a conversational opening, and he finally found one.

"What about a razor, soap—"

"That comes next, Sergeant," Atticus replied. "Until I draw my first pay, Captain Greene is arranging some credit for me at the sutler's store. I'll stock up as soon as I'm finished squaring myself away here."

"Sure." After a moment, "I guess you'll be taking it easy for a while—"

Atticus grinned. "I guess. No patrols for the time being. The Sergeant Major said I'd fill in as Sergeant of the Guard for a bit."

"Sure." In that single word, Tyler expressed his relief that Perry would have little direct contact with the men of Troop E in the field. Beyond sleeping here, taking his meals in the mess hall, Perry's duties and off-duty time need not create a true crisis. Tyler had spent a solid hour arguing and laying down the law—Hatfield's and Riley's and his own—to the other men, at first cajoling, finally threatening.

Tyler looked around at the men. Most had returned to that which had held their attention before the arrival of Atticus, but still they could not keep their eyes off the large Negro, some out of curiosity, others in pure hatred.

"How about some boots? Didn't the QM have any?" Tyler asked.

"None my size. He gave me an order on the sutler for one pair, civilian-type, until he can get some in from the supply depot at Fort Lowell."

Tyler reached for his forage cap and put it on. "Come on. I'll walk you over to the sutler's."

It was an act of generosity on Tyler's part, Atticus knew. To be seen with Troop E's senior sergeant would help establish his presence with those who saw them together, and if he was not accepted by, or acceptable to, the other members of Troop E, at least he could claim the sponsorship, if not friendship, of Sergeant Mike Tyler. It made a deep impression on Atticus, a solitary Negro in an all-white military community.

Early on Sunday morning before Tucson was fully awake, Sam Palmer rose, dressed and began to shave. Marcos awoke with a small groan of protest and asked, "So early, *amigo?*"

"I want to see Jeff Lennon as soon as possible and leave for Lordsburg tomorrow morning if everything works out."

Marcos leaped out of bed and began to pull his clothes on. "I will go with you. I have cousins in Lordsburg."

"If I were going to the moon, you'd have cousins there, wouldn't you?"

Marcos laughed and shrugged. "If there are Mexicans on the moon, maybe I would find cousins there, but in Lordsburg, I am sure."

"Marcos, it isn't an easy ride. We go through Chiricahua country, Apache Pass, Fort Bowie—"

"I was there once, a long time ago. An extra rifle can be useful, no?"

"All right, but I warn you. If I'm able to buy the coaches and wagons, you're going to find yourself saddled with a steady job. I'll need a good man to help me."

"Ah, the choice between freedom and what you call respectability."

"Which will you choose, *amigo?*"

"I will think about it. You once asked me what I have ever won that amounted to anything and I had no answer for you. Maybe it is time to find out the answer for myself."

"I think you're right, Marcos. This would be a good time for that." He wiped the soap residue from his face and threw the towel on the chair. "Ready?"

They ate in the almost-deserted dining room of the Congress then walked down to the Ainsworth Stables, wearing gun belts and carrying rifles, a not unusual sight in Tucson. They saddled up and rode out to Jeff Lennon's place, past Warren's Lane and across a wide expanse of mesquite-covered land along the Santa Cruz River to Lee's Mill, where Jeff ran a small horse ranch.

Lennon was somewhere in that indeterminable age between fifty-five and sixty-five, born and raised in Texas. He had come to Arizona after the war with Mexico to homestead a ranch of his own, but had been burned out by Apaches twice. In '58, he became a stage driver for Butterfield and was made station agent in Tucson in '60 until the line was abandoned the following year. He turned back to ranching then and had built up a fair-sized herd of cattle and horses, only to have his stock "requisitioned" first by Confederate, later by Union forces. Since '65, he had concentrated on breeding, raising and breaking horses which he sold to the Army.

Now he sat on the porch of his adobe house and watched idly as his three Mexican helpers cut out certain horses and hazed them into the larger work corral where their breaking and training would begin the next morning. When he saw Sam and Marcos approaching, he reached for the rifle that leaned against the wall beside his chair and came to the edge of the porch.

They walked their horses in slowly, giving Jeff time to recognize them as friends, and knew that he had when he lowered his rifle and stood it against a four-by-four post. "Light an' have a drink," he called out. "Pablo!"

A young Mexican boy came running out of the house to take their horses. "What you young roosters doin' out here this early?"

"Morning, Jeff," Sam replied. "You know Marcos Espuela, don't you?"

"Shore do. Knowed him since he was a yearlin'. Git down an' come up in the shade. Goddamn heat's enough to shrivel a man's innards. Hey, Carlotta! Bring us somethin' to drink out here!"

They sat in the shade of the overhang and made polite conversation until after Carlotta, who was fifteen and one of Jeff's four children by his common-law wife, Elena, brought a pitcher of mescal and three tin cups. When their cigars had been lighted, Jeff said, "Seen your daddy-in-law not too long ago, month or so. You out of the Army now, Sam?"

"That's right, Jeff. Max is in town today, going to Major Boyden's wedding at the governor's mansion. Thought I'd ride out with Marcos to ask about the old Butterfield coaches and wagons they've got stored back in Lordsburg."

"Wal, like I was tellin' Max, last time I seen it, 'bout a year ago, the stuff was in good shape. They payin' Heine Herzog a little somethin' to see it don't go to pieces, keep it greased an' so forth. Max figgers to buy the stuff, I think he c'n make a good deal for the whole lot. Heine, he's got the 'thority to act for 'em, so I can't see no problem 'cept gettin' the stock an' men you need to haul it all back to Tucson. Was I you, I'd make a deal with Heine to load as much freight as he can find for Tucson an' pay its way for the haulin' alone."

"That's a good idea, Jeff, and thanks. Assuming I can make a fair deal, would you consider a proposition to help us locate and set up the relay stations we'd need between Tucson and Yuma?"

"Wal, if I don't have to give up this place, could be. Fur's I know, you-all c'd rebuild the old ones. Weren't many, but with them to start, you c'd build the couple more you'd need. Problem'll be to get people to man the stations an' keep 'em supplied. Then there's the question of protection from Apache raids out there with nobody aroun' to count on for outside help. Also, the extra stock you'll need, horses an' mules, provisions, hay an' feed to store, water. Shuh, I think it could be worked out."

"Then I'll tell Max we can count on you. I'm leaving for Lordsburg in the morning, Marcos and me. I'll use your name with Mr. Herzog if you don't mind—"

"Mind? Hell, son, Heine an' me, we was the two top drivers an' agents on the line. Both'n us coulda gone with Butterfield when he closed the route here, but, well, neither one of us liked the cold up there in winter. Sure, I'll be glad to come in with you-all. Might even get out to Yuma once in a while—"

Late that night, Sam told Max of his talk with Jeff Lennon, and Max approved of taking the old experienced driver-agent into the organization. Max had also arranged for a $5,000 bank draft for Sam's use as a down payment to bind the deal, and a power of attorney to enable him to sign the agreement with Herzog.

"Somethin' else, Sam," Max told him. "While you're in Lordsburg, see if you can smoke out some news about my cousins, Aaron an' Libby Olmstead an' their son Loren an' daughter Laurie. Our cousins from Fort Leavenworth—"

"I know about them. Ruth used to talk about them coming out here some day."

"Well, they're on their way. Last I heard was five-six months ago when Aaron wrote he was close to a deal an' ready to sell out. He figured it would take him a while to get on the road, comin' down through Santa Fe an' either by way of El Paso an' Sonora, or through Santa Rita an' Lordsburg, dependin' on what they found along the way. By now, they could be in or around Lordsburg if they're comin' that way. If they are, I'd feel a lot better knowin' they'd have company comin' through that Chiricahua country. I'm sure they would, too."

"I'll make inquiries when I get to Lordsburg."

"Check with any freightin' outfits workin' between Santa Fe an' Lordsburg. Could be somebody's run across 'em."

"I'll do that first thing. I'll have Marcos with me. He asked to come along."

Max nodded. "Good boy, once he gets his head on straight. Maybe you could be the one to do it for him."

"I'd like to try."

"Then put him on the payroll as of tomorrow mornin'. Thirty a month—"

"I'll make it forty. He'll be worth it."

128

"Whatever you say—partner."

Sam and Max exchanged grins over that designation. "I'm sure glad we're goin'a be together in this thing, son," Max said. "If you want somethin' in writin'—"

"No need for that, Max. Not between you and me."

"Thank you, son. Had a minute with Major Boyden after the ceremony. He asked about you. Looks like he's jumpin' the traces, quittin' his job as the governor's aide to take over Owen Travis's place at Fort Bandolier."

"He could be a big help to Colonel Hatfield. He proved himself up in Monte de Lágrimas and Mesa Plata. He'll go a long way to make up for the loss of Major Travis."

"Somethin' else he told me. The governor's had General Litchfield close down Camp Brennan, up north of Prescott, sendin' the whole outfit, lock-stock-an'-barrel, down to Bandolier as replacements."

"That's the best news yet. They need everything they can get to cover all that territory."

"Looks like the colonel'll be able to bring back the Fort families as soon as things get settled in. Kind of perk up the place with the women an' children back."

"It will mean a lot to everybody. To us, too, Max—"

Max grinned. "Glad you're beginnin' to think that way. They'll need more supplies, mail, passenger service to Yuma an' Tucson—"

"Better still, if we get that Army contract, we can call on Fort Bandolier and Fort Lowell for escort if things get out of hand."

"All of that an' more. Sam—"

"Yes?"

"How about pickin' up six men from Tres Flechas to take to Lordsburg with you?"

Sam's face cracked into a grin. "I guess you've heard more than you're telling me."

"Well, talk does have a way of gettin' around. You're a marked man. I don't want anything happenin' to you."

"Either do I, Max, but if I take six men with me, it'll be known long before I can get through the mountains. If Marcos and I light out before dawn tomorrow, we can make faster time and slip through some side trails I remember from my courier days. We'll travel light—"

"Any way you want it, Sam. Just get back safely. Don't come back to Tucson. I'll be waitin' for you at Tres Flechas."

"I'll do that. I won't be seeing you in the morning, so I'll say goodbye now."

"And good luck."

They left at three-thirty that morning, carrying food in their saddlebags, blanket rolls, grain for the horses, and extra rifle and revolver ammunition. Without incident, the trip could be made in three days of hard riding, taking normal time out for rest, meals, water and graze the horses. The most dangerous part would come between the approaches to Apache Pass and Fort Bowie. From the peaks overlooking the Pass and the valley approach, they could be spotted miles before they reached the rocky defiles where every shadow could give a traveler cause for fear. The records of slaughter that had taken place here were too well known, too numerous to be counted, for, without question, Cochise's Apaches were dominant in the area. Here, immigrants in small numbers, in large trains, cavalry troops, stages and freight wagons had come under fierce attack; men and women killed, wagons looted and burned, horses, mules, guns and ammunition taken to Cochise's stronghold for distribution among his tribes.

Sam and Marcos pressed hard that first day. They stopped briefly at noon to eat, well-hidden and off the main road. They pushed on until dusk, ate again and rested for three hours, then saddled up and rode all night. Much of the next day they slept, each taking a two-hour watch in turn. Thus, they approached the dangerous Pass at night, rode through it without encounter and arrived at Fort Bowie just after dawn. Late on the third day they rode into Lordsburg and after a hearty meal and a good night's rest, breakfasted early.

"If you have nothing for me to do, *amigo*," Marcos said, "I will begin to look for my cousins."

"If you have any time to spare from your cousins, Marcos, I want you to get around and make some inquiries about the Olmsteads, eh? Check out the trading stores and outfitters, any place they may have stopped to stock up on supplies. Check the Lordsburg–Santa Fe freighters to see if they passed them on the road somewhere. I'll find Herzog and start talking with him and meet you back here around five o'clock."

"By five o'clock, I will know all there is to know about your Cousin Olmstead. Also," with a wide grin, "my cousins."

Heine Herzog could have been cut from the same bolt of cloth (or carved from the same block of granite) as Jeff Lennon. He had been a buffalo hunter for the Rocky Mountain Fur Company, beaver trapper, Indian scout and a sergeant with the Kearney expedition into Mexico. In '48, he had settled in Santa Fe and signed on at Fort Marcy as a civilian scout. When his Mexican wife died in '57, he took her body back to her family in Lordsburg, where he married a younger relative of the same family and remained there. In '58, like Jeff Lennon, he joined the Butterfield Company. Now he ran a livery stable, traded in horses and mules on the side. The Butterfield people employed him to take care of what rolling stock they had left behind until it was needed or could be sold.

"Here it is, Mr. Palmer," Herzog said, throwing open the doors of the first of three buildings that housed the eighteen pieces of equipment. "All blocked up, in fine shape. Dern near like new. Harness oiled, maybe a few straps an' some canvas needs replacin'. Get the whole thing in shape f'you inside a month, six weeks maybe, paint an' varnish included. What's more, I c'n supply the horses an' mules you need. All's you got to do is bring the men in to drive the stuff out."

"How about price?" Sam asked.

"Wal, fust off, let's see do you want it. If'n we get that fur, then we talk price. I'll guarantee it'll be fair, ol' Max bein' the fust man to make an offer in y'ars."

"Let's roll it out and look it over."

Herzog's men rolled the stages and wagons out piece by piece. When Sam remarked over a bad spoke, sprung wheel tire, sagging door or plank, Heine was ready to mark the deficiency with a large round ball of yellow chalk. At the end of the day they had thoroughly checked three coaches and two wagons, all marked for necessary repairs and parts replacements.

At the hotel, Marcos reported both success and failure. He had successfully made contact with numerous "cousins," but had no word of those whom Sam had never seen but only heard of from Ruth and Max.

"By tomorrow," Marcos promised, "all my cousins will be asking questions. If they have been here, or were seen between here and Santa Fe, we will know it."

Next morning, Sam and Herzog were busy checking and marking the other three stages and several wagons and by nightfall, Marcos reported no results in locating the

Olmsteads. They had not been in Lordsburg, nor had he found anyone who had seen them en route.

On the third day, Sam and Herzog completed their inspection and at three o'clock concluded the final financial negotiations, signed the agreement of sale at the bank, where Sam handed over the $5,000 draft as down payment. In four weeks' time, he would return with *vaqueros* from Tres Flechas to drive the vehicles back to Tucson as the property of the new Tucson-Yuma Stage and Freight Lines. Herzog would also supply the required number of horses and mules, this in a deal apart from the Butterfield agreement.

And again, Marcos reported failure. His cousins had checked every rooming house, store, camping grounds in and around Lordsburg and it must be assumed that if the Olmsteads had gotten this far south, they had bypassed Lordsburg on their way to El Paso.

With negotiations complete, Sam was anxious to be on his way. They had an early supper, slept for several hours and started for Fort Bowie after dark in order to arrive there by early morning.

The road west was a good one, well-marked, but night riding was necessarily slow, although much safer from Apache attack. They came into the Fort just as morning colors were being raised and Sam asked for and received permission to eat, have their horses cared for and a place to sleep before moving on. In the mess hall, he ran into several men he had known from his courier days on the run between Bowie and Lowell. Sergeant Major Rusterman, First Sergeant Macklin and Sergeant Frye were having breakfast together when he entered and Rusterman invited him to his table.

After discussing his discharge from the Army and the affair at Monte de Lágrimas, Frye said, "You sure taken a load off'n our backs up here. Word's out that Cochise had to split his forces to send in replacements for the devils you boys taken care of up in Monte. Looks like the Pass'll be a little less troublesome for a while."

"We didn't have any trouble coming through the other day," Sam replied, "but we planned to make it at night, so I didn't think too much about it one way or the other."

"Shouldn't be any trouble right now," Macklin added. "Scout just in the other night reported some movement south out of the Stronghold, probably headin' for Sonora to do some raidin' aroun' the border villages."

"Any pilgrims come through here lately?" Sam asked.

"Not much this time of the year," Rusterman said. "One come through, though, no more'n three—no, two days ago. One wagon, man, wife and a boy. Come all the way from Leavenworth."

"People I'm looking for would be four, also from Leavenworth. Man, wife, son and daughter."

"Well, this party was only three."

"You wouldn't remember their names, would you?"

"Sure. Homestead, something like that."

With growing interest, "Or Olmstead?"

"Could be. You know 'em?"

"No, but Max Potter asked me to keep an eye out for them. They're his cousins, heading for Tubac."

"That's right," the sergeant major said. "The man said they were heading for Tubac. We tried to talk him into staying on the main road for Tucson, but he was kind of hurrying to get to Tubac. His woman was ailing some."

"Ailing?"

"Yeah," Macklin interjected. "They stopped to rest for half a day an' whilst they was here, Doc Metcalf had a look at the woman, but wasn't much he could do for her. I don't rightly know what the trouble was, but I seen her an' she looked mighty peaked, like she had a bad case of road fatigue. Been on the go somethin' like four months or more."

"Where can I find Doc Metcalf?" Sam asked. "I'd like to ask him about her."

"You know where the hospital is, next to HQ."

The missing fourth member puzzled Palmer; and how they had come to Bowie without passing through Lordsburg; unless they had cut west earlier and come across the old, now unused northern pass.

Marcos had eaten with the Mexican kitchen employees, and Sam told him to turn in for a while until he could have a talk with Dr. Metcalf. He found the graying captain in the admitting room at the hospital and made himself known.

"What can I do for you, Mr. Palmer?"

"I'd like to inquire about the condition of a civilian woman you examined a few days ago, a Mrs. Olmstead. She's my father-in-law's cousin, Max Potter of Tubac. He asked me to check on their whereabouts and I'd like to know something about her and the condition of the others."

"Well, in that case—" Metcalf shook his head from side to side as though in doubt. "Tell you, Mr. Palmer, I can't give you too much to go on. The lady seemed to be suffering from severe exhaustion, although I understood from Mr. Olmstead that she'd spent most of the trip in bed in the wagon. I couldn't give her more than a superficial examination because they were in such a hurry to get to Tubac. She was running a low-grade fever, but it would take a number of tests and some controlled observation to discover the causes, but as I say, they were anxious to get along. Left here just two days ago. You catch up with them, I'd urge you to have them get in touch with Captain Wilson at Fort Lowell. He's better equipped there and he's had some good training at Johns Hopkins Hospital before the war."

"Yes, sir, and thank you."

Sam was disturbed by this news and decided to move out as quickly as possible. Shortly past ten o'clock, he woke Marcos and they started for Apache Pass and the southwest route toward the San Pedro River and Tubac.

The Olmsteads had suddenly become vitally important to him.

BOOK II

CHAPTER I

To Aaron Olmstead's knowledge, scavenged from letters, journals and several family Bibles left behind and now in his possession in 1867, there had been Olmsteads in the Revolutionary War, the War of 1812, the Indian, Mexican and Civil wars. Branches of the Olmstead family had settled in New England, Pennsylvania, Maryland, Virginia, the Carolinas, Georgia and Ohio. Aaron's own arm of the family had been brought to Kansas by his father, Esau, with the first trailbreakers West.

There had been an earlier Aaron, a brevet general; a Loren, after whom the present-day Aaron had named his son, and who had been a much-decorated colonel; a scattering of majors and captains, some of naval rank up to captain. From these writings left behind, the present Aaron deduced as he labored to translate almost illegible words, that the earliest Olmsteads were largely uneducated and barely literate, but there was little doubt about their abilities as soldiers and sailors.

Later, more readable documents confirmed the presence of Olmsteads at Bull Run, Shiloh, Chicamauga, Gettysburg, Vicksburg, Atlanta and in the final curtain at Appomatox.

Many, in fact, had died by the time the war had ended in April of '65, and the records Aaron studied had been sent to him by Olmstead widows and orphans with whom he had faithfully corresponded. Ironically, they had fought on both sides of the Cause and letters from the Southern branches evidenced humiliation, anger and even venom at their terrible defeat and losses. Having served on neither side, and living in Kansas, Aaron found little difficulty in assuming the role of a neutral when communicating with both sides.

Among the war dead was Aaron's own father, Esau, who had left his prosperous trading post in Fort Leavenworth in Aaron's hands to ride off to do battle in Olmstead tradition, never to be heard of, or from, after June of

137

1863, when he wrote a brief letter to say he was in Virginia, heading through Winchester toward Pennsylvania. It was later presumed that he was occupying an unmarked grave at Gettysburg. His wife, Lavinia, died the following year. Their other sons, John, Hugh and Kyle died in such landmark battles as Antietam in September of '62, Chancellorsville in May '63, and Cold Harbor in June of '64, this, no doubt, contributing to Lavinia's death.

So it ended finally with nonsoldier Aaron one of the few male Olmsteads left alive, a man embittered from his earliest youth because he had been born with a clubfoot and could never hope to bear arms against the enemies of his country, foreign or domestic. Aaron's wife, Libby, was a distant cousin of the same military heritage, orphaned when her soldier-father (and mother) were killed by Cheyennes while en route to a new post farther west, Libby having been left behind with her Fort Leavenworth relatives until travel was made safer. Libby was perhaps the only Olmstead who was grateful in 1865 that their son Loren and daughter Laurie could boast of two parents, which many children in this sad postwar era could not.

Aaron and Loren, who was saddened that the war had ended before he could get into it, ran the Olmstead and Son Trading Post at the Fort and with it, a subsidiary business, off post, as outfitters of wagon trains heading for California. Libby was an important part of the business, since it was she who kept the firm's accounts, records of orders and shipments, inventory and correspondence, all in neat and comprehensive style. Laurie had no specific duties beyond assisting her mother, which gave her ample time to ride, hunt and shoot with the best of the wagon scouts and soldiers, who had developed a strong protective attitude toward Aaron's daughter, although few thought of her as being a girl. Since Fort Leavenworth was a gathering place for every type of evil known, as well as for the decent, hard-working families who were eager to make a new life in the West, Laurie's hair was cut as short as Loren's, and she wore the same buckskins Loren wore, except on those church and social occasions when a dress and bonnet were mandatory.

On the detailed family tree Aaron had laboriously drawn up, was an offshoot of the Olmstead family, important only in that it belonged to Esau Olmstead's cousin, Jacob, who had been killed at Spotsylvania. A widower,

Jacob had left a daughter, Callie, who had married an Indiana man, Giles Potter, and bore him a son, Lomax. Giles and Callie Potter were drowned in the spring flood of '46 when the Missouri River overflowed some four months after Lomax had gone off to fight in the Mexican War. In '48, when the Treaty of Guadalupe Hidalgo was signed, Lomax remained in Mexico, married, moved from Sonora to Tubac, which became a part of Arizona Territory.

Tubac was a long way from everything Lomax Potter had called home, and although he had begun to raise a family of his own, he wrote a number of letters to his Olmstead cousin, Aaron, who responded with a family historian's eagerness. The two had met as young men, remembered each other with affection, and the correspondence reawakened nostalgia and continued on a sporadic basis after the Civil War had come to an end.

After the war, Lomax had begun a campaign to bring Aaron, Libby, Loren and Laurie to Tubac, using every persuasion possible, but there was the business to tend, although the proposition was tempting to Aaron now that the pressures and demands upon him had increased as more and more immigrants poured into Fort Leavenworth on their way West. Aaron wrote Lomax indicating that he would not be unreceptive, if he could find a ranch near Tres Flechas and learn the mysteries of ranching. Some letters exchanged during this period, but it was not until early in '67, when a personal tragedy overtook the Fort Leavenworth Olmsteads, that the decision to make the move to Tubac became certainty.

It was a bitterly cold Saturday in February and the huge trading post was crowded, as always on a Saturday, with the normal influx of farmer families from beyond the town limits joining with the men, women and children from several large wagon trains forming to leave as soon as the weather would permit travel. Also, it was the day after payday at the Fort and the military families milled about, and Olmstead's clerks were overtaxed to take care of their demands.

At the gun counter, Loren Olmstead's favorite section, westbound immigrants examined, hefted and asked questions about the latest models in carbines and revolvers while Loren proudly displayed his considerable knowledge in minutest detail, demonstrated loading, ease in handling, discussed accuracy and efficiency of the new weapons. His

139

sales talk was as much a lecture as it was a medicine man's pitch to encourage potential buyers.

One man, obviously a city man emigrating West, looked on for a while in fascination, then timidly asked to see the new Colt .44 Loren had been showing with the ease of a seasoned frontiersman, demonstrating such exotic examples as the quick draw, road agent's spin, the roll and border shift; none of which had practical value, but provided a lift to Loren's youthful ego and an entertaining show for his admiring audience.

Loren withdrew the Colt from his holster with a lightning swift move, reversed the weapon and offered it to the man, butt first. Noting how timorously the man accepted the weapon, he asked, "You ever handle one of these before, mister?"

"N-no. I've never had the need."

"Let me show you." In the presence of a dozen onlookers and with the arrogance of an eighteen-year-old expert, Loren took the Colt from the man, twirled it back and forth on his right index finger, holstered it, withdrew it in a flash. It was a childish, yet effective exhibition he would not have performed for anyone but a group of uninitiated pilgrims.

"Finest gun in the West," Loren added, "once you get used to handling it. Practice is what does it."

The pilgrim was duly impressed. "What about bullets?"

"Right here." Loren brought out a box of .44 cartridges, unlocked and spun the well-oiled barrel out, then loaded six cartridges into it and snapped it back into place. "Nothin' to it, mister. Fastest and easiest loading piece we've got. The newest model, too. We just got this shipment in last—"

The Colt was in Loren's right hand, the hammer drawn back as the man stood facing him, admiring its lethal beauty. "How much—?"

From behind Loren, a tall, bearded drover, smelling of the trail and breathing whiskey fumes, pushed through the crowd. He jostled an onlooker with such force that it threw the man against Loren's right elbow. In that split second, Loren's index finger tightened on the trigger. The Colt roared and the would-be buyer clutched at his breast, stunned by the force of the bullet, then fell backward. Every voice, every movement in the store came to an abrupt stop for a moment so that the pilgrim's last words were heard by everyone in the immediate vicinity:

140

"My—God—I've—been—shot!"

Aaron, white-faced, came hobbling from the saddle and harness section, but even before he could reach the immobilized tableau around the victim, the man was dead, his life trickled away in the trail of blood that spread downward on his shirtfront. The Colt fell from Loren's hand to the floor as panic overtook him, his lips trembling soundlessly in his private terror.

The reaction of the circle around him was mixed, accusing and defending at the same time.

"Damn showoff kid—"

"Wasn't his fault, somebody pushed him—"

"—no right to aim a loaded gun at somebody—"

"This is a store, not a damn road show—"

Two employees carried the dead man into a back room while Aaron hustled Loren into the small, cluttered office where, despite the heat given off by the coal stove, he shook as though he had taken a severe chill.

"Loren, for God's sake, what happened?"

"Pa—I don't—know. It went off—somebody pushed me—my arm—my God, Pa, I—killed him—"

"It was an accident, Loren."

"I killed him—"

"Wait here. Don't go out there until I come back. I'll take care of things."

"Where's Ma? Laurie?"

"I don't know. Just stay in here until I get back."

Aaron went back to the confusion in the store and Loren buried his face in his hands and wept.

The marshal came and listened to every witness calmly. The pilgrim was named Leander Bryce, from Taylor City, Pennsylvania. He and his wife had come by rail to St. Louis, then by stage to Fort Leavenworth, hoping to buy a small outfit and join a wagon train West to join his brother in San Francisco, who needed help in running a general store. Bryce had been slowly buying up goods needed by his brother at prices that would more than quadruple by the time they reached San Francisco.

The marshal's inquest declared the shooting an accident, but this was of little consolation to Bryce's widow; or to Aaron, Libby and Laurie Olmstead; and in particular, to Loren. Aaron arranged to take over payment of Mrs. Bryce's hotel bill until he could make arrangements to send her back to Taylor City by train, or on to San Francisco, depending on her choice, which was at the moment justi-fiably indecisive. Apart from transportation and hotel costs, Aaron had withdrawn $5,000 in gold to make up, in part, for her tragic loss.

Loren was inconsolable. He rode out early every morn-ing and remained away all day. At night, he slept in the stables, unable to face Mrs. Bryce, his family, the accusing eyes of the community in which he was so well known. And during this period of his personal anguish, his only companion was his sister, Laurie, who suffered with him.

A week passed and then, early on the eighth morning, Loren was gone, taking his horse, rifle and revolver, a blanket roll and a supply of food. For forty-eight hours his disappearance remained a mystery, then Laurie admitted to Aaron that Loren had gone West, his intention to catch up with a wagon train and sign on as a crew member to work his way to California.

"He told you before he left, Laurie?"

"Yes, Pa."

"Why didn't you come to me then?"

"Because you couldn't have stopped him and he made me promise to give him two full days, else he wouldn't have told me, either. Please don't be mad at me, Pa."

"No Laurie, no. I'm glad one of us knew. He tell you what route he was taking?"

"He said he was going south and west, Santa Fe, then down to Texas, Yuma, Los Angeles, then north to San Francisco. He said he couldn't stand it here, everybody knowing he killed Mr. Bryce, dreaming it over and over again—"

Aaron nodded sadly, then went to Libby to tell her; and Libby did not emerge from their bedroom for three full days.

By that time, Mrs. Bryce was on her way back to Taylor City. The emptiness created by Loren's departure was un-bearable. Aaron could not reawaken his interest in the business and without Libby, upon whom he relied to keep his paperwork in order, he passed more and more respon-sibility on to several of his key employees. Laurie kept her own counsel, but Loren's absence, and her concern for him, gave her little to look forward to each succeeding day.

During those empty days, Laurie could do nothing that didn't remind her of Loren, her most constant companion since early childhood. So it was that when Aaron proposed

142

selling out and accepting Cousin Lomax's offer to come to Tubac, both Libby and Laurie saw merit in the plan. For all of them, the ranch life, away from the bustle and evils of Fort Leavenworth was a chance to become engrossed in a new life. For Aaron, the friendship of Lomax Potter. For Libby, the work of building and organizing a new home. For Laurie, they saw a chance to become a woman instead of a young girl living and dressing like a young man.

But prime in the mind of each was the fact that they might, while en route, run across some word of Loren. They would leave word of their destination with friends, neighbors and the postmaster so that if Loren wrote, the letter could be forwarded to Tubac; or if he returned, he would know where to find them. Already, Aaron had begun placing newspaper advertisements in every city along the southern and overland routes between Fort Leavenworth and San Francisco, hoping to catch Loren's eye.

Aaron had had offers to sell out before; Sublette in St. Louis was interested in expanding his operation. A group from Independence had sounded him out. The Graingers from Springfield. A syndicate from Joplin. The Bernstein brothers from Fort Smith had made the best offer, all cash.

Aaron sent word to Fort Smith and a week later, the Bernsteins came to talk business. An inventory was taken, price agreed upon, papers signed, and the Olmsteads were richer by $43,000, and free to leave at will.

Soberly now, Aaron, Libby and Laurie discussed the move. It was ironical, they realized, after having outfitted hundreds of wagon trains, how little they knew about actual life on the trail, only the means to support it.

"We can't overlook the dangers of traveling alone," Aaron warned.

Laurie took up that question at once. "There's danger everywhere, Pa," she said. "Right here, the past week, a man went into Kelleher's for a glass of beer. Somebody started a fight and this innocent man was killed. Charlie Rhodenbach's horse stepped into a pothole and Charlie died of a broken neck. On Tuesday, a four-year-old girl ran across the street and got run down by a wagon. All in one week, and in a civilized town."

"This is a new and different kind of danger, Laurie, Libby," Aaron said. "We'll be up against nature and a

143

hostile country. Indians, animals, and we don't know what else."

"How much do the pilgrims who leave here know about what's in front of them?" Laurie countered. "I don't want to sit around here to wait for some big wagon train to get started, take orders from some wagonmaster, move when he tells us to, stop when he says so. I think we'd be better off traveling alone, in our own wagon, able to go where we want, sleep when we want, hunt when we want. In that way, we'll have more of a chance to find news of Loren."

"All right, I'm not disagreeing, mind you. I just want us all to be aware that life's not going to be easy from the time we leave here until we get to Tubac. Let's talk about the route now—"

Quickly, unanimously, they voted to go by way of Santa Fe, El Paso, Mesilla, then head directly for Tubac; the trail Loren had told Laurie he would take. All along the route, they would stop to rest and make inquiries. Loren's horse, marked by a white star on his forehead and four white stockings, his saddle branded with his initials, exactly like Laurie's, his close resemblance to Laurie, wearing the same buckskin shirt, jacket and trousers, would give them so many points of identification.

And as to Indians. "Nothin' to worry about between here an' Santa Fe," they were told by a number of trail scouts. "You'll be between supply trains an' Army escorts or couriers most of the way, maybe as far as Albuquerque. No hostiles reported. Weather's cold an' wet right now, so they don't move around too much, 'cept to hunt for food. Y'all take along some tradin' goods for the friendlies, but keep a sharp eye out for stealin'. Give 'em a chance to get too close an' they'll have you afoot in no time.

"Farther south an' west, p'ticularly west, you get into Apache country an' they're tough, but the way I hear it, they move around in small groups, maybe six, no more'n eight, ten at the most. With repeatin' rifles, I figure y'all can put up a good defense, but chances are you won't be runnin' into many takin' the route to Texas, then west from, say, El Paso. Ought to be some protection from Army patrols. All's you need is a good wagon, four strong mules, plenty of food, water, and ammunition. You can shoot birds, turkeys, run acrost a deer for fresh meat—"

They listened to the freighters and Army scouts and finally made their decision. Aaron moved swiftly, and even with Laurie a constant source of help, the details seemed endless, checking against prepared lists, worrying that some item may have been overlooked. Everything came from Olmstead stock before the Bernsteins took over.

For their wagon, they chose a sturdy Moline, weighing about 2,000 pounds. From the ground to the top of its reinforced canvas covering, it stood eleven feet high, giving them good vision of what lay ahead from the driver's seat. It was 24 feet long, providing a bed 14 feet in length and 4½ feet wide. It had a frame of cured white oak and poplar sideboards four feet high. Flooring and sides were 1½ inches thick, the sides reinforced on the inside with thin sheets of iron for added protection. The hinged endgate was held in place by heavy chains, long enough to double into tow chains in case they became bogged down.

The underside was heavily ironed and braced, its bolsters and axles of hickory, with hubs of black gum. The wheel rims were four-inches wide, its front wheels three-feet, six-inches high, the rear wheels four-feet, eight inches, held to the axles by heavy linchpins. Two spare wheels, one front and one rear, were lashed to the bottom. There were three water buckets and two tar buckets, four fifty-gallon water barrels lashed to the sides of the wagon and six personal canteens.

In the iron tool box were hatchets, axes, nails, an auger, saws, coils of rope, spare kingbolts, linchpins and iron strapping. Beneath the left side was a wagon jack, to be used for greasing or changing wheels.

Aaron and Laurie took great pains in choosing the mules, four of the best, strongest and healthiest, averaging sixteen hands high and weighing about 1600 pounds. Aaron's and Laurie's saddle horses would be tied to the rear of the wagon.

Inside, surrounded by boxes, trunks, sacks and crates, was a full-sized bed for Libby's use and comfort, and which she would share with Aaron at night. Laurie decided she would sleep in a special tarpaulin-covered blanket-bed beneath the wagon, and move inside with Aaron and Libby when the weather turned inclement.

There were many choices to make in clothes and personal possessions, with much to sell off and give away. Food came under Libby's and Laurie's supervision; flour, bacon, dried and smoked beef, beans and canned fruits. In the arms department, they carried four of the latest repeating rifles, two shotguns, four revolvers, skinning knives and cases of ammunition, all valuable in Tubac if not necessary en route. Last-minute items included Libby's Singer sewing machine, dress patterns, bolt goods, needles, thread, buttons and dress findings. Gifts, she said, for the Potter girls.

Beneath the wagon, in a separate iron box lashed by iron straps, rode their cash wealth, the $43,000 swelled by another $6,000 gained by the sale of their house, furniture and furnishings, and the 160 acres of land upon which it stood; another $22,000 from Aaron's cash account in the bank.

And on a Monday morning in mid-March, they set off for Santa Fe, each praying for some sign of Loren, any news he may have left along the road to Tubac.

Aaron Olmstead had, while his father, Esau, was alive, taken the trip from Fort Leavenworth to Santa Fe when he was eighteen, as a member of a twelve-wagon freighting team under military escort, for what Esau called a "broadening experience." It had been a most satisfying adventure. Astride a horse, he was able to forget temporarily the misfortune of his birth, the clubfoot, which rode easily in a specially built stirrup. Apart from its educational aspect, the trip had provided Aaron with the intimate association of an entirely new breed of men: muleskinners, freighters, tough mountain-men, scouts and cavalrymen, all of whom added a fresh vocabulary he had never been able to use in the presence of his parents or polite society upon his return.

Almost forty years had passed since that trip and now it was as though it had never happened. There was little he could remember of the terrain, and even the wagon route had changed considerably over the years.

The Olmstead wagon left ahead of a small supply train, knowing there was another only two days ahead of them. South, then west through Council Grove and Diamond Spring, they caught up with the earlier train a few days later and camped nearby, left it behind at daybreak and followed a well-broken trail southwesterly to Fort Dodge. Here, they talked with Army scouts who assured them there were no visible signs of hostiles, but that a number of small bands of friendlies were abroad and should cause no trouble. So far, there was no word of Loren.

The weather, excepting for a two-day period of rain, was bright and clear and warming. The day would begin with

146

breakfast at dawn, a consultation between Aaron and Laurie to determine direction, a "nooning" stop to water the animals and allow for a period of rest and grazing. They would resume at two o'clock, sometimes three, and continue on until they found a protected area for a night camp, generally at dusk, searching for a wooded area where their wagon could be hidden from open view.

Aaron, of course, drove the team of mules. Laurie would mount one of the two saddle horses and ride ahead, careful to remain within sight or gunshot-sound of the wagon. Tiring sometimes, she would return and ride on the seat beside Aaron, both with rifles at their sides, gun belts strapped to their waists, looking from side to side for any movement of man, bird or beast. From the bed inside the wagon, Libby, reclining against two large pillows, kept watch on what went on behind them. They came across a sorry-looking band of a dozen Indian men and women, traveling by horse and travois, whom they could not understand except by the most primitive sign language. They parted with some food, a trade blanket and a few trinkets, Laurie on the alert to keep the more curious away from the wagon, her rifle clearly in evidence.

A few days later, they came upon a small group of bearded, filthy, evil-smelling hide hunters whose appearance alone was frightening. Warily, they politely declined to share a campsite and after leaving some tobacco with them, continued on until well after dark before making camp. The hunters told them they had seen no Indians north of Santa Fe.

A week later found them in Santa Fe where they decided to camp, rest and restock some of their expended food supply. At Fort Marcy, Aaron introduced himself to the post trader, a man he had done business with but had never seen before. Jake Eskridge was perhaps the biggest, fattest man Laurie had ever seen, and his immense girth fascinated her since it took two ordinary belts to encircle his waist, plus a pair of leather suspenders to keep his trousers up. Aaron spent an entire evening with Eskridge discussing routes, weather and road conditions south of Santa Fe.

Their supplies and water replenished, Laurie remained with Libby to guard the wagon while Aaron spent an entire day making inquiries regarding Loren at the Fort and in every store, hotel, boardinghouse and, in final desperation, even the saloons. On that last evening, Aaron ran

147

across an Army courier who remembered seeing someone of Loren's description heading south out of Santa Fe, but he could not remember the exact day or the circumstances. Since this was the first word he had had of Loren, Aaron brought the courier to the wagon for supper that night and at first sight of Laurie, the soldier exclaimed, "You playin' some kinda joke on me, mister? That there's the boy I seen, same clothes, same repeatin' rifle."

Aaron replied, "It's no joke, corporal. This one's two years younger'n the other."

The corporal stared at Laurie, chewing his cud of tobacco slowly. "Mister," he said finally, "you sure by God coulda fooled me. Never seen two boys look so alike."

Laurie listened avidly to the courier who talked between thrusts of food into his mouth, narrating his experiences and exploits, encounters with hostile Indians and narrow escapes, discounting most of it as pure boasting and fantasy; but he did confirm the current reports of Apache raiding parties, Coyoteros in Texas, Mimbreños in southern New Mexico, Chiricahuas in Arizona. To lend substance to the reports, Santa Fe had become a clutter of westbound immigrants, resting, resupplying, waiting for word from travelers heading north and east of Indian sign.

Now, in early '67, the Indian resentment toward the tremendous numbers of whites crossing New Mexico, Texas, Chihuahua, Sonora and Arizona had intensified. There were hardly enough soldiers to ride escort for the many requests from wagonmasters, and limited escort was now being confined, when not otherwise engaged in military patrols, to protect mail couriers and government officials who traveled by horseback, much too fast for slow-moving wagon trains to keep the pace.

This ominous word prompted the Olmsteads to stay on for another week, despite the unpleasantness of overcrowding and shortened tempers. The town was bulging with travelers, drifters, freighters, gold- and silver-seekers, gamblers, former soldiers, Indian agents, minor bureaucrats, women of questionable character and confidence men. No day passed without brutal, ugly fist fights, knifings, shootings and general brawling, becoming more frequent at night. Almost everyone wore a revolver or carried a rifle.

And finally, after considering that this atmosphere was no less dangerous than a chance meeting with hostiles, the Olmsteads decided to break camp and head south to-

148

ward Albuquerque. Two hours out of Santa Fe, rain teamed down upon them, turning the road into water-filled ruts, forcing them off the road to wait the storm out. In mid-afternoon, it was over. The sun came out hot and strong, creating a screen before them of humid earth-vapor that made visibility poor and travel very uncomfortable.

Arriving in Albuquerque, they found it hardly different from Santa Fe, except that it was much smaller and drove through to camp a good six miles south of town. The next morning, they left for Socorro. For all the rumors, they saw no sign of Indians although they passed two deserted, burned-out homesteads, which could have been attacked as long ago as a year or two. Socorro was a small trading town with few supplies and scarcely any whites among the predominantly Mexican population. While resting and making inquiries after Loren, a sergeant and two privates rode in from Fort Bliss in Texas, heading for Fort Marcy with dispatches and Army mail. The men and horses were thoroughly worn and weary and Aaron offered them a better supper than they could possibly buy, which the soldiers accepted gratefully.

The sergeant was named McComb, a man in his forties with a twenty-year Army record, and a sober man not given to exaggeration. He talked of Indian war parties farther south, perhaps thirty miles the other side of Santa Rita.

"Was I you, Mr. Olmstead, I'd forget El Paso right now. Where the damn Apaches leave off, the Comanches take up. I'd go as far as the Kearny crossing into Santa Rita—here, I'll draw you a map—"

It was a grave disappointment to the Olmsteads, but McComb's advice could not be ignored if they were to avoid the raiding parties the three soldiers had come through on their way up from Texas. At first light, McComb and his two men saddled up, thanked the Olmsteads for their hospitality and rode off toward the north.

Because Libby was growing increasingly tired, they spent another full day outside of Socorro to discuss the change in route that McComb had recommended.

Aaron drove the wagon into town for a last-minute check on some minor needs, but such was the shortage of goods that Aaron was offered unheard-of prices for some of the supplies he carried; and so much attention was paid to their wagon, animals and possessions that Aaron and Laurie decided to leave at once.

There was no doubt now that Libby was ailing, although she did not complain. The lines in her face had deepened and it became more of an effort each day for her to get in and out of the wagon to take her meals. She slept much of the time, calling Loren's name in her sleep; tiring quickly, asking for frequent stops in order to relieve herself when nature demanded. They had been pressing harder since Socorro, heading in a westerly direction after crossing the Rio Grande and at the eastern base of the Sierra de los Mimbres. Here, they found an excellent campsite with abundant fresh water, where they decided to rest for a week. The mules needed the rest as much as Libby needed to be spared the jolting wagon. There was good grazing, a critical need since they could use their precious grain sparingly.

Laurie found some tracks and went off to replenish their larder with fresh fowl. She returned with two fat turkeys and six quail, which she plucked and cleaned, cooked enough for three meals and cut the rest of the meat into thin strips to dry in the sun. The next day, to her complete astonishment, she came across a stray heifer, unbranded and coming out of nowhere. She threw a rope around its neck and brought it back to camp, where Aaron killed it and Laurie helped with the butchering. They dined on steaks that night, a large roast the next day, and the remainder was cut and dried into beef jerky.

All was not peaceful. Coyotes shattered the silence of their nights, and other unidentified woods animals rustled about to disturb their sleep. From time to time, Aaron or Laurie would get up to add wood to their dying fire, fearing mainly snakes, mountain lions and rodent thieves, attracted by the smell of food. The mules and horses were in a perpetual state of high anxiety, neighing and nickering their protests. Through it all, Libby slept soundly, too unhealthily soundly, as though in partial coma; a worrisome thing to husband and daughter who kept their opinions to themselves lest one alarm the other.

On the sixth day, Laurie remained close to camp, on guard, while Aaron rode off to find a passable route across the Sierra de los Mimbres that had been marked on Sergeant McComb's map. He returned late that afternnon announcing that he had found an old, little-used trail he thought would be passable. At daybreak next morning,

they left, their private fears now heightened by the knowledge that once across the crest of the mountains, they
would be coming into Chiricahua country, the land of the
most savage of all Apaches.

CHAPTER II

LOREN OLMSTEAD HAD TAKEN ONE CHANGE OF OUTER clothes, two of heavy underwear, extra socks and another pair of boots, and a slicker. He wore his Colt, but had hidden his Winchester rifle inside the blanket roll until he would be far out in the open, well south of Fort Leavenworth. And several sacks of food: bacon, beans, flour, a few cans of peaches, two large canteens and a sack of grain for his horse, Topkick. All this had been gathered bit by bit and hidden in a corner of the stable until he was ready to leave. The money he took was his own, nearly a hundred dollars he had saved from his small salary and gifts at Christmastime and his birthdays. He had little need for more.

On the trail those first days, he passed a few immigrants heading south and west, but declined their invitations to share a meal or campfire, unwilling to become involved in conversations that might lead to his identification. He found his own ground, made camp, fixed his food and, as much as possible, avoided human contact. He supplemented his stock of food with small game and hoarded the beans, flour and peaches until he came to a town or village where those items could be replaced.

There was little physical fear in Loren, yet he was not brash. He rested Topkick frequently so that in an emergency he could call upon him for additional energy. He was more concerned with bushwhackers than Indians and made a wide circle to avoid the smoke of any campfire he saw or smelled ahead of him. Very seldom did he linger at a creek that showed some signs of human traffic, riding above or below it until there were only animal signs.

The night became his friend and closest ally. He reasoned that by day, if he could see, he could be seen, and wherever he could do so, moved off the traveled trails and into whatever shadows he could find. It took him a while to attune his ears to every moving, rustling sound, learning to distinguish those made by the wind, a small or large animal and, of the latter, friendly or unfriendly. Yet it was always at night that his conscience over the killing of innocent Mr. Bryce came back to him, awake or in his dreams. Now, his rifle and revolver were always close at hand.

The Indians he saw were neither friendly nor hostile; men, women and children nomads moving from one camp to another, not unlike himself. Generally, he gave them a wide berth, unwilling to stop, knowing that to do so could cost him part of his precious supply of food. He had heard that all Indians were beggars and thieves and did not care to risk any loss, no matter how small. Strangely, he was not worried that they might attack him. Only the possibility of being robbed deepened his sense of caution.

In Santa Fe, he restocked his food and water supply and added a sack of grain for Topkick, then rode south for six or seven miles before making his solitary camp. In the morning, a courier from Fort Marcy caught up with him and they rode together until noon. They shared a meal and Loren pleaded fatigue and the need for sleep. The courier rode on and Loren was alone once again; and for the first time since leaving home, Loren felt pangs of homesickness. More than anyone else, he missed Laurie, although he felt a terrible anxiety for Aaron and Libby, wondering how they had taken the news when Laurie told them, forty-eight hours after he had left.

Where? This was the question that still faced him, unable to tell Laurie when she pleaded with him not to leave. The question still remained unanswered.

Texas? California?

Or Tubac, where Aaron had so often talked of moving some day. Tubac, to get away from the hustle, bustle and noise of Fort Leavenworth, to settle on a ranch and raise cattle and horses.

And yet, how could he suddenly appear in Tubac and say to Aaron's cousins, "I'm Loren Olmstead. I murdered a man back home. A man who never did me any harm."

Perhaps one day after Aaron, Libby and Laurie reached Tubac and had their own ranch—.

But he had no way of knowing when that would be.

He was young and strong. He could work, if there were jobs available. Ranch work. In the mine fields. Doing what? He couldn't rope or brand and knew nothing of riding with a trail herd. He could learn, but would there be a place for a greenhorn on a ranch or in a mine, one who knew nothing except clerking in a store.

153

He passed through the small towns of Valencia, Tome, Alamillo, Sabilleta, then cut eastward to avoid others until he crossed the Rio Grande at Robedillo, learning here that he was a good one hundred miles below Socorro and perhaps fifty from El Paso. He was out of flour and bought some cornmeal and dried jerky, used the last of his bacon and beans, gave Topkick what grain was left in the nosebag and headed for El Paso.

On arrival there, it surprised him to learn that the town of La Salinera, which he had skirted only two hours before, had been almost completely wiped out earlier that morning by a band of Comanches, at this moment being chased by a troop of cavalry out of Fort Bliss.

In El Paso, he felt safely anonymous among so many strange faces, his own as strange as others were to him. His cheeks and upper lip were covered with fine blond hairs that itched and seemed so ridiculously out of place on such a youthful face. He had a barber shave him, then went out to search for a place to stay. Wearied of the road, he stabled Topkick and moved his saddle and gear into a cheap room at the Lone Star Hotel, where he registered as Earl Madigan of St. Louis, using the name of a soldier he had known back in Fort Leavenworth. He slept around the clock, woke and ate a large meal and went back to bed for another twelve hours.

A few days later, with seventy-four dollars of his cash hoard left, he began scouting the immigrant camping grounds for a job with any train heading west across Sonora, but found none. Two more days passed before he got an offer from a ten-wagon train that would permit him to ride along, but only for meals and a place to sleep in exchange for the use of his rifle in case of attack, and only if he would sign on until they reached Yuma. The train was due to leave within a week, heading for San Francisco by way of Coredada, Terrenate, Tumacacori, Tubac, Tucson, Yuma and Los Angeles. Loren signed on for one dollar, again using the name of Earl Madigan.

Along the way, the train was trailed by Comanches, later by Apaches, but the wagons were pulled up close on one another's tailgates and with twenty-two armed men in the train, the Indians were cautious, testing the reaction of the White Eyes by sending small groups in closely. Four times they came in, firing wildly and howling like madmen, only to run into a heavy concentration of fire, losing half a dozen braves in all, while the white men suffered the

154

loss of one mule shot. Nor would the wagonmaster leave the dead mule for the Indians to butcher, but stood off while buzzards gathered to pick its carcass clean. Loren accounted for two of the dead Indians.

When they left Tumacacori, Loren was tempted to abandon the train and ride off in search of Max Potter at Tres Flechas, but when they reached Tubac he lost his nerve; besides, he had given his word to stay on until at least Yuma, taken a dollar and signed his—or Madigan's—name to the train's rolls. In Tubac, he inquired about Tres Flechas of a Mexican, who was astonished that all the world did not know where Tres Flechas was, that the name of Max Potter, *el patrón*, was not equally well known. Less than six miles west. He could ride out and be back well before dawn, yet he could not bring himself to make his presence known without explaining how he happened to be there. And on the run. A murderer at eighteen.

Tucson was, to Loren, a smaller El Paso, crowded with strange Mexican, Anglo and soldier faces. He rode into town with three drovers from their camp which was north and east of the town, for a change of diet. They ate Mexican food in a *cantina*, Espuela de Oro, then the three men began drinking. From there, they visited another *cantina*, and later, still another. In that one, the three drovers disappeared into back rooms with various of the girls who were present and advertised their availability openly, but Loren, perhaps out of sheer fright, could not be tempted. The men joked about this and Loren, becoming embarrassed, went outside and waited there for them. He waited for almost two hours and when they finally appeared, were quite drunk, but good naturedly so. Loren had to help two of them into their saddles.

They headed back toward the camp, north along Calle Principale, then came into open country and were about three miles from the camping grounds when four armed, mounted Mexicans came pounding up behind them. As they pulled to one side to allow them to pass, Loren suddenly realized that this was not their purpose. The leader reined in, his three companions behind him, and in the pale light cast by the moon, it was difficult to distinguish one from the other, although he suspected they might have been present in the last Mexican *cantina* they had visited.

"*Señores*," the leader said, "if you will hand over your money, no one will be shot. We will take your guns and

155

leave them a mile north of here. You will please to dismount."

But Loren's revolver was already in his hand and as the three wagon men, cursing drunkenly, slid out of their saddles, Loren ducked low and fired, knocking the leader out of his saddle. The other three Mexicans fired, but in the darkness, found no targets. Loren raised up and got off four more shots, hitting two of the bandits, toppling one to the ground. The two still in their saddles turned and ran.

The two Mexicans lying on the ground were dead, and when the three wagon men tried to thank Loren, he mounted up quickly and rode off toward the camp alone. That night, his dreams were more complicated by these two additional victims of his gun.

The next morning, coming through Tucson, the train stopped to report the incident to Marshal Russ Yarborough, who took the two horses of the dead men and sent a wagon out to bring their bodies in. They waited in town for Yarborough's decision, and when the bodies were finally brought into town and examined, the marshal said simply, "Justifiable homicide," and allowed the train to move through. Yarborough's added comment, "A couple of Lizardi's *vagos*," meant nothing to the wagon-train people. They mounted up and rolled westward toward Celeste and Yuma.

Loren, despite the offer of the wagonmaster to put him on the payroll if he remained until they reached San Francisco, left the train when it reached Yuma, weary of living on the road, tired of an atmosphere that was so close to more killing. His cash totaled an even seventy dollars. If he could find a job, he would wait a reasonable length of time, then go back to Tubac and try to learn if Aaron, Libby and Laurie had arrived yet. If he found no work, he would continue west to Los Angeles, on his own, and try to find a job there.

He took a room at the Langtry Hotel and began searching for work, but there was none to be had. He asked among the two wagon suppliers, the largest general store, the ferry operator who carried wagons and passengers across the Colorado to the California side, the ranchers who came in for supplies on Saturday; but most of the local labor was supplied by Mexicans or Pima Indians at miniscule wages.

One night about a week after he had reached Yuma, Loren sat in the Alexandria Café eating his supper and

drinking a glass of beer, since anything other than beer—
mescal, tequila and whiskey—were the only other drinks
available and too strong for his taste. When he went to the
bar to pay the thirty-five cents due, he was ten cents short
and had to reach inside his money cache to get a new bill.
This, because his money was in a small sack and pinned
inside his trousers, caused some amused glances among
the patrons when he paid the bartender and pocketed his
change.

He started to leave when a man who appeared to be in
his early thirties smiled and said, "Have one on me, friend,"
and before Loren could refuse, ordered two beers.

"Thank you," Loren said, unable to refuse to drink with
the man and thus insult him.

"Don't mention it. Name's Ernie Chapman. Chappy."

"Mine's Earl. Earl Madigan."

"Earl Madigan. Where you from, Earl?"

"Uh—St. Louis."

Chapman smiled. "Good town. Been there lots of times.
I'm from Fort Leavenworth. Soldiered there for a while
after the war, got paid off and came West. San Francisco, Los Angeles, San Diego, now Yuma." He grinned
again. "When you came in, I'd swear I'd seen you some
place. Ever been in Leavenworth?"

"Uh—once or twice—with my father. He was a—uh
—drummer."

"What was his line?"

"Uh—saddles, harness."

"Do good at it?"

"I guess. Did a lot of business with the Army at Jefferson Barracks and the wagon suppliers."

"Madigan, hey? I was with the QM at Leavenworth.
Thought I knew all the drummers in those parts."

Defensively, "Well, there were lots of them. You
couldn't know 'em all."

Chapman grinned again. "No, I guess not. Have another?"

"No, thanks. My treat next time. I've got to get to
bed."

"Where you staying, Earl?"

"The Langtry, over on Purcell Street. Just a couple of
streets over."

"I just got in this afternoon. Think I'll try to get a room
there."

"It's clean, nice and quiet."

157

"If you're leaving, I'll walk over with you."

The Langtry was three blocks away. Loren was on foot, so Chapman walked beside him, leading his mare. There were rooms available and Chapman took number fourteen, which was next to Loren's room. He put his horse up in the stable behind the hotel and carried his rifle, saddlebag and blanket roll up to his room.

It was only eight o'clock and Loren was not as sleepy as he had tried to make Chapman believe back in the Alexandria. He came down to the lobby, chatted with the owner, Homer Howell, for a few minutes, then took a copy of the Yuma *Star* and sat on a sofa near a lamp. He turned the pages idly and on the one before the last, saw the boxed advertisement:

Notice to
LOREN OLMSTEAD
Please write to your Father,
Mother and Sister in care of
Postmaster, Fort Leavenworth.
Expect to leave here soon. If
you write, letter will be for-
warded to us. Let us know how
and where you are. We love you
and miss you. *Please write now.*
AARON OLMSTEAD

Loren's eyes filled with tears so that he could not reread the words. He choked back a sob and turned quickly to see if any of the three men seated in the lobby, or Mr. Howell, dozing behind the counter-desk, had heard him. At that moment, Ernie Chapman came down the steps, key in hand, walking toward him with a grin on his face. Loren turned back to the paper, brushing his neckerchief across his eyes. Chapman's alert eyes caught the movement.

"Something in your eye, Earl?"

"A speck of dust, I guess."

"Let me take a look—"

"Don't bother. It's gone now."

"Too early and too hot to sleep. Feel like having another beer, maybe?"

"Not right now, Chappy."

Chapman sat on the seat beside him and picked up the paper Loren had put aside for the moment. He flipped through the pages lazily, scanning the advertisements until he came to the one that had caught Loren's eye.

"Say, how's that for a coincidence?" Chapman said. "We were talking about Fort Leavenworth before and look at this. Now *there's* a name I know. Olmstead. Trading store and wagon freighters. I'll bet your father knew *him*."

"I guess so. He knew all the freighting outfits."

"Well, I know this one. Olmstead. Had a limp, a clubfoot. Nice man. Wife and a son and daughter. The boy was about your age. Boy and girl were so alike you could hardly tell one from the other."

"You knew them?"

"I guess just about everybody did. Saw 'em a few times. Matter of fact, you look so much like the boy, you could pass for him." Grinning slyly, he added in a lower voice, "Or Earl Madigan."

The inference was clear. Loren turned toward him and said quietly, "All right, Mr. Chapman, what do you want?"

"Well, now, that's a little different. What I been wondering, Loren Olmstead, is what kind of a ruckus you're in, hiding under Earl Madigan's name. You see, I soldiered with Earl at Leavenworth. And I've seen you there a-plenty."

"All right. What business is it of yours if I'm Loren Olmstead?"

"Well, I was also wondering if maybe you hiding under another man's name, was there some kind of a reward out for you."

"What are you, a dirty bounty hunter? Anyway, there isn't a nickel reward for me, so you're just wasting your time."

"I've got only your word for that, ain't I? Maybe the sheriff of Yuma would have some word. Or if I answered that advertisement myself, the marshal at Fort Leavenworth would—"

"You do that, Mr. Chapman, and I'll—"

Chapman snickered. "Kill me? Like maybe you killed somebody back home and took to the road, Olmstead?"

Loren leaped to his feet and the three lobby loungers looked up at the sudden move that also brought Chapman to his feet. "Take it easy, boy," Chapman said.

"Stay away from me, Chapman."

"Don't get riled, boy. I'm too fast for you."

"Try me."

Chapman grinned and Mr. Howell, fully awake now, called out, "Here, here, what's goin' on—"

That was the moment when Chapman drew, but not

159

fast enough to level the barrel of his .44 properly. Loren beat him to the draw by a full second, long enough to get his shot off, catching Chapman in the chest. Chapman crumpled against the chair, his face registering complete surprise as he fell into it in a seated position and his .44 went off, plowing a furrow into the floor.

And Loren stood still in shock, staring at the dead Ernie Chapman, saying only, "I'm sorry. I'm sorry. I didn't want to—"

"You're fast, son," Sheriff Jack Kinnick said.

"I don't know," Loren replied dully: "I didn't mean to kill him. I told him to stay away from me. He drew on me first—"

"I know. There were witnesses. Question is, why?"

"I don't even know why. He picked an argument—"

"Over what, Earl?"

"I can't even remember now."

"Well, seems like you hit into a streak of luck."

"Luck?"

"Sure. This here Chapman you killed, I got a notice on him from the Army. His real name is Dewey Corrigan, Army deserter from Fort Leavenworth, wanted in San Francisco and Los Angeles for murder, stage robbery and a few other assorted charges. You're in for a three-hundred dollar reward—"

"I don't want it."

"That's crazy, son. Nobody turns down a reward."

"I said I don't want it."

"Well, we'll see about that later. Tell me, Earl, how come you're so fast? This Corrigan-Chapman, he's shot it out with some mighty fast men in his time, lived through all of 'em 'til tonight. You a gunslinger?"

"Oh, no! No, sir! I—uh—used to demonstrate guns—for my father. He was a—uh—drummer, back in St. Louis."

"Well, you sure learned from a good man." A pause, a squinting of eyes, then, "You ain't wanted anywhere, are you?"

"No, sir!"

"What you doin' in Yuma?"

"I left the Parsons' wagon train here last week. I've been trying to find a job. You can ask around the stores. They'll tell you, sheriff. I've been looking ever since I got here."

"I can and I will, son. If it checks out the way you say, maybe I can find you a job."

"You can?"

"Mm-hm. Pay ain't much an' you got to put a lot of time in, but it's clean work—"

"Doing what?'

"I need a night deputy. I think you might be the right man for it."

Later that night, Loren wrote a letter to his father in care of the postmaster, Fort Leavenworth, Kansas.

The Olmsteads were not complete strangers to Indians. They had seen them in Kansas and Missouri, peaceful Indians with whom they had had only the slightest contact. They had, for that matter, seen few Negroes in their lifetime, and apart from their personal abhorrence of slavery, knew little about these people, their lives, existence and miseries. They had known more Mexicans, had traded with them and could actually understand and make themselves understood by them; but they had no true knowledge of Indians who lived in the open and roamed the land far and wide; Sioux, Cheyenne, Arapahoe and Navajo. Of the Apaches, they knew nothing except what they had heard.

These thoughts, now that they had begun the upward climb into the Mimbres Mountains, were foremost in Aaron's and Laurie's minds, yet they would not speak them aloud for fear of frightening each other.

"Getting closer, I keep wondering just what we're going to do in Tubac, Pa," Laurie said. "What do we know about ranching?"

"What do we ever know about anything until we learn, honey," Aaron replied quietly, happy to get onto a subject that would take their minds off the dangers that might lay ahead of them. "It's like anything else, say, learning to shoot. You want to learn, you've got to get a rifle or six-shooter, then some ammunition, a place to shoot, a target to shoot at. When you have a good teacher, like you had Loren, you learn. Max knows all about ranching and he's got people who can teach us, so we'll learn, too. You've read his letters, and knowing Max as I do, it's got to be right, else he'd never spent all those years coaxin' us to come out."

"I'm not so worried about you or me, Pa," Laurie said. "It's Ma. She's never been too strong and she keeps getting weaker every day. I guess being alone so much makes it harder for her to change her ways than you and me."

"She'll be all right once we get there, Laurie. She'll rest easy. Max says the sun shines 'most every day of the year and there's no such thing as a real cold winter. You—"

"You're not worried about me, are you, Pa?"

"Well, you're coming along now. Pretty near time you started learning things young ladies ought to know at your age. Max's girls, Ruth and Caroline—except that Ruth is married and living out somewhere near an Army fort with her husband, but Caroline will be there at Tres Flechas—"

Laurie snorted. "Married to an Army man—"

"Well, he was studying to be a minister before the war," Max said. "A girl could do a whole lot worse."

"I don't think about it much."

"You're a late starter, honey. I look at you by day, I see a boy, but when I look at you over a fire at night, you're a mighty pretty girl. If you just stop cutting your hair and put a godderned dress on once in a while, maybe I'd remember you're a pretty girl all the time."

"Pa, you're beginning to sound like Mama."

"Well, maybe it's high time—"

Laurie laughed. "How do you think I'd look straddling a horse in a dress, wearing a gun belt?"

"Well, I don't mean right now, today, but you won't always be in a saddle once we get to Tubac, you know."

"Then let's wait 'til we get there before we talk about it."

Not too strangely, the subject of Loren, closest to both, seldom came up in their conversations.

The road up the mountain had become steeper and both now directed their attention to the progress of the mules. This was the most difficult road they had had to negotiate since leaving Kansas and it took all of Aaron's newly acquired expertness to handle the struggling animals, easing them over rocks and malpais that forced them to strain, slipping on the grassy spots. There were times when both Aaron and Laurie had to get off and walk beside the mules to lighten the load somewhat, although this did not count for much; yet they did not feel they could afford to empty any of the water barrels or discard tools they might need later on.

Several times, they roped the two saddle horses to the wagon tongue, well in front of the lead team, to give them additional help; and at other times, they had to stop to rest the animals, placing fallen logs behind the rear wheels to keep the wagon from slipping backward. As they reached for the rim of the mountain, there was snow all around them and the wind brought sharp cold that made them dig into their trunks for additional warm clothing. Closer to the crest, they found a pass that made the going easier, and for which they were deeply grateful. And finally, on the fifth day, they reached the snow-covered crest from which they could look downward to the east and west for miles.

On the crude map Sergeant McComb had drawn for them, it would seem that the most difficult part of the journey was over. There were, in fact, only several markings of importance now; an "X" for Fort Bowie, two squiggly lines beyond it to indicate Apache Pass, then a stretch of emptiness until another wriggly line marked the San Pedro River. Beyond that, another empty stretch and finally a square marked: TUBAC.

Now it was mid-afternoon and they found a good level spot where they could camp and rest the animals. Aaron built a fire and Laurie cut several of the remaining steaks for their meal, which she intended would be a hearty one for Aaron and herself, cutting small pieces of meat into a pot of water to make into a soup for Libby. Later, with the horses and mules watered and given a generous amount of grain, Aaron got into the wagon to sleep beside Libby while Laurie rolled up in her homemade sleeping bag beneath the wagon, thinking over the past four months without even trying to look into the future. More than anything else, she missed Loren and wondered, as she had every night before falling asleep, where he had run off to, if she would ever see him again. They had lived so closely together from early childhood. . . .

Until Loren disappeared, she thought now, she could never remember a day of real unhappiness in her life. They had gone to the post school together, studied together, learned to trap, hunt and shoot together. In a saddle, they were near equals. Loren learned first how to handle a six-shooter and later taught her the fast draw, the fancy spins, but even more important, how to shoot accurately. She was almost as good as Loren with a rifle; and even in their final days together, it somehow pleased her when someone would mistakenly call her by Loren's name. They had been part of a community that respected their father and mother as foremost among its permanent citizens and were welcomed wherever they went; school,

163

church, the Army post, in Aaron's store. Growing up together, they dressed alike, cut their hair in the same manner, this for comfort and convenience; and enjoyed their private joke when people mistook one for the other.

Ah, Loren, she thought now, I wonder if, wherever you are, you are having the same thoughts I'm having now?

She began to feel sleep coming over her, head burrowed under the outside tarpaulin and warmth of two wool blankets that finally drove the last of the cold out of her body.

They had been on the road for four months, traveled miles through strange and wild country of unbelievable beauty, and although they had experienced some discomfort, inconvenience and insecurity that must come to all pilgrim wayfarers in unknown regions, they all had somehow felt secure in their closeness to God and the magnificence of that which only He could have created. It was the closest they had felt to religion in a long time.

The land was nothing like any they had ever seen or could have imagined. No one could have ever adequately described what they had seen with their naked eyes; the vast sweeps of mesa and mountains, of canyons and desert, snow and rivers. They had gazed upon cathedrals of stone, looked down into deep basins as only an eagle could have seen them, upward over fluted limestone mountains that had been carved by a Master Sculptor; awed by splendors that had stood for many centuries before the first humans had seen them.

Indeed, such was the abundance of grandeur that when they looked ahead into an empty desert stretching from horizon to horizon in every direction, the aloneness of a single *butte* rising out of a base of rippled sand gave them the feeling that they well might be the first humans to witness this amazing spectacle, as though they were the only living things remaining on earth.

Here, the first two-legged creatures had come seeking food and shelter and warmth. Indians, conquistadores; and later the trappers, hunters and seekers of rich ores. Here, Nature had poured her rain and snow, heat and winds, driving, slashing, eroding, carving masterpieces beyond man's capabilities to reproduce. Land fissured and crevassed, sugar-coated with snow, ravaged by time and elements, gray by early morning light, washed with gold by day, turned to fiery red by sunset, diminished into purples and blue-blacks by night.

It was a wilderness, yet without wildness; badlands that gave one a feeling of goodness, even holiness, to be witness to such miracles. But not without dangers from Nature herself. From animals. From man.

They had learned to read signs where tracks could be left. Bears, wolves, mountain lions. At night, coyotes howled and yelped. They heard the scurryings of disturbed woods animals and rodents, the chirping and song of birds. Large birds preyed upon smaller forms of life from aloft, and familiar buzzards circled in the distance over a dead or dying animal, perhaps a human, fallen victim to bite, bullet, arrow or sickness; of thirst or starvation.

They had seen old tracks of wagons and hooves of shod and unshod horses; wide and narrow wheel rims, manmade depressions, disappearing as quickly as they had appeared. White men and Indians had passed where they were going. Peaceable or warlike? How long ago? How recently? Whither bound? Signs easily readable to men of the mountains, forests, plains and deserts, but mysteriously inexplicable to people like Aaron, Libby and Laurie Olmstead, who came from that other world of safety, blundering their way south and west, praying they could make it from one center of civilization to the next until they would one day, God willing, reach their destination, Tubac.

The night grew quiet now and the soughing of the wind coming through the pass lulled Laurie into sleep. Tomorrow, she knew, would be better. And she prayed that Libby would show signs of recovering her strength.

And, as it proved, the next day was much better. The weather was clear and the skies bright. Aaron wrapped canvas covers over the hooves of the mules to prevent them from slipping and falling in the snow, and within a few hours was able to remove them, now shredded and useless, the road ahead clear except for small patches of breaking ice and rotted snow that offered no dangers, although the air was bitterly cold.

The slope was gentle and they dropped considerably lower with each mile. The brisk air seemed to lend strength to the mules and they made good time for the next several hours; and when they were approaching the next range of mountains, found to their great delight that there was a good wagon road through a wider pass; even though this increased some small private fears that this could be where an Apache band might be lying in wait to attack westbound travelers. Under this light layer of gloom, they entered the pass and, well on the other side of it, were much heartened when they saw what they believed could only be the fort Sergeant McComb had marked on his penciled map—Fort Bowie.

Several hours later, they were pleased when four blue-coated soldiers rode out to meet and guide them into the Fort. They were welcomed by a Major Leacock, who offered them food and such hospitality as the post could make available. Their animals were watered, fed, stabled, and when Aaron told Major Leacock of Libby's weakened condition, was introduced to a Captain Miles Metcalf, who was in charge of the small, under-equipped hospital. Metcalf took Libby into an examination room for half an hour, then reappeared and suggested that Aaron and Laurie remain for at least a week so that he could make further and necessary tests to determine the cause of Libby's persistent fever and quite noticeable weakness. Aaron and Laurie were willing, but it was Libby who insisted they get on with the trip and bring it to its conclusion; that once she reached Tubac and could rest in a stationary bed for a while, her problems would be resolved.

Captain Metcalf did not agree, but when the threat of hysteria seemed imminent in Libby, he merely shrugged, then advised Aaron to get her to Tucson and into the hands of a very capable physician at Fort Lowell who was better equipped to diagnose and prescribe for her puzzling ailment.

They also learned some news that was frightening; that only eight days before, a wagon train from Lordsburg had been attacked while en route to Tucson, with four dead and three wagons burned. Nine Apaches had been killed. "But," Major Leacock went on, "there's a bright side to the news. One of our scouts came in last night and reported that a large number of Apaches were on their way south from Cochise's stronghold, probably off on a major raid into Mexico. With so many of them heading south, there's only the slightest chance that you'll run into a war party between here and Tubac. Apache Pass was clear when he came through it. You've got something like a little more than a hundred miles to go. At the worst, you might run into a small band, maybe four or five. Two good riflemen could not only stand up against them, but run them off."

"Only two?" Aaron asked.

"I'd say you and your son could handle as many as five

or six with those repeaters you've got. I haven't seen anything like them in the hands of the Apaches. Tell you the truth, Mr. Olmstead, I wish we had them to take the place of our carbines. With that kind of firepower, we'd need fewer men up here."

"Tell you what, Major," Aaron replied, "you people been more than hospitable to us. We've got four of these repeaters with us. When we get to Tubac, I'm going to put one aside for you. You come and visit us and I'll give it to you as a personal gift from the Olmsteads."

A grateful Major Leacock invited Aaron, Libby and Laurie to dine with him that night and it amused the three Olmsteads to hear the major repeatedly refer to Laurie as "your boy." Later, Leacock called in his chief civilian scout and after giving them a rough map of the route from Fort Bowie to Tubac, the scout described certain landmarks they would encounter: Apache Pass, Dos Cabezas, Dragoon Springs, the long stretch of desert after they came out of the mountains, the San Pedro River. "Once you cross the San Pedro, you'll cut south and west toward Tubac. You'll find people on t'other side to guide you, but once you're across that river, you'll be home free."

So easy, thought Laurie.

Too easy, Aaron said to himself.

Yet, they made it through Apache Pass and to Dragoon Springs without sighting man, beast, smoke signal or campfire, lighting none themselves in order to keep from giving their presence away. During this time, Laurie rode beside Aaron on the wagon seat, rifles loaded and within easy reach, moving only at night, slowly, but in safety. They came to a cut-off that led downward to the desert floor and took it, then stopped sometime during the night to rest.

Early next morning, they started out, picking up an old wagon trail, dropping down the rest of the way to the desert floor where the air warmed up and soon became pleasantly hot. At four that afternoon they drew up closer to the foothills to make camp. Behind them, all was hilly and green while ahead lay open desert for an undetermined number of miles, with its multiarmed saguaro jutting upward like organ pipes, already beginning to turn purple in the afternoon sun. Yucca, cholla, prickly pear, Joshua trees and ocotillo spread out before them as they ate their supper amid a cluster of Judas trees which helped conceal them.

At four-thirty the following morning they had a cold breakfast and started out, hoping to make their best mileage before the sun became too strong, the animals too thirsty. At noon, they stopped for more food, watering the mules from Aaron's and Laurie's hats, parcelling out the grain they had gotten at Fort Bowie. The air was clear and they could see low, hazy mountains due west—perhaps forty or fifty miles away, Aaron guessed. By four o'clock they were coming to a stretch of rocky foothills on their right. Laurie, who was driving the mule team then, handed the reins over to Aaron and dropped off the wagon to untie her horse and ride ahead to scout for a stopping place for the night.

She had been gone but thirty minutes when Aaron's eyes caught a rising cloud of dust from the direction Laurie had taken, saw the horse with its head low, ears flattened, coming on as fast as its legs could carry it. He pulled up the team in alarm and moments later was able to make out Laurie, lying low along the horse's outstretched neck.

Then, about a hundred yards behind her, the Apaches came into sight.

He counted nine of them.

CHAPTER III

IT WAS A LITTLE BEFORE DAWN WHEN SAM PALMER AND
Marcos Espuela, pressing hard all the way from Fort Bowie, hammered through Apache Pass as though there were
a hundred of Cochise's warriors on their heels. Sometime
past noon, with the road downhill all the way now, they
stopped briefly to water and feed their horses.

"*Despacio, amigo,*" Marcos cautioned as they lay on
the ground while the horses rested. "It is stupid to kill two
good horses, no?"

"They're solid stock, Marcos, and it's all downhill from
here to the desert floor. They'll make it."

Marcos shrugged. "Of what use is to hurry so? We will
catch them before they reach the San Pedro without pushing so hard."

"I'd like to get to them by the time they make camp.
They're pilgrims. If we come on them after dark, they
might shoot first and challenge after."

"Ai-ee," Marcos said with a laugh, "do you never leave
anything to chance?"

"Chance is for gamblers, *amigo*. The desert and mountains are littered with the bones of men who gambled when
they should have planned ahead."

"Ah, such wisdom, Sam. How many years do you
have?"

"Twenty-seven."

"And I have twenty-two, soon twenty-three. When I am
as old as you, *amigo*, I hope I will be blessed with your
wisdom."

Now Palmer laughed. "You make it sound as though I
were sixty."

"I have known men far from sixty who were not so
wise, and who are no longer around."

A moment of silence ensued, then Palmer said, "Marcos, why do you speak only in Spanish when we are
alone?"

"Because, *amigo*, if I speak only English, I will soon

forget that Spanish is the tongue of my mother. If I speak your tongue to my Mexican cousins, they will laugh at me. I could not stand being laughed at by both Mexican and Anglo. I would be neither."

"But what of the tongue of your father?"

"My father." Marcos spat into the ground to express his contempt. "Martin Van Allen is a rich man. He is married to an Anglo, with a son and daughter of his own whom he has sent east to school. I am the accident of his *aventura romántica* with my mother, a careless mistake who offends his eyes. Yet, there must be something in him, for he has treated my mother well. It was he who bought for her El Espuela de Oro, which supports her well and provides me with money, a good horse, clothes. All the benefits without the name."

"Espuela. In my tongue it means 'spur.' "

"*Sí*. That which I am in the hide of Martin Van Allen. Some day I will dig it deeper into him."

"Marcos, revenge is poor satisfaction. It is much better to forgive—"

"It is not only much better to forgive, but much easier, *amigo*. The difficult thing is to forget."

After a few moments, Palmer said, "If I were you, Marcos, I should not worry so much about wisdom." And when Marcos did not reply, "Let's move out. We can make it out of the mountains well before dusk."

The descent grew steeper and there was little need to urge their mounts along. They could feel the change in temperature, growing warmer as they dropped down closer to the desert floor, feeling coolness only when they passed through the shadows cast by the fanged rocks that formed canyons every few miles; and as the sun began westering, they caught occasional glimpses of the broad expanse of desert beyond the foothills. Then they were clear of the low-lying hills and among the multivarieties of cacti, found the fresh tracks of a single wagon running fairly close to the rocks on their right.

"They can't be too far ahead, Marcos," Sam called out. "Let's try for it. We've still got a good two hours of daylight."

"As you say, *amigo*. All it can cost us is two good horses and a long walk across the desert carrying our saddles, rifles, canteens—"

"If they weaken, we will stop. Come on."

It was an hour later when Palmer, riding a good sixty

yards ahead of Marcos, pulled up. When Marcos drew up beside him, he called out, *"Qué pasó, Sam?"*

"Listen."

For a moment, there was nothing to hear, then the wind carried the sound to them, dull with warning, but unmistakable. Rifle shots. Instinctively, both withdrew their rifles from their saddle scabbards.

Marcos said with impatience, *"Ándale!* Why do we wait?"

"We don't know how many there are. We'll ride close as we can to the foothills and keep in the shadows. When we get there, we'll try to get into the rocks for protection."

"Ándale!"

Now it was Marcos who leaped into the lead, leaning forward, rifle in right hand, the brim of his hat flattened back by the air. Palmer was close behind, occasionally sitting erect to try for a first glimpse of what lay ahead. If it were an eastbound wagon or traveler on horseback, it could not be the Olmsteads. If they were westbound, it could be only the Olmsteads, since no other travelers had been reported to him at Fort Bowie.

He had no need to urge his horse on. His was a cavalry-trained mount who had taken his cue for pursuit by Marcos's magnificent Mano, broken and trained by his own hand.

Up ahead now, a long low arm of rocks jutted out into the desert from the foothills, its rim resembling a mass of tumbling clouds interspersed with jagged peaks. Palmer spurred his horse on to catch up with Marcos, then pointed toward the rocks. Marcos allowed Palmer to pass and Sam, riding in front now, suddenly disappeared into a narrow pass that took him into the rocks. Marcos followed and less than a hundred yards away saw Sam's horse standing alone, foam-flecked, his massive chest heaving to suck air into his lungs. Marcos pulled up, dismounted and ran up the trail to the rim where Palmer crouched, rifle beside him, peering down onto the desert floor.

About two hundred yards away stood the wagon, two of the mules down. One Apache lay dead within fifty yards of the wagon, his pinto standing idly nearby. There were eight other Apaches circling the wagon counter-clockwise, firing into and beneath it. Two saddle horses were tied to the tailgate of the wagon, neighing, rearing, whimpering,

171

pawing the earth, rolling their eyes back into their heads in terror.

And beneath the wagon, lying prone and facing south, two figures lay partially dug into shallow sand graves, firing at the Apaches as they circled around, throwing frequent glances behind them to make sure none was afoot sneaking up on them. And even as Palmer and Marcos watched in momentary suspension, the second Apache fell from his blanket-saddled horse and lay still.

Beneath the wagon, Aaron and Laurie counted and spaced their shots so that both rifles would not be empty at the same time. Aaron's face was sweat- and sand-streaked, but Laurie, under fire for the first time in her life was remarkably calm, even cold and deadly. It was perhaps knowing what would happen to them if they failed that turned desperate fear into grim determination to exact the full penalty from their attackers. Her aim was slow and deliberate, unwilling to waste a shot, remembering to lead her target and squeeze the trigger to avoid jerking the barrel off its target, conscious that she was praying for the first time since she had left Fort Leavenworth.

She missed several targets before she hit on the idea of shooting the larger target, the horse, then at the Indian who had spilled onto the ground. Thus, she accounted for both the first and second Apaches who had fallen. Now Aaron hit one, and when she saw the Indian tumble to the ground, roll over and get to his feet again, she sighted in on him and hit him through the chest. Three down and six to go. Her rifle was empty, but Aaron was still firing. She loaded the repeater coolly, dug in and began lining up her next target.

Along the rim, rifles in position, Sam and Marcos saw the third Apache drop, raise up, then fall again. The first of the remaining six came around and when he was presented with a full head-on target, Sam fired and dropped him. The man behind him fell victim to Marcos's deadly aim. There were four left and they continued the circle, coming around once more. Sam fired and missed, but Marcos got the second in line and now there were three left.

They pulled up then, off to one side, shouting and waving at each other, puzzled. With a quick arm signal, one of the Apaches cut in toward the rear of the wagon, a gleaming knife in his left hand. He pulled up to where the two saddle horses were tied up, his intention clear: cut

172

the horses loose and drive them off. His arm was upraised for the first slash when one of the two figures beneath the wagon rose to cut him down. The second Apache raised his rifle and fired. The man staggered out into the open and fell face down in the sand.

It was a difficult angle for Palmer and Marcos, with the wagon between themselves and the three Apaches, but both were firing together at the two who waited for the one trying to cut the saddle horses loose. From beneath the wagon, a shot killed the Indian with the knife and as the second drove his horse in toward the wagon, Marcos picked him off. The remaining Apache now realized that the shots were coming from the foothills and dug his heels into the sides of his pony and rode off swiftly. From beneath the wagon, the second figure emerged and stood up.

Involuntarily, Palmer shouted, "Down! Down!" but the slender man stood there, legs apart, rifle held midway between waist and chest, pumping bullets into the retreating Apache. One shot caught him, knocking him from his horse to his knees, then flat on the ground, face down.

Then the terrible silence as the gunsmoke rose in soft blue layers and drifted upward, lost against the sky.

Palmer and Marcos mounted their horses and picked their way down the trail, around the peninsula of rock, riding swiftly toward the wagon. When they reached it, the only sign of life was in the man, or boy, who was kneeling beside the older man's body, weeping. When Sam dismounted and knelt beside him, the boy could not speak over his grief.

"Sam!"

Marcos was calling him from the rear of the wagon. He went there, the two saddle horses still tugging nervously at their tie-ropes. Marcos had climbed into the wagon, now looking back soberly over the tailgate.

"What is it, *amigo?*"

Marcos's head nodded toward the inside. "I think you'd better see for yourself, Sam."

Inside was the brass bed and in it lay Libby Olmstead, unmoving, not breathing. There was not a mark visible on her, but she was dead.

Then Laurie came slowly to the tailgate and called, "Ma?"

Sam and Marcos climbed down from the wagon, one on either side of her. Sam said, "Loren—?"

173

She stared past him and Marcos. "She's dead, isn't she?"

"Yes," Sam replied. "She wasn't hit—"

Then Laurie Olmstead collapsed and fell to the ground before either man could catch her.

There was still some light in the sky, but Sam and Marcos felt the need to quit this scene and move westward as quickly as possible since they would be vulnerable to attack at dawn if they spent the night here beside the wagon, the dead Apaches, two dead ponies, the two dead mules still in harness. Now they were encumbered with a heavy wagon with only two mules left to draw it. The two saddle horses were useless in that respect, so the two dead mules must be cut free, the load in the wagon lightened. This close to the San Pedro, they might make it if they were not attacked; if they were, they must flee by horseback and let the wagon go to their attackers.

Water revived Laurie, but she was in a dazed, helpless condition, unable to speak, muttering unintelligible words. Sam and Marcos helped her up and led her to the rocks where they left her, out of harm's way, while they returned to their work. They cut the dead mules free and bulled the other two straining mules to drag the wagon toward the rocky fringe where, out of Laurie's sight, they dug a common grave and buried Aaron and Libby Olmstead and covered the grave with rocks. Marcos prepared a cold meal while Sam watered the mules and horses from his hat and fed them well from the supply of grain he found in the wagon. Then he got into the wagon to decide what Laurie (whom he still thought of as Loren) would want to keep and how much they could jettison to lighten the load. It was a decision, under these circumstances, he did not wish to make alone.

The food was ready and both men ate hungrily, but could not tempt Laurie to either eat or speak. She sat in dazed shock, unable to accept or believe that which had happened, and as darkness became complete, Sam decided they would move on as far as the San Pedro, then cross it in the morning.

They led Laurie to the wagon, but she would not get inside, mounting the box seat instead.

"Loren, can you hear me?" Sam asked.

A nod.

"You're safe now, Loren. I'm Sam Palmer. I was

married to your cousin Ruth. We'll see you get to Tubac safely."

No response.

"Loren, help us. Hold these reins. Marcos, that's Marcos Espuela up front, Marcos and I will rope our horses to the shaft to help pull along with the mules."

Sam placed the reins in Laurie's hands and she held them, properly laced through her fingers, although her action was purely mechanical. "Good boy. Just hold them."

Their horses bucked in protest, but they were roped tightly, and with the two mules pulling, managed to move the wagon through the desert sand. Behind the wagon were the Olmsteads' two saddle horses and two Indian ponies Marcos had rounded up.

Sometime past midnight, the animals became excited and pulled harder and Sam knew they were coming close to the river. An hour later, the wagon creaked to a halt. There was a stand of trees for shelter where they uncoupled their horses and mules, watered all the animals, hobbled and fed them and ate a cold meal. Again, Laurie refused food. The night air chilled them and Marcos prepared their blankets for sleeping. They found Laurie's sleeping bag in the wagon and arranged it between them. Led to it, still in a somnambulistic state, she carried her rifle and revolver with her, lay down and, mercifully, slept.

Marcos took the first watch, sitting with his back to a tree, a blanket wrapped around him. Some time after four o'clock, Sam took over. Other than the yelp of a coyote or distant howl of a wolf, everything was peaceful. There was no moon, so that the river, like the trees and mountains, blended into a single canvas of solid black. In the night cold, even the desert rodents had dug in for warmth.

At daybreak, Marcos awoke. He sat up, looked around and called out, "Hey! *Amigo!* Sam!"

"Here, Marcos."

"You asleep?"

Ashamedly, "I must have dozed off. What is it?"

"The boy. He is gone."

Sam leaped to his feet and went swiftly to where Laurie's bedroll was spread. It was empty. Marcos ran to the wagon, but she was not there. Her rifle and revolver were missing, but the four saddle horses, two mules and two Indian ponies were intact, hobbled, picketed, grazing in the wooded thicket.

"He has taken no food, no horse, only his rifle and revolver," Marcos said in wonderment.

"Hold it, Marcos, here are some tracks. Let's—"

"I will go. You stay with the animals. Your turn to cook, no?"

"All right, but get going. If he went back, we'll have to move fast to find him."

"He is afoot, *amigo,* he can't be far away. I'll be back in fifteen minutes."

Marcos was gone for twice that long and Sam, now deeply apprehensive, began to look over his shoulder as the bacon sputtered and spat in the iron skillet, half-cooked. He removed the skillet and coffee pot from the fire, placed them on a flat rock, then looked around carefully, picked up his rifle and walked in the direction Marcos had taken. Three minutes later, he saw Marcos's boot prints and those of the moccasins Laurie had worn, both leading toward the river. And some seconds later, he saw Marcos, back to him, lying on a rock and looking out toward the river.

Marcos heard Sam and turned swiftly, rifle aimed at Sam's chest. Before Sam could speak, Marcos held a finger up to his grinning lips, beckoned him closer with the rifle.

"*Qué pasó?*" Sam asked.

"*Mira!*" Marcos whispered.

"Where?"

"Over the rock."

Sam peered over the rim of the rock and saw Laurie, standing knee deep in the San Pedro, her back to them, using a cloth to wash her body.

Sam snorted. "It amuses you to spy on a young boy bathing?"

"Perhaps it will amuse you, *amigo,* to learn that our boy is not a boy, but a girl. And ai-ee! Such a girl—"

Laurie turned slightly then and Sam could not deny what his eyes saw. He stood up with his back to the river. "Marcos, it is not an honorable thing to do, to spy on a girl so."

"Then let us say that in such a situation, cousin, I am not an honorable man, but a Mexican *bastardo.*"

"Maybe, but you don't have to act like one."

"I have done her no harm, have I?"

"Not physically. Let us go back."

With a sly grin, "And leave her unguarded?"

176

"Marcos, go back and finish cooking our breakfast. I will wait for her in those trees."

"And you will not spy on her?"

"I will not spy on her."

"Then you are a—"

"Never mind what I am. Get back to the camp. Now."

Marcos shrugged and started back through the woods. Sam waited among the trees, heard the sound of Laurie emerging, drying herself with a towel, clothes being drawn up over her body. When she emerged, he started toward her as though he were at that very moment coming to find her.

"Good morning, Loren," he said.

Her eyes were clear now but the grief in her was heavily in evidence on her face. "Good morning," she replied. Then, "Why do you call me Loren. I'm Laurie."

"I didn't know," Sam lied, "with your short hair and boy's clothes."

"Who are you?" she asked, "and how do you know our—my name? I recall you saved me yesterday. There was another man with you. I saw him this morning when I got up to go to the river. I guess I was out of my head, scared—. I'm having trouble thinking straight."

"You had every right to be scared, Laurie. I'm Sam Palmer. I was married to your cousin Ruth Potter. Her father asked me to keep an eye out for your—party—at Lordsburg, but we missed you there—"

"We didn't get as far as Lordsburg. A sergeant we met advised us to cut west before we got to Lordsburg, across the Rio Grande, then through a mountain pass to Fort Bowie."

Sam whistled under his breath. "You were lucky—" he began, then caught himself. Lucky was a bad choice of words and he saw tears beginning to well up in her eyes.

"Lucky," she said simply.

"I'm sorry. I didn't mean it that way."

"It's all right. I know you didn't. I've got to start getting used to it. Being alone. This morning I awoke and felt that if I could take a bath, I might wash some of it away. It didn't help much, but I feel cleaner."

"Come on. Let's get back. Marcos must have breakfast ready by now."

"What about my father and mother?"

"We buried them last evening. I marked the place.

177

Later on, we can send some men to bring them to Tres Flechas."

"Thank you, Sam. I guess I'm your cousin, too?"

"By marriage, yes."

"You said you *were* married to Cousin Ruth. Does that mean you're not married to her now?"

"Laurie, she's dead. The Apaches killed her and our infant son, so you can believe me when I say I know something about how you feel. I'm terribly sorry—"

"Oh, Lord, and I am for you."

"There were only three of you. Where is Loren?"

"I don't know. I wish I did. I miss him more than ever now. He's got to know what happened. I've got to find him."

They were back in camp now and over breakfast she told Sam and Marcos of Loren's misfortune and disappearance in swift, compulsive words, her eyes filled with tears again, yet so preoccupied with the story that she cleared every bit of food on her plate; bacon, balls of dough browned over the fire, a can of peaches divided between them, and coffee. She insisted on washing the plates, but Sam sent Marcos to perform that chore while he talked with Laurie.

"We've got to lighten the wagon load, Laurie. The crossing isn't too deep here, but the horses won't be effective and the mules will bog down. I hate to ask you to throw anything away—"

"I don't mind. There's lots we can unload. The water barrels, heavy tools, spare wheels and axles, chains, extra harness. I won't need any of mother's things, or father's."

"All right, we'll go through it and see what we can leave behind. We can bury most of it and have some of the *vaqueros* come back in a few days and bring it in to Tres Flechas."

He reached into his shirt pocket and brought out a thin gold chain and a wide gold wedding band. "I took these from your mother before—"

Laurie took them into her own hands. Silently, she unhooked the chain, slipped the wedding band onto it, then placed the chain around her neck. "I'm ready," she said. "Let's see what we can do about the wagon."

They forded the river with considerable difficulty, but were across by eleven o'clock. Now there were less than forty miles of more or less firm ground to travel, swinging north of Fort Buchanan, again using the horses to make

better time. Their nooning was briefer this day, and by
two o'clock they were rolling through a pass into the
Sonoita Valley. Before dusk fell, they pulled up for a
breather and Sam called out, "Look ahead, Laurie. That's
Tubac, that dark haze in the distance."

His words were anticlimactic. Here was the goal of
Aaron Olmstead's dream; new country, new home, cousins
they had never seen. How much would it mean now
without Aaron, Libby or Loren? she wondered.

They skirted the village and reached the slope leading
up to the *hacienda* at a little past eight o'clock. Two
Tres Flechas riders saw them as they came over the rim
and started down into the valley. One rode forward to
meet them while the other hastened back to the *jefetura* to
announce their arrival. Max Potter sent an escort of
vaqueros to guide them in. On their approach, Sam
loosened his end of the lariat attached to the wagon shaft
and rode on ahead to warn Max and Caroline of the tragic
encounter, so that when the wagon came through the
gates, the guitars would be put aside and the songs of
welcome remain unsung.

Laurie's first meeting with Max and Caroline had an
emotional impact on everyone within sight and hearing.
There were few words spoken. Behind them stood Emelita,
Marguerita and a knot of ranch wives and children, hushed
by the drama and with sympathy for the young *señorita*
who had lost both parents only two days before. Max
embraced Laurie first, then Caroline took her into her
arms.

Max said, "Welcome to Tres Flechas, Laurie Olmstead.
You have a family and many friends here."

Caroline added, "Our home is yours, Laurie, for now
and always."

Laurie's words of reply were choked in her throat. With
Emelita and Marguerita in tow, Caroline led Laurie to
her bedroom, the large one originally intended for Libby
and Aaron. Emelita began issuing orders; a tub to be
brought to the room, hot water from the bathhouse, food
from the kitchen, flowers from the garden. Caroline returned with a nightdress and robe until Laurie's clothes
could be unloaded from the wagon and brought to her.

Outside, Sam and Marcos unbolted the iron box that
had been strapped beneath the wagon which contained
Aaron's cash wealth and his family records, which they
now carried into Max's study. While Sam continued to

tell Max of the circumstances under which they had come across the Olmsteads, the ranch carpenter arrived and was instructed to built two coffins. In the morning, Marcos would lead a party of *vaqueros* to the graves of Aaron and Libby and return them to the destination they had dreamed of but would never see. On the return trip, they would pick up the goods and tools that Sam and Marcos had buried beside the San Pedro.

For the next hour, with the bustle and excitement of welcome in the air, however restrained, there was little time for Laurie to reflect or remember; not until they were all gone and she was alone in the largest bed in the largest room she had ever seen or slept in. It was then that she wept in private for Aaron and Libby. And for the missing Loren.

CHAPTER IV

TO SAY THAT COLONEL DION HATFIELD WAS PLEASED WAS A monumental understatement. He had trusted his judgment and given command authority to Major Kane Boyden without knowing anything more than that Governor Brett Mitchell, a former general of considerable reputation, had personally chosen Boyden as his staff aide, a position most officers would have given much to have. Hatfield had risked much to send Boyden into Monte de Lágrimas to seek out Anaka and a reported two hundred braves, but his decision was, fortunately, vindicated. Boyden had not only defeated the much-feared war leader with far less men, but followed the remnants of the Indian band through the Carancho Valley into Mesa Plata and inflicted additional losses there.

Anaka was dead, but Hatfield's Indian scouts had brought word that Cochise had already sent another war leader, Bokhari, into Monte Babiacora with sufficient men to replace Anaka's losses. Revenge for Anaka's death and defeat would be paramount in Bokhari's plans, and that revenge must surely be directed at Fort Bandolier, the symbol of the white man's strength west of Tucson and south of the Gila River. To destroy it would be of immense psychological value to Cochise, who would then have proof that the bluecoats were not invincible; and this alone would be effective in convincing Chamuscada—and all Apaches now on government reservations—to join under a single leader and wreak death and destruction on all White Eyes in Arizona.

Boyden, before returning to Tucson for his confrontation with Governor Mitchell to urge him to exercise pressure on General Litchfield to bring Fort Bandolier up to full strength, had indicated that he had "an idea" that might accomplish his purpose, one he did not wish to divulge until he had presented it to Governor Mitchell. Hatfield, in face of numerous previous requests which had been rejected by the Territorial Military Commander, secretly expressed doubts that this could be achieved, but withheld any adverse comment that might discourage Boyden.

In Tucson, Boyden had outlined his idea to Governor Mitchell and won immediate approval. Camp Brennan, outside Prescott, was one of two military installations activated during the period when Prescott had been the Territorial Capital. When the capital was moved to Tucson early in this year of 1867, the two camps, Brennan and Harridge, remained with little enough for either to do. It was Boyden's suggestion now that Camp Brennan be deactivated and its entire complement of eight officers and 168 men be sent directly to Fort Bandolier; one company of infantry, one of cavalry, plus forty headquarters men and specialists.

Mitchell at once sent for General Litchfield, who opposed the idea and made the countersuggestion that the Brennan men be posted to Fort Lowell and kept there. Mitchell protested, and when Litchfield hinted that he might use his not-inconsiderable influence in Washington to win his point, Mitchell stated that he would immediately send dispatches to the President. At once, Litchfield recognized that this would amount to a showdown, one in which he would be the loser, and gave his consent to the transfer to Fort Bandolier. Also, Governor Mitchell had approved Major Boyden's request for transfer to active duty as replacement for the late Major Owen Travis.

This news, told to Captain Greene by Colonel Hatfield, overheard by Greene's clerk and passed on from mouth to ear throughout the Fort (in the traditional transmission system of every Army post) was electrifying to the command.

Rumor became fact when work details were set to repairing and cleaning old, abandoned enlisted men's quarters, officer billets and storage facilities. Stables, blacksmith shop and corrals, now only in partial use, were opened and prepared for occupancy. Quartermaster, Ordnance, Engineering and Hospital requisitions were hastily forwarded to the Tucson Supply Depot by special courier while laundry, kitchen and mess facilities were being expanded.

Hatfield toyed with plans for a new chapel, a post school and library, a recreational hall for enlisted men; and juggled the present married officers' quarters around in anticipation of one of his first proposed plans—to permit the return of Army wives and children as soon as possible after their long absence.

But foremost in his mind lay the pertinent fact that with a complement of 331 officers and men, plus civilian employees, patrols would be able to issue forth in proper full strength under officer command and without danger to the Fort.

A week later to the day, the Camp Brennan men arrived and the problems of integrating the new with the old began; of establishing seniority of rank, quarters and command, readjusting company and troop strengths. Greatest and most natural of all problems was that of the Camp Brennan men in evaluating their new Commanding Officer.

Boyden, himself a recent acquisition, carefully examined personnel records and interviewed each officer and ranking noncom before working out with tact new assignments; yet he realized that the Fort's present infantry and cavalry field officers, all of whom were lieutenants, must necessarily be displaced by the two senior officers, a captain and first lieutenant, and wondered how this would affect the Fort's morale and cooperation.

The two new officers, Captain Reed Ahearn, tall and belligerent, and his executive officer, First Lieutenant Kermit Vickery, short, heavyset and aggressive, showed little willingness to be helpful. Ahearn, close to fifty, had been Acting Camp Commander at Brennan and now showed open resentment toward being suddenly placed in a subordinate company-grade situation.

On that morning, Colonel Hatfield sat at his desk listening as Major Boyden skillfully interviewed Ahearn and Vickery. Hatfield scanned reports, requisitions and correspondence and seemed more preoccupied with the work at hand than in Boyden's conversation. At one point, finally, Hatfield cleared his throat. Boyden looked in his direction and caught the colonel's eye, turned back with a smile at Ahearn and Vickery and said, "I think that will be all for the moment, gentlemen. We will continue this discussion later." The two acidy officers rose, saluted and left.

"Major," Hatfield said when they were gone, "have all the new officers assemble in this office after the noon meal. I will have a few words to say to them."

At one-thirty, the eight new officers trooped past Adjutant Greene into the large room occupied by Hatfield and Boyden, but only Boyden was present and he could feel a certain conspiratorial hostility in the air, little different from the mood imparted earlier by Ahearn and Vickery. Boyden greeted the officers casually and noted that none had come to attention or saluted formally upon entering; and this caused him to smile inwardly to himself. A few minutes later, he heard Colonel Hatfield's boots clump across the outer office floor. Boyden stood up behind his desk as the door opened, called out, "Attention!"

The eight officers responded as Boyden had expected; they rose slowly to their feet and saluted in a most relaxed, if not sloppy, manner. It was a test, Boyden knew, and he was already anticipating the colonel's reaction with some sympathy for the four first lieutenants and three second lieutenants who were following Ahearn's lead.

Hatfield reached his desk and stood behind it facing them, tall, trim, militarily neat and firm. He did not return the salute, but stared at each man without a smile or other sign of welcome.

"Unsatisfactory, gentlemen," he said finally. "I will have it one more time and only once more. You will come to attention properly and salute in the prescribed manner. Drop your hands. I will not return a salute that any of my enlisted men can execute more precisely. Now!"

Their arms dropped. Again, Boyden called, "Attention!" and this time the eight men braced as rigidly as boards and eight hands flew upward in unison, correctly. Hatfield stared for a moment, then returned the salute. As the eight officers dropped their hands and sought their chairs again, Hatfield said crisply, "You will remain standing at ease until I tell you you may be seated."

Captain Ahearn almost sputtered aloud. Vickery threw a swift glance at Ahearn, then stared ahead at Hatfield and waited.

"That, gentlemen, is how it will be," Hatfield said. "In this organization, we will perform all duties explicitly and properly. Even friendly. But if you choose otherwise, I will accommodate you, either as a group or singly. I will have one thing understood clearly and now. I am the commanding officer and my orders will be obeyed without question unless I ask for an expression of your judgment. My next-in-command is my executive officer, Major Kane Boyden. In my absence, or by my direction, he will at all times speak for me.

"I well understand the emotional difficulties of switching

184

loyalties from one command to another. I have had that same experience, just as Major Boyden and others of this command have, so let us clearly understand one another. Your assignments will be made by myself or Major Boyden, and you will accept them. You will function as company and troop officers in harmony with the officers now present in this Fort.

"Do not presume upon your rank or seniority, such as it may be. I warn you that I can, and will, break any officer or enlisted man who reluctantly performs, or refuses to perform, his duties. I don't know how Camp Brennan operated. You don't know yet how Fort Bandolier operates. I can assure you, gentlemen, you will learn, and learn quickly.

"One last word of caution. Don't ever again test my strength by flexing your muscles at me. I want each of you to pass the word down to your noncommissioned officers and their men. I think you know now what that word is. Dis-*missed!*"

The eight officers braced, saluted, executed a "right face" and marched out.

The word had indeed been passed.

There were problems in the officers' quarters and enlisted men's barracks as well. The Fort officers, First Lieutenants Douglas Kennard and Lewis Carpenter, Brevet First Lieutenant Philip Zimmerman and Second Lieutenant John Mason-Field, occupied the choicest rooms in the bachelor-officers' building. Captain Morris Lapham, Quartermaster-Ordnance, Captain William Breed, Medical, and Captain Marcus Greene, Adjutant, occupied married Quarters numbered two, three, four. Numbers five, six, and seven had been occupied by civilian ranchers who had come into the Fort for protection during the recent escalated Apache raids, and were now evacuated. Also, an entire empty barracks had been occupied by other civilians, all now returned to their ranch homes—or what was left of them.

Ahearn and Vickery, whose families had remained in Tucson, were assigned to Quarters numbered six and seven, Captain Lapham to number five, since number two would be taken over by Major Boyden when his new bride would return to the Fort with the other wives and children as soon as it was practicable. First Lieutenants Greg Albee, Laurence Benjamin and Frank Tennant, Second

185

Lieutenants Gordon Lynch, Dean Farmer and Russell Isaacs, took the rooms that remained in the bachelor-quarters building, complaining that their seniority demanded some adjustment with the Fort officers who occupied larger rooms; although since their meeting with Hatfield, none voiced his objections or opinions openly.

The quartering of 168 additional enlisted men posed the greatest problem of all. The seventy new cavalry men were divided between Troops E and K. The fifty-eight infantry men retained their Co. B designation and half were installed in the barracks preempted by the civilians, the other half in Sibley tents behind the Co. G barracks temporarily, while the forty Headquarters and special duty men found rooms in the Headquarters barracks without much difficulty.

Sergeant Major Riley had his hands full with these problems of adjustment. The immediate demand for mess hall space was such that meals were now being taken in two shifts. Drill periods for both mounted troops and foot soldiers had to be scheduled meticulously. Patrols were organized so that at least half the men were experienced in the area; the other half, without experience, made up of Camp Brennan men; a situation in which officers and noncoms were frequently under command of others to whom they were senior. Mike Tyler was promoted to the rank of First Sergeant.

Food, clothing, arms, ammunition, equipment and supplies of every military type at once fell below normal minimal requirements. Pay records showed that some of the newcomers had not been paid in three months. Requisitions to Fort Lowell were slow in being filled and one of the shipments was ambushed in the Malhado Pass by a band of Apaches in strength, with four of the escort troop of twenty-four men killed, six wounded, the supply wagons and most of the freight burned.

The first patrol under a Brennan officer was undertaken by Captain Reed Ahearn, the new C.O. of Troop E. Sixty-four men, with its former C.O., First Lieutenant Doug Kennard, First Lieutenant Greg Albee, First Sergeant Mike Tyler, Sergeant Tim Kilkarrick, civilian scout Ira Gorton and Pima scout Han-Ti. The patrol was by far the largest mounted in well over a year, heavily overstrengthed but equally divided between Bandolier and

Brennan men, the latter to gain experience in the desert. They left before dawn on a Friday.

Ahearn, with twenty-four years of service, which included four during the Civil War, had served only two years on frontier duty in Wyoming Territory and sixteen months at Camp Brennan in an administrative capacity. With Lieutenant Kennard as "watchdog," which he resented, Ahearn operated by the book. The six-day mission was a light one for such a force, a one-day sweep east through Malhado Pass, a swing south for two and one-half days, then two and one-half days back to Fort Bandolier.

"Your mission, gentlemen," Hatfield said in his briefing, "is dual. You are to cover as many ranches as possible to give reassurance to the ranch families, and to be seen in full troop strength by Apaches known to be in the mountains close to and across the border in Sonora. You are under strict charge to make no special effort to engage in unnecessary combat with hostiles unless attacked or in pursuit of any raiders you may come across. This is a patrol for the purpose of show only, so that the word will be spread among the Apaches that we are at our peak strength and that other patrols will follow in similar force. Good luck."

Once out of sight of the Fort, Ahearn called for a rest halt. He sent Trumpeter Colin Galt to summon Lieutenants Kennard and Albee to his side. Scouts Gorton and Han-Ti were already there.

"Gentlemen," Ahearn announced, "I am changing our order of procedure. I want four men from each of your platoons, under Sergeant Trent, to ride a full mile in advance of the column. At the end of two hours, they will be relieved by First Sergeant Tyler and eight other men."

Ahearn saw Gorton and Kennard exchange a swift quizzical glance. "Any questions, Lieutenant Kennard?" he snapped suddenly.

Gorton said, "Cap'n—"

"I didn't ask you, Mr. Gorton. Well, Lieutenant?"

"Sir," Kennard replied quietly, "I understood by the colonel's orders that we were to remain in a single body of force with scouts on point, flankers, and a rear guard. With nine men riding a mile ahead on flat ground, I can see little possibility of attack, but when we get into the foothills and canyons of Malhado Pass, that squad of troopers could be bushwhacked—"

"Lieutenant, those nine men can hold off any attackers until we arrive."

"But they're being used as decoys to invite attack—"

"And we will not attack unless we are attacked first, according to our orders."

"Cap'n—?"

Exasperatedly, "What is it, Mr. Gorton?"

"I think we're lookin' for trouble the colonel didn't intend. He said—"

"I know what the colonel said, Mr. Gorton, but we are on our own and I am in command here. Regulations state that if, in the opinion of the troop commander in the field, a departure from ordered procedure is deemed necessary or wise, he shall change that procedure. I do now deem it necessary and wise. Mr. Kennard, Mr. Albee, the men. At once."

Gorton said, "How about a scout to ride ahead of 'em?"

"Mr. Gorton, I've given the order. Scouts will remain with the main body. Let's move, gentlemen."

Kennard shrugged and Lieutenant Albee grinned as both officers rode back to their platoons to select the men for the advance guard.

Thus the advance body came into the foothills and by five o'clock had entered the first of the walled canyons. Sergeant Trent had been relieved by First Sergeant Tyler and two hours later had himself been relieved by Trent and the original eight troopers. A full mile in advance of the column, Sergeant Adam Trent led his men into Malhado Pass, four with little or no patrol experience and four veterans of over two years in the lower Arizona desert, the latter apprehensively sighting along the ragged upper rims of the walls which reached upward some forty or fifty feet high. The road underfoot was well-traveled but narrow, its walls barely wide enough to accommodate a stage or freight wagon. Behind them, the main body was approaching the foothills.

As they moved upward toward a crest, it seemed that the height of the canyon walls was shrinking. With the sun lowering in the west, the interior canyon was in shadows, turning from gray to purple.

From behind, Corporal Mannie Zentz called out to Trent, "Hey, Sarge, how about movin' a little faster?"

Trent swung around in his saddle. "What's the matter, Corporal, you got piss in your blood?"

"I don't know, Sarge," Zentz replied as the snickering of the Brennan men began, "but what the hell ever it is I got in it, I don't want none of it leakin' out through an arrow hole."

"Just shut up and ride, Corporal. You're out with a real company commander now, not no desk colonel."

Zentz, Miller, O'Shea and Broadbent, the Bandolier men, flushed angrily at the insult to Colonel Hatfield. The Brennan men, Corporal Chester, Privates Harrigan, Russo and Easter grinned with approval.

Thirty seconds later, Privates Miller and Easter were dead with arrows through their bodies. Zentz, O'Shea and Broadbent leaped from their horses and found cover among crevices in the wall, searching for targets above them and finding none. Six or seven more arrows came flying down from the rim above before the rifles began answering. Chester and Harrigan were hit, Chester through the neck, spouting arterial blood in a thick stream, Harrigan taking an arrow through his upper right shoulder.

The horses were plunging and rearing in frenzy. Russo was thrown to the ground and struck by the hooves of Easter's excited horse. Trent, still mounted, cried out, "Back! Get back to the column!" and tried to rein his mount in that direction.

Zentz shouted, "Take cover, you goddamn dummy! Get off that horse an' use him for a shield!"

Then Russo, trying to get to his knees, took an arrow through the center of his chest. Harrigan lay flat on his back looking past the feathered guides of an arrow shaft that protruded from his shoulder, praying, "Jesus, oh, Jesus—"

Zentz, O'Shea and Broadbent were firing their weapons at the rims, seeing no targets but the flashes of the Apache rifles, hoping the column was close enough behind to hear the shots. Trent had dismounted, but held on to his horse's reins, using the animal as a shield, urged by Zentz to huddle close to the wall, using its projection and shadow as a cover.

Then, as suddenly as the attack had begun, it was broken off, and in the silence that followed from overhead, they heard the clatter of hooves coming into the canyon. Ira Gorton was the first man in, Captain Ahearn directly behind him, the rest of the column only a few lengths at

189

their rear, rifles at the ready. Kennard had already sought for the trail to the upper reaches of the canyon wall, found it and ordered twelve men to follow him. Lieutenant Albee's platoon shot past him into the canyon behind Ahearn. Then Corporal Chester died.

Four dead, one wounded. Trent, Zentz, O'Shea and Broadbent were, by some miracle, untouched. Ira Gorton looked on in silence while Ahearn's curses seared the air and those men who could crowd into the narrow space stared with fascinated horror at the four dead men. First Sergeant Mike Tyler leaped from his horse and went to Zentz, who was looking after the wounded Harrigan. With a sharp knife, Zentz had cut the arrow shaft about eight inches above the entry point while Kilkarrick tried to hold the writhing Harrigan still.

Zentz said, "It's almost all the way through, ain't it, Mike?"

"Almost," Tyler said after a brief examination. "Two men here! Hold him."

While the two troopers, along with Zentz and Kilkarrick, held Harrigan tightly, Tyler shaved the shaft to a smooth point, then signaled the men to turn Harrigan on one side. When this was done, Tyler removed Harrigan's neckerchief, wadded it into a ball and shoved it into his open mouth. "Bite on it, trooper," Tyler told him. "This is going to hurt like all hell." To the others, "Hold tight."

In one swift move, Tyler grasped the arrow shaft and forced the arrowhead through the remaining half-inch of flesh. When the flinthead appeared, he grabbed it with his neckerchief-covered hand and pulled it the rest of the way and threw the bloodied cloth to one side. Harrigan fainted, which was a blessing to Zentz, who cleansed the entrance and exit wounds with alcohol from the medical kit and began binding them. "Think he'll make it, Ty?" Zentz asked.

"Well, if that flinthead wasn't poisoned, no reason why he shouldn't," Tyler replied.

Meanwhile, Sergeant Trent was reporting to Captain Ahearn what had happened, and Ahearn, knowing he had willfully disregarded not only Colonel Hatfield's orders, but the considered suggestions from Kennard and Gorton, was sweating far more than mere heat exacted from a man's body. His questions were larded with angry curses, but there were still four dead troopers and one wounded for whom he must account to Hatfield. Not too curiously, all but Miller were Brennan men.

Then Kennard and his twelve mounted troopers returned and Ahearn glowered at him. "Well?"

"All gone, Captain. About twenty as far as I could count. Rode out through the east end of the trail. Apaches, of course. Rawhide-shod horses."

"How—?" Ahearn began when Gorton interrupted.

"From up that high, Cap'n, they could see us comin' cross the open. All they figgered to do was hit the advance party an' git out before the main body come up. They done just that."

When Ahearn did not reply, Gorton added, "Let's get out of this canyon—"

"What about the men—the dead?"

Kennard said, "We'll carry them through the Pass and bury them in more yielding ground. Then I'd suggest we send an escort back with Private—uh—"

"Harrigan," Tyler supplied.

"With Private Harrigan, to report the, uh, engagement to Colonel Hatfield while we continue the patrol, sir."

A detail of three Bandolier men was chosen to return with Harrigan. The dead were placed across their saddles, covered with blankets and tied on. The column continued eastward through Malhado Pass until dark, when they camped, buried Miller, Easter, Chester and Russo, then took care of their horses and prepared supper. There was little or no conversation. Captain Ahearn ate alone, paced about, personally checked the sentries and horse pickets at least four times during the night.

And he thought of five days hence, when he must face Colonel Hatfield and report his negligence.

After supper that evening, Sergeant Atticus Perry sat on the edge of his cot working a leather-softening compound into his new boots. The sky was still light and the Troop E barracks were otherwise empty. Outside, some of the men sat or sprawled on the narrow porch and on the steps. Others had gone visiting friends in various barracks, or to the sutler's store.

Corporal Dick Hudson came into the barracks, whistling his way to his cot while removing a sweat-marked shirt. He threw it on the cot, opened his locker box and picked out a towel and bar of soap, then noticed Perry, half a dozen cots away, kneading one of his boots.

Curiously, "What are you doin', boy?"

Perry stiffened at what he knew was intended for an insult. His hands worked slower, but he did not reply.

"What's the matter, you deef, boy? I asked what you're doin'?"

"I heard you, Corporal. I'm sitting here minding my own business and softening these boots up."

"Don't get smart with me, boy—"

"Where are you from, Corporal?" Atticus asked.

"Macon, Georgia, if it's any of your business."

"And how much time have you got in the Army?"

"Is that your business, too, boy?"

"Well, Corporal, if today was your first in the Army, I couldn't expect you to know that a man wearing three stripes rates being called 'Sergeant,' and not 'Boy.' "

Hudson laughed. "Well, maybe you ought to know that where I come from—"

Atticus put the boot aside and stood up. "The point is, Corporal, neither of us is where we come from and I'm *Sergeant* Atticus Perry and you're *Corporal* Richard Hudson."

"That ain't been proved yet, that you're a sergeant. Maybe you ain't got no more right to them stripes any more'n your name is Perry."

"Then it's lucky for me I don't have to prove anything to you, Corporal. Now why don't you go on doing what you've got to do and leave me to my work."

Hudson flushed angrily. "Look, boy, I don't give one good goddamn if you're a major general, no nigger is goin'a bigmouth me."

Atticus took his time replying and finally said, "If I wasn't so much bigger than you, white trash—"

"Outside, nigger. Take off them stripes an' let's settle this in the bull ring."

"That suits me just fine, Corporal," Atticus said and began stripping his shirt off. "Just fine."

At that early evening hour, a large crowd was a certainty. When the cry, "Bull ring!" went up, every barracks within hearing emptied out, and within minutes, the ring, a twelve-foot by twelve-foot square with two strands of rope held up by a series of four by fours sunk deeply into the ground, was completely surrounded. There were excited yells and shouts, all favoring (or encouraging to) Hudson, who was not only white, but somewhat smaller than Perry and had fought in numerous amateur boxing

192

bouts held in the Fort as part of its entertainment program. Bets were made with what little cash was available, verbal I.O.U.'s against the coming payday, or for cigars and plug tobacco.

As the Fort's top noncom, it fell to Sergeant Major Riley to act as referee. He first tried to get the opponents to call the fight off, but Hudson insisted that it was legal and refused to give in. Perry quietly waited until Riley shrugged, then called the men together in the center of the ring and announced the rules in a voice intended for all to hear.

"This here fight will be with bare knuckles for twenny rounds, the round lasting until one man is knocked down. If he don't come out in one minute, the fight is over and the man who comes out is the winner. If it goes twenny rounds an' both men are on their feet, the fight is a draw an' it's all over. Use your fists only. There'll be no usin' your feet, knees or fingers, no bitin', eye-gougin' or hittin' below the belt. Understood?"

Both men nodded.

"Go back to your corners. When I call, 'Time!' come out fightin'."

Hudson was shorter than Perry by three inches and lighter by about twenty pounds, but he was fast and an accurate puncher, which most Fort Bandolier men knew. A few Brennan men, knowing neither of the antagonists, but gauging the opponents by size, chose to bet on Perry.

When they came out in response to Riley's call, Hudson came on fast, trying to get inside Perry's open arms. He danced back, then inside, feinting with right and left, missing two roundhouse punches by the large black man, taunting him with sneering words and curses, then he stung Perry with two slashing punches to the jaw and mouth. Perry shook the blows off and circled, warding off several light jabs with his longer arms, taking a solid punch in his mid-section, all to the shouted approval of the onlookers.

"Git inside 'im, Hudson!"

"Murdelize the booger, Dick!"

"C'mon, nigger, quit backin' off!"

Perry looked topheavy and ineffective as Hudson danced in, weaving out of the way of the larger man's solid blows, jabbing Perry's mouth, drawing first blood; and when Perry's hands went up to protect his mouth, he caught a smashing hard right in his belly.

Sweat drenched both men and blows were sliding off arms and sides harmlessly. Perry drove in with a flurry of smothering lefts and rights, but Hudson backed off, riding with the punches. Hudson landed another hard blow into Perry's middle. Perry gasped as the sweat flew. Hudson got to Perry's jaw with a hard left and Perry's knees buckled as he went down. Riley stepped in and sent Hudson to his corner for the one-minute rest before Round Two.

There was water and a towel in Hudson's corner, two men to wipe and rub him. There was no such second for Perry, who drew up two handfuls of water from his bucket, drank some of it and wet his face with the rest, drying his hands on his trousers. Over the heads of the crowd, he could see several officers looking on from the porch of the bachelor-officers' quarters nearby, not permitted, by tradition and social restriction, to give a fight between enlisted men quasiofficial recognition. Guards on the upper ramparts within sight of the bull ring gave the area their undivided attention.

Round Two began with Hudson, encouraged by shouts from the crowd, attempting to finish what he had begun when Round One ended. He rushed in with confidence and took a solid and stunning left on the jaw, froze momentarily with shock, then another to the chin that dropped him flat on his back. Round Two was over within three seconds and the next thirty were silent with astonishment; then the air was filled with yells of encouragement as Hudson rolled over and got to his feet quickly, yet shakily, stumbling to his corner.

He waited for Perry to come to him as Round Three got under way, moving backward, coasting until his head could clear and his eyes were able to focus clearly. Perry moved in slowly, stolidly, twisting his body from side to side to provide a leaner target. Then suddenly, Hudson leaped forward in a crouch that brought him inside Perry's swing and rained several blows into the big Negro's middle, backing him against the ropes.

"Get 'im, Hudson!"

"Kill the nigger, Dick!"

Perry slid along the rope out of reach and again, overly confident, Hudson rushed in. Perry spun off the rope quickly and when Hudson wheeled around to find him, found a hard right waiting for him. It landed on the point of his chin, followed by a left to the jaw, a right

194

to his belly and another left to the chin. Still, Hudson refused to go down. With buckling knees he stood flailing away at Perry, who now had time to take careful aim and deliver his blows when and where he wanted. A right to Hudson's eye closed it. His mouth was bleeding and swollen. Perry backed off then, as though unwilling to punish the corporal any more, but Hudson staggered toward him, clawing, throwing weak, ineffective blows. Perry looked around at Riley and saw no sign that the fight would be stopped by anyone but himself; and he now undertook to do just that.

Measuring Hudson carefully, he drove a hard right to the corporal's jaw and stopped him in his tracks. Hudson wavered but remained on his feet. Perry then threw a left to the jaw, a right to the chin, a left to the mid-section and was about to deliver a lethal right to the jaw again when Hudson toppled over. He was a long way from Fort Bandolier when Riley raised his hand and called, "Time!" for the fourth round to begin.

A few moments later, Riley raised Perry's hand in victory, to the angry booing from the losing bettors and the shouts of approval from the winners, although everyone ignored the winner himself. Two men climbed into the ring on Riley's order and carried the unconscious Hudson back to Troop E barracks.

Perry climbed out of the ring and walked back to the barracks alone and without a glance to either side of him. He went to his cot and picked up a boot and resumed kneading its stiff leather and did not look up when the two troopers brought Hudson to his cot.

Several of the Troop E men came in and went to Hudson's cot where they talked in low voices, throwing furtive, antagonistic glances toward Perry, who worked on in silence. Finally, Private Halleck walked down the aisle toward him, stood with his feet apart, hands on his hips. Perry still would not look up and kept his eyes on the boot in his hands.

Halleck said, "Nigger boy, you sure didn't make yourself no friends tonight."

Eyes still turned downward, Perry replied, "You better go along, Private. I'm holding on to myself as best I can right now."

When they were within a mile of the Fort late on Thursday afternoon, with Captain Ahearn at the head of

195

the column and in no way resembling the erect figure who had led them out into the desert five days before, it was Lieutenant Kennard who signaled Trumpeter Galt to his side.

"Sir?"

"Pass the word along the line to smarten up. The colonel will be on hand as we come into the Fort."

"Yes, sir!"

The trumpeter wheeled and rode back, passing the word to Lieutenant Albee and First Sergeant Tyler who, in turn, relayed the order to the troopers. The men came alert, spaced their mounts properly, sat a little more erectly in their saddles and tried to take on the smart appearance of a fresh cavalry column.

Which they were not. Since the attack in the Malhado Pass on their first day out, they had seen no sign of Apaches. The ranches they had visited reported no sight or contact with hostiles. They had ridden across desert wastes in enervating heat, short of water because of dried waterholes, and poisoned wells, unable to get up into the mountains because of the distance, where there were several natural limestone tanks. Had it not been for his bad judgment on that first day, Ahearn would probably have tried for the Dos Viudas tanks, but with one mischance behind him, he was reluctant to take a second risk.

The effect of a bad patrol showed on the men. After that abortive first day, Ahearn had kept to himself, ate and slept apart from the officers, scouts and men, brooding. The men, in turn, were silent and sullen. The shortage of water forced rationing and plagued men and animals alike. A sandstorm on the third day out had not helped matters. By now, their uniforms were crusted with sand and dust. It was imbedded in their hair, beneath their clothes, in their throats and nostrils and nothing could shake them out of their black mood.

In this manner, they rode into the Fort under the eyes of Colonel Hatfield and Major Boyden, who stood side by side on the porch of the headquarters building and watched as Ahearn returned the O.D.'s salute, reported the return of the patrol, the four dead and one wounded, although this was already known. The column was then turned over to Lieutenant Kennard for dismissal while Ahearn rode on to the HQ building, dismounted and began a verbal report to Hatfield.

"Not now, Captain," Hatfield interrupted. "When you have made yourself presentable, I will send for you."

Ahearn handed his horse over to an orderly and turned toward his quarters, but took note that Scout Gorton was heading in Hatfield's direction and knew that by the time the colonel sent for him, he would have already been enlightened by the scout. And, no doubt, Lieutenant Kennard.

The call was two hours in coming and an hour before supper. Meanwhile, Ahearn had bathed, shaved and dressed in a fresh uniform, but had little taste for food. He took a bottle from his locker and drank from it, then poured more into a glass, added a splash of water and sat on his cot sipping at the drink and smoking a cigar; thinking it curious that none of the Camp Brennan officers, knowing he was back, had come to talk with him; knowing also that the word of his failure was well known by now.

The colonel's orderly knocked and Ahearn bid him enter. "Sir, Colonel Hatfield requests Captain Ahearn to report to him at once."

"Very well. Inform the colonel that Captain Ahearn will be there directly."

"Yes, sir." The orderly executed a smart salute, faced about and marched out.

Ahearn finished his drink, put on and buttoned his blouse, strapped on sidearms, adjusted his Kossuth hat and walked to the HQ building. As he mounted the steps, an alert orderly leaped to his feet and saluted. Inside, Captain Greene said, "Go right in, Captain. The colonel is waiting."

Ahearn went to the closed door, paused to take a deep breath and knocked. On Hatfield's "Come!" he entered. At the desk beside Hatfield's, Major Boyden sat examining some documents.

"Stand at ease, Captain," Hatfield said after Ahearn reported, and when Ahearn glanced at the chairs arranged in front of the desk, Hatfield added, "Remain standing at ease, Captain."

Ahearn planted his feet about fourteen inches apart, hands clasped behind his back, eyes averted and looking over Hatfield's head.

"Look at me, Captain," Hatfield ordered.

Ahearn dropped his gaze and the eyes of both men locked upon each other. "Yes, sir."

"Now, Captain, you will repeat the orders I gave you on the morning you left here in command of your column, with specific reference to formation and my implicit instructions to do nothing to invite or engage the enemy unless attacked first."

"Sir," Ahearn replied, "I respectfully submit that we were attacked first."

"Not acceptable, Captain. Contrary to orders, you split your intact body by sending an advance party of nine men a full mile ahead of your point, thus presenting the enemy with a tempting target and thus sustained a loss of four dead and one wounded. Unnecessarily so, and in direct disobedience to my orders."

"Sir," Ahearn replied in a voice almost shaky with emotional heat which was becoming more difficult to control. "Sir, I was in the field and circumstances dictated—"

"Not circumstances, Captain, but your own judgment, or a desire to show your command your indifference to my instructions and your reluctance to bow to a new commanding officer." And as Ahearn started to reply, "You will listen without interrupting, Captain. Now. You were in open desert when you ordered an advance party to move up, not a wise move, and not necessarily dangerous, but of little use or benefit and, perhaps, forgivable. What is not forgivable, however, was permitting those men to enter the foothills of Malhado Pass and into a high-walled canyon, against which you were warned by an experienced scout and an officer, whose advice you chose to disregard. True or not?"

Ahearn squirmed and the sweat began to dampen his face, which was now reddening with anger.

"Your answer, Captain."

"True, sir."

"You may be seated now, Captain."

Ahearn remained standing.

"I said, Sit down, Captain!"

Ahearn sat in the chair, body erect, ankles extended and crossed. "Sir," he said, "may I request a transfer?"

"Request denied while a matter of insubordination, subject to possible inquiry for the purpose of a court-martial, is in effect."

Ahearn's face, beneath its tan, blanched and paled to gray.

"Now, Captain," Hatfield continued, "I will ask you to answer this hypothetical question. Let us assume that you

198

are in command of this Fort and I am sitting where you are, in these exact circumstances. The question: How would you handle the present situation?"

Ahearn swallowed and took his time before replying. After a full fifteen seconds he said, "Sir, I find it impossible to express an opinion."

"You are an officer of considerable experience. Twenty-four years of service with at least two years on frontier duty, four years of war, breveted a captain in '64, and with sixteen months at Camp Brennan, the last six of which you were acting commander. I think an officer of your rank and varied duties should be able to answer the question. Your opinion, Captain Ahearn."

"I'm afraid I can't."

"*Sir!*"

"Sir," Ahearn added.

"Very well, Captain. For the present, you will remain within the confines of this Fort, temporarily unassigned. You will have no contact with troops and are relieved from your command of Troop E, which will revert to Lieutenant Kennard as of now."

"Am I under arrest, sir?" Ahearn asked.

"You are not. You are free to move about the Fort from your quarters, to mess or to the sutler's store, but you will not answer Officer's Call or participate in any military duties or functions until I direct otherwise."

"Sir, may I write a letter to Tucson requesting transfer?"

"I will allow it, of course, Captain, but if you do, it will carry a negative endorsement from me, giving my reasons why, and supported by sworn affidavits from those present on the patrol. Understood?"

"Yes, sir."

"You are dismissed, Captain."

Ahearn rose, saluted and left. When the door closed on him, Hatfield said to Boyden, "See to the transfer order, Major, but do not record the restriction into his official record. Yet."

"Yes, sir," Boyden replied.

"An opinion, Major, if you please."

"I have none to offer, sir."

"I think I denote a reluctance on your part to tell me you thought my treatment was, ah, unduly harsh."

"Not necessarily, Colonel, although I couldn't help putting myself in his place."

"You can't, Major. You don't think Ahearn's way. He knew better than to do what he did. His personal resentment toward serving a new commanding officer became stronger than his judgment and therefore, he must accept punishment for what I consider to be a crime, although a court-martial board would never convict him."

"Then why not allow him to transfer out?"

"Because until he changes his attitude, he is my responsibility to train and make into a good officer. If I permit him to transfer before he changes, other men elsewhere may die for no justifiable reason. That, Major, is also the burden a C.O. carries upon his shoulders along with his rank, to see that a man not fit to command does not command."

"A question, sir."

"Ask it."

"By remaining unassigned, how will Captain Ahearn learn?"

"What he must learn first of all, Major, is humility. On the day Captain Ahearn requests permission to speak to me, I will recognize that as the beginning of his willingness, not necessarily to learn, *but to remember what he learned long ago*—to place his mission above all personal considerations and protect the lives of the men under his command at all costs. When and if I restore him to command, I will expect no repetition of his recent behavior. I cannot order a man to change his inner feelings, but I can help him find the means to do so for himself."

"That's a lesson I've never found in the *Officers' Handbook* or *Tactics*," Boyden said with a smile.

"No, Major. It is for each man to find for himself and pass on to the next man. There was little enough reason to lose four enlisted men through a laxity of judgment or out of personal pique. Nor is there any reason to lose a good officer who can be saved and, God knows, we need good officers."

BOOK III

CHAPTER I

DURING THE MONTHS OF AUGUST, SEPTEMBER AND October there were few empty days for Sam Palmer and Max Potter. Max had bought the former Butterfield Stage Station on the corner of Calle Alvarado and Mariposa, long vacant and requiring much repair and refurbishing. He bought additional land on either side and behind the original property and set crews to work building more office and storage space, stables, corrals and a blacksmith shop. By mid-September, the new headquarters of the Tucson-Yuma Stage and Freight Line was ready to receive the stages and freight wagons that Marcos and a small army of Tres Flechas *vaqueros* had brought in from Lordsburg.

Meanwhile, Sam and Jeff Lennon had reestablished the old Butterfield relay stations, contracted to have the additional four stations built and manned, wells dug, arrangements made to keep each supplied. On Max's firm insistence, four of his best *vaqueros* accompanied Sam everywhere, sworn to guard him around the clock against any attempt on the part of bounty hunters or Apaches to deliver him to Bokhari or Cochise.

Lennon was remarkably successful in locating former drivers, agents and hostlers for the eight intermediate relay stations at Celeste, Encantado, Malhado, Fort Bandolier, Mesa Plata, Denton, Matape, Corozal, and the end depot in Yuma, which Lennon agreed to manage until a suitable replacement could be found and permit him to return to his horse ranch.

In Tucson, Max Potter had undertaken the task of soliciting hauling contracts from local merchants and arranging connections with independent carriers from as far east as St. Louis through Santa Fe, Lordsburg and El Paso, to act as forwarding agents to Yuma, connecting with the San Diego–Los Angeles–Yuma Line. With this important "middle link" established, regular service would encourage a steady flow of passengers, mail and freight for the T-Y Line.

With a pocketful of signed contracts, Max then called directly on Governor Mitchell, who not only voiced his complete approval, but assured Max that if T-Y could deliver private passengers, freight and mail safely, he would exert the full influence of his office to secure Army hauling contracts and a valuable mail franchise by the end of the year. In the meantime, Mitchell agreed to talk with General Litchfield and the new Quartermaster at Fort Lowell, Colonel Taggart, and arrange for T-Y to haul Army freight on a load-by-load basis.

Locally, there were expressed doubts that T-Y could operate with the safety Max Potter promised. Historically, stages and freight wagons had always been attractive targets for Apache raiders, Mexican and Anglo renegades and, therefore, there was little enthusiasm among those Max had tried to interest as investors. Potter was not overly disturbed. He had complete faith in himself and Sam Palmer, and his personal financial resources were adequate to offset initial operational losses until T-Y proved itself.

Toward the end of October, announcements began appearing in the Tucson *Star*, on wall posters and in handbills advertising the Inauguration Run, leaving Yuma and Tucson simultaneously on Friday, November 1st. Thereafter, stage schedules would operate on Mondays, Wednesdays and Fridays, with freight service on Tuesdays and Thursdays. The stage fare was set at $50.50 either way, or 18½¢ per mile, and between-station rates at 25¢ per mile. Freight rates were established on the basis of $35.00 per ton per one hundred miles. The distance between Tucson and Yuma was 273 miles, far shorter, if no less difficult than following the Gila River route farther north.

With a week before the inauguration service, Max, Sam and Marcos rode to Tres Flechas for a breathing spell.

In the three months that had passed, Laurie Olmstead had passed only one birthday, but seemed to have matured by years. She had permitted her hair to grow and no longer wore her boyish garb. Caroline's seamstress had fashioned a new wardrobe of ranch attire for Laurie; dresses for normal wear, split riding skirts when she accompanied Caroline over the range. Apart from the new

204

Winchester repeating rifles, shotguns and revolvers which had been part of her remaining possessions, and were a delight to the *vaqueros* to whom she loaned them, the object most prized by the ranch wives was Libby's sewing machine, the latest Singer model, which was entirely novel to Tres Flechas. Laurie was drawn into demonstrating the fascinating machine and instructed the seamstress and others in its use.

Laurie was an excellent horsewoman and enjoyed nothing better than riding out over the open range, although this disturbed the *vaqueros* who were charged with the security of the home range; yet there was so much ground to cover and Laurie seemed to want to cover it all during her first weeks there. She was a good hunter and it was not long before the *vaqueros* were spreading the word of her accuracy and precision with rifle and revolver.

At first, Caroline spent considerable time with Laurie, but soon the newness of Laurie's presence seemed to wear off and each sought her own way to keep occupied. Caroline was somewhat introverted and less energetic by nature, but Laurie could not stand inactivity, eager to learn as much as she could of the language and customs of the Mexicans, of the land itself, perhaps needing to keep her mind from dwelling on the new double grave in the Tres Flechas cemetery; and Loren.

Laurie was forever visiting the small *casas* of the ranch families, inventing games for their children, organizing school classes, giving the women pieces of dress materials from the several dozen bolts of cloth, spools of colored thread and ornamental buttons Libby had insisted on taking along. At other times, she rode out with the day riders, eating mid-day dinner with them, returning home by dusk. And some nights, sleepless, she wandered through the home grounds, standing on the ramparts with the silent sentries who kept watch over the sleeping ranch to protect it from Apache marauders who might come at any time.

At supper on the first night of Max's and Sam's return from Tucson late in October, she was vibrant and alive, sparkling with anecdotes of the ranch, asking endless questions about Tucson and T-Y Lines. Caroline refused to be drawn into the babble of conversation and, Sam thought, seemed more withdrawn and reserved than ever before; or perhaps it was only by comparison with Laurie's natural enthusiasm that made her appear so. Neither he nor Max could help remarking on the amazing change in Laurie's appearance, her emergence as an attractive young woman; and again, Sam noticed the insularity of Caroline's complete detachment from the conversation, and wondered if there had been some break between them.

Caroline's interest was finally awakened when Max turned to the subject of investors in T-Y Lines. "Once we've made a dozen or so trips," he said, "they'll all want to come in. When they do," he added with a chuckle, "they're goin'a find it'll cost 'em a sight more for holdin' out so long."

"There's still the safety factor to solve, isn't there?" Caroline asked. "You won't get the Army or mail contracts until the danger of attack is over."

"Sure, sure," Max replied easily, perhaps too easily, "but Sam'll whip that once we get rolling."

"How?" The question was asked of Max, but Sam recognized that it had been intended for himself.

"It can be solved," he replied. "All it takes is money. Not cash, but manpower."

"You said manpower was a big problem in Tucson before. How much more will you need?" Caroline asked.

"I figure about sixty men for the next few months before T-Y begins paying its way with that Army contract and a Federal mail franchise."

"Where do you expect to get sixty more men that easily?"

Max said, "From Tres Flechas."

"Won't that leave the ranch shorthanded?"

"For a while, Caro, yes," Max replied. "I'll try to recruit more men down in Chihuahua and Sonora. Meanwhile, we'll spread our lines a little thinner here. By the end of the year, I hope, we'll be able to hire other men for Tucson and Yuma and bring our own people back here."

"It all sounds so big," Laurie broke in excitedly. "It must be costing a fortune."

Max said, "You're not far off. It's taken as much loose cash as I had on hand. Close to sixty thousand dollars."

"What about operating expenses, monthly payrolls, hay, grain, upkeep, food and provisions for passenger stopovers?" Caroline interjected suddenly, and Sam realized then that for all her show of indifference, she had been listening intently all the time. "Then there are the sixty extra *vaqueros* to take care of."

206

Max said, "We'll make it, Caro. I can borrow as much as I need, or more, on our herds, the land itself—"

"You want investors, don't you, Cousin Max?" Laurie asked. "I'd like to do something with Loren's and my money. There's over seventy thousand dollars lying in that iron box. Some day Loren will come back and he'd have something to work at. Please—"

"You're serious, Laurie?"

"Yes. Very serious."

"We'll talk about it later," Max said. "If you want to do it, I think it will make a sound investment for a good return."

Laurie turned to Caroline. "Isn't it exciting, Caroline?"

"If you like that kind of excitement," Caroline replied coolly. "I should think you'd have had enough excitement to last you forever."

When Laurie looked perplexed, Max said, "Nobody really wants the kind of excitement you're thinking about, Caro, but it's out there and we've got to fight it to protect our lives and property."

"Papa," Caroline said stiffly, "if the Indians had been treated fairly in the beginning, none of this fighting would be necessary. Because of it, I've lost my mother and sister. Laurie has lost her father and mother—"

The spell was broken. Laurie, tears moistening her eyes with the abrupt reminder, stood up and walked out of the room. Max said, "Caro, that wasn't a kind thing to say. Laurie has got to try to forget, but she can't if you keep reminding her."

"Papa, she won't forget any more than I can. Maybe a man can do that and go on as though nothing had happened, but it's not possible for women."

And again, Sam felt that most of this exchange was being directed at himself, although Caroline's anger-brightened eyes were on Max, and for him, the sparkle of the evening died, too. He stood up and said, "Excuse me," and left Max and Caroline together in the dining room.

He found Laurie sitting in a rawhide-covered chair on the porch in the cool evening air. From the Mexican quarter came the soft guitar chords and singing, voices chattering, the dim light of candles and oil lamps from the kitchen, *vaquero* barracks and adobe quarters of the married couples, the patter of children's running feet, the barking of the dogs that chased after them.

207

"Laurie," Sam said softly.

"Hello, Sam."

"She didn't mean it, Laurie."

"Then why did she say it?"

"I don't know—something—"

"It's always something—to remind you of those you loved and lost, isn't it?"

"Yes, and we have to learn to live with it. Mostly, it's innocent, with no harm meant, but it's always there. Laurie—"

"What?"

"Listen. We can't crawl into someone else's grave to be with them, but it doesn't end life for the living. Believe me, I know how you feel, but you've got your own life to live now."

He couldn't see her face in the darkness and had no way of knowing whether or not she had been affected by his words, or how. He sat in the chair beside her and said, "Laurie, time is a merciful healer. Give it a chance to work."

For a few moments she was silent, then she said, "Is it too soon to ask you a question?"

"I won't know 'til I hear it."

"Maybe I'd better not—"

"Go on, Laurie, ask it."

"Do you think—the time will come when you'll—ever feel you want to marry again?"

He waited before replying, using the time to light a long, thin cigar, and Laurie thought, I've hurt him the way she hurt me. "I'm sorry, Sam," she said aloud. "I didn't mean—"

"No, it's all right, Laurie. It's just that I haven't really thought about it before. No reason to." He paused again, then said, "I suppose in time, I'll think about it and if the right girl is willing, I'd say 'yes' to your question."

"Can a person—?"

"Marry again without feeling guilt or disloyalty?"

"Yes. Is it easier for a man than a woman, what Caroline said?"

"Laurie, it's not easier for one than the other. I loved Ruth as much as any man can love a woman, with all my heart, mind and body, but I lost her. I can't feel so much guilt that I've got to condemn myself to a solitary existence for the rest of my life. I don't think Ruth would want that or ask it of me. I'll probably remarry some

208

day, and have children, but I'll never forget Ruth any more than I can forget my mother or certain other things that happened in my life long ago."

"Sam—"

"What, Laurie?"

"I—nothing. But thank you. I'm glad you're here."

Sam smiled and said, "And I'm glad you're here, Laurie. Try to forget it and be happy. There's a lot in this world to be happy about. A husband some day, children, a home, a good life."

"I wish—"

A voice broke through the darkness. "Hey, *amigo!* It is your cigar I see?"

It was Marcos, spurs jingling musically as he came toward them and mounted the lower step of the front porch. As he came closer, he saw Laurie. "Ah, Señorita Laurie. I interrupt?"

"No, Marcos," Laurie replied. "Come up and sit with us."

"Ah, *gracias,* no. I think maybe if you would like to hear the singing, the guitars playing—"

"Yes, I think I would. Sam, will you excuse me?"

"Sure, Laurie, go ahead. I've got some thinking to do."

Alone with Laurie, a change came over Marcos. He was no longer playing the part of a *mestizo,* but chose his words carefully, using only correct English and not larding it with Mexican phrases. "Are you enjoying Tres Flechas?" he asked.

"Yes. It's a beautiful place, but after a while there's so little to do."

Marcos laughed pleasantly. "The girls and women here would hardly agree with you."

"You're teasing me, Marcos. You know what I mean."

"Yes, of course."

"I want to move to Tucson."

"To live?" Marcos's voice rose with incredulity at the suggestion.

"Yes. I'm going to talk to Cousin Max about it."

"What would you do there?"

"Maybe I could work at the T-Y Lines office."

"And where would you live?"

"I could find a nice family to board with."

"Tucson. Such a bad town for such a pretty girl—a nice girl."

209

"Thank you. You know, Fort Leavenworth wasn't what anybody could call a very nice town, Marcos."

"But that was different. You had someone to protect you. I'm sorry, Laurie, I didn't mean to remind you—"

"It's all right. I remind myself a hundred times a day here. If I were working, it would be easier not to remember."

"And at night? At least you can walk around here among friends, without fear. In Tucson, no nice woman goes out after the sun goes down, except to visit other nice families, and only when a man is with her in the carriage."

"I'm not as concerned about the nights as I am about the days, keeping busy. You don't approve, do you?"

His voice turned brighter. "Only as long as I am in Tucson."

Laurie laughed. "You are very nice, Marcos."

"And you are very young."

"You're not much older than I am."

"I am close to twenty-three, but it is not the years that make one young or old."

"That's a little deep for me to understand, but I'll think about it. When my mother was eighteen, she was already married over a year."

"I don't mean young in that way. Or old."

"Marcos, tell me something else—"

"Anything I can."

"Why is it that when you are with the Mexican people here, you are completely Mexican and when you are with Anglos, you become part-Mexican, part-Anglo. With me, now, you are all Anglo, your speech, your manner."

"Ah, Laurie, I have been discovered, exposed. I will try to explain. I am a *mestizo,* a half-breed Mexican-American. So, Anglo prejudice says I must be Mexican, act like a Mexican, live like a Mexican and talk like a Mexican who has learned his English in the streets, although I was educated by the priests at San Xavier del Bac. If I display my knowledge in front of Mexicans or Anglos, I am what is called *bronceado* by Mexicans, brazen by Anglos, for acting above my station. So, in order to live with both, I play the part of both. I compensate in other ways."

"How?"

"By doing all things better than those who take pleasure in looking down on me."

"Then why do you play the part of Anglo with me?"

"Ah, there is a difference, Laurie. You are too new to Arizona, not long enough here to learn Anglo prejudices against someone who is not the same as you, a little darker in color, a little different in pronouncing English words, the food he eats, the clothes he wears. In time, you will learn—"

"I will not!"

"I said, in time."

"And I say, I will not."

"And I say, I hope not."

They stood at the rails of the family corral and watched the shadowy forms of the horses and several young colts. One came up to them and placed his muzzle into Marcos's outstretched hand. "This one is mine," Marcos said. "I love him." He said the words so simply and sincerely that Laurie felt a wave of emotion sweep through her.

"What is his name?"

"Mano. In English, it means Hand, but when I call him, *Mano!* he knows it means he is my *right* hand, which is very important and necessary to my life. Without it, I would be nothing. Without him, I would feel lost."

Laurie put out her own hand and caressed Mano, who nuzzled her palm. Marcos said, "He loves you."

"How do you know that?" she asked.

"Because I know him as well as he knows me. What he feels, I feel. What I feel, he feels."

Laurie suddenly realized what Marcos was trying to say, unable to say it openly. "I think I'd better go back to the house," she said.

"Yes. It has grown much cooler."

With the coming of late autumn in the southwest, the desert furnaces were banked by cooler winds and the days, with the exception of noon and early afternoon hours, became less hot and more pleasant, the nights colder. At Fort Bandolier, the former Camp Brennan officers and men had become satisfactorily integrated in drills, patrols, desert maneuvers and range firing to the point where they were now considered a single operating force, a fact that pleased Colonel Hatfield to the extent that he had permitted word to be passed that the Fort families would be allowed to return by the end of the year.

The news created a beehive of activity and men who

211

had never wielded hammer, saw or paint brush, made adobe brick or handled a hoe or rake, volunteered to build needed quarters, a recreation center for enlisted men, a smaller one for officers, a chapel, school-library, lay out an athletic field, dig a new well and erect a windmill. Private Alex Dickson, a shy, scholarly man from Troop E, was chosen to be schoolmaster and set about requisitioning necessary school books for grades one to eight for the two dozen or more children who would be arriving with their mothers.

The new activity was gratifying to Colonel Hatfield, who suffered the loneliness of all field commanders. He remained in constant touch, but aloof, refusing all personal attachments lest his judgment be impaired by emotional considerations. He had lost his oldest and closest friend when Major Owen Travis died in the Chancla Canyon massacre. He and Travis had been classmates at the Academy, served on frontier duty together on their post-graduation assignments. They had married within a year of each other and their wives had become inseparable friends. During the Civil War, Hatfield and Travis had become separated, although on several occasions their units were brought together in battle and these, despite the conflict, were times of happy reunion.

Travis was gone and Hatfield knew he would never see his widow again, would hear of her when his own wife came back to the Fort to live with him. It was not an isolated case. It had happened before to himself, to others, but it was the way of Army life and one had to steel oneself against the death of old and good friends.

Now fully staffed for three months, patrols out of Fort Bandolier moved in strength and had reduced Apache activity in the area to a new, effective low. Except for isolated hunting parties to seek food, Bokhari's braves were being well-contained in the Dos Viudas region, a few miles north of the Mexican border within easy retreat to Monte Babiacora in Sonora. But Hatfield's vigilance never relaxed. He knew that Bokhari lacked only one vital element—rifles and ammunition—and when these fell into his hands in sufficient quantities, the peace enjoyed for the moment would come to an abrupt end.

Closer to the silver mining town of Mesa Plata which lay west of the Fort, the Apaches had been more active, raiding in the fertile Carancho Valley for cattle and horses, but continuous sweeps by Army patrols managed to keep

212

the Indians at a safe distance except on occasions when, in desperation, forays were made to gain needed food. However, these raids were far less successful now and civilian losses were negligible compared to those sustained by the Apaches.

At this point, the return of the Fort families in another month was the most important thought in the minds of the military.

Out of Tucson and Yuma, the T-Y Lines had begun operating on its announced schedule and traffic was heavy, but so were the operating costs to Max Potter, requiring as many as four extra guards for each stage and six for each freight convoy. Goods from the East began arriving for trans-shipment to Yuma and the West Coast, passenger service picked up, and local merchants were now shipping supplies to all relay stations where local ranchers came to pick up their ordered merchandise, saving them the extra days it would take to drive all the way into Tucson at great personal risk.

In the two years since the war had ended, inflation had continued at an uncontrollable upward spiral. The price of hay had leaped from $30.00 a ton to $70.00. Coal oil sold for $8.00 a gallon, brandy at $40.00 a gallon. A bar of soap sold for 60¢, a broom for $6.00, sugar was $3.00 a pound, coffee $4.00, flour $30.00 for a one-hundred-pound barrel, lard $1.50 a pound, eggs $1.75 a dozen. At a time when beef was critically short in the East and brought an average of $40.00 a head at railhead in Abilene, after a long and costly drive from Texas, ranchers in the Tucson-Yuma area were charging the Army $62.00 a head for locally raised beef. For food and supplies freighted in from St. Louis or Fort Smith, prices were forbiddingly outrageous. Lumber, cut and hauled down from the mountain areas by civilian contractors, sold at prices which fluctuated upward as the Army's needs increased. Yet there was a good enough reason for the runaway inflation.

The white man's malignant greed.

When certain local merchants saw that the reservation Indians, with the help of Army overseers who supplied tools, seed and advice, were becoming proficient to the point of being able to sustain themselves on what they were growing, they formed a protective group consisting of certain politicians, contractors and other interested parties to bribe and otherwise influence the Indian Bureau's chief agent in Tucson, Marcus Rodman, to put an end to this practice of self-support. Rodman, who had the necessary authority from Washington, ordered the Army overseers to discontinue furnishing the necessary seed, tools and supervision, claiming jurisdiction over all Arizona reservations; thus forcing the government to buy all meats, vegetables, fruits, blankets, clothing and other needed supplies locally. Not only did prices soar, but the reservation Indians had little or nothing to do but ponder their plight and the white man's injustices.

The original plan of the Indian Bureau to eventually make the Indian reservations into self-sustaining, peaceful communities and reduce the size of the Army in those areas, was doomed. The plotters, who became known as the Tucson Ring, went even further. They furnished the Indians with whiskey, rifles and ammunition and encouraged many to bolt the reservations and rejoin their former tribes, thus perpetuating a state of continual unrest and warfare and creating an even greater need for more Army troops, all at increasing profit to the infamous Ring members.

Marcus Rodman, as chief purchasing agent for the reservation Indians, became a rich man. Blankets bought for 62¢ were billed to the Bureau in Washington at an even $3.00; 24¢ wool socks at 80¢; $1.10 hats at $3.75; $1.50 trousers at $4.15; Indian-made moccasins that cost 30¢ were billed as shoes at $3.60 a pair. Ring merchants and collaborators, of course, shared in the abundant profits by supplying Rodman with the necessary certified bills at the exorbitant prices.

When the Fort Lowell Inspector General, General Reese, in protest, asked the Quartermaster General in Washington to ship all such supplies to Fort Lowell for distribution, a storm of protest was received by members of Congress and Department of the Army from Tucson merchants and their political henchmen, arguing that this "interference with our free enterprise system" would bankrupt them. General Reese's request was promptly refused, and the Fort Lowell Quartermaster sternly ordered to buy all nonmilitary goods and supplies on the open market and forbade him to "continue this unwarranted harassment upon the merchants in the Territory of Arizona."

Corruption breeds corruption, and since the Quartermaster at Fort Lowell was the principal source of supply for all Army posts in Arizona, certain carefully selected officers and noncommissioned officers became silent participants in Ring activities by accepting the shipper's count and weight with one eye closed, thus saving themselves many time-consuming chores and lining their pockets with cash. Likewise, requisitions from other camps were shipped short in count and weight. In this manner, valuable goods disappeared from Army warehouses and reappeared in the hands of Ring members, only to be resold to the public and, in some instances, to the Army Supply Depot from which it had been stolen. Inventories were faked and shipping invoices forged to make good the shortages.

Thus, rifles and ammunition, items under strict control of the Army, managed to come into the possession of the man who had conceived the Tucson Ring and effectively organized it.

Martin Van Allen.

Martin Van Allen had been born in Texas, the son of a blacksmith, Andreas Van Allen, and a mission-raised half-Navajo, half-American woman twenty years his junior, who had died giving birth to her son. Martin was subsequently raised by a succession of women whom Andreas brought to his home, and as he grew from childhood into young manhood, spent most of his time in town among older men whom he thought were wise and worldly.

Martin worked sporadically on several ranches, but the work was hard and not to his liking. Equally at home among Mexicans and Anglos, he learned to gamble in the *cantinas* and saloons and discovered that he had excellent card sense, which he developed into a fine art when the game of *poque*, later renamed poker, became more popular than faro and other frontier games of chance. A shrewd judge of human nature, he studied the odds carefully and found that the game, apart from pure chance or luck, was one of strategy and required a knowledge of his opponents's personal traits, mannerisms and idiosyncrasies. Soon he was able to leave Andreas and his assortment of women and move into town permanently.

He did very well in turbulent El Paso. Within a year or two, he had won a good-sized stake, which he loaned out at high interest rates. He put $1,000 into a saloon, brought in several attractive young Mexican girls from below the border and made it into a showplace for tran-

215

sients and local men willing to risk their money at the gaming tables. He bought into a livery stable and a general store, then built a hotel next to his saloon and continued to prosper. When the law interfered with his activities, he bought off the town marshal with money and saloon girls. Men running for political office sought his support, which he gave on a *quid pro quo* basis. No favor was ever granted without demanding one in return.

When he was twenty-eight years old, he shot and killed a man during an argument over a card game. The man happened to be a wealthy rancher who was driving a herd of cattle back to his ranch in New Mexico and within a few hours his crew of trailherders had burned the saloon and hotel to the ground. Martin Van Allen escaped, but the furious trailherders gave chase and drove him across Chihuahua and Sonora before they gave up. Afraid to return to El Paso, Martin headed north until he reached Tucson. Here he rested until he was certain he was no longer being pursued.

Within a short while, he began to reconstruct his life along lines not far different from what it had been in Texas. He found an abandoned cabin north of Tucson along the Santa Cruz River and moved in. Here, he took stock of his total possessions: horse, saddle, rifle, revolver, blanket roll and the $800 he had had in his pockets when he left El Paso on the run.

In Tucson, he found willing gamblers and a streak of bad luck. When he was down to two hundred dollars, he stopped gambling long enough to give his luck a chance to change. Taunted by a rancher one night, he accepted the man's challenge and put up his last $200 in an all-or-nothing attempt to either increase his stake or move on.

That game made history in Tucson and propelled Martin Van Allen into local prominence.

In a six-handed game, he won steadily after a shaky start that had reduced his capital to less than fifty dollars. With false confidence, he bluffed the next hand with a pair of deuces and his luck returned. The game went on hour after hour into the next day, with men ready to sit in for those who had dropped out for a few hours of rest. By nightfall of the second day, Martin had won over two thousand dollars in cash and gold, held I.O.U.'s amounting to fifteen hundred dollars and a piece of land a mile south of where his cabin stood. He dropped out for a while to sleep and returned to the game at midnight, feeling fresh and confident, to find that several of the men who had started the game originally were back again.

Martin's luck held. The game had attracted so many onlookers that it became the only game in progress. A space had been cleared around the table and the only other activity in the saloon was at the bar. The stakes became progressively larger and Martin gauged each hand as carefully as he observed the other five players. He refused drink after drink and only puffed on his cigar as he studied his cards, considered the odds-for and odds-against his chances before throwing in his hand or deciding he could better it.

The game continued for four days and nights with brief periods of rest for each player. Each time Martin returned refreshed, a place was made for him as the biggest winner and the most attractive target for the other players. In the early hours of the fifth morning, the game ended with a winning hand. Martin had drawn three kings, a ten and an ace. He discarded the ten and ace and drew a king and the six of diamonds. One man dropped out. Three men drew two and three cards and one stood pat.

The center of the table looked as though it had rained money; silver and gold coins, sacks of weighed gold dust, bills and several I.O.U.'s. At the final call, the pat hand, the only one Martin was concerned with, turned out to contain four jacks. Martin's four kings took the pot and broke the game. He slept in a room at the hotel that night, the door barred with a chest of drawers and his revolver within reach of his hand. The money, gold dust and I.O.U.'s were stuffed in a pillowcase upon which his head rested in peaceful bliss. He slept the clock around and opened the door only for a waiter from the dining room who brought him his one meal and a bottle of whiskey late the next afternoon, then slept again.

The following day he carried the money to Boyd Kiner's bank and was surprised that everyone he saw en route called him by name. He deposited $27,000, then totted up his paper. He owned the ranch of the man who had taunted him into the game that first night and two other smaller pieces of land. Two merchants owed him a total of $4,800. There were I.O.U.'s in much smaller amounts and in a burst of sudden generosity, he returned these to their owners, thus making a number of friends.

He took over his newly won ranch and moved in. There were a Mexican *mayordomo* and three other Mexican families as well as a dozen range hands to do all the work, leaving Martin free to come and go as he pleased. He spent a month at the ranch before returning to town to make a deal with the merchants who owed him the $4,800. At mid-day dinner at the hotel to which he had invited both men, he agreed to pay each an additional sum for a half interest in their businesses. Both agreed. He used six thousand dollars to build the Congress Saloon, where he spent most of his time as owner-host. Life was very good to Martin Van Allen.

On his ranch, he took the daughter of his housekeeper, an attractive young Mexican girl named Inez, to his bed, and in the following year, she became pregnant. Martin sent her and her mother back to Tucson and bought a small house for them in the Mexican quarter. The year was 1845. On the thirteenth day of May of 1846, the same day the United States declared war on Mexico, Inez Espuela gave birth to a son whom she named Marcos.

After Inez's mother died some two years later, Martin visited Inez and Marcos frequently, resuming the illicit relationship. When the war ended and with the signing of the treaty in 1848, borders were realigned and Mexico ceded United States claims to Texas, New Mexico, Arizona, California, Nevada, Utah and part of Colorado, for which the Mexican government was paid fifteen million dollars.

Then the United States Army moved in to control the rampaging Indians, who were greater enemies of the Mexicans than of the Americans. Martin Van Allen saw profit in the sudden influx of troops and went to Washington to seek Army contracts to supply the armed forces. He was as persuasive as he was liberal and soon found a champion in Congressman Willard Harmon of Massachusetts, who headed the Committee on Indian Affairs, and who arranged conferences between Martin and the Secretary of War.

Martin convinced the Secretary that, while no merchant himself, the Army should turn over the supply of all non-military supplies and goods to local merchants in order to win their support and permit the new territories to expand. In a few months, with the supply problem a major source of trouble, the Army was glad to be rid of the headache, and the Secretary acquiesced to Martin's pressure. The Committee on Indian Affairs also agreed to permit local merchants to supply all Indian reservations through Bureau agents. Martin came away with these agreements and a wife, the daughter of Congressman Harmon, who was named Abigail, and who had fallen victim to Martin's enthusiasm for the frontier country.

Abigail was sick most of the way across the country, appalled at her first sight of the adobe-walled, predominantly Mexican town of Tucson, aghast at the primitive ranch home to which Martin had brought her. With no knowledge of the language, she was helpless to remake the house into her Boston-oriented idea of what a home should be. Thus she lived as a stranger among strangers. Had she not been pregnant, she would have attempted to return to the safety of Washington. Or Boston.

Abigail's son was born in 1849 and her daughter in 1851. Her next two children were stillborn. In 1856, she took her children back to Boston, insisting on the need to educate them properly. Through her father's offices, she received military escort to St. Louis and from there, managed to reach Boston in safety by rail. It was Martin's understanding that after the children were placed in a good school, Abigail would return. Instead, she sought and received a divorce and remained in Boston.

Martin Van Allen no longer needed his ex-Congressman father-in-law. He was his own power in Tucson and had other lines of communication into Washington. He enlarged the Congress Saloon and built the Congress Hotel beside it. He recruited a shadowy following and arranged his own private treaties with Cochise, trading guns, ammunition, horses, mules and cattle for gold. Casimiro Lizardi became his shadow commissioner, and the latest chief Indian Agent in Arizona, Marcus Rodman, like his predecessor, became Martin Van Allen's pawn.

T-Y Lines had added two Abbott-Downing and two Concord stages to its passenger service, four heavy freight wagons, two celerity and utility wagons for short distance hauls and fast express, plus two tank wagons for hauling water. To expedite freight shipments from the east, the four new wagons were assigned to a trial Lordsburg-Tucson run, which required a heavier guard and drained more *vaqueros* from Tres Flechas. After the first two trips in November, and at Max Potter's insistence, Sam Palmer put Marcos in charge of the Tucson-Lordsburg freight run.

"We need you where you're more valuable, Sam," Max insisted. "The Tucson-Yuma run is what's keepin' the Line alive, and Marcos can use the experience on the Lordsburg run."

"You still worried about me being in Cochise country?"

"That, too, but there's no use sticking your neck out. We ought to be getting that Army contract and mail franchise out of Washington pretty soon, then we can ease up a little."

"When?" Sam asked. "We keep running into Army convoys time and again. Either we or they are wasting a lot of manpower and equipment."

"Soon as Colonel Taggart at Fort Lowell can get an acceptable contract drafted and approved by General Litchfield. The mail thing ought to be coming through from Washington next month some time."

"We'll need both if we expect to last another six months, Max."

"You let me worry about that end of it, Sam. By next year we'll have our contracts and plenty of people trying to buy into T-Y."

Schedules had been worked out so that all runs would come to an end in Tucson on the Tuesday before Thanksgiving in order to give the hard-pressed *vaqueros* a full day to receive their pay, do some shopping, and leave for Tres Flechas in time for the holiday. Some had not been home in over three months. On Tuesday night, Max Potter sent Santiago Reyes and three other *vaqueros* ahead to notify the ranch people to prepare a suitable welcome for their men. They arrived at daybreak on Wednesday.

Caroline and Laurie were at the gate to meet them. As they dismounted, Santiago embraced his wife and son, then went to Caroline and gave her the message so all could hear the news that the others would arrive by nightfall.

"And Papa?" Caroline asked.

"*El patrón* and Señor Palmer will be with them, *señorita*. They are well and eager to be here."

"And Marcos?" Laurie asked.

Santiago turned to her with a smile. "He is well, *señorita*, a fine *caudillo* for such a young man."

"He comes with the others?"

"Yes."

Caroline said, "You and your men are tired, Santiago. Eat and rest."

"Sí señorita, gracias." Santiago bowed and rejoined the men who had accompanied him, now being deluged with questions from the men, women and children who surrounded them.

On the way back to the house, Caroline said, "Laurie, don't ever question any of the men about another man."

"Why not?"

"Because no matter how innocently you mean it, there will be talk. Santiago will mention it to Lupe that you asked about Marcos. Lupe will tell Celestine, who will tell Rosa, who will tell Chita and soon it will be all over Tres Flechas that the white *señorita* longs for a *mestizo*."

"I only asked—"

Caroline's crisp retort cut her words off. "I know. I heard you. Everyone within hearing distance heard you."

"I don't see anything wrong in asking about someone you haven't seen in months, Caroline."

"Laurie, Marcos is a half-breed."

"Well, aren't you—"

"I am half-Spanish, half-American."

"And Marcos is half-American, half-Mexican."

"I shouldn't need to tell you that out here, there's a big difference. Besides, his mother and father weren't married. He is illegitimate, a *bastardo*."

For a moment, Laurie was silent, then she said quietly, "That's not his fault, is it?"

"No, Laurie, but it is a hard fact of life. He is accepted by most Mexicans, but only tolerated by Americans. Except for Papa and Sam, for whom he works."

"That's not fair!" Laurie exclaimed.

"Maybe not, but there's a lot of reality that isn't fair."

"I—" Laurie stopped, then laughed uncertainly. "I've been making a lot over nothing, haven't I?"

"Unless you're interested in Marcos."

Laurie tossed her head impudently. "I don't know if I am or not." Caroline smiled stiffly and Laurie arched her eyebrows and added, "Not any more than you are about Sam."

Caroline's smile turned wintry cold. Without a further word, she quickened her pace and went into the house.

Laurie had not intended touching on a subject which she had come to believe would be sensitive to Caroline and now, for the first time, she realized that her suspicion was true; that unfair as it was to Sam Palmer, Caroline refused to admit her own interest in her brother-in-law.

Unfair. Fair.

Laurie remembered now how Libby had taken so many pains to teach Loren and herself the meaning of fairness. Little examples, explanations. One came back to her mind now.

When they were eight and six, Loren and Laurie had come home from the post school at the Fort, hungry as usual. Both ran to the pantry off the kitchen, only to find that Libby had used the last of the fresh apples to make several pies for the church social that Friday night. Then Loren discovered one apple that Libby had overlooked. He grabbed it and ran, teasing Laurie by shouting, "I've got one! It's mine! It's mine!"

But Libby caught him before he could escape outside and took the apple from him. "It's not yours, Loren. Shame on you. It's Laurie's as much as it is yours. Now you divide it between you."

"I'll divide it!" Loren shouted. "Give it to me."

Laurie said, "You divide it, Mama. If Loren does, all I'll get is one little bite."

"No," Libby said, "I'll tell you how to do it fairly. One of you will divide the apple in half, but the other will have first choice."

Finally, Loren agreed to cut the apple. Laurie had first choice, but she recalled that no apple had ever been cut more precisely in half. A lesson in material fairness.

It did not bother her at all that Marcos was half-Mexican or illegitimate. He was warm and gentle, his eyes (which were Laurie's standard guide for judging people) were kind. His lips were full and generous, his hair black and with a soft wave. His skin was somewhat dark, but no darker than her own or Caroline's or Max's after exposure to the sun. Then, she argued with Caroline's suggestion, how can anyone blame him for something that happened between a man and a woman long before he was born?

It was something she could not resolve alone, so she did what she had learned to do when she needed to occupy her mind.

She thought about Loren.

Cousin Max had told her two months ago he would send an advertisement to be placed in a dozen cities where he thought a westbound runaway might land; perhaps as far away as Oregon Territory. Two months were not long enough time to have any replies, yet she pinned every hope on him seeing the advertisement and writing to her in Tubac. He might even be on his way now.

CHAPTER II

ON THAT THANKSGIVING EVE, FORT BANDOLIER WAS thrown into a state of high excitement when a courier arrived from Tucson with dispatches and the scuttlebutt that the traveling paymaster would arrive at Bandolier late on Friday night. The Fort had not been paid in almost three months and this was cause for celebrating; a general clearing of all debts, additional money in most pockets, plans to be made for spending it.

On Friday morning, although the word had not yet been officially released, company first sergeants were busy drawing up pass lists for the two towns nearest the Fort; Mesa Plata, sixteen miles west, and Malhado, thirty-four miles east, through more dangerous territory, but where the welcome would be greater and with more opportunity to satisfy male appetites.

After breakfast, Major Boyden ordered the trumpeter to sound Officers' Call. All but the Officer of the Day and Captain Ahearn, who was still under restriction, assembled and sat in chairs arranged in two rows facing Major Boyden and Colonel Hatfield.

Boyden formally announced the arrival of the paymaster, due late that night, "—which I am certain you gentlemen were aware of via the grapevine only moments after we received the news by courier. At ten o'clock, one hour from now, Lieutenant Zimmerman and twenty-four men will ride to Malhado to meet the paymaster's detail and escort them the rest of the way in.

"Tomorrow, pay lines will be mustered immediately after breakfast. Only guard and necessary housekeeping details will be scheduled for duty, and the usual Saturday inspections will not be held. Passes will be granted to forty men. Under the ten percent regulation, only thirty-one are eligible, but we will add nine to round out that number rather than subtract one to reduce the number to an even thirty. Pass parties will be on mounted leave with forty-eight hours to spend at their destinations, Mesa

224

Plata or Malhado, plus travel time to and from. No passes will be extended as far as Tucson or Yuma. When the first forty return, forty others will go on pass each weekend until all who so wish have had their passes. Officers who desire leave will be accommodated after the enlisted men have had theirs.

"All men on pass will wear sidearms and carry carbines en route to and from their destinations. Any man arrested for misconduct of any kind will most probably be jailed and fined locally. Let me add, however, that if he returns here overdue, he will serve double time in the stockade with heavy extra duty and forfeiture of pay unless he can prove his innocence beyond all doubt. Colonel Hatfield?"

Hatfield took over now. "Gentlemen," he said, "we cannot prevent a certain amount of drinking, gambling and brawling when pockets are bulging with money. Former Camp Brennan troops, I understand, haven't been paid for four months. Fort Bandolier hasn't seen a paymaster for three months. To some degree, I will look aside at minor infractions for the next few days, but I will not tolerate excesses and will hold all officers and senior noncoms responsible for the conduct of this Fort's personnel while on post.

"There are now eight laundresses in this Fort, all of Mexican extraction. Three are unmarried, five are the wives of Mexican employees. If any one of those women is molested, even touched or insulted in any manner, I promise the harshest penalties I can order will be meted out. You will see that this word is passed.

"I expect that my officers will show firmness in dealing with the men, but I shall also demand fairness. Very well. As the men are paid, I insist that all personal debts, company fund loans, and credit extended by the sutler on official orders will be paid first. If the Camp Brennan men will follow the examples of the Fort Bandolier men in this case, I think all will go well.

"Finally, there will, after this payroll has been met, no longer be any references made to Camp Brennan. In the future, all officers and enlisted men will officially and unofficially regard themselves as Fort Bandolier men. Any questions?"

There were none. Boyden rose. "Atten-*tion!* Dis-*missed!*"

Ten minutes after the officers trooped out, Captain

Greene returned. "Sir," he said to Hatfield, "Captain Ahearn requests permission to speak with the colonel."

Boyden threw a quick side glance at Hatfield and saw him weighing his answer. "Show the captain in," he said finally. Boyden stood up to leave and Hatfield added, "Please remain, Major."

Ahearn entered and saluted Hatfield briskly. "Be seated, Captain," the colonel said as he returned the salute.

Ahearn sat down, still at attention. "Well, Captain Ahearn?"

"Sir, I respectfully request that I be considered to lead the patrol to Malhado to escort the paymaster detail to the Fort."

Hatfield studied Ahearn for a moment. "It will be a detail of only twenty-four men, Captain, hardly enough to warrant a lieutenant in charge."

"Nevertheless, sir, I would appreciate the assignment. I feel I should learn more about the area, with specific reference to Malhado Pass."

"Ah, yes. Does this request negate your previous verbal request for transfer, Captain?"

"Yes, sir, it does. I wish to remain on duty at Fort Bandolier, sir."

"Very well. Major Boyden will rescind Lieutenant Zimmerman's orders and have them made out in your favor. On your return, we will discuss your permanent assignment."

"Thank you, sir. I would also like to apologize for my earlier behavior and attitude—"

"Don't apologize, Captain, except by the performance of your duties in the future. Be ready to leave at ten o'clock. That will be all for now."

As Ahearn marched out, Hatfield caught Boyden's slow smile and said, "Well, Major, it's a beginning. We shall see."

Shortly after midnight, Captain Ahearn led the paymaster's detail into Fort Bandolier to be welcomed by an almost wide-awake camp of men who had stayed up to satisfy their own curiosity.

Before reveille on Saturday, the men were up and about, washed, shaved, in clean uniforms with boots and shoes glistening. At the first note of reveille, not a man remained in the barracks or tents. They answered roll call, rushed through breakfast and loafed about until as-

226

sembly was sounded, then marched in company formations to where the paymaster's table had been set up in the open. As each man's name was called and answered to with a loud, "Yo!" he stepped up, signed the payroll by name or with an "X," gathered up his pay and headed off to count it, despite the fact that it had been counted out before his eyes only moments before.

Nearby stood the two or three moneylenders, men who preyed on the needy between pay days, loaning "four-for-five" in the early days of the month, "three-for-five" by mid-month, and later, as the need for gambling, cigars, chewing tobacco, beer or whiskey grew, at fantastically exorbitant rates of interest. These were the most sought-out, yet the most resented men on the post, but regarded as a necessary evil and beyond discipline, since they had been created by the men themselves. Prominent among the lenders was Sergeant Brigham Quitt, notebook in hand.

After the laundresses, moneylenders and other debtors had been paid, the pass parties mounted up and left for Malhado or Mesa Plata. The others dispersed to their barracks to gamble at cards or dice, to the sutler's store to lay in a supply of tobacco, toilet articles and what sundries were available from his familiar and not too full stocks, to sample his beer and whiskey. Before lights out, considerably more than a few would be broke again and turn to the moneylenders.

While the men were being paid, Sergeant Major Riley sought out Sergeant Atticus Perry and told him to report to the adjutant. On reporting, Captain Greene told him, "Sergeant, there was no way to have you included on the regular payroll, but Colonel Hatfield has signed an emergency authorization on your behalf for thirty dollars. This will in no way affect the back pay due you when your records come through from Fort Bliss."

"Thank you, sir, very much."

Greene counted out the thirty dollars and placed the money on the desk. "It will be necessary for you to sign this pay voucher," he said. He moved the yellow oblong slip headed, *Receipt For Emergency Payment*, across the desk and handed Atticus the pen. When Atticus tried to sign the slip, the pen point was dry.

"Here," Greene said, moving the ink bottle closer to Perry, who thrust the pen point into the narrow neck of the bottle. In withdrawing it, he did so hastily and the

227

small bottle tipped over and spilled on the green blotter pad. Some of the blue ink touched a corner of the receipt, but most of it spread toward the money. Atticus grabbed for the bills and succeeded in picking up all but the single ten-dollar bill which lay on the bottom. A thin, widening streak of the dark blue ink ran across the face of the bill for about four inches before Atticus rescued it, leaving a design similar to an arrowhead on it.

Captain Greene leaped to his feet, moving papers out of the way, his face showing his annoyance, brushing off Perry's apologies.

"I'm sorry, Captain. Been a long time since I held a pen in my hand. I guess I'm still a little shaky—"

"It's all right, Sergeant," Greene replied somewhat testily. "Get a rag or something—"

Atticus whipped a handkerchief out of his pocket and mopped the rest of the ink up.

"You didn't have to do that—" Greene began.

"It's all I had, sir. I apologize for my clumsiness."

Perry's contriteness somehow softened the situation. "No great harm, Sergeant. I have another desk blotter to replace this one. That will be all."

"Yes, sir. Thank you, sir." Atticus stiffened to attention and saluted, did a proper about face and went out.

Outside, he took the folded bills from his pocket. The ink was almost dry now, but had bled off from the ten-dollar bill onto the five that was next to it. There was another five, three twos and four ones. Thirty dollars. The first money he had held in his hands in over eighteen months. And a lump sum of $372 in back pay due him; enriched by enforced savings due to circumstances beyond his control.

Whoo-ee-ee!

It was a field hand's expression of joy he whistled under his breath, yet if he were off alone somewhere, he would have emitted it in an exuberant shriek. Cash money and $372 to come! Hallelujah!

He owed seven of the thirty dollars to the sutler for supplies drawn by him on the adjutant's order, but he would pay it tomorrow, unwilling to brave the crowd he could see through the store window. Meanwhile, he had all of it to touch and fondle at will.

By mid-afternoon, the buying at the sutler's store was generally limited to the bar. There was warm beer and whiskey, but it had to be consumed at the bar and none sold to take out; although there were those who were able to overcome that minor difficulty as long as there was cash, plus a premium, to be exchanged for the service. In every barracks building there were serious poker games and noisier dice games in progress. Money changed hands frequently as curses of the losers and chortles of the winners mingled and warmed the smoke-laden air.

Sergeant Perry lay on his cot and dreamed of his $372 and a possible future. His enlistment was nearly up and he would be faced with the decision whether to enlist again or be discharged. There were advantages and disadvantages to consider. A civilian life in relative safety at home (relative only, considering the rise of the Ku Klux Klan in the South), or Army life and the perils of death or recapture. He might remain in Tucson as a civilian or go on farther west to California to see what life had to offer there.

It was a choice. Or was it?

He turned away from the wall and faced the long row of cots that ran the length of the barracks. The two empty spaces next to his cot were still there, silent evidence that his presence among white men was still resented, although he had performed his duties as well as any sergeant on the post.

Opposite him, a poker game was in progress on Corporal Zentz's cot, six players and four watchers. Farther down the line another group, noisier, occupied a huddle of eight men. Private Alex Dickson, perhaps the oldest man in Troop E, lay on his cot reading a book; a rare sight at a moment like this. The first sergeant, Mike Tyler, was not present, having drawn duty as Sergeant of the Guard.

No one spoke to Atticus or looked in his direction. It made little difference to him. He was well-clothed, well-fed, warm and rested. And he had thirty dollars, twenty-three which belonged to him, clear, and nothing he needed to spend it on at the moment. And no chance of being invited to join a poker or dice game.

Before supper, First Sergeant Tyler, with permission from the Officer of the Day, asked Atticus to take over the rest of his watch as Sergeant of the Guard, a request Atticus was glad to comply with. The O.D. was Lieutenant John Mason-Field, spending his first day on duty since he had been wounded in the battle of Monte de Lágrimas. Mason-Field was the youngest officer in the Fort, an Academy man on his initial tour of active duty since leaving West Point, and whose hobby was archaeology. He had become interested in Atticus the very first time he saw him, but this was the first time they had been on duty together, and the two talked at great length. Mason-Field's side, where he had taken a lance wound, was still tightly bandaged, which made moving around a bit difficult, and Atticus extended himself to take whatever responsibility he could so that the young officer could remain inside the guardhouse. Atticus inspected the guard, climbed the watchtower, leaped up at the first call of any sentry, and sent one of the off-duty men to the kitchen to bring hot food and coffee to the O.D.

At eight o'clock that night, a sentry call was relayed to the guardhouse, reporting a fight in the sutler's store. Mason-Field got up stiffly and began buckling his sword on, but Atticus said, "Let me take it, Lieutenant. I can be there in thirty seconds, sir."

Mason-Field said, "Go ahead, Sergeant. I'll come along in a few minutes."

The fight was still going on when Atticus came into the store. The two men involved were Corporal Hudson, his old antagonist, and Corporal Simon Lanier, a specialist on duty with the supply office. Hudson had just rammed his bullet-shaped head into Lanier's stomach and thrown him back about six feet into a table laden with merchandise. Gathered around the battle arena were about twenty onlookers, corporals, privates, and one sergeant, none making an effort to stop the fight.

Mr. Sherman Pierce, the civilian sutler who operated the store on Army contract, was trying desperately to keep the men apart and bring the fight to an end, but received little help. His three Mexican employees, two men and one young boy, remained behind a counter. Pierce saw Atticus enter the store, wearing his duty belt and holstered revolver, symbols of the authority of his office. "Here! Here! Sergeant of the Guard!" Pierce shouted loudly, but the combatants paid little attention.

Atticus, taller than either Lanier or Hudson, pushed through the ring of watchers and stepped between the participants. "All right, men, you'd better break it up—"

Someone shouted, "Take off, nigger!"

Hudson, brought face to face with Atticus, snarled, "Get the hell out of my way, booger!"

230

Lanier backed off, fists still balled up, but remained silent, panting heavily from exertion, wiping a sleeve across his bleeding lip. Atticus took a grip on Hudson's arms and said, "Break it off now, Hudson, and I won't put you on report. If the O.D. walks in here, you'll be telling it to the adjutant and Colonel Hatfield come Monday morning. You've got just one minute—"

Hudson, further enraged by the idea of a Negro sergeant giving him orders, attacked. He threw one punch which Atticus blocked, and a second which got through. Atticus pushed Hudson off, braced for the next assault. He warded off the first punch, blocked the second, then stepped in with a hard drive to Hudson's midriff and a left to his unprotected jaw. Hudson dropped and stayed down.

Someone called, "O.D. comin'! Watch it!"

Atticus said, "Get him under cover or he goes to the stockade. Quick!"

When Lieutenant Mason-Field entered the store, Atticus greeted him at the door. "Nothing to it, Lieutenant. It was all over when I got here."

Mason-Field did not believe this, but was willing to accept the sergeant's word. "All right, Perry," he said. "Thank you."

"Yes, sir. I'll be back directly, sir. With the lieutenant's permission, I'd like to pay Mr. Pierce a little bill I owe him while I'm here."

"Very well, carry on." Mason-Field left. Mr. Pierce said, "Thanks, Sergeant. I'll get some of the boys to get the corporal out of the back room and to his barracks."

"That'll do fine, Mr. Pierce." Atticus pulled out his thin wad of money and handed Pierce a five and two ones. "I owe you this, the stuff I got last month."

"Sure, Sergeant. Wait a minute and I'll check it off the books." He took the seven dollars and added it to a large roll from his pocket.

Taps sounded at ten and some of the activity slowed down, but did not come to a complete halt. Gambling and drinking continued in the stables and nonbarracks buildings, but the sutler's store was closed. Making his ten o'clock rounds, Atticus looked in on the Troop E barracks to see how Corporal Hudson was getting along, but the corporal was not in his cot, nor in the latrine behind the building. There were lights in the stable, but he passed this up, not wishing to be an official witness to the

231

gambling he knew was going on there. He passed by the sutler's store again and tried the doors, found them locked. He peered through the window and saw Mr. Pierce counting the day's income, a stack of bills and piles of coins, two canvas money sacks on the counter beside him. Pierce looked up at the sound of the front doors rattling, waved a hand toward Atticus, who waved back and moved on to check the warehouse doors and sentries in the east area.

Slowly, the Fort settled down. Returning to the guardhouse, Atticus reported an "All's well" to Lieutenant Mason-Field, who so recorded that fact in his O.D.'s book.

At eight o'clock on Sunday morning during the informal guard mount, the colors were raised, the new and old guards presented arms to each other and Lieutenant Laurence Benjamin took over the duty as Officer of the Day. Lieutenant Mason-Field signed the O.D. book, handed over the Orders of the Day and, relieved of further duty, left the guardhouse with Sergeant Perry.

"Thank you for making my burden lighter, Sergeant," Mason-Field said. "It would have been a lot more difficult without you."

Atticus smiled. "My privilege to serve a gentleman, sir," he replied.

At the one crossroad, the two men parted and went their own ways, Perry in the direction of Troop E barracks, Mason-Field toward the bachelor officers' quarters. On a Sunday morning following a Saturday payday, there was no reveille roll call. Very few men had gotten up for breakfast and the Fort lay hung over in sleep, except for the sentries on duty.

At 8:20 A.M. Hernando Opoca, his brother Luis, and Hernando's sixteen-year-old son, Manuelo, civilian employees of Sherman Pierce, were seated on the wooden platform in front of the sutler's store, waiting for Pierce to arrive and unlock the door for them. The store was not open for business on Sundays but after a payday there would be much cleaning up to do, shelves to be restocked from the storeroom in the rear. Hernando's and Luis' wives were two of the eight laundresses on the post and lived in the northwest corner shacks next to the laundry building, an area known as Soapsuds Row.

Pierce was late this morning and Hernando said, "He has been late before, yes, but not this late."

Luis ground out his cigarillo in the dirt. "When the *soldados* are paid, he has much money to count. Ai-ee, how I would like to have as much money as he took in yesterday."

Manuelo said, "The black one, he came in too soon last night. It was a good fight."

"Fight!" Hernando spat into the dirt contemptuously. "With the hands, like women."

"Among themselves, Anglos do not fight to kill," Luis remarked, "only to punish."

"Punishment is for children, not men." Hernando lit a fresh cigarillo and looked up at the sun, now reaching higher into the sky. "Manuelo."

"Sí, papá."

"Go to the *casa* of Señor Pierce and see if he is awake."

"Sí." Manuelo slid off the platform and walked slowly to the end of the building, then turned left toward the one-room shack of the sutler which stood about forty yards behind the store. As he reached the rear of the store, something caught his eye beneath the outer edge of the loading platform off the back door to the storeroom. He stopped and stared for a moment or two until he could distinguish that what lay there in the shadows was a leather boot. From that distance of ten feet, he knelt cautiously and peered into the dim recess beneath the platform. It was too dark to make out *who,* but he was certain of *what*—most likely a soldier who had had too much to drink and had crawled beneath the platform to sleep it off.

Manuelo's mission to find Señor Pierce was momentarily forgotten. He returned to the front of the store and reported what he had found to his father and uncle. Luis got up to go to the soldier's aid, but Hernando put out a hand to restrain him. "No, Luis. It is better to send Manuelo to the guardhouse to bring the *soldados.* If we go along, he will say that we first robbed him."

Manuelo ran to the guardhouse, which was on the opposite side of the Fort. Lieutenant Benjamin was having coffee at the officers' mess, so he reported his find to the Sergeant of the Guard, Art Petrie. Petrie could not understand Manuelo's Spanish or his broken English, but Corporal Hardy Davis, who was standing nearby, understood both.

"He's telling you there's a soldier lying beneath the

233

rear platform of the sutler's store, sleeping off a drunk," Davis interpreted.

Petrie mumbled his displeasure, looked around the room. To two of the relief guard, he said, "Haverstraw, Cusack, come with me. If the lieutenant comes back, Davis, tell him I'm checking the west wall sentries. You take over here. If this trooper doesn't give us any trouble, we won't give him any. We'll just get him to his barracks and forget it."

Petrie, Haverstraw and Cusack followed Manuelo back to the store where Hernando and Luis Opoca waited. As they walked to the rear of the store, Hernando again remarked that Pierce was now a full hour overdue. Luis, as two of the soldiers knelt beside the extended boot and crawled back under the platform, said, "Hernando, you think—"

Cusack, from beneath the platform, called out, "Sarge, this ain't no trooper. And he's sure by God deader'n hell."

"Pull him out," Petrie ordered.

The two men did so and discovered that the body, the back of its head caved in, was that of Sherman Pierce.

The three Mexicans crossed themselves and moved their lips in silent prayer while Petrie, Haverstraw and Cusack stared into Pierce's open but unseeing eyes in disbelief. They had seen violent death many times before, but murder was something else again, and there was little doubt that this was murder.

Petrie broke the silence. "Cusack, get over to the hospital and notify Captain Breed. Haverstraw, keep an eye on these three and hold them here. We'll need them for witnesses. I want to check the doors."

Front and rear doors were locked and Petrie could find no broken windows or signs of forced entry. He returned to where the body lay. "Haverstraw, fetch Lieutenant Benjamin. Go past the officers' mess first. If he's not there, he'll be back at the guardhouse. Move, man."

Minutes later, Captain Breed arrived with two hospital orderlies carrying a stretcher. He examined the body briefly and made his obvious pronouncement of death as Lieutenant Benjamin came upon the scene alone, having sent Haverstraw to Colonel Hatfield's quarters to report the incident. The colonel and Major Boyden arrived together and by this time, the word had swept through the Fort. Men in semidress stood within a respectful distance

234

of the body and the small knot of authority surrounding it.

Hatfield, unable to find Pierce's keys, ordered Sergeant Petrie to break the lock on the rear door. He, Boyden and Benjamin entered to investigate. Inside the storeroom, all was in order, but in the store area, they found signs of a struggle—a table turned on its side, one leg missing; some merchandise in disorder; a smudge of what was probably Pierce's blood on the floor. Behind the counter, in a heavy strongbox which was unlocked, they found a large canvas sack filled with coins. Boyden suggested that if robbery was the motive, as apparently it was, the thief-killer would have found the sack of coins too burdensome to carry or hide, and had been satisfied with the paper money only.

Sentries were posted at the rear and front doors with orders to permit no one to enter. Captain Breed's men removed the body to the hospital for further examination. Sergeant Major Riley arrived and Hatfield, Boyden and Riley went to the sutler's quarters. Riley broke the lock and it was discovered that the bed was still made up. There was no sign of the considerable amount of paper money they knew Pierce had taken in on a payday.

By now, the entire Fort, sentries included, knew that Sherman Pierce had been murdered by a person or persons unknown, for the purpose of robbery. Somewhere within the Fort was a thief-killer at large.

Major Boyden was placed in charge of the investigation by Colonel Hatfield.

The major sent Riley to round up as many men as he could find who were present in the store during the hour before closing time. Within an hour, between forty and fifty men were waiting at the HQ building to give their statements to Captain Greene and Riley while Boyden interviewed Lieutenant Mason-Field and Sergeant Atticus Perry.

In questioning both men, Boyden elicited from Perry the true story of the fight between Corporals Hudson and Lanier, which he had withheld from the O.D., this irregularity being dismissed by Boyden as a natural occurence under payday circumstances. Perry also added that he had checked the store after taps, that the front door had been locked and he had seen Mr. Pierce alive, alone, counting his receipts at the rear counter.

"Then, Sergeant," Boyden said, "the signs of struggle we found inside the store could be the result of the fight between Hudson and Lanier and not of one between Mr. Pierce and the man who attacked and killed him. Is that your opinion?"

"No, sir, I don't think so. Any disorder that occurred during that fight would have been cleaned up and put in order because there was still some time before taps went. My opinion is that there was a fight that followed after I had seen Mr. Pierce about ten minutes past ten."

"Very well, then. That will be all for the present." Mason-Field and Perry left.

Later, while eating his supper in the mess hall, Atticus looked across the room and saw Corporal Hudson eating his meal slowly, his jaw red and somewhat swollen. He then recalled his visit to Troop E barracks at taps to see if Hudson was all right, and that Hudson had not been in his cot or in the latrine. The thought niggled at him. Was it possible he had been in the stables, involved in a card game? Or taken a walk in the cold air to clear his drink-fogged brain? Had he then found the rear of the sutler's store open, entered, attacked and killed Pierce, stolen the money, then dragged Pierce outside and placed him under the platform, locked the rear door and thrown Pierce's keys away?

Or was Atticus seeing and reading something into the business that did not belong there; perhaps because Hudson and he had been involved in the fight in the bull ring?

He finished his meal and left the mess hall as he had entered it, alone. As usual, no one had sat near or opposite him at the table; an untouchable, to be disregarded in the presence of others. But he had overheard the conversations all around him which concerned the foremost topic of the day, the murder of the sutler.

Sherman Pierce, he gathered, had not been a popular man to most of the enlisted men. For one thing, he was a civilian, an outsider. For another, he was believed to be wealthy. Pierce never extended credit unless in an emergency, and then only on written authorization of the man's company commander; or by the adjutant, as in the case of Atticus Perry. Pierce's wife lived in comfort in a house in Tucson and the sutler, according to the gossip now emerging, had been dallying with one or two of the laundresses from Soapsuds Row after dark, a practice forbidden the Fort personnel under threat of harshest punishment. Unofficially, Pierce would loan an enlisted man ten dollars in exchange for a signed I.O.U. for twenty. In short, there were many men who might have what they considered sufficient reason, or grievance, to murder him.

Atticus was recrossing the quadrangle on his way to Troop E barracks when he heard footsteps behind him. Without turning, he moved to his right to make room for whoever was coming up on him and was surprised as the man came up beside him and slowed down to match his pace to Perry's. "Sergeant—"

The man was Corporal Hudson. "Evening, Corporal," Atticus replied.

"Sergeant, I want to apologize for last night. I'd been drinkin' with Lanier—"

"It's all right, Corporal. I didn't mean to hit you. I just wanted to keep both of you out of trouble with the O.D."

"Thanks for not puttin' us on report. Lanier an' I could of lost our stripes."

"You're welcome. Next time, better use that bull ring."

"Well—I'm kinda sorry for that, too."

"It's forgotten."

"The thing with Lanier an' me, it wasn't that important. Just drinkin' an' temper."

"I understand—"

"The boys tell me you come by lookin' for me last night."

"That's right. I wanted to make sure you got there all right."

"I did. I wasn't feelin' so good, so I went out to get some air."

"Where?"

"Oh, behind the stables."

When Atticus didn't reply, "Listen, Sergeant, I didn't go anywhere near the sutler's—"

"I didn't say you did, did I?"

"I just wanted you to know."

"I heard you."

"Listen, I—uh, well, just so you know." Hudson suddenly stepped up his pace and turned west toward the latrines. Atticus continued on to the Troop E barracks, entered and lay on his cot wondering which had been more important to Hudson—to apologize, or to impress upon

237

Atticus that he had not returned to Pierce's store after hours.

He was lying there in deep thought when the inevitable poker games began on this second night after payday, while there was still a considerable amount of money in circulation. He saw Tyler and Zentz setting up one game, Walker and Michaels arranging another. At the far end of the barracks the dice were rolling. But no one invited Atticus Perry to join the games, nor was he anxious to lose any of his remaining twenty-three dollars.

Only to be asked.

During the first week in December, Sam Palmer rode with the *vaqueros* guarding the stage from Tucson to Yuma. Inside the stage, one of the passengers was Vern Skelly, drafted from the Tucson depot to take over the Yuma office from Jeff Lennon, who wanted to be home on his horse ranch with his family for Christmas. Vern would remain until Jeff returned about the middle of January, permanently if he could be persuaded to make the move.

They picked Jeff up at the Yuma depot and Jeff arranged for Vern to take over his room at the Langtry temporarily. At supper that night, Jeff asked with impatience, "What the hell's holdin' up that Army freightin' contract, Sam?"

"Any day now, Jeff," Sam replied. "As soon as the Quartermaster can work out the contract details to Max's and the Army's satisfaction."

Vern Skelly said, "The way the Army does things it won't never get done."

"You said a mouthful," Jeff agreed. "What's more, Marty Van Allen's got Taggart sewed up in his hip pocket."

"You hinting that Van Allen and Taggart have a stake in withholding the contract?" Sam asked.

Lennon and Skelly exchanged knowing glances, then Jeff said, "Sam, either you ain't been around Tucson long enough or else you Army an' ex-Army people got a way of lookin' sideways at what's been goin' on for years. Van Allen's got a big stake in Tucson, mighty big. He's got most of the merchants buffaloed into doin' what he says. Long as goods is in short supply, prices stay sky-high. Everybody pays through his nose, but the Army pays the most. Van Allen can't afford to have T-Y bringin' in

238

supplies from Lordsburg to private citizens an' more p'tic'ly, Army supplies. It runs the Ring's prices an' profits down, an' everybody knows Van Allen *is* the Ring."

"We've gotten through so far," Sam said.

"So far. You start bringin' it through in big payloads, goin' around the storekeepers direct to the ranchers, all of a sudden you goin'a find every Apache b'tween Bowie an' Tucson hittin' your wagons."

"Now you've got Van Allen tied into dealing with Cochise."

"I ain't sayin' fer positive, but you c'n bet your last horse an' bridle he's somewheres mighty close to it."

Vern Skelly nodded in affirmation. "Don't look so danged surprised, Sam. Marty Van Allen is a big operator. He don't care where it comes from. Ask Max. He'll tell you."

"I've heard all these rumors before. If they're true, why haven't we been hit before, especially the Lordsburg-Tucson run?"

"Well," Jeff said, "so far, we ain't been haulin' what you'd call train-sized loads. Second, you got your *vaqueros* ridin' herd on the wagons. Third, when Cochise or Bokhari get their hands on enough repeatin' rifles, enough to match yours, they'll make their move, count on it. You notice they don't back off no Army convoys on account of them Army carbines ain't no better'n the stuff the Apaches got. In fact, they got exactly the same as what the Army's got. One of these days, they'll get those repeaters an' they'll be lookin' down our throats."

These old timers, Sam thought, had been around. Only a simpleton would take their opinions lightly.

Homer Howell, the Langtry's owner, came over to their table and exchanged a few words with Jeff and Vern, whom he knew. Jeff said, "You know our boss here, don't you, Homer? Sam Palmer, Homer Howell, owns this place here."

Sam said, "When Vern and I checked in, Mr. Howell wasn't around. Glad to meet you, sir."

"Likewise. Sam Palmer," Howell repeated. "Man come by a little while ago askin' about you. Looked at the register an' wanted to know if you was from Tucson."

"What was his name?" Sam asked.

"Don't know. Never seen him before. Looked like a saddlebum drifter. My boy, Otho, told him to check over to the T-Y Depot."

239

Sam's eyes drifted to a table across the room where a young man sat eating his supper. There was something strangely familiar about him and yet he was certain he had never seen him before. He looked back at Howell and asked, "That wouldn't be the man, would it?"

Howell looked across the dining room over his steel-framed glasses. "Him? Shoot, no. That's Earl Madigan. Young fella drifted in off a wagon train outfit coupla months ago lookin' f'r a steady job. Killed a gunslinger right out there in my lobby. Sheriff Kinnick hired him as a night deputy. Nice boy."

"Madigan, you said?"

"Earl Madigan," Howell repeated. "Kinda quiet. Don't think he's too happy here. Keeps to hisself mosta the time. Sleeps all day, works at night."

"He doesn't come from Kansas, does he?"

"Don't rightly know, Mr. Palmer. I never ast an' he never said."

"Well, it's not important. I may have seen him passing through Tucson."

Jeff said, "Well, you boys want to see the night life in Yuma? There's a coupla saloons, not much of anything else—"

In the Homestead Saloon, Sam, Jeff and Vern sat at a table drinking beer and discussing the T-Y operation, its expansion to Lordsburg for freight-hauling purposes. "Hell," Jeff said, "no reason why T-Y can't some day stretch all the way up to Santa Fe or even St. Louis or Fort Smith, all the way to San Diego an' Los Angeles, same as Butterfield back in '58 to '61. Five years, maybe. Alls you need is the manpower, break in drivers as you go along—"

"Sure," Vern agreed, "an' every Apache in Arizona an' New Mexico tucked in safe on some reservation—"

"Guns'll do it, too, Vern," Jeff said.

"Not as long as they get 'em as good or better'n we got—"

A tall, hard, lean man came to the table and stood behind the one empty chair. When the three men looked up at him, he smiled ingratiatingly and said to Sam, "Man over there said you was Sam Palmer of T-Y Lines, out of Tucson."

"That's right," Sam replied without returning the smile. The stranger wore a cartridge-studded belt with a Navy

240

Colt .44 suspended in a worn holster, looking as though both had seen much service.

"I'm Harry Penn. I was on my way to Tucson to look in on T-Y. Thought I'd try hittin' you up for a job, Mr. Palmer." Jeff and Vern were scrutinizing the man carefully and when Sam did not reply at once, he continued, "I know horses and I'm good with a rifle, shotgun or this." His right hand caressed the grip of the holstered .44.

Sam looked toward Jeff Lennon and said, "Jeff?"

Lennon shook his head. "Don't need no more hands on this end. What about the Tucson-Lordsburg run, Vern?"

"Maybe." Vern looked back to Harry Penn and said, "Could be a trouble run, though."

Penn laughed easily. "That won't bother me much. I rode for Clark & Williams on the San Francisco–Los Angeles run, the Sacramento run, too. Plenty of trouble with bushwhackers an' gold highjackers."

"You a driver?" Lennon asked, inspecting Penn's long, delicate hands.

"Some, in emergencies. Mostly I rode shotgun an' gold guard."

"You'd be up against Apaches in these parts," Vern said.

"Makes no difference to me, a bushwhacker is a bushwhacker whether he's wearin' furs or feathers."

Again, Jeff looked at Vern and Vern nodded imperceptibly. Jeff said, "Well, I'll be in Tucson 'til the middle of January. You get there, come see me an' we'll talk about it."

"All right with you, Mr. Palmer?" Penn asked.

"If Jeff says so, it's all right with me, Mr. Penn," Sam replied.

"Harry," Penn said, smiling again. "Thanks. I'll ride into Tucson sometime next week. I'm obliged to you, Mr. Jeff." He turned and left the saloon.

"Gunslinger," Jeff snorted with disdain.

Vern nodded. "Maybe what we need on the Lordsburg run."

Sam said, "If you hire him, Jeff, keep him on the wagon next to the driver. I don't want him riding with the *vaqueros*."

"If'n I hire him at all."

At eleven, Jeff yawned and said, "I'm fer bed. What time we leavin' in the mornin', Sam?"

241

"We'll go out with the eight o'clock stage, tie our horses on behind and ride in comfort. Got room for us, Jeff?"

"Sure. On'y three passengers for Tucson an' some light freight to carry in the boot."

They walked back to the Langtry together. The lobby was empty and only one oil lamp burned on the desk-counter. Vern and Jeff shared the same room, Sam down the hall in number twenty-two. He hung his gun belt over the head of the bed, undressed and was asleep as soon as his head hit the pillow.

How long Sam slept, he couldn't tell. When he came awake suddenly, it was pitch dark outside and the earlier night wind had died down. The thin curtains at the two windows hung still with the window farthest from him open from the bottom about three inches.

Three inches?

He could see that the window was open all the way now and instinct told him he was not alone. He lay still for a few seconds, listening, hearing nothing, then slowly began reaching for his gun, no more than twelve inches from his head. As his hand touched the leather belt, he heard the man say in a low whisper, "It ain't there, Palmer. Just keep your voice down low. I got a .44 aimed at your head, less'n six inches away."

The voice came from close beside the bed and Sam recognized it at once. "You're Penn—Harry Penn," he said slowly.

"That's right. Tell you once more, you raise your voice to call out, you won't live to see what happens next."

"Not a smart way to go about getting a job, is it?"

Penn chuckled. "You got a good sense of humor, Palmer. No, what I was doin' was sizin' you up."

"What do you want, Penn, money? It's in my pants on the chair, other side of the bed."

Again Penn laughed throatily, softly amused. "The kinda money I want, Palmer, you ain't got an' never will have. But with you, I know where to get it."

The contempt in Palmer's voice was obvious. "You're a bounty hunter?"

"Call it what you want. And I ain't in this thing alone, so don't take no fool chances or make any dumb moves. I got three men waitin' downstairs at the back of this here hotel." Sam heard some movement, the strike of a match on the tabletop, saw the flame touch the wick of

242

the bedside candle from the corner of his eye. "Now you take it real easy an' do it the way I say. Sit up slowlike, then stand up an' put your clothes on. You'll need 'em. You got a long way to go an' it's cold as a welldigger's ass outside. When we walk out of here, you first, turn left an' go down the back stairs. Once we get outside, that's all you got to worry about 'til we turn you over to the paymaster. Even dead, you got a big enough price on you, so take your choice, dead or alive. All right, start moving now, Palmer. Careful—"

Since midnight, Loren Olmstead had made one full turn of the commercial area, checking the doors of the bank, two general stores, the gate to the blacksmith's shop, barber shop and public bathhouse, three restaurants, hardware store, gunsmith's shop, saddle and harness store, and every small shop along his way. He had stopped at the livery stable and talked with Charley Ten-Gallon-Hat, the Pima night man. By the time he reached the Homestead and Golden Eagle saloons, both had closed down at the two o'clock curfew hour and, like the four Mexican *cantinas*, were dark.

He drew the collar of his jacket closer around his neck and throat and jammed ungloved hands into his pockets as he walked along. Yuma, gratefully, was finally asleep and at peace. A night lamp burned in the front office of the T-Y Depot and he tried the door, found it locked and moved past the doctor's office, the veterinarian's place next door, checking doors mechanically.

With the rest of the world abed, his thoughts turned to Aaron and Libby and Laurie, wondering if they had reached Tubac by now. Only a week ago, with nostalgic memories of many Thanksgivings back in Fort Leavenworth, he had been sorely tempted to turn in his deputy's badge to Sheriff Kinnick and ride into Tucson to inquire whether the Olmstead family had reached Tubac yet; but he had delayed his decision and out of desperation accepted an invitation from Laura Kinnick to share their Thanksgiving dinner. For the Kinnicks and their five children, it had been a memorable event; for Loren, an emotional disaster.

He wondered what had happened to the letter he had written to Aaron in care of the Postmaster at Fort Leavenworth; if it had gotten through or lay on a dirt road somewhere, victim of an Indian attack.

243

Now, Christmas would be here soon and the memories of it brought back a longing almost too much to bear. If he left Yuma only to find that Aaron, Libby and Laurie had not yet arrived, he would be in an even stranger world in Tucson than in Yuma, where he was getting to be known. He could, of course, go directly to Tubac and Tres Flechas to be with Aaron's cousins—strange that he could never think of the Potters as his own cousins—but that would only arouse curiosity and questions he felt he could not answer comfortably.

Up ahead, he saw dim light spilling out of the front windows of the Langtry Hotel where he still maintained his room at a special low rate from Mr. Howell. He wondered if Howell's son, Otho, who took the night turn, was awake, and if so, knew there would be a pot of coffee on the stove in the back room; a few minutes of respite from the biting cold. There was no wind blowing, but the December night had dropped to near-freezing temperatures.

He opened the front door which was always unlocked, and stepped into the lobby, closing the door softly behind him. Otho Howell stirred in his sleep on the long leather sofa, then sat up.

"It's me, Otho. I'm sorry I woke you."

Sleepily, " 'Sall right, Earl. Everything quiet?"

"It's quiet."

"Cold out, hey?"

"Yeah. Real cold."

"I'll make some fresh coffee."

"Don't bother—"

"Shoot, it's no bother. What time is it?"

"Close to three o'clock when I checked the T-Y Depot. I guess about three now."

"Got me three hours' sleep. C'mon, I'll put the coffee on. Won't take long."

In the room directly behind the counter, Otho put a few more sticks of wood in the stove and put the coffee pot on, then came back to the lobby and sat on a high stool and turned up the oil lamp. "Boy," he said to Loren, "you look frozen. How about somethin' to eat?"

"No. Just the coffee. That'll be enough."

"If I had your job, I'd find me a bed this time of night, maybe with somebody in it to keep me warm."

Loren grinned. "Sheriff Kinnick told me that's how the last deputy lost his job."

"Yeah, but I'll bet it was fun while it lasted. Anybody in the lockup?"

"Not a soul. Turned the last drunk loose this morning."

Somewhere in the rear, a horse neighed and pawed the earth. Loren said, "You forget to lock the stable door, Otho?"

"Not me. I checked it when I came on just before midnight. It was closed and locked."

"Sounds like a stray out back. I'll take a look."

"I'll come with you. If it is, I'll stable him 'til morning."

Otho got the keys to the stable from a hook on the key rack, put on a fleece-lined coat and followed Loren down the hallway toward the rear of the building.

When Loren opened the back door, he was momentarily startled by the sight of three men sitting there on their horses, one holding a riderless fourth. One of the men called out, "Hey—!" and Loren instinctively drew back, his hand going on his gun. Otho pressed forward to see what was going on, but Loren blocked his way.

"What's out there, Earl? What are they—?"

The man on the near horse fired and the bullet chipped several splinters from the edge of the door, only a few inches from Loren's face. He crouched, returned the fire and knocked the man out of his saddle. "Get back, Otho!" he called out.

The other two men began firing and now the four horses were rearing and bucking, interfering with their aim as they milled about. They heard Homer Howell's voice calling from his first floor room, "What the hell's goin' on out there—?"

When the first shot came, Sam Palmer was walking down the steps which led to the back exit to the stables, feeling the hard end of Harry Penn's gun in the small of his back. At that moment of the surprising sound of gunfire, the pressure on his back was relieved and he knew that Penn had been taken unaware and had moved the muzzle just enough to allow Sam to leap suddenly to one side. He heard Penn's muffled curse and the words that followed immediately, "Hold it, Palmer, don't—"

But Sam had already moved, turned and grabbed for Penn's body, aiming to pin his arms to his side. He felt a blow in the darkness, chopping downward from one step above him, but the gun barrel missed and only Penn's wrist struck him alongside his neck, glancing off his shoul-

245

der. He grabbed for that hand and held it, knowing it was the one which held the gun. Penn kicked at him and missed. Sam twisted the hand, yanked it forward, but Penn wrapped his other arm around Sam and the two struggled for a moment before they fell, tumbling the rest of the way to the bottom of the stairs. On the ground level, still in darkness, Sam struck out and with some satisfaction felt his fist connect solidly with bare flesh and bone. He followed that blow with another, then Penn moved, rolled to one side. Sam pounced on him and found his arm, twisted it upward behind his back. His other arm curled around Penn's neck and he put as much pressure into it as he could command. Penn gasped and squirmed, but could not break the hold.

Outside, the firing continued. From his crouched position, Loren dropped the second man from his saddle. The third man was still seated on his rearing, milling horse and now, with other voices rising from the hotel and Harry Penn not in sight, he wheeled his horse and streaked out of the alley and out of sight just as Homer Howell and Otho, both now armed with rifles, returned to the scene.

Loren ran out into the alley, Otho beside him. The two men lying on the ground were dead, their horses wandering toward the far end of the alley. From the stable came the nickering and neighing of other horses, the barking of the two stable dogs. Homer Howell, wearing a nightshirt under a fleece-lined outer coat, was joined by Jeff Lennon and Vern Skelly, both in long underwear, guns in hand, demanding to know what was going on. "And where's Sam Palmer? I looked in his room an' he ain't there," Vern demanded.

They heard the scuffling against the other door at the same time Homer went to it, opened it. On the landing, Sam Palmer sat upright astride Harry Penn's body, his face down, both arms pulled tightly upward.

"Good mercy o'God!" Homer exclaimed.

Now other residents of the hotel, all in various stages of undress, poured into the alley. "We'd better get inside before we all freeze to death," Homer said, helping Palmer up. To Otho, "Son, you round up them horses an' stable them."

Sheriff Jack Kinnick, notified by Loren, arrived and got the story from Palmer, Loren and Otho in the warmth of the lobby over steaming cups of coffee. Harry Penn, wrists and ankles tied, refused to talk or identify his companions. Sam Palmer dismissed the whole affair as an attempted robbery, keeping the matter of the bounty out of the discussion; but Kinnick quietly refused to accept the fact that four men would attempt to rob only one man.

By daylight, Kinnick had had the two dead bodies hauled away to the cemetery. Loren's tour of duty was over and he remained at the Langtry, Sam's guest at breakfast while Vern and Jeff went off to the Depot.

"Mr. Madigan," Sam said, "I wish I could tell you how much I appreciate your being where you were at the right time. You saved my life."

"I just happened to be there," Loren replied.

"Lucky for me you were. I'll tell you what I didn't want to tell the sheriff and have the news spread around. If it hadn't been for you, I'd be on my way with four bounty hunters riding herd on me."

"You—you're wanted?"

"Not by the law, deputy. By some people who've put a big price on my head."

"Glad I could be of help."

"You know, I can't help thinking I've seen you somewhere before, Mr. Madigan. You ever spend any time in Tucson?"

"I came through Tucson with a wagon train a couple of months ago. Dropped off here in Yuma to look for a job. Sheriff Kinnick made me his night deputy."

"I hope you'll overlook a personal question, but are you from Kansas, or have relatives there? You look so much like an Olmstead, I can't help remarking on it."

With a sudden sharp quickening of his voice, Loren said, "Olmstead? You know any Olmsteads in Tucson, Mr. Palmer?"

"Not exactly, but there's one in Tubac who—" Palmer stopped abruptly, staring closely at Loren's face. "Of course," he said softly, "you're Loren, Laurie's brother."

Excitedly now, "You know Laurie? She's in Tubac? you said—where are the others, my father and mother?"

"Let's go up to my room, Loren," Sam replied. "I'll tell you all about it."

By eight o'clock, Loren had turned his badge in to an unhappy Sheriff Kinnick, packed his few belongings and was ready to leave on the Tucson stage with Palmer, Jeff

247

Lennon and the three passengers. With them would be the driver and stage guard, and six *vaqueros* riding escort. Loren was inconsolable at the news of the deaths of Aaron and Libby but, thank God, Laurie had been spared. He sat alone with his guilt and grief, guilt at not having been with them in the desert where his gun could have made the difference; huddled in a corner and well out of the initial sporadic exchange of conversation between a whiskey drummer, an attorney and an ex-miner returning East to rejoin his family. Sam Palmer, rifle across his lap, kept his eyes on the landscape and disposition of the *vaquero* escort. Jeff Lennon slept soundly.

They passed through Corozal, spent the night at the Denton Wells relay station. Next afternoon they rolled into Mesa Plata, where they spent the second night. In the morning they left with fresh horses, heading for Fort Bandolier. From there, another 124 miles would bring them into Tucson, then only fifty-four more miles to Tres Flechas and Loren's reunion with his sister.

En route to the Fort, the stage threw a wheel, which smashed into an unseen rut and over a rock, shattering it beyond repair. It took only thirty minutes to jack the body of the stage up and replace it with the spare carried beneath the coach body, but only three miles later, that one-in-a-thousand chance mishap occurred. A second wheel collapsed and there was no spare left. Two *vaqueros* rode out and cut a small tree, trimmed it and anchored it in place to act as an Indian travois. The stage was forced to creep along at a snail's pace, stopping several times to allow the *vaqueros* time to relash the tree pole back into place. They reached Fort Bandolier at ten-thirty that night, seven hours overdue, and were furnished sleeping quarters until morning, when the blacksmith would be able to put a new wheel on.

At five-thirty next morning, the wheelwright was at work and Palmer took advantage of the delay to visit old friends with whom he had soldiered during his year and a half on duty there. He had time for a brief chat with Major Boyden, Captain Greene, several of the junior officers, Riley and Willy Logan. Others whom he would like to have talked with were out on patrol.

"You'll soon be haulin' furniture an' household goods 'til y'r eyes bug out, Sam," Riley told him.

"Whose?"

"Order's been out f'r over a month. Comes the new

year, the Fort families'll be movin' back in, wives, children, the whole kit'n kaboodle. Y'seen all the new construction work goin' on, didn' ye? New quarters, chapel, recreation huts."

"Sounds like a grand reunion."

"Aye, the grandest. It'll be a thing to see, petticoats an' bloomers hangin' on the wash lines ag'in."

"Anything new on the man who killed Sherman Pierce?" Sam asked.

"Nary a thing. All the thievin' goslin' took was paper money, no tellin' how much, an' hard to trace as a gust of wind. Pierce's wife come in, brung her brother, Fred Wheeler, out from Tucson to take over the store."

"Too bad."

"That it is. Not that anybody had too much love for Pierce, but it gives the Fort a bad name."

A patrol had been forming and now, led by Lieutenant Lewis Carpenter, passed by Riley and Palmer. Scout Willy Logan, on Carpenter's left, waved his iron hook at the two men. Behind him rode Sergeant Atticus Perry, then twenty-four troopers in a column of two's. The patrol stopped at the Main Gate to be checked out by the O.D. and once through the gates, headed east.

"That sergeant—?" Sam began.

"He's the 10th Cavalry booger Lieutenant Zimmerman found in the Apache camp in Dos Viudas. We're still waitin' for his records to come in from Fort Bliss."

"I heard something about him at Fort Lowell. He any problem?"

"Not him, but some of the men are. We'll ship him off to Bliss soon as we can. He thinks his time is about up. Be a good man to keep on as scout an' we could sure use another one. Reads sign, knows Apache talk. On'iest thing is, he's a booger."

"We might be able to use him at T-Y."

"You c'd do a whole lot worse. We been usin' him on rotation guard duty. This is his first time out on patrol, special orders from the old man hisself."

"I'd like to get a chance to talk to him. Where's Carpenter headed?"

"This side of Malhado Pass. Got a big Army freight train comin' through from Lowell. New rifles, ammunition, rations, hardware, sawed lumber, paint, clothin'. Got a full house to take care of now, plus the women an' children'll soon be comin' in."

249

"We'll catch up and ride along part of the way."

"You'll be another hour with that new wheel. How about a little coffee?"

"I could use some."

Riley called out to Mike Tyler, who was Sergeant of the Guard, "We'll be over in the mess hall, Mike. Send us word when that wheel is fixed."

The supply train from Fort Lowell was the largest destined for Fort Bandolier in the little over two years since it had been reactivated, and the first since the Fort Brennan contingent had been added to its table of organization. Twelve high-sided freight wagons, each drawn by six mules, were laden to full capacity, driven by an Army teamster and a relief driver to take over every two hours. Because of recent decreased activity of the Apache this far north of the Mexican border, Colonel Simon Taggart, the Supply Depot QM had requested an escort of only twenty-four troopers, these under command of Lieutenant Claude Ericson.

Ericson, a recent arrival at Fort Lowell, had been on similar escort duty twice before, to Fort McDowell on the Rio Verde and Camp Grant on the San Pedro. This was his first trip west of Tucson and he looked forward to seeing the terrain in the Western desert. On receiving his orders, he checked his map with his senior sergeant, a veteran who suggested that they plan to ride through Encantado at night in order to reach Malhado just before dawn. This would permit them to move through the treacherous Malhado Pass, six miles west of the town, in early daylight. Once through, the train would come into the open desert, where they could water, feed and rest the animals and allow the men to sleep for a few hours before the patrol from Fort Bandolier arrived to escort them the rest of the way.

The convoy reached Celeste by day and rattled into Encantado the following afternoon where a rest for the animals and four hours' sleep for the men was ordered. By ten-thirty that night they were well on their noisy way to Malhado on a wide, hard-packed sand road, the pace slowed down considerably because of a lack of visibility, yet able to proceed by the light of a full moon. The point rider was a good two miles ahead of the train, and because of heavy desert brush on either side of the road, all flankers had been drawn in close beside the wagons.

250

At approximately three o'clock in the morning, the point rider came upon a roadblock of logs and rocks stretched across the road and there was no doubt in his mind that its purpose boded nothing but evil. He wheeled his mount around instantly to ride back and warn Ericson, but as he did, he was cut down by an arrow from a distance of only a few yards. His horse was caught and led well off the road to a stand of trees where it was tied to a picket line.

When the train reached the obstruction, it was hit by repeated volleys of rifle fire from both sides of the road. The escort, totally unprepared for the sudden assault, took heavy losses even before they could unlimber their carbines from saddle scabbards. Milling about in confusion, it was impossible to return accurate fire at the flashes which came at them from stationary positions behind previously prepared rock and log barricades. A dozen troopers fell during the first moments of the attack. The others dropped to the ground hoping to use the wagons for cover, but the frightened mules and riderless horses were turning and twisting in terror, increasing the dangers of being killed beneath the heavy, iron-rimmed wheels of the wagons. Before they could regain their wits, the attackers came from behind their barricades, drove in quickly from both sides of the road and were among them.

Within fifteen minutes it was all over. The few dead mules were cut out, the troopers and teamsters scalped, the wagons driven off toward the south.

The T-Y stage, with its driver, conductor, five passengers and six *vaqueros*, left Fort Bandolier at seven o'clock in the morning and caught up with Lieutenant Carpenter's slower moving patrol less than four hours later, then fell in behind about a quarter of a mile and adopted a more leisurely pace.

"Why don't we get ahead of 'em?" the whiskey drummer asked.

"If we do," Palmer replied, "we just might meet the Army supply train inside the Pass and won't have room to get past them or turn around. Malhado Pass is narrow and twisty and about three miles long, so we couldn't back out of it. We'll make up the lost time between Malhado and Encantado, all flat ground."

The drummer mumbled a reply, then settled back into sleep, hat brim pulled down over his eyes. Jeff Lennon snored peacefully. Loren Olmstead had been rocked to sleep, too, while the ex-miner and lawyer chatted amiably and smoked cigars. Sam Palmer's mind was on Laurie, her surprise at seeing Loren again, some measure of happiness, yet a reawakening of the tragic deaths of their parents. Somewhere, somehow, Loren must be fitted into T-Y Lines and the Potter family. He wondered what Caroline would think of Loren, what her reaction would be.

Up ahead, Lieutenant Carpenter had stepped up the pace and when it slowed down after a few miles, Palmer looked out and saw the yawning mouth of Malhado Pass about four miles to the east. The patrol came to a halt three miles farther on and the stage driver pulled up closer to the escort patrol. Sam got out and saw Carpenter riding back toward the coach.

"Something wrong, Lieutenant?"

"I don't know, Sam. I understood the train would be camped on this side of the Pass. I was ordered to take it easy to give them time to get some sleep. I sent Willy Logan ahead half an hour ago and he just came back with word there's nothing in sight."

Palmer thought for a moment, then said, "Give me your sergeant and Willy and I'll take the stage and my six *vaqueros* and ride through to Malhado. They may have had a breakdown."

Carpenter made his own decision. "No, Sam. I think we'd better go on through. We'll take the lead while your *vaqueros* fall in at the rear of your stage. Will you ride ahead with me?"

Sam nodded and gave his driver and *vaqueros* their orders. He untied his horse, mounted and flanked Carpenter's left while Sergeant Perry rode on his right, Logan taking the point.

They moved through the Pass with carbines and rifles at the ready, eyes fixed on the upper rims of the canyon, but there was no sight of anyone above them, nor did they receive any warning shots from Logan. Once out of the long narrow, twisting canyon, they picked up speed. The stage took a brief ten minutes at the relay station for a change of horses, fresh coffee, picked up a new spare wheel and information, but neither the Mexican in charge nor his hostlers had any knowledge of the westbound Army convoy.

Carpenter then decided to go on as far as Encantado

and if they did not run across the convoy during those next twenty-six miles, he would consider that it had been delayed at its point of origin and return to Fort Bandolier.

Twelve miles east of Malhado, they found the bodies of the two dozen soldier-teamsters, the twenty-four trooper escorts and Lieutenant Ericson, scattered on both sides of the road, along with the carcasses of eight of the original seventy-two mules in the train. Logan, who had ridden ahead, was standing at the near edge of the macabre scene when Palmer, Carpenter and Perry galloped up. Carpenter sent Perry to keep the others far enough back in order to avoid unnecessary trampling of the grounds until Logan and Palmer could read and evaluate all tracks and signs.

When Logan and Palmer had concluded their examination, Carpenter ordered all personal belongings of the dead to be gathered and marked for identification, a common grave dug. Perry set the men about the grisly task, then walked among the tracks to study the markings left behind while Logan and Palmer reported their findings to Carpenter.

"Sam?"

"I make it between thirty and forty attackers," Palmer said. "From some of the horse droppings and body temperatures of the men, I'd say it happened somewhere between two and four o'clock this morning. Horses were hidden in those trees on the right side of the road, the roadblocks set up and the train hit from both sides of the road."

"Willy?"

Logan nodded in agreement. "I make it the same way, Lieutenant. I picked up these .56-.56 cartridge casings. Looks like they were using Spencer 8-shot repeaters against Army single-shot carbines. Plenty of .36 and .44 revolver casings, Starr or Colt Navy '51 models. Could of been the troopers—"

"Something doesn't add up here," Carpenter said.

"The night attack, Lieutenant?" Palmer said. "What it adds up to is that in spite of the arrows and the scalpings, they weren't Apaches. Whoever it was, they wanted the Army to think so, using unshod horses."

"They slipped up a bit," Logan added.

"How?"

"Except for the scalpin', no other mutilation. An Apache has time to scalp, he takes time to mutilate.

Wasn't nobody around to worry about, so they had the time. Another thing, them revolver shell casings are scattered all over the place, shows the attackers were usin' them, too. Apaches use rifles for both distance an' close up. A revolver is just so much useless weight for 'em to carry."

Perry returned then with added confirmation. "Over there, south of the road, Lieutenant, a couple of their horses fell and got up again, but left saddle markings in the sand. Mexican saddles with hooded stirrups. Here—" Perry held up a length of braided rawhide—"this is part of a *reata* tore loose. Pure Mexican. Apaches use a woven grass rope. Also, some of them got careless and smoked cigarillos while they waited. A dozen butts over in that thicket where they picketed their horses. Then, all these barricades, no Apache would use anything like that. I'd say there were between thirty and thirty-five of them."

"Well—" Carpenter was studying the situation.

Palmer said, "We're going all the way into Tucson, Lieutenant. If you want, I'll take your report in to Fort Lowell."

After a moment, Carpenter said, "No. I'll send three men back to the Fort to report this and go on to Lowell and break the news in person." To Perry, "Sergeant, I want Corporal Keller and two men for that detail."

"Yes, sir."

Loren, Jeff Lennon, the *vaqueros*, stage driver and stage guard worked with the troopers to complete the work. The three passengers remained apart, in the vicinity of the stage. When the mass interment was finished, Carpenter said a brief service over the grave. Corporal Keller and his two men rode westward to Fort Bandolier while the patrol and stage began its ride toward Encantado, Celeste and Tucson.

Palmer, meanwhile, had sent two of his *vaqueros* southward to follow the trail of the stolen wagons, with orders to keep out of harm's way, then return to Tres Flechas to wait for him there.

Benito Macias and Alonso Maderos, as usual in the presence of Anglos, kept their own counsel during the discovery, discussions and burial of the bluecoats, but now, riding southward on orders from Palmer, they followed the elaborately written trail left in the desert sand by the dozen iron-tired wagons, horse and mule tracks.

"It is child's work, this," said Alonso, the younger of the two.

"For now, yes," Benito remarked.

"And later?"

"You will see. They will find a place and rid themselves of that which they do not want. They will burn the wagons and use the mules to carry away on their backs that which they wish to keep. Then they will ride over loose stones in the dry river bed until they come to the malpais in the foothills. Once they cross the mountain into Sonora, they will be safe. And rich."

"*El hijo del patrón*, he has the eye of an eagle, no?"

"Señor Sam? Ai-ee, he can read the trail of a hawk in flight."

"Then these were not the Indios?"

Macias snorted and spat in the sand. "No, *muchacho*. They were our own. Evil men. Lizardi's *vagos, bandoleros* who deal with the Apache for gold."

"You know it is Lizardi?"

"Who else has so many *bandidos*? It is Lizardi. I know him well. He comes from my village, Cienguilla, south of Monte Babiacora where the Apaches have many camps and are safe from the Anglo *soldados*. The *rurales* fear them. The villagers fear them. So they live together thus. Renegades like Lizardi bring guns and food to the Indios and take gold to spend in Sonora and Tucson on tequila and women. For them it is a quicker way to earn money than by working."

Alonso said nothing and Benito suspected that his young companion was thinking that perhaps Lizardi's way of life was not too far wrong. "Do not linger too long with your dreams of such riches and glory, *joven*," he said. "Better to think of the girl you will one day marry, the children she will bear you, the joys of living in peace with a good woman instead of like a pig among whores."

Late that afternoon they came to a shaded woods and followed the tracks to its edge. Benito signaled Alonso to dismount and stay with their horses while he scouted ahead on foot. An hour passed before Benito returned.

"We will eat and go back. It is as I have said. They have burned the wagons and lumber and taken the mules to carry the stolen goods. They have left behind the Army clothes, tools, nails, paint. The food, guns and bullets are gone, south toward the mountains."

"We will not follow them?"

"There is no need. They are six hours ahead of us and will reach Sonora long before we can catch up with them. And if we did, what can two do? Therefore, we will ride east and south to Tres Flechas. It will be good to be home again, even for the few days, until *el patrón* and Señor Sam come from Tucson."

Lieutenant Carpenter reported the attack on the convoy first to Colonel Michael Hardy, deputy commander of Fort Lowell, then to General Edwin Rossiter, the Fort commander. Rossiter at once sent word to General Lucius Litchfield, then sent for Colonel Simon Taggart, the QM, and Major Norman Rood, the Inspector General's deputy. Sam Palmer was then brought in and repeated substantially what Carpenter had told the four officers. It was Colonel Taggart who was not entirely satisfied with the story.

"Much of what you and Lieutenant Carpenter have told us, Mr. Palmer, is pure assumption, is it not?" he asked.

"I was not there when it happened, Colonel," Sam replied. "I have reported what we all saw. The rest was clearly indicated by sign."

"Sign?"

"Yes, sir."

"You are an expert interpreter of sign, Mr. Palmer?"

"Sir—" Lieutenant Carpenter interrupted.

"I am addressing Mr. Palmer, Lieutenant," Taggart barked with severity.

General Rossiter said gently, but firmly, "Colonel, I might suggest that this is an informal inquiry. Let the Lieutenant speak. Mr. Carpenter?"

Carpenter, mollified now, said, "I merely intended to add that Mr. Palmer was on active duty as a sergeant at Fort Bandolier until his discharge some five months ago. He was highly regarded as a scout and tracker as well as a student of the Apache language and their customs. Also, since Colonel Taggart was not here at the time, it was Sergeant Palmer who brought in Anaka's head after the Monte de Lágrimas battle, and for which he was commended by Colonel Hatfield, General Litchfield and Governor Mitchell. His opinion in this matter is backed up by our chief civilian scout, Mr. Logan, and by Sergeant Perry, who lived among the Comanches, Navajos and

256

Apaches as a prisoner for almost nineteen months. My official account is based on their expert findings."

Rossiter turned to Taggart with a faint smile. "Any further questions, Colonel?" he asked.

"No, sir," Taggart replied, adding, "and I thank the Lieutenant and Mr. Palmer for enlightening me."

"There will be a further inquiry, gentlemen," Rossiter said. "I am certain that General Litchfield will so order it when he has conferred with Governor Mitchell. I want a written report from you, Lieutenant, and if Mr. Palmer will oblige us similarly, I will appreciate it. Also, one from Mr. Logan and Sergeant Perry. Will you see to it, Major Rood? For the present, that will be all, and thank you very much."

CHAPTER III

IN THE GOVERNOR'S STUDY, THE REPORTS OF LIEUTENANT Carpenter, Sam Palmer, Willy Logan and Sergeant Atticus Perry lay on his desk while Governor Mitchell paced the floor. Earlier, he had discussed the matter with General Litchfield, the politically-oriented son-in-law of United States Senator Oren Beall. It was Litchfield's position that the fault lay with the Fort Bandolier command for having failed to maintain wider-ranging patrols since its complement—"on your orders, I might add, Governor—was substantially increased over two months ago."

When Litchfield left the governor's mansion an hour later, Max Potter and Sam Palmer arrived and were shown into the study by the governor's aide.

"Thank you for coming, Max, Mr. Palmer. I know how busy you must be."

"Always have time for the Governor of Arizona, Brett," Max replied. "What can we do for you?"

"I have the reports filed by Lieutenant Carpenter, Scout Logan, Sergeant Perry and Mr. Palmer on my desk. I want to hear Mr. Palmer's version in support of these reports in less formal terms."

"Sir," Sam said, "those reports are substantially accurate in every detail. I have read the others—"

"I want more than surface details, Mr. Palmer. Facts. You state that the attackers were not Apaches. If not, who were they? What is behind all this? How do we prevent it from recurring?"

Max said, "Brett, the best anybody can do is read and interpret what signs are left behind. I think Sam and your people have done the best they could. They are sure it was done by Mexicans, but if you want names, you've got to go on pure assumption—"

"Then, dammit, let's do some assuming. I've spent too many years in the Army not to recognize when something is out of kilter, and I want to know what it is. I'm not as satisfied to dismiss this as easily as Litchfield is. We've lost

258

forty-eight men, seventy-two mules, twenty-four horses and twelve wagonloads of hard to replace food, guns, ammunition, clothing and other supplies. We can't afford to have this happen again, not ever. Dammit, if we can't protect our own, how can others expect us to protect them? Mr. Palmer?"

"Well, sir, if we can assume, I'd say the animals and ammunition and guns will find their way into the hands of Bokhari's Apaches, even though I am certain the raid was not committed by them. The food will be put to use or sold off along with some of the other hard goods. The clothing is of no use to anyone but the Army, so it will have been burned along with the wagons—"

"Who?" Mitchell spat the word out.

Max Potter shrugged. "Renegades who've been dealing for years with Juan Jose, Mangas Colorados, Cochise, Anaka, Tan-Hay, Bokhari, Vicenzo and others I can name. Cochise has gold that's got no use except to buy what he can't steal. Look at the manifest of that convoy. Two hundred and fifty brand new repeating rifles, sixty cases of rifle ammunition, thirty of revolver. Everybody knows Bokhari needs guns to make up for what Anaka lost and he'll pay upwards of one hundred dollars in gold for every rifle he can lay his hands on, more than double that for a new repeater. That adds up to one hell of a lot of money for any bushwhacker or renegade to take chances Bokhari can't afford right now. You can bet Colonel Hatfield's boys are goin'a begin feeling the effect pretty damned soon. Or Mesa Plata, the Carancho Valley ranchers, everybody west of here and south of the Gila."

"Admitted, admitted," Mitchell said, then, "Max, could you have gotten through where the Army failed?"

"I'll let Sam answer that one, Brett. He's in charge of operations and logistics."

"Well, Mr. Palmer?"

"I've given it a lot of thought, Governor, and I think we could. We'd never send out twelve wagons that heavily loaded. I think we'd use twenty-four wagons, carrying lighter loads and send them through in six groups of four so they could travel faster and lose less if they were hit, each group with six men riding well enough ahead and on either side to scout."

"But this was at night."

"And it should have been by day, making better time, resting at night. The Army's problem, sir, is that it has no

259

relay stations between Lowell and Bandolier to rest the men and change tired animals for fresh ones. T-Y Lines has three. We may take a little longer some times, or go faster at others, but we have a safety factor the Army hasn't.

"Another thing, the manifest shows that all the rifles were in one wagon, the ammunition in another. We'd divide everything equally among all wagons so that if we lost one, two, even three or four wagons, we wouldn't lose all of any one item."

"Goddamn it," Mitchell barked angrily, "why can't those dunderheads at Lowell think the same way?"

"Well, Brett," Max said slyly, "maybe it's because they're soldiers first an' freighters second. All the more reason why the Army shouldn't be in the freightin' business."

Mitchell stood up and resumed pacing, then went to the door and threw it wide open. To the sergeant-orderly on duty, he snapped, "Get my aide in here at once."

"Yes, *sir!*"

He closed the door and said, "All right, Max, no more shilly-shallying from Colonel Taggart. By tomorrow morning, he'll have a contract ready for you to sign. Be in his office no later than ten o'clock. And Palmer, I want you to give Taggart's warehouse men instructions on how you want your wagons loaded."

Max and Sam rose and Potter said, "Thank you, Brett. Always a pleasure to do business with you."

That night, Colonel Simon Taggart and Martin Van Allen met in an unused line rider's cabin on the Van Allen ranch on the Santa Cruz River.

"I couldn't do a damned thing about it, Van," Taggart said. "I've stalled that contract ever since T-Y began operating, but I couldn't say no to a direct order from Litchfield after the governor got through raking him over the coals. As of tomorrow, T-Y takes over hauling Army freight to any point outside a thirty-mile area of Fort Lowell."

"How long and how much, Si?" Van Allen asked.

"One year, starting tomorrow. Fifteen hundred tons minimum at thirty-five dollars a ton per hundred miles. Also, because it relieves a lot of teamsters for other duty, we supply escort on certain hauls into known hostile country when requested."

260

"That's better than fifty-sixty thousand dollars minimum for the first year, enough to show a good profit."

"I did my best, Van. That damned raid did the trick for T-Y. What's more, they'll be getting their mail franchise pretty soon and—"

"Yeah. All right, Si, you did your best. I'll have to work out something else. Also, I want you to know I didn't have anything to do with that raid."

"Then it must have been Lizardi and his people working on their own. The reports show definitely it wasn't Apache work."

"That's something else I've got to look into. You might as well go back now. Keep me posted on what goes out and where. And when."

"Of course, Van, but if it was Lizardi, you ought to—"

"I'll handle Lizardi, Si. Leave him to me."

It was close to midnight when Martin Van Allen entered Espuela de Oro. He went directly to the bar and ordered a drink, then turned, leaned his back against the top rail and looked across the room to where Casimiro Lizardi sat at his usual corner table playing cards with his three lieutenants, Julio Campos, Orlando Vega and Hector Moreno. He knew Lizardi had seen him when he came into the *cantina,* yet Lizardi did not look up or in any other way acknowledge his presence. Van Allen ordered another drink and waited.

Out of the corner of his eye, Casimiro Lizardi was indeed aware of Van Allen's presence and hesitated to show the Anglo he had seen him, formulating answers for the questions he knew Van Allen would ask. He studied his cards carefully until Campos said, "Casimiro, it is your play."

Lizardi looked up, glanced back to his cards, then threw them face down in the center of the table. "It is not my night, *amigos. A bruja* rides on my shoulders." He gathered up the money in front of him and pocketed it. "Play among yourselves. I will return soon."

Lizardi circled past tables with late diners and drinkers, spurs clinking as he moved along, touching a shoulder here and there, responding to several who greeted him. Lizardi was a tall, dark man with sharp, angular features, a drooping mustache over thin lips. His clothes were traditional Mexican in style, with a short vest-jacket of black, embroidered with rows of silver thread, its buttons made of large, pierced Mexican silver coins. His black trousers were close-fitting to show the strength of his legs and his boots were high-heeled and treated with silver-threaded designs.

Casimiro Lizardi had no known occupation, owned no land or house or business, yet he was never without money and always with at least three or four followers in attendance, to drink and gamble with, share the girls who were readily available to men with money. He could be charming or cruel as called for, despotic in his demand for loyalty. His hand gun was a late model six-shooter with mother-of-pearl and silver handgrip, and it hung loosely at his right side in a silver-ornamented holster within easy reach of his hand.

Where he came from originally in Mexico was known by only a very few and very few were inclined to inquire deeper; but there were rumors that he had ridden with at least two notorious guerrillas, Aragon in Chihuahua and Galindo in Sonora, both now dead. There were others, rumor or legend, that Lizardi had, in his youth, lived with a tribe of Apaches, married into the tribe, then left when his wife was killed, victim of a raid by U.S. Cavalry troops. Only this much was known to be true: his deep hatred for white men everywhere, with particular emphasis on soldiers, either Mexican or American. It was one of his deeper disappointments that the son of Inez Espuela refused to align himself with what had come to be known as Lizardi's *vagos,* or vagabonds. In Tucson, his informal headquarters was Espuela de Oro, but for security reasons he seldom slept twice in the same house.

He made his way past the bar without showing the least sign that he had recognized Van Allen, then went through a door that led into a hallway to the rear of the building. He walked to the last door on the right side and knocked three times, then three times more. From inside, he heard Inez Espuela call out, "Casimiro?"

"Yes."

"I come."

He heard the grating of a key in the lock, then a bolt sliding. The door opened and he entered a two-room apartment, Inez's private quarters, which was large and comfortable, with many pieces of furniture scattered around. In the room beyond, to which he had retreated, Inez stood before a long mirror, in the act of changing her clothes. There was a large brass bed, clothes heaped across chairs and bulging out of two large wardrobes. A partially eaten meal stood on a tray on the table beside her bed. Inez was clothed except for her dress. She was past her mid-thirties, a woman whose face and figure belied the fact that she was the mother of a twenty-two-year-old son. She had borne Marcos when she was fifteen, as tall and womanly then as she was now.

When Casimiro entered, she was tugging a tight-fitting bottle-green dress over her voluptuous figure, showing no qualms at his presence.

"Help me, eh?" she said. "I can shout my lungs out and that *gorrón* Tereza stuffs her ears with cotton so she cannot hear me."

Lizardi helped draw the dress down over her body. "Green becomes you, Inez," he complimented.

"Gracias," she replied, pleased. "What is so important you cannot wait until I am finished here?"

"He is outside. He will be here in a minute." There was no doubt who Lizardi meant by *he.*

"Eh? I will be ready by then. What is it this time?"

Lizardi shrugged. "Do not ask questions, *querida.*"

"So. You use me, he uses me, but I am to keep quiet and know nothing."

"He uses you and I use you, but in different ways, no? And you are well-rewarded by both of us, so it pays you to keep quiet and know nothing, *es verdad?"*

"Ah, Casimiro, men think they are so clever. If you are close-mouthed, you believe all men are close-mouthed. But you are fools, all of you."

"Eh? *Cómo?"*

Inez laughed. "You are so clever, I will tell you. An hour after you returned to Tucson last night, I knew who had attacked and robbed the soldiers between Encantado and Malhado. Mules, horses, guns—"

"Hold your tongue, Inez."

"Tell that to your *vagos,* Casimiro. I am much better at holding my tongue than they, or the girls they sleep with."

Lizardi frowned, then smiled. "Yes. Yes, you are."

"Have you traded the goods yet?"

"Not yet. There was no time. It lies buried and guarded in Sonora. In a few days I will go to see Bokhari."

"A profitable night's work."

"A costly one. We lost nine men dead and four wounded. We had to carry them away with us."

"Where are they now?"

263

"We buried the dead in the mountains and sent the wounded to Clemente to heal. Speak not of this to anyone, not even *him*."

"You did this without his knowledge?" Inez asked in surprise. "You are a fool, Casimiro. He will be angry."

"Then let him be angry. I cannot wait around for him to make up his mind while valuable goods move from fort to fort. One day, I will no longer need him—"

They heard Van Allen's knock on the door. Inez patted her hair into place and went to open the door. As Van Allen entered, she said in Spanish, "Martin, I greet you. My house is yours."

"Hello, Inez. You look well, as usual."

"*Gracias.* I go now to visit with my customers."

When she left, Van Allen bolted the door and turned to Lizardi, who was pouring a drink for himself. "Tequila, *amigo?*" he asked.

"Not now. We have business to discuss."

"So?"

"The business of the Army convoy you raided four nights ago."

"I, *amigo?*"

"You, Lizardi. There is no one else who can muster so many men to take on the Army, except Bokhari, but this was not the work of Apaches. Also, you were stupid to try to make it look that way."

"So."

"So. I will tell you once more, Casimiro. You have grown fat doing my bidding. If you go into business for yourself, it will be without me."

"Then maybe I have grown fat enough that I do not need you, Martin."

Van Allen flinched at this new familiarity. "So it is 'Martin' now."

"I am Casimiro to you, why should you not be Martin to me, eh?"

Van Allen let it pass for the moment. "What do you intend to do with the Army goods, Casimiro?"

"I will tell you, Martin. I will do what I have always done with guns I got from you. I sell them to the Apaches. Bokhari needs them and I have waited too long to get them from you. So now I have 250 fine guns and much ammunition which I will sell to him for gold, which I need to keep my men together."

"Then we do not work together any longer?"

"It is as you wish. I can work with you or without you."

"You need me, Lizardi. This one time you were lucky. Next time, the Army will not be fooled. Even this time, it was I who told you of the shipment and told you not to touch it."

"But I did and I have what I wanted, no?"

"Yes, but who will tell you next time, *amigo?*"

Lizardi remained silent.

Van Allen said, "You cannot fight the Ring *and* the Army, Casimiro. It has been tried before and failed. I work with others and between us we have arranged to keep the Apaches armed, in blankets and horses so that the Army must be kept here to spend much money in Tucson. We cannot allow you to compete with us. It is because of us that you have followers, money and horses. If we turn on you, the Army will wipe you and your men out first. We will see to that."

"Then whose guns will you hire, *amigo?*" Lizardi asked.

"Ah, Casimiro, you are a fool. You were not the first, nor will you be the last. Once your money is spent, what comes next? Think it over before you measure your size against mine."

Lizardi thought quietly and quickly. "You wish a share of this thing?"

"On the same basis as before."

"I have my men to answer to. I have promised them a larger share than before. They will expect me to keep my word."

"And I expect the same of you. The thing is, do you wish to continue on your own or work with me?"

Casimiro took a full thirty seconds before he answered. "I will work with you, *señor,*" he replied finally.

The *"señor"* was Lizardi's capitulation and Van Allen knew when to stop pressing. "Very well, Casimiro. You will conclude the business with Bokhari. First, you will give me a list of what you have kept, goods and animals, then I will set the amount of gold you must get from him."

"I will send the list to you tomorrow."

"Good. And in the future, you will not work alone or separate from me. I will give the orders. You and your men will follow them." Van Allen held out a hand and Lizardi shook it in agreement. Then Van Allen said, "Go back to your card game. And send Inez here to me."

Lizardi went out, cursing the Anglo under his breath.

In Monte Babiacora, an hour's ride from his main camp, Bokhari sat alone in his wickiup, deep in thought. On the night before, he had held a council with Vicenzo and the twelve subleaders whose braves were scattered through these hills in strategically located camps, ready to move in any direction at his given word.

The members of his council were young and eager to show their courage in the field, but Bokhari had held them in restraint. Each brave had spoken his thoughts, shown a strong desire to go foraging into Anglo territory, and this was good. He had listened with great patience as his father, Heah-Lik, had taught him, giving each of them his time to speak what was on his mind. He was in no great hurry.

And then Bokhari spoke. He was pleased, he said, and proud of each of them. Eagerness and courage were Apache virtues that would bring their own rewards, and this was good. Their words reflected honor upon themselves as individuals and upon the entire tribe, and this, also, was good. However, he added, one must temper anxiety with wisdom.

"If we seem to do little but wait, then we do so for a good reason. Listen, brothers. Our rifles are old and worn and in use, sometimes they do not fire well or at all. Many of our braves have no rifles at all. I have told you that I arranged with the Mexican, Lizardi, to bring new rifles. He promised me fifty or sixty soon and these I will give to you for your braves who lack them. But they are not enough.

"Now, word has reached me that many wagons of the White Eyes, carrying many more rifles and bullets, have been attacked and the White Eyes soldiers killed. We are here together, so we know this was done by someone else and it is my belief that it was the Mexican, Lizardi, because I have promised him much yellow iron for every new rifle he brings to us.

"In a short time, he will come and we will have many times the fifty or sixty rifles he promised me. New rifles that shoot straighter and for longer distances every time. Hear me, brothers, I say now that when we have those rifles, each brave in these mountains will have one for his own, with many bullets. When this happens, we will gather once more in council and make our plans to use them. No longer will we sit and wait—"

This morning, Bokhari had left the main camp with his young wife, Lo-Kim, and sons Malha, who was now eight, and Tanzay, who was seven. With him also was Vicenzo

266

and his wife, three other subleaders, their wives, and six
armed braves to serve as guards. Among them, there were
five children. They reached this camp beside a small
mountain stream in peaceful surroundings, a valley whose
Indian name meant Where-Fresh-Water-Runs-Between-
Mountains, and which was reserved for the use of Bokhari and his chosen guests.

While the others raised their wickiups and the children
bathed and played beside the stream, Bokhari slept with
Lo-Kim for a while, then sent her to fetch Malha and
Tanzay. As he did on every occasion possible, and as
Heah-Lik had done for him, he instructed his sons in the
history, legends and lore of the Apaches. They repeated his
words after him and he questioned them in depth, pleased
with their answers. Two hours later, Lo-Kim brought food
for her husband and stepsons and when they had eaten,
Bokhari sent the boys away with Lo-Kim so that he could
be alone and meditate in peace.

He was disappointed that he had not yet led his braves
against the White Eyes as he had promised Cochise. Without new guns, they were vulnerable to the ranchers and
soldiers, except in large numbers, and even then it was
easy to see that a small victory was not worth the heavy
losses they would sustain. He knew that the White Eyes
fort now contained over 325 men and not the hundred he
had been led to believe. He had himself scouted Mesa
Plata and the Carancho Valley and knew the miners and
ranchers there were heavily armed. And in Sonora, he had
taken as much food and as many animals that he could
without driving the villagers off their land. So it was all a
matter of guns and ammunition. For this, he must con-
serve the gold Cochise had given him. And so meditating,
he fell asleep.

Some hours later, when the sun was westering, he was
awakened by soft footsteps beside his pallet. He rose on
one elbow and saw it was Lo-Kim.

"Eh?"

"Tarqua comes with word from the camp, Great One.
The Mexican has come with three others."

Bokhari sat up. "Bring Tarqua to me. And Vicenzo."

They came in together and Bokhari said, "Speak, Tarqua."

"The Mexican, Lizardi, comes with three men. He is in
the main camp and asks to speak to the Great One."

"The guns. He has brought the guns?"

"He has brought no guns, but he and his men have them nearby. Many guns. Many bullets. He waits for the Great One."

To Vicenzo, "We leave at once. The men only. The women and children will remain here with the six guards."

The horses were ready. They rode off swiftly, crossing the valley, climbing upward and disappearing over a crest. Within the hour, they had reached the base camp where the four unarmed Mexicans sat in a wickiup guarded by six braves, with most of the camp gathered around it watching; waiting for Bokhari's arrival.

They spoke in Spanish, Bokhari's somewhat difficult to understand beneath his guttural Apache. "Where are the guns?"

"I have them," Lizardi replied. "Two hundred and fifty new pieces and many bullets."

"Where?"

"Three hours' ride from here. First, we will talk about the gold."

"I have the gold. Tell me about the guns."

"They are new, never used before. Each can fire many times before there is a need to reload it. They are the best anywhere."

"Bring them here."

"When I have the gold. I must ask two hundred dollars for each gun. Ten ounces of gold for each piece. There are also sixty cases of bullets for the guns and I must ask twenty ounces for each case."

The elated Bokhari was in no mood to dicker. "I will have it measured out. The guns, where are they?"

"When we have the gold, made up in four sacks, four of your braves will follow us and carry it to where the guns and bullets are hidden. When they see that all is as I have said it is, we will take the gold and go. Then one of your braves will ride back here and bring many men to carry the guns and bullets back with them."

"What of the mules and horses?"

"Next time we will bring the mules and horses."

"*Enju*. Vicenzo!"

"Yes, Great One."

"Begin measuring the gold."

The exchange was made in the rocky foothills of the Oro Blanca Mountain where the guns and ammunition had been cached. Lizardi, Campos, Vega and Moreno each took a sack of gold and tied it firmly to his saddle pommel. Vicenzo sent one of the men back to bring more men and animals to pack the rifles and ammunition back to the main camp, sending one rifle and a small box of bullets to Bokhari so he could sample his buy.

Lizardi and his men left at once, wary of a possible trap. By nightfall, they had reached Pena Oro Lake, where they made a dry camp, watered and fed their horses, then ate a cold meal of meat, beans and tortillas, huddled together with blankets covering their bodies against the night cold, unwilling to light a fire.

None was pleased when Lizardi told them that the gold must be shared with the Anglo, Van Allen. For the first time there was serious dissension over the fact that this had been a thing of their own doing and why should they give up half the rewards to one who had nothing to do with it? But Lizardi overcame their objections by explaining to them that without Van Allen, none would have known of the supply train and thus there would have been no attack; also, that if they broke their ties with the Anglo over the gold, it would not be long before the soldiers would be out hunting them instead of the Apaches.

Yet, here at Pena Oro Lake, the thought rankled Lizardi no less than the sore that festered in the bosoms and minds of his three closest lieutenants.

Campos again brought his feelings into the open. "The Anglo," he said suddenly. "Maybe we should kill him."

"It is a thought," Moreno said.

Vega, munching on a tortilla, added, "It would not be a difficult thing—"

"You are fools," Lizardi snapped. "All you can see is the tips of your noses. So we kill him and keep all the gold. What then? Tomorrow, next month, next year, eh? Who will keep us informed? Who will supply us with other guns, blankets and goods that we sell to the Apaches, eh?"

"But half the gold—" Campos muttered.

"So it has always been, no? We will give him his share and still have more to divide among us than ever before. And I say it is nothing."

"Nothing?" Campos parrotted. Moreno and Vega looked toward Lizardi.

"It is nothing to compare with what I have in mind for us, *amigos*, a thing in which the Anglo will have no share."

The others were interested to the point of remaining re-

269

spectfully silent. "You have trusted me before, *compadres*, so trust me now," Lizardi continued. "I will say no more to you except that I am planning a thing that will bring us more gold than any of you has ever seen. What it is must remain with me for the time because it is a fact that when one man knows a secret, it remains a secret. When two or more know it, it is no longer a secret, eh?"

But Lizardi had not reckoned with Campos' intelligence. He looked up and said, "More gold than any of us has ever seen? Then you speak of the reward for the Anglo Palmer, no, Casimiro?"

Lizardi showed his disappointment and Moreno and Vega smiled at Campos' clairvoyant suggestion. For a moment, Lizardi merely looked at Campos angrily, then said, "Yes. It is Palmer."

Vega snorted. "With *vaqueros* always at his side wherever he goes, *amigo?*"

"There is a way, Orlando. I have thought it out carefully during many sleepless nights. We four can carry out the plan and thereafter live like kings. Mexico, California, anywhere we please, not as *bandoleros* but as *caballeros*, with our own estates and servants."

"To take Palmer," Moreno said, "we would need an army—"

Lizardi smiled with complacent laziness. "Such is the beauty of my plan, Hector, that four will be enough. It is why Casimiro Lizardi leads and others follow. With my plan, *we do not take Palmer*. He will give himself up."

"Give himself up—it is insanity to think that he would do such a thing. Even you—" Vega began, but Campos cut him off sharply.

"Let Casimiro speak before you pass judgment, wise one."

"Listen well," Lizardi said. "I have lived among Anglos longer than any of you. I have worked with them, dealt with them, know them well, how their Anglo minds work. They are hard in battle, but soft as children in other matters. Trust me, *amigos*—"

They brought the gold into Tucson two nights later. A boy was sent with a message to Martin Van Allen, who came to meet Lizardi in the back room of Espuela de Oro. With a few changes, Lizardi related the details of his meeting with Bokhari and the exchange of gold for rifles and ammunition. On the table between them lay three sacks of gold.

"The price you set, *señor*," Lizardi said, "was too high. Bokhari had not that much gold, only enough to pay a little more than half of what I asked."

"You accepted?"

"What else could I do, *señor*? If I refused, what would I do with such a load? If I left him without taking the gold, he would send men to track back and discover the guns and ammunition and take everything without payment. I took the three sacks of gold."

"Lizardi, you are lying to me."

Lizardi shrugged. "I have three witnesses—"

"Your own men."

"Who else would I have with me, *señor*? If you do not believe me, there is Bokhari—"

"Whom you know I cannot afford to meet."

"Then—" Lizardi raised his hands, palms upward and outward in a suggestion of hopeless stalemate.

There was little else Van Allen could do but accept Lizardi's story. Inez brought the scales in. Two of the sacks were of equal weight. The third was divided and Van Allen left with one full and one half-filled sack, leaving the rest with Lizardi. It was over and Lizardi took great delight in having cheated the Anglo out of a full sack of gold, giving each of his scattered henchmen a larger share.

Back at his table with Moreno, Campos and Vega, their earlier disappointment was somehow softened by Lizardi's clever handling of the distribution of the gold, and over a bottle of tequila, Campos asked, "And now?"

"Tomorrow we will ride out and give the others their shares. After that, we four will ride south and keep our eyes open. Be wise, *amigos*, and do not let your tongues flutter with drink or in the presence of your women."

It was Loren's second day in Tucson and his restlessness to see Laurie was apparent. While Max rode to Fort Lowell to see Colonel Taggart about the new contract, Sam tried to occupy Loren by showing him through the T-Y Depot and explaining in detail its operation; but at the moment, Loren found little interest or enthusiasm in his examination.

"How soon," he asked, "will we be going to Tres Flechas. I want to see my sister."

"You've waited this long, Loren, another day can't hurt.

Max wants to clean up this Army contract business and Marcos Espuela is due in from Lordsburg sometime tonight. There's a report the Apaches are on the move between Dos Cabezas and Fort Bowie and he might have run into trouble. If all goes well, we'll leave for Tubac in the morning."

"I'm anxious to see her."

"No more than she has been to find you. Also, you can stay on for as long as you want when Max and I come back here on Monday."

"Who is Marcos Espuela?"

"A good friend who works for T-Y."

"A Mexican?"

Sam ignored the question. "Marcos was with me when we came on your father, mother and Laurie while they were under attack. Laurie—"

They were interrupted by the entrance of Max Potter, his face alight in triumph. "Got it," he said, waving a folded document. "Signed, sealed and delivered. We'll have to make some plans to work around our regular schedules, Sam. For the time being, we'll have to cut down on the Lordsburg run to take care of this new deal."

"How about the offer to take some of the heavy equipment off their hands?" Sam asked.

"I brought it up. We're to meet with Colonel Taggart one day next week to discuss it. Any new word on Marcos?"

"Not since the courier came in yesterday. If there's no trouble, he should be here tonight."

"Good. Then we'll go home for the weekend and thrash this thing out." To Loren, "Hold your horses just one more day, son, and we'll have a lot to celebrate." Turning to Sam again, "Word's out already. Stopped at the bank and Boyd Kiner wanted to know if he couldn't put a few thousand into T-Y. By Monday, when the word spreads, there'll be a dozen more wanting to come in." And again to Loren, "Son, you and your sister are going to own a piece of a gold mine. Won't be long before your investment doubles itself."

"Thank you, Cousin Max," Loren replied. "I can't believe it's happening. Finding Laurie, being in business." He grew solemn and added, "If only Pa and Ma—"

Max put an arm around his shoulder. "Don't look back too hard, Loren, except to remember the good years you had with them. It's happened to me, to Caroline, to Sam, to lots of others, something we have to live with."

"Yes—"

At eight that night, Marcos brought the four-wagon train into Tucson, showing physical evidence that the Apaches were on the move. The wagons showed ample signs of the attack: bullet holes, scorched canvas where burning arrows had struck, and even more convincingly, three dead *vaqueros* whose blanket-wrapped bodies lay in the last wagon. Four of the twenty-four mules were dead, left behind in Apache Pass.

"We came through at night," Marcos explained, "but they had rolled some boulders down the mountain to block the road. By the time we could clear enough away to get through, daylight had come and we were still in the Pass. That's when they hit us. All we could do was run until they hit the mules in the lead wagon, so we made a stand and fought back. Lucky for us they ran out of ammunition first."

"How many?"

"Up in those rocks, hard to tell. Maybe twenty or thirty. Hard to see. We got eight of them, maybe ten. We brought our three dead out, cut the dead mules away and came on as fast as we could. This side of Dragoon Springs, it was clear all the way."

"All right, Marcos. We'll unload and take the three men to Tres Flechas in the morning, bury them there."

"Who will go?"

"Max and I. You, if you'd like to come along."

"Yes. I will talk to the wives of the men who were killed."

"We'll leave at first light. Get something to eat and turn in early, eh?"

"Yes. Sam—"

"What?"

"The Apaches. They had repeating rifles as good as ours. Somebody is dealing with them."

"We know. Also, we expect Bokhari will start moving, too." He told Marcos of the raid on the Army train. "Two hundred and fifty new Winchester repeating rifles and sixty cases of rifle ammunition."

Madre de Dios! We'll need more men—"

"Don't worry about it now. Go over and get a good meal under your belt—. Wait a minute. I've got a surprise for you." Sam gripped Marcos' arm and led him inside the Depot, past the front counter and into Max's office. As

273

they entered, Loren looked up from a schedule he had been studying. At first glance, Marcos' eyes opened wide.

"Marcos, this is—"

"Laurie's brother! *Madre mio,* it can be no other!" Such was his surprise that he spoke in Spanish.

Loren got to his feet slowly. He was taller and more filled out than Laurie, but the resemblance was unmistakable. Marcos approached Loren in awe, took his hand and held it. In English now, he said, "Boy, you don't know how much we've wanted to see this happen. You haven't seen Laurie yet? She knows—?"

"No," Sam replied. "By tomorrow night she will know."

"Ah! What a thing it will be to see!"

CHAPTER IV

At first light on Saturday morning two new groups of troopers left Fort Bandolier on a forty-eight-hour mounted pass, twenty-two riding east to Malhado, eighteen west toward Mesa Plata. In the latter group, led by Sergeant Major Peter Riley, were First Sergeant Mike Tyler, Sergeant Atticus Perry and a mixture of Troop E, Troop K, and two men from the Headquarters Company. On arrival at Mesa Plata, they turned their mounts into Kendall's new livery stable and headed for the Silver Queen for a nonmilitary meal of steak, eggs, flapjacks and coffee, the answer to one of their most persistent dreams while on duty at the Fort and on desert patrol.

Coming into town, most local eyes were focused on the large Negro sergeant, whose appearance in Army uniform caused much comment and conjecture in this Confederate-oriented mining town that showed no respect and little love for Union bluecoats—except among the merchants, saloonkeepers and restaurant owners who profited by their presence.

In the Silver Queen, there was some question whether Perry would be served, but Riley put an end to the doubt by informing the owner that not only would all eighteen men leave (a doubtful threat), but that Colonel Hatfield would place Mesa Plata off limits to military personnel if Perry were not treated in the same manner as white troopers (false). When the quiet agreement was finally reached, Riley, Tyler and Private Dickson sat with Perry over a gargantuan meal while the other fourteen troopers occupied nearby tables.

"When do you think we'll be getting some word from Fort Bliss, Top?" Perry asked.

"Last we heard, Atticus," First Sergeant Tyler replied, "there was some trouble locating your records. They had you listed as missing for a year, then sent the records back to Washington as 'probably dead.' Soon as Washington sends the records back to Bliss, they'll send them on to us. You'd be about ready for discharge, wouldn't you?"

"I think so, but I don't rightly remember."

"Well, shouldn't be later than next month. Meantime, you're eating and sleeping good."

After the meal, some of the men lined up at the bar. The others drifted out to look in on the various shops, crowded with the usual Saturday afternoon traffic coming from the Carancho Valley and neighboring ranches to the south. Since the last Apache attack, new buildings, as yet unpainted, had been built or were in the construction stage to replace those burned out.

Riley and Tyler strolled up to the Bolton House to arrange for rooms for the night, found only six available and reserved them for their party of eighteen; then remembering that Atticus was one of their members, reduced the number to seventeen and would arrange for one accommodation in the livery stable for Perry.

Atticus wandered along the main thoroughfare, conscious of the eyes staring at him in confused wonder, even enjoying the attention he was receiving, careful not to nudge or jostle anyone in passing, apologizing politely when someone brushed against him. The windows of Calhoun's General Store attracted his attention and he stepped inside to examine the merchandise he hadn't seen since before the war began.

At one counter, Corporal Lanier and two privates were buying chewing tobacco and cigars to take back to the Fort for themselves and others. At one showcase, Corporal Dick Hudson, Privates Cleary and Dunton were inspecting a display of new rifles and revolvers. Atticus wandered over to a display board on which a circle of hunting knives and razors were being exhibited. Inside the circle, the legend read:

IMPORTED FROM ENGLAND
WORLD'S FINEST STEEL

The razors, each in its own blue velvet-lined box, took his fancy and Atticus, remembering Dr. Perry's set of imported razors, decided to buy one if the price was reasonable. He noted, too, that other prices here were far lower than those charged at the sutler's store at the Fort, and this brought to mind once more the brutal murder of Sherman Pierce; and that the thief-killer was still at large.

276

Then Hudson, Cleary and Dunton were beside him, staring at the arrangement of hunting and pocket knives, discussing their merits.

"Hey! All the way from England," Hudson exclaimed. "Look at that scalp lifter, the one with the pearl handle."

"If them pocket knives ain't too much, I'm goin'a get me one for whittlin'," Dunton replied. He turned and called out, "Hey, Mr. Calhoun, how about these knives?"

"Be there in a minute," Calhoun dropped several items into a paper sack, handed it to a woman customer, accepted her money and came over to where the four troopers stood. Out of the corner of his eye, Atticus saw Tyler and Riley enter the store and head for the tobacco counter.

Calhoun had removed the hunting knife for Hudson, pocket knives for Cleary and Dunton. "Finest steel blades ever made," Calhoun said enticingly. "Hold their sharpness longer'n any made in this country. Real Sheffield, see the name there?"

"How much?" Hudson asked.

"Six-fifty for that one. The pocket knives run from a dollar-fifty to three-fifty."

"How much for the razors?" Atticus asked.

Without removing the razor from the display, Calhoun said shortly, "Seven-fifty," and turned back to the white men. "Got a leather sheath goes with the hunting knife, Corporal, no extra charge. Six-fifty for both."

"I'll take it," Hudson said. Cleary and Dunton had lost interest in the knives and went back to the gun display.

"Can I see the razor, please?" Atticus asked.

"Sure." Calhoun detached one of the razor boxes and handed it to Atticus. It was a beauty, just like Dr. Perry's, he thought as he ran the ball of his thumb along its finely honed edge. The one he had bought from the sutler had cost three-fifty and was a poor imitation of the fine instrument he now held. Calhoun added, "Leather strop goes with it. No extra charge."

Meanwhile, Calhoun had found the proper sheath for the hunting knife and Hudson thrust the blade into it. He put the holstered knife down on the counter, pulled out a small wad of bills from his shirt pocket and counted out a five and two ones. Calhoun reached for the bills, remarking, "Out of seven. You got four bits coming to you."

But not before Atticus noticed the five-dollar bill.

No other bill could be marked like it except the ten-dollar bill in his own pocket at this very moment; the thin line that had spread into an arrowhead design when he spilled the bottle of dark blue ink on Captain Greene's desk. And later, had paid that same bill, along with two ones, to discharge his seven-dollar debt to Sherman Pierce on the night Pierce had been murdered.

"Well, boy, you want that razor?"

Atticus awoke from his reverie. Hudson, hunting knife in his hand, had rejoined Cleary and Dunton at the gun display. Riley and Tyler were waiting at the tobacco counter and civilians were everywhere in the store impatiently calling for service from Calhoun and his three clerks.

"Yes, sir," Atticus said, "I'll take it." In his pocket was the ten-dollar bill that was marked identically as the five Hudson had paid over to Calhoun. He also had two fives, a two and a one, aware that he must now retain the ten. He took the money from his shirt and put a five, the two and one on the counter.

"And four bits change for you." Calhoun put the razor and strop into a paper sack and placed it on the counter with a fifty-cent piece beside it. Atticus picked up the sack and coin and stood contemplating the immensity of his discovery. He walked toward the tobacco counter where Riley and Tyler stood, waited beside them.

"You stockin' up some t'bacco, Atticus?" Riley asked.

"A little."

"Best chewin' is Great Frontier Brand. Best cigars are them Mexican stogies. Cost half as much here as in the sutler's."

"Thanks." For a moment he was silent, then said in a low voice, "Can I see you for a minute, Sergeant Major?" He glanced at Tyler and added, "In private."

Tyler had heard, frowned at his exclusion, and moved to one side. Riley said, "Somethin' botherin' you, Atticus?"

"It's a mighty troublesome thing." In a low voice, he spoke swiftly, telling Riley of the spilled ink incident, his payment to Sherman Pierce, now seeing the telltale five-dollar bill in Hudson's hands.

"You sure, Atticus? You c'd be standin' a man up against the wall for somethin' like this."

"I'm sure—"

"An' it ain't because you an' Hudson had a brannigan in the bull ring?"

"I swear it, Sergeant Major."

"Ty," Riley called, "c'mere a minute." When Tyler rejoined them, "Atticus, you tell Sergeant Tyler what you just told me."

Atticus repeated his story and Tyler shook his head from side to side. "Hudson? Hell, he's got a temper like a cottonmouth, but kill a man and rob him in cold blood? That's hard to believe."

"Well," Riley said, "we can't just do nothin'." He thought for a moment, then said, "You two stay here with me. I'll need a couple witnesses."

When one of Calhoun's clerks came to serve them, Riley said, "We're waitin' for Mr. Calhoun. Somethin' special we want to ask him about."

Hudson, Cleary and Dunton had left the store by the time Len Calhoun was free. Riley and Tyler gave him their orders for tobacco and Atticus bought a box of fifty Mexican cigars with his fifty-cent piece. Riley's bill came to $3.75, Tyler's to an even five dollars. Tyler handed Calhoun a ten-dollar bill and was rewarded with the marked five-dollar bill as his change.

"Funny thing," Atticus remarked on seeing it. "I got a ten marked the same way." He pulled it from his pocket and put it down beside the five to show its identical marking. Calhoun stared at both bills.

"Could of had the same daddy and mamma," he said with a short laugh.

"Where'd you get this one, Mr. Calhoun?" Riley asked.

"Where'd I get it? From a customer, of course. One of your own boys, come to think of it. The corporal who bought a hunting knife just a couple of minutes ago."

"Corporal Hudson?"

"I don't know what his name is. He was standing alongside this boy here," indicating Atticus.

"It was Corporal Hudson," Atticus said.

"Something wrong, Sergeant?" Calhoun asked.

"Maybe," Riley replied. He took a deep breath and said, "Mr. Calhoun, would you write out a statement an' sign it, with us three as witnesses?"

Through pursed lips, the merchant said warily, "Look, I don't know what this is all about, but I'll do it, long's I don't lose my five dollars."

"I'll give you one to take its place."

"All right. I'm busy right now, but I'll do it while I'm eating my supper. Come back later and I'll have it for you."

279

When Max Potter, Sam Palmer, Loren Olmstead and Marcos Espuela rode through the gates at Tres Flechas, Laurie was standing in the center of a circle made up of more than a dozen children whose ages ranged from two to nine. Hands clasped, they circled from left to right as they sang a song in their native tongue. At a certain point, Laurie called out a key word, at which the children were to reverse directions from right to left, and which resulted in a confusion of bumping and piercing laughter.

At the moment when the confusion was at its peak, she looked up, saw and recognized Max, Sam and Marcos; and finally, Loren. She broke from the circle of children and ran wildly to Loren, flinging herself at him just as he dismounted. Locked in a tight embrace, the target of every eye surrounding the newly arrived group, Laurie drew back and through tears, her eyes, which were duplicates of Loren's, inspected his face which so closely resembled her own, touching his cheek, neck and shoulders.

"Oh, Loren, Loren! Where on earth did you come from? You're so—thin!"

"I'm fine, Laurie, just fine. You look—so grown up. You're a—fine lady. Golly—"

Max and Sam walked toward the house where Caroline waited on the porch. Marcos turned and walked toward the *vaquero* quarters, leading the four horses to the corral for the younger boys to feed, water and rub down. Those men and women in the vicinity stared at the reunion between the young woman and man, murmuring silent thanks that they were happily reunited. Emelita began issuing orders and the ring of curious men and women at once began to dissolve.

In the house, two servants began carrying food and drinks to the dining room, Emelita chattering, complaining that Tucson was bad for them, they were not eating well, they looked tired, they needed food and rest, their baths were being prepared.

After the meal, Max and Sam went to Max's study for a talk. Caroline had not joined them at the meal, but had gone for her daily ride and now Laurie and Loren sat on the porch, each filled with questions only the other could answer. They sat and talked for several hours, saw Caroline return from her ride, spoke with her as she came onto the porch and leaned against the rail, asking questions of Loren.

The change in Laurie was remarkable. She had found

warmth and gentleness from Max, Sam, Marcos, the *vaqueros,* their wives and children, but there remained a wall between herself and Caroline; a tendency on Caroline's part to treat her, with only two years' difference in their ages, as an unworldly child, despite the tragic loss of Aaron and Libby; and that she had helped fight off the Apache attack, killing several of them.

It was Caroline's own loneliness, Laurie had decided, that forced her to withdraw from contact with others; the loss of her mother at an early age, Ruth's "desertion" when she married Sam, and later, Ruth's death, for which she blamed Sam. For those reasons, Laurie had hoped to leave the ranch, and Caroline, and move to Tucson where there was life and activity. Now, with Loren's arrival, her determination was strengthened. Soon, she suspected, Loren would want to move to Tucson and it would be most natural for her to want to be with him. There was more than enough money to buy a house, perhaps a small ranch of their own on the outskirts of Tucson. For the moment, she would wait and talk it over with Loren after a few days had passed.

The weekend, for Marcos, was not a pleasurable one. Seeing Laurie and Loren happily together, scarcely out of each other's sight, Marcos was swept with envy, even jealousy, and for the first time felt a wave of hopelessness in the situation in which he found himself; in love with the Anglo cousin of Max Potter, her brother now injected into the picture as her protector, far wealthier than he, Marcos, could ever hope to be and, in fact, their employee, since she and Loren owned an investor's interest in T-Y Lines.

And there was sadness throughout the *jefetura* once more. Three *vaqueros* to bury in the Tres Flechas cemetery; two had been married, one unmarried, leaving two widows and seven children. The service was held on Sunday morning, all attending except Marcos, who had ridden out the night before to visit one of the distant range camps.

After the burial, Sam Palmer sought out Benito Macias and Alonso Maderos, who had been sent to track the attackers of the Army supply train. Benito gave Palmer an accurate account of their findings and drew a map on the ground with a pointed stick. One final trail led in the direction of Sonora.

"Where in Sonora, Benito?"

Macias shrugged. "A *conjetura, señor.* First, I think

these were the *pícaros* of Casimiro Lizardi, for no one else commands so many followers. If this is so, then I think he would go to a place he knows best, his home village, Cienguilla. It is south of Monte Babiacora, which was the home camp of Anaka, now of Bokhari, where the Anglo *soldados* are not permitted to cross the border."

"I know of Monte Babiacora, Benito. You know it?"

Macias grinned. "I, too, was born in Cienguilla, *senor*. As a child, I played in those hills, learned to hunt for deer there until the Indios drove us out. When hunting is forbidden us, food becomes scarce and many move away. When I was sixteen, my uncle Ignacio brought me to Tres Flechas. I became a man here, also a father. Twenty-seven, no, twenty-eight years I have been on this land."

"And Babiacora?"

"The Indios came many years before your war. One leader, then another, then Anaka, now Bokhari. There are many camps there, to the north, the east, south and west, wherever there is grass and water for the animals. In the center is the big camp, *la ciudad principal*, where the council meets and many live. The outer camps are for the braves who wait to go raiding and hunting in any direction when the orders come from the big camp."

"Bokhari lives in *la ciudad principal?*"

"I do not know Bokhari, *señor*. Anaka took for himself a place in a valley where a stream runs and the grass is sweet. He lived there and went to the big camp for councils."

"You know this place well, Benito?"

Macias smiled. "If I say no, I may live to be an old man. If I say yes, I may be told to guide you into Babiacora to die there."

"And which do you choose to say, *amigo?*"

There was no hesitation in Benito's reply. "One cannot hope to live forever. I say yes, *señor*."

"*Gracias*, Benito. If it becomes necessary, we may one day go with many *vaqueros* and see this place for ourselves."

"*Con Dios, señor*."

"When we do, I hope He will ride with us."

For a while, it appeared to Sergeant Major Riley that Corporal Hudson might not be alive by the time the pass party was due to return to Fort Bandolier.

On Saturday night, drinking in the Silver Queen, Hudson caught the eye of one of the bar girls and invited her to sit at his table with Lanier, Cleary, Dunton, Svoboda and Hecker. For their own protection, Riley had insisted that the troopers leave their carbines and sidearms with their horses in Kendall's livery stable, but the miners and ranchers were under no such restrictions.

The girl, Amelia, was the younger of the group of saloon girls whose purpose was to keep patrons contented, happy, and ordering more drinks. Amelia sat with the soldiers, performing her prescribed duties, unmindful of the occasional caresses from roughened male hands as long as the drinks flowed and certain limits of conduct were not exceeded.

At ten-thirty, Ward Gallagher, a shaft superintendent at the Argonaut Mine, came into the Silver Queen. He had a drink at the bar and looked around for an empty chair at one of the poker games in progress. Finding none, his eyes wandered around the large, crowded room until they rested on Amelia. Well-known for his sympathies toward the defeated Confederacy, still aware of the bullet wounds in his thigh and leg, the sight of his favorite bar girl sitting with a group of bluecoats brought him to a level of mild rage, which was fanned into flaming hatred by more whiskey.

Someone began playing the piano and in various parts of the saloon men rose to dance, if it could be called dancing, with the acquiescent bar girls. As did Dick Hudson with Amelia, ardently, if not gracefully. Ward Gallagher, well on his way to the point of explosion, finally reached it when he saw Amelia in the arms of Hudson. With a suppressed grunt, he pushed himself away from the bar and toward the laughing, dancing couple and took Amelia's arm in one hand, Hudson's in the other, trying to pry them apart.

"Somethin' botherin' you, mister?" Hudson asked.

"You damn well right," Gallagher retorted. "The sight of any Yankee bluebelly bothers me a lot."

Unwilling to precipitate a fight, Hudson restrained himself for the moment. "Well, old hoss," he replied, "why don't you stumble down to Kendall's an' find yourself a nice mare?"

Gallagher swung, Amelia screamed, and Hudson found himself lying in the middle of a no-limit poker game. As he came up, shaking the fog out of his eyes, Gallagher rushed in. Hudson sidestepped and the table, money, and

283

card players hit the floor together, bowled over by Gallagher's flying body. When he picked himself up and focused on Gallagher, who stood braced for the oncoming attack, Gallagher was drawing his revolver. At once, Hudson's hand snaked behind him in search of his new hunting knife, then realized the ridiculousness of attempting to defend himself against a six-shooter with a six-inch steel blade.

Someone called out, "Drop it, Ward. He's got no gun."

Gallagher, in the vortex of his tempest, shouted, "I'll drop him first, the bluebellied bastard!"

But before he could raise the .44 to aim it, two arms had clamped around him and swung him off balance. One hand gripped his gun wrist and turned the weapon's muzzle into his belly. "You can pull the trigger any time you want now, mister," Sergeant Major Riley's voice said coldly.

Gallagher's hand went slack and Riley took the .44 from him, emptied the six cartridges and handed the gun back. To Hudson, "You had enough, Corporal. Hit the sack."

Hudson glared angrily, turned on his heels and went outside. Instead of returning to the Bolton House, however, he walked in the opposite direction toward Kendall's livery stable. In the dim yellow lamplight, he searched among the stalls for his horse. Saddle and blanket were racked on the edge of the riser that separated the stalls, gun belt hanging from its pommel, carbine in the scabbard. As he withdrew the revolver and checked its load, he heard soft footsteps behind him, wheeled around to face Atticus Perry, who had been asleep on a straw-filled mattress in an empty stall nearby.

"Pretty late to go hunting, ain't it, Corporal?" Atticus said.

"What I do is my business an' none of yours," Hudson replied.

"You take a weapon out of here, it's my business. The sergeant major gave me orders to see—"

"I don't care what your orders are. Nobody pulls a gun on me an' gets away free an' clear."

"Well, if it was an Apache you're going hunting—"

"Don't get funny with me, booger boy," Hudson snapped.

"Hudson, I've been overlooking that 'boy' for some time now. I'll remind you I'm a sergeant. I outrank you and my name is *Sergeant* Atticus Perry."

284

"Well, Sergeant Atticus Perry, where I come from, people like me own people like you."

"Not own, Corporal, *owned*. You might remember that President Lincoln cleared that little misunderstanding up a few years ago. Now put that gun back and go sleep it off. You're disturbing me."

"Boy, you're disturbing *me*. Now stand out of my way." Hudson replaced the revolver in its holster, took the belt from the saddle pommel and began strapping it around his waist.

"I said for you to put it back, Corporal."

"For all of me, you can go outside and howl at the moon, nigger."

Atticus hit him flush on the jaw. Hudson staggered back inside the stall as the gun belt, not yet buckled, fell to the floor. His horse, startled when Hudson bumped into him, reared and began pawing the air with his forelegs. Hudson rolled to one side out of the way, with Atticus Perry's hands gripping his arms to help him. The gun lay on the floor beneath the excited horse's thrashing feet, out of reach. Hudson suddenly turned and threw a punch toward Perry's jaw, but the whiskey he had been consuming all evening had altered his judgment of distance considerably. He swung loosely again and missed. Then Atticus measured Hudson with patience and accuracy and hit him flush on the chin. Hudson dropped to the floor and lay still. Atticus picked him up, carried him to his own mattress in the empty stall nearby and covered him with a blanket.

"Lord," he said softly, "how long does it take a man to learn? Even a white man."

On Monday morning, the pass group to Mesa Plata rode out before dawn and, sparing their horses as much as possible, or unwilling to return behind guarded walls, did not reach Fort Bandolier until late in the afternoon. Since they would be free from duty until reveille the next morning, the men filed into the mess hall, ate a meal of liquefied hash and went to their respective barracks to catch up on the sleep most had missed over the preceding forty-eight hours.

Sergeant Major Riley reported at once to the adjutant and asked permission to speak with Major Boyden on a matter of grave importance. Captain Greene told him that Boyden had been up all night on a false alert and was at the moment resting in his quarters. Riley went there, found the major awake, and asked if he could speak with him, "kinda off'n the record, sir."

"What is it, Riley?" Boyden asked with a smile. "Some of the boys misbehave in Mesa Plata?"

"Well, sir, yes an' no. A little bit of a mixup, but nothin' important to report official. But there's this other thing." He pulled a sheet of brown paper from his shirt pocket, unfolded it and handed it to Boyden to read. It was the affidavit from Leonard Calhoun, merchant, attesting to the fact that he had received a certain curiously marked five-dollar bill from one Corporal Richard Hudson in payment for a hunting knife. The statement included a description and sketch of the arrowhead marking, its serial number, and had been witnessed by Sergeant Major Peter Riley, First Sergeant Michael Tyler and Sergeant Atticus Perry. The bill also bore the signature of Calhoun and the witnesses.

"Anything beside Perry's word that this was the bill he paid to Mr. Pierce, Riley?"

"This, sir." He pulled the ten-dollar bill from his pocket, marked identically with the five-dollar bill described in the statement and which was in Boyden's hand. "I didn't want to say anything to Captain Greene, sir, but you can check up with him whether this is the bill he saw when Perry spilled the ink, then put it together with the other bills in his pocket."

"All right, Riley, leave these with me. Has Perry been reimbursed for this ten-dollar bill?"

"You mean did I give him a ten for this one? No, sir. Wasn't another ten dollars left amongst the lot of us time we left Mesa Plata."

"Very well, I'll see that he is reimbursed. And keep this to yourself, Tyler and Perry as well. I'll talk with Captain Greene and we will look into this more thoroughly. You will be called as witnesses before any decision is made."

"Yes, sir. I'll talk to Tyler and Perry right away."

At sundown on Sunday, Marcos returned to the home ranch, put his horse in the corral and went to the mess hall to eat with the *vaqueros*. The funeral earlier that morning had had a sobering effect on the Tres Flechas community, and those men who were on watch ate in shifts with the unmarried men. There were no Sunday

286

serenades in the compound, nor would there be the usual rest day gaiety and dancing.

Venustiano Carras came in and sat at the lower end of the table, next to Marcos. "A sad day, *joven*," he said as he signaled a mess attendant for his supper.

"Death always brings sadness," Marcos replied. "I was with them when it happened. I knew them well."

"Yet you did not attend the service or the burial."

"It is enough to see good men die. Where they have gone, they do not know who watches to see them buried."

"If one believes so, then it is so. There are over sixty *vaqueros* now working in this new business. When will they return to Tres Flechas?"

Marcos shrugged. "The Indios have begun to move again. You have heard this. Also, there will be more work and *el patrón* talks of taking more men from here to Tucson."

"This I have not heard. And who will protect the range and the *jefetura* here if the Indios come?"

"That is something to discuss with *el patrón*, Venustiano."

"Ai-ee, I will do this before he leaves."

"He has said when he rides north?"

"In the morning."

"Then I will get a good night's sleep."

In the main house, Max and Sam had discussed the new contract and listed their equipment and manpower needs to accommodate it. There were drivers to be shifted, wagons to be taken from regular runs, routes planned to the various forts and camps outside the thirty-mile circle around Fort Lowell. The main problem would be guard support.

"We'll have to take another twenty men from here, Sam. Seven from the *jefetura*, the others from the north, south and west camps. That will make the men cover longer lines and force some of the younger boys into men's jobs for the time being, but there's no outside source we can count on and we need to support that contract, particularly when the mail franchise comes through."

"I'm thinking of Tres Flechas, Max. If Cochise—"

"He won't come this far in a hurry, Sam. The walls will hold and Venustiano will have to space his men to cover more ground, just as the range foremen will. There's at least two dozen young'uns can start learnin' to use a rifle. Once we're better organized up north, we can start sending some of the men back."

"I'm worried about those guns and ammunition that were taken in that raid, Max. New repeaters, better than Army carbines. That's a lot of fire power."

"Well, we'll have to do the best we can. We'll leave at first light. I've already told Venustiano."

"What about Loren?"

"We'll leave him here with Laurie and Caroline for the time being, a sort of reacquaintance period. Later on, I'm sure he'll want to come to Tucson—Laurie, too."

"I'll go see Marcos and fill him in."

Marcos had left the mess hall and was on his way to the bunkhouse when he heard Laurie's voice call out, "Marcos!"

He turned and made out two shadowy figures standing at the family corral, the familiar silhouette of Mano reaching his long neck over the top rail, nuzzling Laurie's palm. With her was Loren. When he came toward them, Loren spoke to him first.

"I want to say my thanks again for what you did to help Laurie, my mother and father," Loren said. "I know more about it now. Laurie told me."

Marcos studied Loren for a moment, then said, "To say 'It was nothing' would be to belittle the value you place upon your sister, so I will say simply that I am glad I was there with Sam to do what we could. Unfortunately, we were not there sooner—"

"I know. I wish I could repay you—"

"Who knows? Perhaps one day you will, but I ask for no repayment or thanks."

"Cousin Max tells me you're going back to Tucson with him in the morning."

"Yes. And you?"

"I want to—"

"Loren!" Laurie interjected.

"—but Laurie wants me to stay here for a while. We've got some catching up to do."

"As it should be. I hear more of the *vaqueros* will be moving north for a while, so an extra hand to keep an eye on Caroline and Laurie will be a good thing."

"It sure will, but I guess we'll be moving up to Tucson ourselves pretty soon."

"If you will be there, it will be a good thing. I go to

the bunkhouse to get some sleep now, if you will excuse me."

Laurie said, "Wait, Marcos." To Loren, "Will you wait in the house for me, Loren? I want to ask Marcos something."

Suddenly, what little cordiality there had been in Loren vanished. He hesitated only long enough to impart that impression in one swift look at Laurie and Marcos, then turned and walked toward the main house without another word.

"You shouldn't have done that, Laurie," Marcos said softly.

"Why not?"

"Because—because Loren has been in the West long enough to learn that Anglo girls and Mexican men do not speak privately at night."

"Marcos, Loren isn't like that. It's something you see between you and all Anglos, a social barrier. Admit it. Is there that same wall between you and Sam, or Cousin Max?"

Marcos grinned. "No, but I do not walk or ride or talk with Caroline, and Sam has no sister—"

"Stop it, Marcos. You are looking for difficulties where there aren't any."

"And you, dear Laurie, do not see what you do not want to see. I will go now. Your brother waits for you."

"You will be leaving early?"

"At first light, before you are awake, so *hasta*—"

Before he could finish the sentence, Laurie reached up on her toes and kissed him. Marcos drew back for a moment, startled by this first fleeting kiss between them, then took her into his arms and kissed her soundly. "Ah, *querida*, we should not have done this. For every star above us, there is an eye that sees."

"I wanted to do it, kiss you. I won't see you for a long time."

"The kiss," Marcos said, "is only a moment out of our lives. The memory is forever."

"Then remember it. I want you to."

"Ah, yes—" He stopped and stared at her, then said, "In my whole life, the things I remember best are those things that happened to me for the first time. My first dog, my first gun, my first horse. Now this, to remember always. Laurie—"

But she had turned swiftly and was walking toward the
289

house. Marcos leaned against the corral rail and watched until she disappeared into the darkness, then saw her again as she mounted the porch steps, standing in the lighted doorway. She turned back to look toward him and raised one hand in a final wave, then went inside and closed the door.

Marcos felt Mano's soft, damp muzzle against the back of his neck. Still staring at the point where he last saw Laurie, he said softly in Spanish, "Horse, do not be too happy for me too soon. There are many deserts and mountains and rivers to cross."

On her way to her room, Laurie saw light spilling into the hallway from Loren's room and paused at his doorway. Loren lay on the bed, boots off, but otherwise clothed, hands cupped behind the back of his head.

"Come in, Laurie," he said, sitting up and swinging his legs around to the floor. She entered the room, noticing at once the change in her brother, his face flushed with brooding.

"What is it, Loren?" she asked.

"That's what I thought you could tell me."

"What is it you want to know?"

"What's between you and him?"

"Who?"

"You know who I mean. That Mexican, Marcos."

"He's half-American," Laurie said defensively.

"So he's a half-breed Mexican."

Laurie sighed. "Loren, don't be angry with me. You don't know what I've been through since we left Fort Leavenworth—"

"I've been through a lot myself, but I haven't taken up with any greasers yet."

"Please, Loren. He's a fine person. If you took the trouble to know him—"

"I don't want to know him and you're talking like a silly child. My God, Laurie, can't you see what you're doing? Who'd ever want to marry you if they knew about you and a Mexican, even if he is a half-breed?"

She said quietly, "I'm hoping Marcos would be the one who wanted to marry me, Loren. I love him."

"You're crazy! Something has happened to your mind!"

"Loren, please don't. Marcos is a fine, decent man. Educated, too, better than either one of us. What's more, he and Sam Palmer saved my life."

290

"And you're paying him back with kisses? And maybe more? I saw you out there at the corral from the porch."

Laurie's face flushed with anger she was trying hard to conceal. "That's not true, that last. I don't—even know you any more, you've changed so much in six months. You weren't like this before, so narrow-minded and prejudiced—"

"Before I killed Mr. Bryce, you mean?"

"That was an accident. You couldn't help it."

"What difference does that make? He's dead, isn't he, and I killed him, didn't I?"

"Loren, is that what's changed you so much, living with a guilt that wasn't your fault?"

Loren laughed grimly, without humor. "If you only knew."

"Knew what?"

"Laurie, I'm a killer."

"You don't know what you're saying. You're—"

Heatedly, "Don't I? You think I don't?" He stood up and began pacing the floor in agitation, suddenly turned and picked up his revolver in one hand, the Winchester in the other. "Since Mr. Bryce, I've killed seven men with these."

Laurie's eyes opened wide with shock. "Seven—"

"Eight, counting Mr. Bryce. Two Indians who attacked the wagon train somewhere between El Paso and Tucumcori, two Mexican bushwhackers just outside Tucson, a man named Ernie Chapman, and two bounty hunters in Yuma. Eight all told. I guess that makes me a gunslinger, a killer, doesn't it?"

"Loren—"

"It's the truth. Eight men, and I'm only nineteen."

"You did it in self-defense—"

"What difference does that make? I did it, didn't I? And how many who are nineteen can say that? It's different out here, Laurie. The choice is between the quick and the dead—"

"Don't say things like that. You almost sound as if you're proud of it, like you're enjoying it."

Loren sat down on the edge of the bed, still gripping the two weapons tightly, his body trembling. "Laurie, I don't know why or how. I've asked myself a hundred times, why did it always have to be me? It's as though it keeps following me around, like it's going to keep on happening. I've been lucky so far, but the next time it could be the other way around. It scares me." Laurie sat beside him and hugged him tightly. He said, "Maybe it was being so alone. I was never alone before I left home."

If confession is good for the soul, it seemed to be having an opposite effect on Loren. Sitting there cradling the two weapons, Laurie had never seen him more abjectly unhappy, like a small boy enveloped simultaneously with fear and remorse he was ashamed to show. Without releasing her hold on him, Laurie said, "Loren, that part is over now. You're safe here and I'm with you. You're not alone any more. Only, please don't be angry with me. Or Marcos. I love him. It's a good thing we have between us."

"You don't know what love is. You're only seventeen."

"I know as much about it as I need to know. Mama was only seventeen when she was already married—"

"He's a Mexican and nothing can change that, Laurie."

"Don't make it hard for me to keep on loving you. We're all that's left of our family. You're my brother, but you can't be my father, mother and guardian. I'm a woman now, Loren, not a child."

"Maybe that's what's wrong with both of us, we're not children any more. All right, Laurie, I can't tell you what to do or not to do, but I don't have to lie and tell you I like what you're doing."

"Thank you for that much, Loren. Marcos will be going back to Tucson with Max and Sam in the morning and we'll be here to talk it out and decide things."

He stood and walked to the window, looked out into the compound and up at the stars, then turned and said, "No, I think I'll go back to Tucson in the morning with Max. I'll take a few days to think things out. When I do, I'll come back here."

"Promise you won't say anything to Marcos, start something—"

"I won't if he doesn't."

"He won't, Loren. He's a good person."

"If he doesn't, I won't. I'll promise you that much."

Three hours after Max, Loren, Sam and Marcos left for Tucson, Caroline knocked on Laurie's door waking her. Caroline was dressed for riding, carrying her gun belt in one hand.

"Have they left yet?" Laurie asked.

"At first light. I'm surprised you weren't up to see Marcos off."

"Caroline, I know how you feel about Marcos, but this doesn't concern you."

"It should concern you. By now, everyone on Tres Flechas knows you were kissing him last night. They've been talking about it in the kitchen."

"I don't care who knows about it," Laurie replied defiantly.

"If Loren should find out—"

"He already knows. We've talked about it."

"Laurie, listen to me, please. Marcos is a Mexican with—"

"I don't want to hear any more about that."

"In these parts, he's counted as all-Mexican and white girls don't kiss Mexicans. Can't you understand that?"

"All I can understand is that when you like—love—somebody, it doesn't matter. Your mother was Spanish. If Cousin Max felt the way you do, where would you be?"

"I've told you before, there's a great difference between being half-Spanish and half-Mexican."

"Caroline, I don't care what the difference is. As far as I'm concerned, it's too little to pay any mind to."

Caroline's deep annoyance showed in her rigid expression. "All right, it's your business. I hope you know what you're doing."

"Caroline, please don't be angry—"

"I can't help being angry with anyone who makes a fool of herself."

"The way you thought of Ruth for marrying a soldier?"

Caroline flushed angrily. "You didn't know Ruth, so you can't know what you're talking about."

"Maybe not—"

"Besides, what would your father and mother have said?"

"You didn't know them, so I think I know better than you what they would have felt and said, and I don't think they would be nearly as upset as you."

"And Loren?"

"Loren is my business, not yours. Caroline, I've tried to be friends with you, but you won't let me, not any more than you'll let Sam be your friend. You're taking something out on all of us, Sam, Marcos, me, even Cousin Max sometimes."

"Taking what out on you?"

"Look, I'm—"

"What?"

"You don't need me to tell you."

"How will I know if you don't?"

"All right. You can't forgive your father because he wasn't there to save your mother. You can't forgive Sam because he wasn't at home when Ruth and her baby were killed. You won't forgive me because I don't feel the same things you feel, and I don't. I can't."

Caroline's face was flushed, her eyes blazing. "You—you're—that is a monstrous thing to say to me. I hope you do move to Tucson, your brother with you. And as long as you're here on Tres Flechas, don't you dare speak to me again!"

Caroline ran from the room, slamming the door behind her. Moments later, Laurie watched from the window as Caroline mounted up and rode furiously out of the compound.

In Yuma, the Homestead Saloon, except for Sheriff Jack Kinnick and Bob Ehrlacher, the owner, was empty. It was close on to two in the morning and Kinnick had made his rounds, with this his last stop before checking the jail.

"Long day, hey, Jack?" Ehrlacher said, wiping the long bar with a beer-dampened towel.

"Makes for a longer night without a deputy, Bob," Kinnick replied, one gnarled hand gripping the handle of his beer mug. "I could sure use me another one like Earl."

"Another one, Jack? On the house."

"No, thanks. Only takes two to make me sleepy an' I'm sleepy enough as it is."

The loss of his night deputy, without replacement thus far, had placed a heavy burden on the aging sheriff, not only requiring his presence by day, but forced to keep watch over his four prisoners—two drunks, an assault-and-battery case, and Harry Penn, all waiting for their trials within two days—and had presented domestic problems by his extended absence from home and family.

"Well," Ehrlacher said, dropping the cloth beneath the counter, "might as well shut up shop an' get to bed."

"Yeah. See you tomorrow, Bob."

Kinnick went out, drawing his sheep-lined coat about

him as he braced himself to face the bitterly cold night. He crossed the street and turned left toward the jail, boots clattering along the raised wooden sidewalk past several dozen darkened shops whose locks he had tested earlier. He looked back as the lights in the Homestead went off, heard its doors slam shut as Bob Ehrlacher locked them and headed toward his home in the opposite direction.

Kinnick gave in to a few moments of self-pity. A damned nuisance, running his job without proper help, by day as well as by night, with little enough help or money from the Town Council; having to sleep at the jail since Earl Madigan—or Loren Olmstead—left. One of these days, if nothing better showed up, he'd have to give in and hire a couple of Mexican deputies, and wouldn't *that* blow the lid off the kettle with the Council and white population of Yuma.

He stepped off the walk and turned right into Calle Cañada, reaching for the ring of keys that hung from his pistol belt, when the man stepped out from the narrow alley between Olsen's Saddlery and the Yuma *Star* building. Kinnick heard the two steps behind him and turned, but the ring of keys were already in his right hand, too late to drop and go for his gun.

"Take it easy, sheriff," the cold voice said.

"Who the hell are you?" Kinnick demanded angrily.

"You wouldn't know if I told you. Keep them keys in yore right hand an' keep movin'. I don't like makin' widows an' orphans." The man waved his gun in the direction of the jail. "Go ahead, sheriff, an' open it up."

Inside the jail, the man kicked the door shut behind him. The room was small and cluttered, the wick in the oil lamp turned low. A battered desk littered with papers and Wanted notices, more of the latter lining the walls; four straight chairs, a table, a pot-bellied stove in the corner with a dying fire, a neat stack of cut firewood beside it. There were two doors which were shut, one evidently leading to the prisoner cells. Holding his gun on Kinnick, the man went to one door and opened it. The small room contained a made-up cot, a chair and a washstand with a water pitcher and bowl. No windows.

The man kicked the door shut and went to the other one, opened it and grinned. In one of the four cells were three men, all asleep, snoring and mumbling. In another stood Harry Penn, awake, gripping the vertical bars.

"What took you so long, Dutch?" Penn asked.

"Had to lay low for a coupla days. Won't be long now," Dutch replied. To Kinnick, "All right, sheriff, unlock the cell an' let 'im out. You behave an' I'll let you keep them other three slobs. Come on, old man, move!"

Kinnick moved past Dutch into the cellblock. He unlocked the door to Penn's cell, eyes on the barrel of the gun that was aimed at his abdomen, wishing he were younger, swifter, braver; or at home and in bed beside Laura.

"You got horses, Dutch?" Penn asked.

"Sure. Out back. You'll need an iron." He motioned toward Kinnick. "Take his."

Penn did so from behind the sheriff. He buckled the gun belt around his slimmer waist, removed the heavy .44 and checked its load, reversed it in his hand and brought the butt down sharply on Kinnick's head. The old man gasped and went down. Penn dragged him into the vacated cell, picked up the ring of keys and locked it from the outside. In the next cell, the two drunks slept and snored on, but the assault-and-battery prisoner lay on his cot, eyes wide open. Penn returned the wide-eyed stare. "You want out, friend?" Penn asked.

The man said nothing, but continued to stare.

"To hell with you, friend," Penn said and followed Dutch into the outer office. Another key on the ring unlocked the gun rack. Dutch chose a rifle and shotgun for himself and Penn took a similar pair of weapons. On the shelf overhead were several boxes of ammunition and both men filled their pockets. As a parting gesture, Dutch added several sticks of wood to the dying fire in the stove.

In the alley outside, the men mounted the two horses and came into the main street in a slow walk. "Where we headin', Harry?" Dutch asked.

"East," Penn replied laconically.

"East means Tucson. That could spell trouble when they find that old man in there."

"Us an' trouble ain't strangers, Dutch. South is piss-poor Mexico, an' north ain't much better. There's too many nooses waitin' for us back in California, so we ain't got too much of a choice. You ever been to Tucson, Dutch?"

"Nope."

"I was there once, a few years ago. Even then, it was a

296

wide-open town. Ought to be big enough and crowded enough by now to lose ourselves in. Besides—"

"Besides what?"

"—Tucson is where Sam Palmer is, an' I got a big score to even up with that hombre. Dead or alive, he's goin'a make Harry Penn an' Dutch Macklin a coupla rich men. Even richer now that we only got two ways to split, 'stead of four."

"Yeah. An' I'd give a good piece of it to get my hands on that smart deputy who got Andy an' Floyd. I'm with you, Harry. *Ándale!*"

Harry Penn and Dutch Macklin turned eastward and headed for Tucson.

CHAPTER V

MAJOR KANE BOYDEN, WHOSE INVESTIGATION OF THE murder of Sherman Pierce had been frequently interrupted by the press of normal Fort business, resumed his private questioning of Corporal Richard Hudson at the first available opportunity.

On the desk before him lay the sworn statements of Sergeant Atticus Perry, Sergeant Major Peter Riley and First Sergeant Michael Tyler, along with the witnessed affidavit of the merchant Leonard Calhoun of Mesa Plata.

Boyden had already interviewed Lieutenant Mason-Field and Perry on the events of the tragic evening, checked into Perry's story of the ink-blotted ten- and five-dollar bills with Captain Greene, questioned every man known to have been present during the fight between Hudson and Lanier, the three Mexicans who had discovered Pierce's body, Sergeant Petrie, Privates Cusack and Haverstraw, who were present when Pierce's body was pulled from under the sutler's building.

"The question, Corporal," Boyden said now, "is how you happened to be in possession of this—" holding it up— "five-dollar bill which you paid to a Mesa Plata merchant in exchange for a hunting knife, an act witnessed by Sergeant Perry, attested to by Mr. Calhoun, and verified by Sergeant Major Riley and First Sergeant Tyler."

"I don't know, sir," Hudson replied firmly. "I told you before. It was payday. A lot of money changed hands, debts to pay, drinkin', gamblin'—"

"I would advise you to try to put your thoughts in proper order, Corporal. I'm sure you understand the seriousness of a murder charge, the penalty for which is death."

"Major, sir, I ain't been thinkin' of nothin' else. You got to believe me," Hudson pleaded.

"You understand, don't you, Hudson, that I am trying to help you by giving you every opportunity to remember what happened that night."

"Yes, sir. Like I said, I was in the sutler's that Saturday

night. We were drinkin' an' talkin', I remember that clear. Then Corporal Lanier come in an' we started horsin' aroun', nothin' serious. I said somethin', I don't know exactly what, an' Lanier called me a lousy redneck. That's what got me mad an' we started the fight. A little later, the nigger sergeant come bustin' in an' stopped it. I think he hit me, 'cause the nex' thing I know, I'm in my bunk in the barracks, feelin' kinda sick to my stomach an' woozy. I got up an' went outside to throw up an' I remember taps goin'.

"The men were comin' back to the barracks about then an' I didn' want to talk about the fight, or the nigger bustin' me, so I went over to the stables where Brig Quitt, the stable sergeant runs some games in his quarters. I taken a hand in a small game on account of I didn't have too much money left, then I got lucky for a spell an' won some good pots, so I moved over to a bigger game. About an hour, maybe a little more, I quit an' went back to the barracks an' turned in."

"Can you remember this bill at all, if you got it in change at the sutler's store or during the poker game in the stables?"

"No, sir, but it had to come from some place. I wasn't anywheres else."

"All right. Can you remember who the other players were in the stable games you played in?"

"No, sir, not specially. There must of been thirty-forty men there, some playin', some just lookin' on."

"In two poker games?"

"No, sir. There was a faro table runnin', a couple of crap games an' four or five poker games goin' all the same time. A man goes broke, drops out, somebody else sits in. Lots of men just come in to look aroun', didn't play at all."

"Is this a usual practice in Sergeant Quitt's quarters on paydays, Corporal?"

"I—uh—don't rightly know, sir."

"Hudson, don't try to protect anyone at this stage of the game. Remember that I'm trying to do what I can for you. An effort at gallantry may cost you your life."

"Yes, sir. I mean, it happens every payday. Sergeant Quitt sets up the games. He don't play, just takes a cut out of each game for the use of the stables an' supplyin' the cards an' dice."

"Sergeant Quitt is a very enterprising man, wouldn't you say, Corporal?"

"Yes, sir. He lends money on the side, too, between pay-days."

"Let's get back to this five-dollar bill. You've heard how Sergeant Perry was able to identify it, which was confirmed by Captain Greene. Also, that he used that same bill to pay his outstanding debt to Mr. Pierce on the night Mr. Pierce was murdered. However, I know that he paid that bill to Mr. Pierce after the fight between you and Corporal Lanier took place and you were no longer in the store. Therefore, if it came into your possession later, it had to come from one of two sources; from Mr. Pierce's cash taken in that night, or later, in the game in the stables, from someone who had robbed and murdered Mr. Pierce.

"After taps sounded, Sergeant Perry, who was Sergeant of the Guard, checked the Troop E barracks and found you were not in your cot, although you were not the only one missing at the time. However, you told Sergeant Perry later that you had gone out for a breath of air, but didn't mention you had gone to the stables to gamble."

"That was a lie, sir. I didn't want to go on report for gambling an' I thought the nigger would tell on me."

"Very well, I will accept that for the moment, but I insist that when you speak of Sergeant Perry in the future, you use his rank and name."

"Yes, sir."

"Can you take it from there?"

"I told you, sir—"

"I'm aware of what you've told me, Hudson, but you can't recall anyone in the game you were playing in, nor can I find anyone who is willing to testify that you were present. It is very likely that the men do not wish to incriminate themselves in this gambling business, so their identities are up to you. Is it that you can't remember or out of some false sense of loyalty don't wish to involve anyone else?"

"Sir, I—just don't remember. I was woozy. One face didn' look much different from another. All I was interested in was the cards."

"Can you remember how much you won or lost?"

"Yes, sir. I must of won because nex' mornin' I had over eighty dollars in my pockets. After I drawn my pay, paid off the laundress and a coupla guys I owed, an' spent some at the sutler's, I on'y had six or seven dollars left, enough to get into a small game, so I know I won."

"Including this marked five-dollar bill which matches this ten-dollar bill perfectly?"

"I—I guess so, sir. I don't know any other way I could of got it."

Boyden sighed deeply and said, "All right, Corporal, that will be all for the moment. I'll talk with you later. In the meantime, you are restricted to barracks except for meals."

"Yes, sir." Hudson stood up, saluted and went out. Boyden checked his list again and saw that Sergeant Brigham Quitt was next in line for questioning, postponed until now in order to amass as much evidence as possible against him for permitting his stables to be turned into a gambling den. He also had Quitt's military record before him.

Quitt, he remembered from an initial visit, was a brutish man, bald, short and stocky; a rough customer. The record showed he had twenty-two years' service, had enlisted in 1845 at the age of sixteen as a bugler. With the exception of the four years of Civil War, all his time had been spent on frontier duty. His record was spotty with reprimands and fines for minor offenses of drunkenness and disorderly conduct, one civil arrest in South Dakota. He had been a good bugler and orderly, a moderately good trooper, but was at his best running a stable operation, breaking and training horses. It was in that assignment that he had won his sergeant's stripes with no blemish on his record thereafter.

What the record did not show was that for Quitt, the Army was home. Orphaned in an Indian raid in Sioux territory at the age of nine, he had run away from a foster home at the age of twelve to be on his own. For the next four years he lived by his wits, working at odd jobs for meals, wandering on foot or by lift from one town to another. He had, at times, entered a small town late at night, broken into a store to steal food, clothing and shoes, but no more than he could wear or safely carry on his person.

When he was barely sixteen, he broke into a well-stocked store in East St. Louis late one night and after filling a small bag with food, appropriated a new pair of shoes, then rummaged about and found a cash box with a hundred and ten dollars in coins and bills. Buoyed up by these sudden riches, he slept in a nearby woods and returned the next morning to eat a hearty meal in a restaurant, then audaciously, or absentmindedly, went to the very store he had robbed and asked to see a rifle.

The storekeeper, perturbed by his loss, finally recognized the new shoes Quitt was wearing and sent his son to fetch a constable. When over a hundred dollars was found on his person, for which he could not account, Quitt was arrested and charged with the burglary. Three days later, he admitted the charge. Since the money and shoes were returned, he was given a choice—join the U.S. Cavalry or go to jail. Quitt chose the cavalry.

Now he came into Major Boyden's office, reported and was put at ease when the major asked him to be seated. Boyden assumed a "man-to-man" attitude, which astonished Quitt, who had always regarded all officers as Deity— or the natural enemy of all enlisted men. He was nervous and unresponsive, clearly showing his apprehension, a condition not entirely unknown to Boyden in certain enlisted men of Quitt's type.

Boyden, therefore, instead of attempting to question Quitt, related what he had learned from others; that Quitt loaned money at usurious rates of interest; that he used government property for gambling purposes; that both were against Fort regulations. Boyden did not add that either of these charges was sufficient reason to strip Quitt of the three stripes he wore, a fact already well known to the sweat-marked sergeant who sat stiffly in his chair, nodding his understanding of the charges.

"Now, Sergeant, I ask you who was present during the games you were operating in your stable quarters on the night the men were paid."

"S-sir, I couldn't say. Men came an' went. I wasn't payin' no mind to the men, only the games."

"Was Corporal Richard Hudson present during that Saturday evening?"

"He coulda been, sir."

"Was he or wasn't he?"

"I couldn't swear to it, sir."

"Can you remember any of the men who were present?"

"Well, sir, there were a lot of men. Corporal Zach Ingram, Privates Zeno, Best, Peters, Harrigan, Schwartzkopf, Garrigan, Sergeant Delevie—"

"What about Hudson?"

"Jeez— 'scuse me, sir—I can't remember, sir."

"Were you present at all times?"

"Yes, sir. I didn't leave the stables."

"Sergeant, are you in this alone or do you have—ah—partners, or associates, or assistants, to help you keep watch on the games?"

"Ah-h—"

"Speak up, Quitt. I have other ways of getting information. If you lie to me and I learn of it later, I can assure you there will be no leniency shown you."

"I—uh—Private Zeno an' Private Best kinda help me keep an eye on things. It's too much for one man—"

"Zeno. Best. They are on stable detail, are they not?"

"Yes, sir. An' Corporal—ex-Corporal Ingram, sir, but he don't help. Or Private Peters."

"All right, Sergeant Quitt, you may go now. I'll look further into your extracurricular activities and have you back later."

A sorry, time-consuming procedure, Boyden thought, but a necessary one. Each man he had questioned had turned up new names to add to his list, but no new evidence. The longer the inquiry dragged on, the more firmly was Hudson tied to the ghost of Sherman Pierce, all on the circumstantial evidence of possession of a five-dollar bill known to have been in the sutler's possession on the night he had been murdered, later discovered in Hudson's hands.

Captain Greene entered the office as Sergeant Quitt went out. "Ready for the next man, Major?"

Boyden looked up wearily. "How many are out there, Marc?"

"Seven."

"I'll take one more and see the rest in the morning. I'm getting nowhere in a hurry."

"Major, may I suggest two more?"

"Which two?"

"They're not on your list. Privates Ingram and Peters—"

"Stable detail?"

"Yes, sir."

"I've just added their names after talking with Quitt. How did you turn them up?"

"I didn't. The Sergeant Major suggested them. In fact, they practically volunteered themselves to Riley."

"Willingly?"

"I'd say so. They, ah, don't particularly like Quitt."

"Prejudiced testimony, Marc?"

"Possibly, even probably, but it might be enlightening."

303

"All right. Send Ingram and Peters in, dismiss the rest, and have the orderly get me some coffee, please."

Ingram, the ex-corporal, was belligerent. Peters, a pale-eyed man who wore steel-rimmed glasses, seemed hesitant. Boyden put his first questions to Ingram. Both, Ingram volunteered, had been present in the stables the night of the murder.

"And you were no part of the games, either as participants or as Sergeant Quitt's watchers?"

"No, sir. You see, sir, on game nights, Sergeant Quitt needs our stalls—uh—quarters—to give him room enough to set up the games. Peters an' me, we have to wait 'til the games are over before we can get to sleep."

"Private Peters?"

"Yes, sir," Peters agreed, nodding his head affirmatively.

"Very well. Did either of you see Corporal Hudson in any of the games that were in progress?"

"I seen him, sir," Peters said.

"Me, too, sir," Ingram acknowledged.

"On Saturday night?"

"Yes, sir," Ingram said. "He come in, must of been close to taps or a little after. I remember because he looked kind of bunged up, maybe a little hung over."

"Which game was he playing?"

"Poker, sir. I remember now, the time, I mean. It was just after taps. Some of the men quit the games an' there was an empty seat. Hudson came in an' took that seat. I was lookin' on."

"Then you saw him when he first came in?"

"Yes, sir. He sat down, pulled out some money—"

"How much money?"

"I wasn't that close, sir."

"Was there much of it, Ingram, a thick wad of bills—?"

The orderly knocked and entered with the coffee for Boyden, who said, "Bring two more cups," and the young orderly's eyebrows, like those of Ingram and Peters, rose. He brought two tin cups from the outer office. "For them, sir?" he asked, still not believing.

"For them." The orderly poured the three cups of coffee and placed the pot on the desk. When he left the room, Boyden said, "Drink up," then turned to Ingram. "The money, Ingram."

"I been tryin' to remember, sir. It wasn't much. He reached inside his shirt pocket an' pulled out some, just a few bills, maybe four or five ones."

304

"Was Sergeant Quitt present?"

"I don't remember, sir."

Peters said, "No, sir, he wasn't. He left around taps, said he was goin' over to the mess hall to get somethin' to eat. I heard him tell Zeno and Best to keep a sharp eye out on things."

Boyden's attitude became one of alertness. "When did Sergeant Quitt return?" he asked, trying to keep his voice casual.

"I can't say, sir. Not for a while," Peters replied.

"How long a while, half an hour, an hour?"

"Somewheres in between. Maybe forty-five minutes."

"And he went to the mess hall, you said."

"I didn't say that, sir. I said, he *said* he was goin' to the mess hall to get somethin' to eat. I didn't see him go there. All I wanted to do was go to sleep, but I couldn't because the players were in our quarters."

Boyden scribbled a note, called for the orderly and told him to give the note to Captain Greene. He then turned to Ingram. "While you were looking on, Ingram, did you notice how Corporal Hudson was doing?"

"Well, sir, I wasn't just watchin' him alone, but I know he won a few pots. There was other poker games goin' on at the same time. This was a low stakes game Hudson was in. The others was ten-dollar limit."

"When do you remember next seeing Sergeant Quitt?"

"I guess when he come back from the mess hall. He come in an' Best an' Zeno talked with him for a bit. Quitt started checkin' the tables an' the crap game."

"Did anything happen when he checked the game Hudson was in—something out of the ordinary, the game you were watching?"

"No, sir—wait—yes, sir. Hudson was winning, I remember, shovin' some big bills in his pocket, leavin' a couple of ones on the table. He was callin' a bet an' raisin' it, an' then he was out of money on the table. Somebody tellin' him, 'You a dollar light, Corporal,' an' he pulled out a twenty an' throwed it on the table. I remember he said, 'Change it, somebody. Ain't enough on the table,' but nobody had that much in front of him in a low stakes game. Then Quitt says, 'Don't slow the game down, boys, I'll change it,' an' he picked up the twenty an' changed it. I remember because Hudson won that pot with a full house an' moved over to the high stakes game."

Boyden paused to sip at his coffee, Ingram and Peters

doing likewise. Boyden put his cup down and said, "You saw Sergeant Quitt change the twenty-dollar bill for Hudson, Ingram?"

"Yes, sir. I was standin' between Hudson an' a corporal from K Troop."

"Can you give me the names of the men who were in the game at that time?"

"Maybe two or three, sir. A corporal from HQ, sir, his name is Janowicz—"

Boyden jotted the names down as Ingram called two other names off. To Peters, "You saw no part of this?"

"No, sir. I guess I wasn't payin' close attention."

"Very well, Peters, you are dismissed. I want you to remain, Ingram."

When Peters left, Boyden took the marked five-dollar bill from his desk drawer and placed it directly in front of Ingram, and saw a flicker of recognition in his eyes. Boyden waited for a few moments, then took the similarly marked ten-dollar bill from the desk drawer and placed it beside the other and noticed Ingram's eyes shifting back and forth from one to the other. "Look at these carefully, Ingram, and tell me if you have seen either bill before, and if so, when and where."

Boyden watched Ingram's face carefully as the ex-corporal's attention was riveted first on the five, then on the ten, then back to the five. Finally he extended a hand and pointed to the five-dollar bill. "This one, sir," he said.

"You're absolutely sure?"

"Yes, sir."

"Where?"

"It was one of the bills Sergeant Quitt gave Corporal Hudson in change for his twenty, sir."

"Think carefully, Ingram, this is very important. You are certain beyond all doubt?"

"Yes, sir. I remember Hudson kinda held it out an' stared at it for a coupla seconds, then put it back in his pocket."

"And this was after Sergeant Quitt returned from his visit to the mess hall for something to eat?"

"Yes, sir."

"About what time was that, Ingram?"

"Like I told you, sir, maybe a quarter to eleven."

"Thank you. Please remain where you are." Boyden turned his head toward the door and called out, "Orderly!"

When the orderly appeared, "Has Captain Greene returned yet?"

"Not yet, sir."

To Ingram, "I want you to wait outside until Captain Greene returns. He will take down your statement as you have given it to me, as you will give it to him, and ask you to sign it if it is correct. I want you to tell him in your own words exactly what you have told me just now, with regard to the exchange of bills, your identification of the five-dollar bill, and the time the exchange was made. Also, the times Sergeant Quitt left the stables and returned, and the names of the men present whom you remember."

"Yes, sir."

"Orderly, find Sergeant Major Riley and send him to me at once."

"Yes, sir."

Within fifteen minutes, Captain Greene returned with the two Mexicans who had been on duty in the mess hall on the Saturday night in question, Jose Garcia and Bernardo Rojas. They were interviewed separately by Boyden and disclosed what they had told Greene; that they had been in the kitchen and mess hall from eight o'clock until midnight, preparing coffee and sandwiches for each guard shift. The question put to each, and their replies, were almost identical.

"At any time during those four hours, did anyone but the guard details going on duty, or coming off duty, come to the mess hall for food?"

"*Sí señor*. One trooper came for coffee to take to the O.D. The sergeant major, he come for a cup of coffee maybe half past nine. Lieutenant Kennard come for coffee and one sandwich maybe fifteen minutes to ten."

"Anyone else?"

"No, *señor*."

"And Sergeant Quitt?"

"Of the stables, *señor?*"

"Yes."

A moment of thought, then, "No, *señor*. He does not come."

"You did not see Sergeant Quitt between the hours of eight o'clock and midnight that night?"

"No, *señor*."

"Think hard."

Another few moments, then more positively, "No, *señor*."

"*Gracias.* You will please go outside where the captain will write out your statement. When you are sure it is correct, you will sign it and swear to its truth."

The orderly knocked and entered. "Sergeant Riley reporting, sir."

"Send him in."

"Riley," Boyden said when the formalities of reporting were over, "I want you to handpick four men who know how to keep their mouths shut. Then I want you to send Sergeant Quitt to my office. While he is here, you will find some excuse to get Zeno, Best, Peters and Ingram out of the stables for an hour. During that hour, I want you to direct your chosen men to conduct a thorough search of the stables. I want every stall, every storage box, every locker, every inch of the floor, walls and upper gallery checked out carefully and thoroughly; not merely looked at or into, but physically moved to see what lies beneath or on top of it. In particular, I want you to personally check Sergeant Quitt's private room there. Move every tool, every chair, the bed, everything in his clothes locker, the locker itself. Is that clear?"

"Yes, sir, exceptin'—beggin' your pardon, sir, what'll we be lookin' for?"

"Money, Sergeant Major."

"Ah—how much money, sir?"

"About as much as a sutler's store would take in on a payday."

Sergeant Quitt's first visit to Major Boyden's office had left him considerably shaken, aware that having been forced to admit his illegal money-lending and gambling activities, his position as Stable Sergeant was now in jeopardy along with the three stripes of his office and authority. With so many men being questioned, it would have been foolhardy to deny that he was the Fort's most prominent gambling entrepreneur and moneylender, having the largest amount of space available to accommodate the greatest number of men.

Over the last ten of his twenty-two years in the Army, Quitt had learned that by not sitting in any game and simply operating as landlord, the cut he received from every poker, faro and dice game pot made him the biggest winner in camp, with no possible chance to lose. Add this to the usurious interest he gathered in on small loans made between paydays, Quitt had accumulated a considerable hoard of cash during those latter ten years.

He knew there was more to Boyden's inquiry than the discovery and exposure of a gambling operation. On most Army posts, payday gambling was more or less taken for granted and from the C.O. to the lowliest O.D., officers willingly looked aside during the first three days which followed a payday.

Therefore, Quitt knew, Boyden was after something more important, and that 'something more important' was causing the bald, stocky sergeant to sweat even more when Riley came to his quarters in the stable and told him to report to Major Boyden's office on the double.

Over his own jumbled thoughts, he heard Boyden saying, "Sergeant, I have been rechecking my notes taken during our earlier conversation."

Quitt sat tensely still, neither speaking nor nodding.

"Sergeant, I want you to go over your actions during the night of—ah—the Saturday night following the morning the men were last paid."

"Yes, sir. Well, sir, 'twasn't no different than any other payday night—"

Quitt rambled on at great length, describing in detail how the games were set up; folding camp tables in the empty stalls; the largest poker game on a table made up of bales of hay and covered with a canvas tarpaulin, using camp stools for seats; Quitt and two assistants in constant circulation, taking a cut from each pot; men coming and going at all hours of day and night—

"And you were present all night long, Sergeant?" Boyden asked quietly.

"Yes, sir. Except maybe once or twice, sir, to answer a call of nature."

"How long would you say each of those calls of nature took, Sergeant?"

"Oh, no more'n a couple two-three minutes, sir."

"And those were the only two times you were absent? Keep in mind, Sergeant, we are speaking of that Saturday night only, not the night that preceded it or those that followed."

"Yes, sir, them were the only two times I left."

Rustling through a sheaf of papers, showing no impatience, Boyden hesitated over one sheet as though he were reading it carefully, then looked up suddenly and said,

"Do you in any way wish to change what you told me relative to your absence from the games on the night in question, Sergeant?"

Quitt said, "No, sir."

"Very well. I have here the statement of a man who was present at the stables. In it, he states that somewhere around ten o'clock he heard you say you were going to the mess hall for something to eat. I can call other witnesses to testify to the same thing."

Quitt's bullet head jerked upward, his eyes locked onto Boyden's. "Well, Sergeant, what about it?"

"I—uh—I don't remember, sir, with everything goin' on."

"Perhaps I can refesh your memory by pinning it down a little closer to the time. In connection with this statement, it would appear you left the stables somewhere about the time taps were sounded, that would be around ten o'clock. I have that here in a signed, sworn statement, Sergeant."

"I—uh—lemme think, sir. Yes, sir, I recall now. That was Saturday night. I remember I didn't have nothin' to eat since breakfast, sir, no dinner, no supper. By taps, my belly was growlin' somethin' fierce, so I told Privates Zeno an' Best to look out for things whilst I grabbed a quick bite an' some coffee at the mess hall—"

"How long would you say that took, Sergeant?"

"Well, the mess hall bein' so close to the stables, sir, no more'n ten-fifteen minutes, sir. You see, sir, Zeno an' Best ain't as sharp as they could be, so I hurried back to take over—"

"Sergeant, did you see anyone in the mess hall at that hour who could testify to your presence there during those ten or fifteen minutes?"

"Well, like I said, sir, I was hungry an' in a hurry, so I wasn't payin' no attention to who was there. I guess if I got around an' did some askin' among the men, I could—"

"Sergeant, let me suggest that you couldn't find a single eyewitness to your presence in the mess hall that night between the hours of eight and midnight for the simple reason that you were not there."

"S—sir?"

"Suppose I told you that I have sworn statements from at least two witnesses who were present in the mess hall from eight until midnight, who claim you were not there. And another statement which claims you were absent

310

from the stables from about ten o'clock until ten forty-five."

"I—sir—well, you see, sir, a man like me, makes money cuttin' on games, lendin' money, he don't make many friends. I got a idea there's a lot of men would like to see me court-martialed for runnin' games—"

"Sergeant, I want you to tell me where you were between the hours of ten o'clock and ten forty-five that Saturday night, why you left the stables for at least forty-five minutes, where you went, whom you saw, and who, if anyone, saw you during that time. I will remind you, as you no doubt already know, that I have been interviewing quite a number of men. These documents you see on my desk are the sworn statements they have made and signed. Now let's get down to the facts of those forty-five minutes without wasting any more time."

Quitt sat speechless, his face darkened with strain and beads of perspiration, hands fumbling with his neckerchief ends, shirt collar and pocket flaps.

"Answer me, Sergeant! At once!"

"I already told the major everything I know."

"You refuse to answer?"

"I already answered all I can, sir."

"I'll give you another ten minutes, Quitt, to think about it. I will only add that your answer, ten minutes from now, could be the most important one you have ever made in your entire life. If you refuse, I can assure you that my next action will be one of the most serious consequence to you. Think it over carefully, Sergeant."

At the end of five minutes, while Boyden continued to scan the statements on his desk, every word of which he had read and digested numerous times before, and as Quitt sat hunched forward, elbows resting on the arms of his chair, both heard the rap of knuckles on the door. Boyden called out, "Come in."

Captain Greene entered, went to Boyden and whispered a message. Boyden looked up and said, "Very well, Captain. Show them in."

Quitt's head turned to follow Captain Greene, who walked to the door, opened it and called out, "All right, Sergeant Major."

Riley came in and reported formally to Major Boyden. Behind him came two enlisted men, carrying a regulation foot locker which was scarred and scratched with years of

311

movement, a lock hanging from its broken hasp. Quitt's face turned an ashen gray.

Boyden said, "Sergeant Quitt, have you considered your answer?"

Quitt's head rocked from side to side, his mouth drawn in a grim, tight line, but he did not answer the question.

"Where did you find that locker box, Riley?" Boyden asked.

"Sir, we found it buried in the stable under the planks 'neath Sergeant Quitt's bunk."

"Open it."

"Yes, sir." Riley motioned to the enlisted men, who raised the lid. Inside, filling the box to above the three-quarters mark, were many neatly tied bundles of currency, stacked one atop the other. To the right were several canvas bags of gold and silver coins, and a wooden box which contained almost a dozen watches and a score of rings.

"Sergeant Quitt, can you identify the contents of this locker box?" Boyden asked.

Quitt's mouth began to move in convulsive jerks. "Yes, sir. Yes, sir. It's mine. Mine. I been savin' it for over ten years. Ten long years. It's all mine. Nobody's got any right to go bustin' into my personal b'longin's. It's mine—"

Riley lifted one of the canvas bags and placed it on the desk. "Take a look at the bottom of this, sir," he said to Boyden.

Boyden examined the bag and found nothing unusual about it. He looked at Riley questioningly. Riley said, "Sir, take a look at the bottom."

Boyden turned the bag over, the bottom towards him, and examined it carefully. The barely legible letters read:

PROP'TY OF
S. PIERCE
Army Sutler

During the five days that had elapsed, Lizardi and his three companions had remained out of sight in the house of Julio Campos' woman, Maria Elena Duarte; the house stood on Calle Maricopa, only a few steps across the alley behind Espuela de Oro. Confined to two rooms, drinking, eating, sleeping in cramped quarters while in possession of more gold than any had ever possessed, wearied of playing cards, nerves were beginning to wear thin.

On the sixth day, Lizardi's woman, Ema Arboleya, came

from the *cantina* before noon with word. "The Anglo marshal comes seeking you, Casimiro. Inez told him she has not seen you for a week. He left word he would return at five o'clock."

"*Gracias,* Ema."

"You will come?"

"I will come. Go back and tell Inez."

When Ema left, Campos, Vega and Moreno waited through the heavy silence that followed for Lizardi to speak and tell them what lay in his mind; but Lizardi poured more tequila for himself and began laying out the cards in a familiar pattern. Finally Campos came to the table and sat in the chair opposite him. Lizardi looked up.

"Six days now we have lived like roaches in these two rooms, Casimiro," Campos said.

"So?"

"We have gold we cannot spend and the air grows foul with the smell of our bodies. We could be many miles from here, in Sonora, even Californio, enjoying our money. Now the Anglo marshal seeks us."

Lizardi smiled crookedly and said slowly, "But for me, Julio, you would not have that gold. But for me, you would be in jail because you could not explain how you came by it. But for me, you would be hanging from an Anglo gallows or a tree by now. As for the Anglo marshal, he does not seek you, but me."

"You will see him?"

"Why not? It would not be polite to run like a coward when he comes seeking me, no?"

"Casimiro—"

"What disturbs you, Julio? Speak out like a man."

"Casimiro, why do we wait here?"

Lizardi laughed patronizingly. "Perhaps to teach you patience. Perhaps to—." He suddenly turned cold and snapped angrily. "When it is time for you to know, I will tell you. Now do not disturb my thoughts, eh?"

In the sullen atmosphere, Lizardi waited until a little before five o'clock, then went to the *cantina* and sat at his corner table, ordered a bottle of tequila and one of whiskey, with two glasses. He consumed four small glasses of tequila before he saw the rangy figure of Marshal Russ Yarborough enter from the street door. Yarborough pushed his hat back on his head and glanced around the room until he saw Lizardi, then strode toward the table with purpose. He was slight in build, but lithe in movement,

313

a man in that indefinable age between forty and sixty. Years of outdoor living had darkened and dried his skin to an almost parchment quality, drawn tightly over a lean frame and bony skull in a way that emphasized his stern, foxlike features.

Without an exchange of greetings, Yarborough slid into the chair opposite Lizardi, while Lizardi poured a generous glass of whiskey and pushed it toward the older man. Not until they had finished their drinks was the silence broken, then by Yarborough. He spoke in a slow drawl that was a mixture of Georgia, Texas and Arizona, and when he spoke, poured more whiskey for himself then waited for a response from the Mexican.

"Señor," Lizardi said finally, "if you have the proof of your accusation that I, Casimiro Lizardi, am guilty of the attack on the Army supply train, would we be sitting here in a *cantina* talking over a drink, or would I be in your jail, or the Army prison, talking through iron bars, eh?"

Yarborough leaned back in his chair, one hand toying with the empty whiskey glass, his piercing gray eyes staring directly into Lizardi's, forehead wrinkled as though puzzled why he had even taken the trouble to come here, wasting his time.

"Lizardi," he replied, "if I had anything to pin on you besides strong suspicions, we both know where you'd be. All's I'm tellen you is I know it wasn't no Apaches did that job an' you're my next likely prospect. No, I'n got no proof right now, but somewheres along the line, I'll git it an' when I do, I'll see you an' yore whole gang of cutthroats hangin' from a gallows or a tree limb."

"Señor Yarborough, you do me honor to come here to see me, but I do not like this talk of cutthroats and hanging. I am what you see, a citizen of Mexico which once owned all this land that was taken from us by the Anglos. There are laws and treaties that protect honest men—"

Yarborough stood up abruptly. "All right, honest man, I git the point. But I don't like takin' a lot of guff from the Army Provost Marshal whilst you're walkin' aroun' like a fat cat with a full belly. Tell you one thing, Lizardi, from now on, wherever you go, whatever you do, just keep lookin behin' you. The one time you don't—" He stopped short, then added, *"Adios, hombre.* Thanks for the whiskey."

To Yarborough's retreating back, Lizardi replied, *"Adios,* Marshal. Come back as my guest any time."

He poured more tequila and downed it in quick tosses. Tucson was getting a little too warm for comfort and the thought of free-spending in Sonora, in total safety, was becoming more appealing. Ai-ee, it was time to make a move.

After two more drinks, he went to the back room of the *cantina* and spoke to Inez for a few minutes, then crossed the alley to Maria Elena Duarte's house where Campos, Vega and Moreno awaited his return. Campos spoke first.

"The marshal, he knows?"

Lizardi snorted with contempt. "Rumors. He suspects. He threatens. But he knows nothing. There is no proof. *Amigos,* I think we have had enough of Tucson for a while. After sundown, we will ride out. Vega, Moreno, we will pack food for ten days. Campos, go to the *cantina* and bring tequila, then put fresh water in our canteens."

"Where, Casimiro?"

"Sonora first. Later, we will see."

BOOK IV

CHAPTER I

THE RIDE FROM TUBAC TO TUCSON WAS A SWIFT ONE, with one stop for a noonday meal and a brief rest for the horses. There was little talk between the four men, and Sam Palmer somehow identified this remarkable reluctance to talk with the presence of Loren Olmstead and Marcos Espuela. If Max Potter suspected anything, he did not remark on it. Usually, Sam and Max rode side by side, but at the outset early that morning, it was Loren who chose that position, with Sam and Marcos riding behind. Since Marcos held his own counsel, Sam let the matter pass without comment.

They reached Tucson at dusk. At the Congress Hotel, Max, Sam and Loren dismounted. Marcos said, "I will take the horses to Ainsworth's and stable them."

"Thanks, Marcos. Come back and have supper with us," Max invited.

"*Gracias,* Señor Max, but I will go to the Espuela de Oro to see my mother, if you will excuse me."

"Sure, son. Sam and I will walk over to the Depot afterwards if you want to join us there. Got that Army shipment to Fort Bandolier to figure out."

"When I am free, *señor.*"

While Max, Sam and Loren went into the Congress, Marcos led their horses down Calle Principale to the public stables. Inside, two men, their faces heavily shadowed with beards, were lifting saddles from the backs of their weary horses. Placing the saddles on racks, the men took their rifles from the scabbards, and from blanket rolls, each withdrew a double-barreled shotgun. Meanwhile, Luis Perez, the attendant on duty, led each horse into a separate stall.

"How long you stay in Tucson, *señores?*" he asked.

"A few days, more or less, maybe a week," Harry Penn replied. "Give 'em a good rubdown an' some grain. They come a long way today."

"*Sí señor.*" Luis looked over the edge of the stall as

319

Marcos dismounted. In Spanish, he called out, "Ah, Marcos, you return from Tubac. All is well?"

"*Sí*, Luis, all is well," Marcos replied in Spanish.

"Four horses this time."

"Four. The cousin of *el patrón* rode with us."

"And his sister?"

"She is well. It was a happy reunion."

"You will want these tonight?"

"No, Luis. *Señor* Potter and the others are at the hotel. Tomorrow, maybe."

"*Bueno*. I will take good care of them. Your mama sends word she would talk with you when you return."

"*Gracias*. I go to see her now. *Hasta*—"

"Hey, boy!" As Marcos turned on the sound of Penn's voice, "You speak any English?"

"Enough to get by on," Marcos replied easily.

"Good. My friend an' I just rode in from Lordsburg an' we're a little shy of cash. You know anybody in town might be interested in buyin' a coupla good shotguns?"

"No, but there's a gunsmith a few doors up from the Congress Hotel. He might be interested if the price is right. His name is Murtagh."

"Thanks." To his companion, "Let's give it a try, Dutch."

"Did you say Lordsburg?" Marcos asked. "You have any trouble between Fort Bowie and Dragoon Springs, coming through the Pass?" When Penn failed to answer at once, "Apache Pass. You had to come through it—"

"Uh—yeah. Yeah. We didn't have no trouble at all."

As the two men walked out into Calle Principale, Luis Perez said, "An act of God. There has been much movement in the Pass. Cochise has been active. The *soldados* were in a battle there only two days ago."

Marcos said, "Why would they lie about coming from the east?"

"Who knows why Anglos lie," Luis replied with a shrug. "Maybe it is second nature to them."

Marcos walked up Calle Principale and in passing Murtagh's Gun Shop looked in and saw the two strangers at the counter talking with Coley Murtagh, who was examining one of the shotguns. Giving the matter no further thought, he crossed over to Maricopa and went directly to Espuela de Oro with thoughts of Laurie and Loren commingled with the added problems created by the return of the latter.

But soon, in the warm embrace of Inez, the familiar aroma of food and an atmosphere of congeniality, he put Loren and Laurie to one side temporarily. Inez sat with him at a table and ordered a bottle of tequila and food for both.

"You are thin, Marcos," Inez said examining his face.

"But I have grown hard. The work I do agrees with me. I am outside and in the saddle. What more can a man ask, eh, Mama?"

"You grow farther away from me and closer to the Anglos."

Marcos laughed and covered one of his mother's hands with one of his own. "As long as your blood runs through me, Mama, I will never forget what I am."

"It is told that you hunger for an Anglo girl."

"And who is it who tells you this story?"

"If it is true, it is not important who tells me."

"Then hear it from the best source. It is true that I have such thoughts, but they may come to nothing."

"You are not good enough for her?"

"I am good enough for her, yes. For others, perhaps not."

Inez muttered a curse and said angrily, "For whom are you not good enough, eh?"

"Mama, do not concern yourself with this matter. I am a man and a man solves his own problems. What will be, will be, no?"

The food arrived and the subject was put aside for the moment. As he ate, Marcos glanced at the table next to the corner window. "Espuela de Oro does not seem the same without Señor Lizardi and his three *vagos.*"

"They rode out three days ago."

"They are lice in the hair of decent men."

Inez shrugged. "They are no better or worse than your Anglos who rob, cheat, murder and steal from Mexicans and Indios alike."

"My Anglos? My papa is an Anglo, no, Mama?"

"Eat your food, Marcos, and let us speak of other things."

"Yes. It is not pleasant to talk about those who walk through our lives like shadows."

"Marcos, I beg you, do not push Casimiro too hard or evil days will fall upon both of us. Already, he looks upon you as his enemy."

"And but for you, I would be dead, no?"

"Perhaps, perhaps not. All I ask is that you keep out of his way. If he must die, let it not be at your hands."

"*Sí*, Mama. Now, let us forget him."

At nine o'clock, Marcos embraced Inez, kissed her cheek and departed. Outside, he walked in the direction of the T-Y Depot, only a few blocks away. He reached for a cigar and found he had smoked his last one after supper. Across the street from the Depot was a restaurant-*cantina* and he crossed over, went inside to replenish his supply. Jorge, owner of El Gaucho, greeted Marcos warmly as he proferred a box of cigars. Marcos counted out five cigars, paid for them and accepted a light from Jorge. As he turned to leave, Marcos saw the two strangers he had encountered earlier in the stable. They sat at a table sharing a meal and a bottle of tequila. Evidently, he thought, they had made a deal with Murtagh for their shotguns.

"You know the two Anglos there, Jorge?" Marcos asked.

"No, I have never seen them before. They drink, eat and ask questions."

"What questions?"

"About the Depot. When the next stage leaves for Yuma. Who are the owners. Where do they live. I tell them to wait until morning when it is open, then ask their questions across the street."

Marcos glanced at the men curiously, then turned back to Jorge. "How long have they been here?"

"Over two hours. They sit there at the window and look across the street at the Depot where Señor Potter and his son-in-law work in their office. Also, another young Anglo with hair the color of gold."

"*Gracias,* Jorge. If those two ask questions of me, tell them nothing, eh?"

"*Sí*, Marcos. *Hasta la vista.*"

"*Buenas noches, amigo.*"

With the two strangers watching the front of the Depot, Marcos did not approach it. Instead, he walked up Maricopa for a short distance and stood inside the darkened doorway of a *farmacia* and waited. Across the street, light came from one window to the right side of the main entrance, which was locked at this time of night. Through the window, he could make out Max seated at his desk, Sam pacing back and forth, stopping occasionally to converse with Max. Loren was not in his line of vision and

322

Marcos had no way of knowing if Loren was with them or back at the hotel.

He stood in the dark doorway, braced against the cold night and wondering over the coincidence of the two strangers who had lied about the direction from which they had come, needing to sell their shotguns to raise a few dollars, now spending them liberally at El Gaucho and asking questions about T-Y Lines and its owners. Since their horses were stabled at Ainsworth's, what need for them to know when the next stage left for Yuma? What was their particular interest in the owners and where they lived?

These were the questions Marcos wanted answers for; enough to outwait the two strangers. To see what, when they left El Gaucho, were their plans.

Across the street, Loren sat quietly looking on and listening as Max and Sam outlined plans for T-Y's first major assignment under its new Army contract—the logistics of transporting replacement supplies for those which had been looted en route to Fort Bandolier. Most of the items were on hand in the warehouses at Fort Lowell, the need was urgent, and T-Y would be forced to postpone certain civilian shipments in order to accommodate the Army.

The intricate details being discussed by Sam and Max were lost on Loren, who felt no part of the new life he felt was being forced upon him. Since leaving Fort Leavenworth, he had become part of an entirely new world, one in which he felt he had achieved a certain maturity and manhood, seeking help from no one and surviving its dangers and hardships. His sadness over the loss of Aaron and Libby was monumental, yet he felt a certain release in the knowledge and feeling that he was on his own to go where he pleased, do as he pleased. When he first reached Tres Flechas and was reunited with Laurie, he felt that he had reached a certain goal, but now, he realized, she had no further need of him; that they were farther apart than ever before in their lives, with a Mexican, Marcos Espuela, standing between them.

Yet, as Laurie had told him firmly, she was a woman and not a child. He could see no way in which he could convince her that she was making a grave mistake. From what he had seen, Marcos stood high in the favor of Max and Sam and he could not expect moral support from that

323

quarter. Therefore, he stood alone; as much alone as he had been these last six months.

Well, being alone was not the worst thing in life. He was a man and many men lived alone. There would be no problem with money. He would draw off his share of their investment in T-Y and head for California, make a life for himself in San Francisco, about which he had heard so much.

When? Perhaps at the turn of the new year. A new year, a new life. A good omen.

He looked up when he heard Sam say, "Well, Max, I think that's about it for now. If we can borrow four wagons from Colonel Taggart, I think we can make up the complete train and leave no later than Thursday. Without any trouble on the road, we can be at Fort Bandolier by Sunday."

Max said, "All right, Sam. I'll see Governor Mitchell first thing in the morning. Since he's puttin' all the pressure on us, I'm sure he'll clear the way." Max pulled his watch from his vest pocket. "It's after ten. Let's get back to the hotel an' get us some sleep."

Loren stood up and drew on his outer coat as Max gathered up his papers, and Sam turned the oil lamp down. Outside, Sam checked to make sure the four night guards were alert, rejoined Max and Loren and began walking down Maricopa toward Calle Principale and the Congress Hotel.

"I wonder what happened to Marcos?" Max said, thrusting his hands deeply into his coat pockets.

"Probably spending the night with his mother," Sam replied. "He'll show up in the morning."

Loren pulled his coat collar up over the back of his neck and said nothing.

From the doorway of the *farmacia*, Marcos watched as Max, Sam and Loren walked slowly along the darkened street. Moments later, he peered around the edge of the doorway and saw the two strangers emerge from El Gaucho, cross the street and turn in the same direction Sam, Max and Loren had taken. There was no one else on Maricopa, a street of small shops, all dark at this hour except for El Gaucho and another small *cantina* farther down on the opposite side of the street.

Marcos moved quickly across the street, half a block behind the two strangers, and followed, keeping close to the building line. In the middle of the next block, he moved up closer, faster, now within thirty yards of the two men. From sheer instinct, he opened his coat and drew the right side back to clear his gun.

His instinct was working. One of the men touched the sleeve of the other and now both began opening their outer coats and moved up more rapidly on Max, Sam and Loren. Calle Principale was still a good three blocks away.

Stepping away from the building line into the center of the sidewalk, Marcos took a few running steps, closing the distance between himself and the two strangers to a mere yard and a half. The men heard his boots on the wooden walk and half turned in his direction.

"Hold it!" Marcos called out.

Up ahead, he saw Sam turn first, then Loren, and finally Max. Loren already had his gun in his hand and Sam was drawing his own .44. The two strangers were caught between them, Harry Penn looking toward the threesome to his left, Dutch Macklin toward Marcos.

"Drop the guns!" Marcos ordered, but Harry Penn raised his weapon and shouted a curse. Loren's gun spat and Harry Penn wheeled around, hit. The gun in his hand went off and the bullet bored a hole in the doorway of the store on his right. Dutch Macklin raised his hands, but Loren's second shot cut him down. Macklin fell to the ground, but Penn, knees buckled, was still on his feet.

The whole thing had happened in a matter of seconds, no more than three. The gun fell from Penn's hand to the walk with a sharp clatter as people began to emerge from the *cantina* and from the side streets off Maricopa. Harry Penn had fallen to his knees, one hand clutching his middle. Marcos and Sam ran to him as Max and Loren came up behind them. Dutch Macklin was dead.

"You know this one, Sam?" Max asked.

"He's Harry Penn, the bounty hunter who was locked up in Yuma. Must have broken out somehow."

"The other one," Loren said. "I think he was the one who lit out after I shot the other two in the alley that night."

"Git me a doctor," Penn gasped.

Two Mexicans lifted Penn and carried him down toward Calle Principale to Dr. Hogan's surgery. By that time, Sheriff Yarborough had arrived and taken charge. While Dr. Hogan was being wakened in his quarters above his office, Yarborough said, "Just got a wanted notice on this Penn this mornin'. The other one fits the description of the man who pistol-whipped Sheriff Kinnick an' sprung Penn loose. Stole two rifles an' shotguns on the way out."

"Any word on Sheriff Kinnick?" Loren asked.

"I guess he come out of it. He's the one signed the message. You all go ahead. I'll take care of this fella. Be a nice little reward to collect on him. Who got him?"

Marcos said, "Loren here. He got both of them."

"Good shootin', son," Yarborough complimented.

"They weren't very fast," Loren replied.

In his room at the Congress, Max said to Loren, "You sure come up fast with that iron, son."

Loren looked back at Max and smiled.

"Can't figure it was that necessary," Max continued, "what with Marcos holdin' his piece on them from one side, you an' Sam on the other."

"Looked like he was ready," Loren said.

Sam said quietly, "He wouldn't have fired, looking into the barrels of two guns, Loren. Besides, Macklin had his hands up over his head."

"I just wasn't taking any chances, Sam."

"Well, maybe Penn will live to be hanged. The other one won't have even that much of a chance."

Somehow, Loren felt his sense of pride dissipating, hearing in Max's voice, now in Sam's, a note of disapprobation. He said, "Good night," abruptly and left the room to go to his own.

Alone, thinking over the event, he felt a glow in himself he had not felt before, together with mild anger for Max's and Sam's attitude toward him, feeling they were ungrateful for what he had done. Yet he took satisfaction in knowing he was fast, faster than Sam, faster than Marcos. He undressed slowly and got into bed, experiencing an almost sensual gratification in his feeling of total maturity.

The next day, over Colonel Taggart's protests, General Reese authorized the loan of four freight wagons to T-Y. This brought forth a stormy reaction from Chief Indian Agent Marcus Rodman, who insisted the wagons were needed to supply the Indian reservations under his control. Not only were Rodman's protests nullified by executive order of Governor Mitchell, who declared the mission to Fort Bandolier an extreme emergency, but an experienced rifleman was ordered to ride guard beside the driver of each of the twelve wagons. T-Y supplied thirty-

326

six *vaqueros* to round out the escort detail. At the last moment, Loren asked permission·to accompany the train and Max approved his request. Total manpower came to sixty-three.

Under Palmer's direction, the supplies were so distributed that clothing, food, hardware, paint, tools, tentage and other goods were carried in equal amounts in each wagon. The train was planned to move out in three sections of four wagons each, Palmer leading the first section, Loren with the second, Marcos with the third, each section two hours behind the first. The new rifles and ammunition, so highly prized by the Apaches, were placed among the four wagons of the second section. Last to be loaded was the sawed lumber which acted as a protective cover for each wagon, then covered with heavy canvas tarpaulins and lashed securely in place.

The trip to Fort Bandolier, despite apprehension and misgivings, was made without incident. Once arrived, the prime topic of conversation was Sergeant Brigham Quitt's confession and arrest for the murder of Sherman Pierce, almost overshadowing the news that the Fort families would be returning sometime after the new year.

Third topic of discussion was the arrival of the new repeating rifles to take the place of the older carbines. There was not a man in the entire Fort who wasn't eager to get his hands on the new weapon and take his turn on the rifle range.

There were few in the Fort who had liked or admired Sherman Pierce, for all sutlers were notorious price-gougers; nor was the brother of Pierce's widow, Fred Wheeler, any exception. He was no better or different than Pierce, already the butt of derision from the troopers who were forced to deal with him. First to benefit from Quitt's arrest was Zach Ingram, who regained his two stripes and was temporarily in charge of the stables. Quitt's courtmartial had been set for sometime in March in order to allow him a choice of adequate defense counsel and time to prepare his case.

In the meantime, Atticus Perry's records had arrived from Fort Bliss with authority for his discharge if he so desired, listing the back pay and unused clothing allowance due him. He received the news from Major Boyden, who asked him to stay on until after Sergeant Quitt's trial, since he would be called as a principal witness. Atticus agreed.

"The booger c'd be useful to you, Sam," Riley said. "Make a hell of a scout for T-Y Lines an' he knows how to talk Apache as good as you or Willy Logan."

"What makes you think he'd want to stay in Arizona, Pete?"

"I got a feelin' he ain't got nothin' much to go back to in the South."

"What about the 10th Cavalry?"

"He'd make a lot more ridin' for T-Y, wouldn't he?"

Palmer thought the matter over. While there would be little love lost between the *vaqueros* and a Negro, the animosity would be far less than that for a Negro in an all-white Army community. "I'll have a talk with him," Palmer said.

"I'll send him over to see you."

He had seen Atticus on the one abortive escort patrol, when the previous supply train had been attacked and carried off. He recalled that the Negro had joined Logan and himself in accurately reading the signs left by the Mexican renegades who had masqueraded as Apaches, heard him make an articulate, skillful report at Fort Lowell, and later on remarked over his written account of the affair.

When Atticus arrived at Riley's quarters, where Palmer was staying, he submitted to Palmer's questions without hesitation, even speaking the Athapascan tongue and showing a superior knowledge of Apache customs and manners.

"How would you like to work for T-Y Lines, Sergeant?" Palmer asked finally.

"Doing what, sir?"

"Riding escort, scouting, doing what needs to be done to get our wagons and stages through."

"I think I'd like that mighty fine, sir."

"When you're discharged, come to Tucson and see me."

"What about getting on with your people?"

"Atticus, there won't be any problems you don't make for yourself. You'll be judged on performance, not color. With the *vaqueros*, you'll make your own friends and your own enemies. With the whites, unfortunately, you'll have to tread easily and see how it goes. But you'll have Max Potter and me on your side, that much I can promise."

"That's good enough for me. If I can get permission to ride back to Tucson with you now and be ready to come back for the court-martial, will that be all right with you?"

"If Colonel Hatfield agrees, it will be just fine with me."

"Thank you, sir."

An hour later, with that provision clearly understood, Atticus Perry became a civilian and an employee of T-Y Lines. Four hours later, he started back for Tucson with the empty wagon convoy.

As the Christmas holiday approached, freight and passenger bookings were reduced substantially and arrangements were made to bring freight operations to a halt on the night of December 23, which fell on a Monday, and would not be resumed until Thursday, January 3. The intervening ten days would provide a long and well-deserved holiday for all T-Y employees, particularly the *vaqueros* who were anxious to spend that time with their families.

On that Friday before Christmas, Max, Loren and Sam were abroad early in Tucson, ransacking the stores for gifts for Caroline and Laurie. For the Tres Flechas headmen, the *vaqueros* and their families, Max had sent a wagonload of bolt goods, serapes, blankets, foods not grown on the ranch, shoes, boots, dresses, guitars, saddles, bangles, trinkets, toys and confections ahead. Other than the gifts for the home ranch, the balance was made up into three caravans for shipment to the three outlying range camp communities to the northwest, south and southwest on Sunday, in time for the big fiesta celebration on Monday.

The advance shipment was received at Tres Flechas on Saturday. Caroline and Venustiano Carras supervised the make-up of the three mule packs which were to leave early the next morning. It was decided that Laurie, Caroline and Bernardo Aragon would each accompany one of the caravans and deliver the gift goods to the camp headman of each community, together with a speech purported to come from Max Potter, with an apology for his absence.

At dawn on Sunday morning, three groups of six mules were ready, two armed *vaqueros* riding with each group. Caroline had chosen to ride with the goods intended for the southwest camp, farthest from the home ranch, Laurie to the northwest camp, which was closest to the home ranch.

To Caroline, this was a nostalgic journey. Long before Sam Palmer had come along to marry Ruth, she, Max and Ruth made the trip to all three camps, spending a full day at each before returning home for the Christmas Day celebration there. Always, these had been joyous occasions, featuring huge *bárbaros,* speeches, singing, dancing and drinking. Once, in the midst of a speech by Max, a herder had ridden in to warn of an Apache attack. Every man present mounted up and rode off to protect the herds, leaving the women and children with a minimum guard made up of boys, who could hardly be called men, but were skilled in the use of their rifles. The men were gone for seven hours and when they returned, the festivities were resumed with even greater enthusiasm, although three of the *vaqueros* had been wounded, one seriously.

Today, Caroline rode through the sunny morning in advance of the two *vaqueros* and six pack mules. Before noon, they caught up with her at Cobre Creek, so named for the coppery color of the stones which lined its bottom and sides. At this time of the year, the rippling stream was full and sweet, no more than three feet at its greatest depth. Here, the two men fed and watered the mules and horses and permitted them to graze, then spread a clean blanket for their light meal.

At three o'clock, they reached the southwest camp. Word had been sent ahead, so that the riders, dressed in their finest clothing, came out to meet and ceremoniously escort the daughter of *el patrón* into the camp. Over a pit, a choice steer had been roasting since before dawn, turned by two men on each end, basted by two women who dipped long-handled mops into deep pans of sauce and coated the bronzing flesh until it glistened. Long tables were covered with cloths and everyone, it seemed, had been given tasks to perform—men, women and children alike.

The headman, Eduardo Castillo, and his wife, Rosalina, welcomed Caroline who, in turn, apologized for the absence of *el patrón* and spoke her memorized speech; after which, she presented the laden mules to the community on Max Potter's behalf, the gifts to be opened on the following day.

The mules were then led away and the carving of the steer began. There were also mountains of tortillas, tamales, enchiladas, beans, peppers, fruits, cakes, coffee and chocolate. The meal, as usual, was a huge success and a number of the men rode off to relieve an equal number of herders so they could ride in and participate in the pre-Christmas Day feast in honor of the daughter of *el patrón*.

The guitarists played, everyone sang, then the dancing began. Caroline took part in the start of the festivities, then sat among the older women and men to watch the younger dancers. And she remembered the days when her mother was alive, when she and Max sat among the elders while Caroline and Ruth danced with the boys and girls and sang these very same songs.

There was a break in the dancing for a special event; the marriage of Yolande Segura to Jose Orduna, a ceremony in which Caroline participated. Then the dancing was resumed.

Everything was as she remembered it from the past, and yet everything was different. In the women, she saw pleasure; in the men, pride; in the children, happiness. And all she could feel was desperate loneliness and depression within her. Suddenly, despite the warmth of the sun, she felt a chill and shuddered. A woman sitting next to her on the bench offered her a black shawl, but Caroline refused it with a smile. She stood up, her eyes seeking Rosalina Castillo, saw her sitting at a rear table with Eduardo, and went to them.

"Please do not stop the singing and dancing, but I must ride back to the *jefetura*," Caroline said apologetically.

She saw the protest in their faces, knowing they had expected her to spend the night, the usual custom on this rare occasion. "I am sorry," Caroline added. "I must be home when my father arrives from Tucson in the morning with the men."

Eduardo said, "The people will be disappointed, *señorita*."

Again, "I am sorry, but I must."

"I will have your horse saddled and the men and mules ready to accompany you."

"No. It is not necessary. I will return alone—"

"But it will be dark within three hours, *señorita*. I cannot permit it."

"Do not fear, Eduardo. I can find my way back with my eyes closed. Let the men enjoy themselves and return with the mules tomorrow."

"*Señorita*—"

"Please. I would never forgive myself for spoiling their

pleasure. I have my rifle and revolver. No harm will befall me. When I have gone, please express my regrets and wish everyone another *felices navidades* for my father and myself."

A few moments later, she slipped away to the stables, mounted her horse and rode off, wondering why a happy occasion should bring her nothing but the feeling of total emptiness. As she rode along, giving the mare her head, she noted a few cattle grazing in a shallow draw, but saw no *vaquero* nearby. Well, tomorrow, some of the men would be out to gather up the strays. Later, she came upon a shepherd's hut that needed some work on its roof and made a mental note to report this when she reached the *jefetura*.

She was riding in a northeasterly direction, the last of the sun creating an elongated shadowy caricature on the grass ahead of her. The mare, well-rested and fed, became fractious and she put her into a gallop for a while, then slowed her down to a walk. After a mile, the mare went into a gallop again and Caroline permitted her the exercise. After another hour, when the sun had dipped behind the mountains, the mare veered south and Caroline realized they were nearing Cobre Creek. When they reached it, the mare nuzzled for the water eagerly so that Caroline had to restrain her from drinking too greedily in her overheated condition.

She loosened the nosebag of grain hanging from the pommel, slipped it over the mare's head, then tied the reins to a low-hanging branch on the edge of the thicket of trees. While the mare munched contentedly, Caroline lay flat on her stomach and edged her own mouth over the clear water, sipping its delicious coolness, hearing nothing more than the rippling of water and the soft breeze, now turning cooler, rustling through the leaves and branches; and suddenly, she stiffened at a strange sound, the human sound of boots crushing the grass behind her.

She rolled over on her left side, swiftly, expecting to see one of the Tres Flechas *vaqueros*, yet in that same move, her right hand reached instinctively for her revolver.

Too late.

She saw the grinning, unshaven face towering over her just as his boot tip kicked her hand to one side, then saw the small round hole of the muzzle of his own revolver aimed at her chest. Behind him, three other

332

men stood like grinning statues and she saw the evil in their faces, in their eyes. The man with the revolver reached down and took hers from its holster, threw it behind him to one of the others without even looking backward.

"Get up, woman," he commanded.

Caroline rose slowly to her feet. "Who are you?" she demanded in Spanish. "What do you want here?"

"It is of little importance who we are. What we want is still another matter."

"You are trespassing on my father's land, *señor*. If you have no business here, I warn you, his *vaqueros* will kill you."

The man laughed and said to his companions, "You hear, *amigos?*" Then to Caroline, "First, *señorita*, they must find us. We saw you riding south and followed. When you were preparing to leave, we rode on ahead. Had your *vaqueros* ridden with you, it would have been necessary for us to kill them. We are grateful you did not change your route home."

"*Señores*, whoever you are, wherever you come from, I warn you—"

In one swift move, the man took a step forward and struck Caroline across her face with the flat of his hand. "No woman warns me but once, *señorita*," he snapped angrily.

Caroline put a hand up to her aching jaw, shock rather than fear registering on her face, knowing it would be useless to argue, wondering what would come next. Theft of her horse, rifle and revolver? Or worse?

"Moreno, the horses. Vega, take the rifle from her saddle. Campos, the *reatas.*"

While Moreno brought their horses from the thicket and Vega removed the rifle from her saddle scabbard, Campos brought several rawhide thongs to Casimiro Lizardi, who tied Caroline's hands behind her back. Both men then hoisted her into her saddle and Campos lashed her ankles to the stirrups while Lizardi led the mare to the other horses. Finally, Lizardi untied her neckerchief and placed it in her mouth, retying the ends at the base of her neck.

The others mounted their horses. Lizardi looked around carefully, then waved his hand forward to indicate the direction due south toward the Oro Blanca Mountains and Sonora.

Long past midnight, they came to Pena Oro Lake, where they camped. By now, Caroline knew the names of three of the men: Campos, with the sullen face and evil eyes; Vega, the youngest, who tried to make himself appear older with an awkward swagger and a heavy, drooping mustache; Moreno, who stared at her as though she did not exist. The fourth, obviously the leader, had not been called by name. He affected the dress of a *caballero* at a fiesta, with jingling oversized spurs, the black *sombrero*, trousers and jacket decorated with silver piping, embroidery and silver coins in place of buttons. His saddle, likewise, was more liberally decorated with silver and, when he lifted it from his horse's back, was heavier than the others.

The leader called to Moreno, who was busily engaged over a small fire, arranging food in heated pans, and when Moreno called back, "It is ready," said to Campos, "Untie her hands and remove the cloth from her mouth."

Campos went to where she sat on the ground with her back to a tree. He bent over her, allowing his stubbled growth of beard to graze her cheek and when she drew back from his foul breath, he lurched toward her, implanting his lips on her neck. She twisted away and he laughed, untied her neckerchief, then her wrists, but her ankles remained tied. When she reached toward them, he slapped her hands away.

"They remain tied. When you have eaten, your hands and mouth will be tied again."

"You filth of a pig!" Caroline exclaimed.

Campos laughed. "Ah, your Anglo blood heats easily, *señorita*. It is good. I like a woman with spirit. I would like to tame you in my bed. Come."

He moved behind her, stooped and placed his arms under hers as though to help her stand, cupping his hands over her breasts. At his touch, she twisted out of his grasp and rolled away from him toward the campfire. Campos uttered a curse and leaped at her squirming figure and in the dimness, fell across her body. She rolled over face down and he turned her over, his face close to hers. She reached up with both hands and raked her nails across his face, drawing a howling curse from him. He raised an arm to strike her, but the leader suddenly appeared, caught it in mid-air and said, "Campos! Let her alone! She has value to us only if she is alive and unharmed, you fool!"

Campos' body rolled away and Caroline's hand touched his holster. She found the handgrip of his revolver and when he moved, his own hands extended outward, pressing the earth to lever himself upward, she pulled the weapon from the holster and drew the hammer back. Then Campos regained his balance and sat up, facing her, seeing the glint of highlight upon the barrel of the gun.

"Anglo *puta*—!" he screamed and lurched downward toward her, but before he could touch her, Caroline pulled the trigger. In the stillness of the night, the noise was like the roar of a howitzer. Then Moreno and Vega were upon her, the revolver twisted from her grasp. Moreno retied her wrists behind her back while Vega replaced the gag in her mouth. The leader stood looking down upon her, Campos' revolver in his hand.

They carried Campos to the fire and examined his wound. The bullet had entered his left side and the blood was soaking through a layer of underwear, shirt and vest.

"Her *enaguas,* quickly," Lizardi barked.

Vega ran to where Caroline lay on her side, reached under her riding skirt and tore her petticoat away. He returned to the fire where Lizardi ripped the garment into strips, using part of it to wad up the hole. On closer examination, he found that the bullet had passed entirely through Campos' body, leaving a larger, uglier hole where it had exited. He made a second wad and plugged that hole, then bound the strips tightly around Campos' waist.

"Kill her! Kill the Anglo *ramera!*" Campos groaned.

"Quiet, Julio," Lizardi said coldly. "One does not deal with a woman so valuable as this one as though she were one of your tramps." To Moreno, "Let us eat quickly. I want to be gone within an hour."

"If we move him, he will bleed to death," Moreno replied.

"And if we wait for him to heal, we will be hunted down by *el patrón* and his *vaqueros* and shot to death. He brought it on himself. If he dies, there will be one less to share the gold. Hurry."

"And the girl?"

"Leave her to her misery. She will eat when we reach Cienguilla. Vega, prepare the horses."

Within thirty minutes they had hoisted the groaning

335

Campos and a well-trussed Caroline into saddles, tied them there securely and were on their way.

Early that morning Sam Palmer and Marcos Espuela met Max Potter and Loren Olmstead in the dining room of the Congress Hotel for breakfast. Max decided they would leave for Tres Flechas as soon as the meal was over, with the *vaqueros* following later.

"What of the new one, *el negro?*" Marcos asked.

"What about him?"

"He will be alone in Tucson without the protection of his uniform and without friends among Anglos or Mexicans. It will be a long ten days. He could find himself in trouble."

"Marcos is right, Max," Sam said. "Could we take him along with us? He'd be safer there and it would give us a chance to get better acquainted."

Max thought for a moment. "I don't see why not," he said finally. "He can ride down with the *vaqueros.*"

"It might be easier all around if he rides down with us," Sam suggested. "Most of them have never seen him before and that could make things embarrassing."

"All right," Max agreed. "Marcos, find Perry and get him started. Where is he staying?"

"In the back room of the Depot. I will go now and get the horses at the same time."

Atticus joined them with mixed feelings. He had found the last few days difficult to adjust to, missing the security of his blue uniform with its three yellow stripes. After a few days as a civilian, he was simply a black man who had been freed by presidential proclamation, regarded with tolerant curiosity by the Mexicans, with open animosity and resentment by former Southerners and Confederate sympathizers who made up much of the population of Tucson, and ignored by others. As he saddled up for the trip south, he wondered what his reception there would be like; acceptance or rejection. The experience might well force him into a decision to move on elsewhere, either West or back to the South where he would be among his own.

Conversation while riding was limited, and for this Atticus was grateful. They stopped shortly past noon to water and feed their horses and eat their midday meal, resuming at two o'clock. An hour later, riding ahead of the others, Marcos saw two riders coming toward them from the south and spurred his horse on to meet and identify them. When they were fifty yards apart, he recognized Venustiano Carras and his son, Tomas.

"Venustiano! *Qué pasó?*"

"*El patrón*, Marcos, he is with you?"

"Behind me, with the others. What—?"

"Thank God. I ride to Tucson to call him home."

The alarm in Venustiano's voice, in Tomas' face, was transmitted to Marcos. Without further question, he wheeled Mano about and the three closed the distance between themselves and the rest of the party, who had also stepped up their pace.

"What is it, Venustiano?" Max asked.

"*La patrona, señor*. Yesterday she rode out to the southwest range with two men and six mules carrying *los regalos de navidad*. This morning, the men returned with the mules. Señorita Caroline was not with them. She had ridden back yesterday afternoon alone, but did not reach the *jefetura*."

Sam Palmer's body jerked around in his saddle, his eyes on Max's face. "What have you done?" Max asked.

"I have sent men to seek her trail, two more toward the southwest camp to see what they can learn."

"The other two, Señorita Laurie and Bernardo?"

"They returned with the men and mules before I left."

"And those you sent to find her trail?"

"They have not returned yet. I did not wish to waste time, so I came—"

"*Ándale!* Let us make haste."

Their mounts were rested and they pressed hard, leaving the main road to take the shorter way across open desert, over rolling hills, more desert, finally dropping down into grazing land that was the northernmost rim of Tres Flechas property. They flew past a herd of cattle and several startled *vaqueros,* who waved and were soon lost to sight, splashed across the upper Cobre Creek, topped a rise, dipped into a draw and an hour later caught their first glimpse of the walls of the *jefetura* compound. They thundered into the enclosure through gates held wide open for them, dismounted and went inside the main house. Atticus remained on the front porch. All around the house, men, women and children stood gaping in silence. Max greeted Laurie soberly, nodded to Emelita and Marguerita as he went through the

337

large front room to his study, Sam, Marcos, Loren and Venustiano on his heels.

Inside, Max went to his desk and while lighting a cigar said, "Venustiano, tell me everything from the beginning. Which horse she rode, what time she left. Tomas!"

When Tomas appeared in the doorway, "Find the two men who accompanied *la señorita* to the southwest camp and bring them here. Well, Venustiano?"

Carras filled them in as best he could; time of departure, the two *vaqueros* and six pack mules; riding her favorite horse, Lucero, wearing a gun belt and revolver, Winchester repeating rifle in her saddle scabbard. "It had been expected she would remain in the camp overnight and return in the morning with the two men and mules, just as Bernardo Aragon and Señorita Laurie had—"

"Did the *vaqueros* say why she had changed her mind?"

"Only that she told Eduardo Castillo she wished to be here when you returned from Tucson. She did not tell them at the time she was leaving. If they had known, they would have followed her. This they learned from Eduardo later in the night when they saw she was not among them, that she had ordered them to remain. It was then too late to follow her."

They were interrupted by a knock on the door. Marcos opened it to admit the two *vaqueros*. The elder, Ortega, began talking at once. He described their arrival, the barbecue, singing and dancing. "And then, the *señorita* was gone." He had spoken to Castillo, who told them the *señorita* did not wish to interrupt their fiesta. He had thought to follow, but by then it was full darkness and would have been impossible to pick up her trail. "Early in the morning—."

"The route, Ortega."

"We went and returned by the straightest route, the one we always take, but saw nothing to indicate the presence of Apaches, although we tried our best to find some sign."

Venustiano said, "The trackers were sent from here to cut wide circles around the route to the camp to pick up fresh sign, especially along Cobre Creek in case someone rode up or down the stream to cover his tracks. At the first sign, one will return to bring the word."

Despite his inner anguish, Potter said, "You have done well, *amigos. Gracias.*"

"What can we do now, *señor?*" Venustiano asked.

"We wait for word from the trackers. Let me know as soon as one returns. Go now."

Max sighed deeply and sought Sam's eyes, finding only concern and no comfort. Marcos walked to the window and looked out, saw the huddle of ranch families gathered around Venustiano and Ortega, questioning them. Emelita brought food and coffee and bowed out tearfully. No one in the study touched the tray.

"Sam?" Max said quietly.

"I wish I could guess, Max, but we'll have to wait for some word, anything, from the trackers. If they come up with any sign at all, we'll know what we've got to do. If there is none, we'll have to get out and cover fresh territory. If she were thrown and hurt, Lucero would probably have come back on his own, so it can't be that. My only hunch is that she was taken."

"Apaches?"

"I don't know. I don't think so. They'll take captives in battle, but if they were out looking for beef or sheep, chances are they wouldn't bother with one woman, riding alone. A steer would be more valuable. They'd have kept hidden, let her go by and continued on until they found some strays or a herd guarded by one or two men. We can guess anything we want, but we'll still have to wait for word from the trackers."

They waited in the study for another hour before Marcos, still at the window, stirred. "Someone just rode in," he announced briefly. Moments later, Venustiano appeared in the study with Benito Macias, one of the four trackers he had sent, and who bore definite news.

"While the others rode in wide circles, *señor,*" he reported to Max, "I backtracked over the southwest range and picked up *la patrona's* trail. I followed it to Cobre Creek. Where Señorita Caroline stopped to water her horse, I found more sign. In the woods nearby, there were the tracks of four horses, all wearing iron shoes, bootprints of four men who smoked thin cigarillos, the remains of an eaten meal. Later, they crossed the creek on foot and waited among the trees. There is the sign of *la señorita's* horse and smaller bootprints among the others, then the arrival of the horses of those who waited in hiding for her. The trail disappeared into the creek and perhaps four or five miles south, reappeared once more, then headed in the direction of the Oro Blanca Mountains and Sonora. Five horses now instead of four. I and the other men went south for a few miles and then I decided to return here to bring the word. The others will follow the trail until dark."

Palmer thought, four men, bootprints, ironshod horses, ruling out Apaches. Benito's description of the food particles and cigarillos indicated Mexican tastes. He looked toward Marcos and caught his tense, reflective stare. Marcos came toward him while Max took over the additional questioning of Macias.

"You know, Sam?"

"A hunch. Lizardi."

"And his three *comadrejos*. Vega, Moreno, Campos."

"Ransom?"

"I hope so, else she can come to great harm. I do not like to think about it."

Macias had concluded his findings and was sent out with Venustiano Carras. Max said, "What do you think, Sam?"

"I'm leaving at once, Max. I'll want Macias to go along. If we leave now, we can save four or five hours' riding in the morning. Before daybreak we can pick up the others and take over."

"How many more men do you want? Take as many as you need."

"I'll have Macias—"

"And me," Marcos interjected.

"And Marcos. That makes three, and more than enough. Any more could give us away long before we can catch up—"

"Sam, you know the risks if you're caught—" Max began.

"We'll keep a sharp eye out for Apaches. We think we know who we're after."

"Who?"

"Lizardi and three of his men. If we're right, they've taken Caroline for ransom and won't hurt her."

"If that's it, Sam, make a deal, anything he asks, only get her back safely."

"I promise you, Max, we won't do anything to hurt her chances."

There was a problem with Loren, who insisted on going along, but Max diplomatically persuaded Loren he would be needed to defend the *jefetura* since the *vaqueros* who would be coming in from Tucson would, on arrival, be riding out to the three camps to be with their families.

Laurie was distraught and sought comfort in Max's calm front, which was purely a pose designed to keep the emotional Mexicans from being plunged in despair. To Loren and Laurie, Max said, "If Sam Palmer and Benito Macias weren't two of the best trackers in the whole southwest, I'd be out there myself. There ain't a man on Tres Flechas don't want to be out hunting for Caro, but what we don't need right now is a lot of meaningless movement and shooting. We're sure she's alive. If they were goin'a kill her, they'd of done it right off an' we'd pretty well know about it by now. Question is, where is she and what's behind it. That's what we've got to know an', hard as it is, all we can do is wait 'til we find out."

Marcos watched as Horacio Quiroga brushed Mano's silky coat in the family corral. "He is a fine animal, that one," Horacio said admiringly.

"The best, *amigo*. He was a present from my mother."

"It is a pleasure to care for him. Some day I will have one like him for my own."

Marcos laughed pleasantly. "When I was sixteen years old, Horacio, I spoke those same words. Then it was only a dream. When I became twenty-one years old, the dream came true."

"Then mine will come true." The task was finished. Marcos took a silver coin from his pocket and flipped it at Horacio. *"Gracias, señor,"* the boy said.

"Saddle him for me, eh?"

"Willingly." As he lifted the saddle from the top rail, Horacio said, "It is a sad homecoming for *el patrón.*"

"Yes. There is no joy in this celebration of the natal day of our Lord."

"The prayers are useless. The gifts are joyless—"

"Marcos—"

He swung around and saw Laurie facing him. "Ah, Laurie."

"When are you leaving?"

"Before it grows dark."

"Marcos, do you think you can find Caroline and bring her back?"

"There will be three of us, Sam, Benito and I. We will do our best. Put your trust in us."

"My trust and my prayers, Marcos. In you."

He touched her elbow lightly and guided her away from

341

the corral toward the main house, out of Horacio's hearing. *"Gracias, señorita,"* he said.

"De nada, señor," Laurie replied.

"Hey, like a real native! Smooth, no hesitation. You said that like a fine Spanish lady."

"Or an Anglo girl who pursues a *mestizo?*"

"Laurie—"

"You won't say it, Marcos, so I have to. If you want me to, I mean."

"Laurie, you can't say things like that. Everything, everybody would be against it, and us."

"Not anybody I would care about."

"Not your brother, *el patron,* even Sam? And my mother, Laurie, she is not your kind—"

"I don't care about that. I'm Laurie Olmstead and I'm my own self, with my own mind and feelings. I know what I feel—"

"Laurie, listen. It—it's crazy. They won't let it happen. I know. And—"

"What?"

"—if we don't bring Caroline back, you know what will happen then?"

"What has that got to do with us?"

"You will become more than a cousin to *el patrón.* You will take Caroline's place in his life, become his daughter. He would never permit—"

"Marcos, I'd still be Laurie Olmstead who loves Marcos Espuela."

"Ah, Laurie, if it could only be."

"We can make it be."

"Your brother—"

"Loren will be my problem, not yours."

Marcos laughed without mirth. "For that, I wish I could take you in my arms and kiss you."

"Why don't you?"

"Because there are too many eyes, your brother's among them, there on the porch. I will leave you now, Laurie. Let us not anger him and make things more difficult."

"For now, I will obey you. Good luck, Marcos. *Vaya con Dios.* You carry my love with you."

CHAPTER II

THEY LEFT AT DUSK AND BEFORE DAWN, MACIAS HAD LED them to where the other three trackers were camped in the foothills of the Oro Blanca Mountains. In the early morning light, sign of the passage of five iron-shod horses was in evidence, even over hard rock; scars where iron shoes had nicked and chipped stone, still fresh and clear; horse droppings, patches of urine-drenched grass, both checked for moisture content in estimating age in terms of hours. Branches broken, crushed grass, disturbed earth where horses had been picketed and fed; bootprints, one set with small heelmarks; and again, crumbs of leftover food, eaten cold while riding, small grains of feed dropped from a horse's nosebag. To the average eye, the small signs would have meant little or nothing, but to the tracker's eye no detailed map could be clearer.

After a quick breakfast, the first three trackers were sent back to the home ranch. Palmer, Marcos and Macias continued upward into the mountains, following the sign, moving steadily, removing their fleece-lined outer coats by mid-morning when the sun had beaten down the cold and the wind had abated. Well into the afternoon, they crested the mountain and stopped to eat and rest their weary horses. Here, the terrain was well-covered with low-growing bushes, trees and grass. There were two trails now, one leading downward toward the south, another to the west. Macias rode down the west trail, Palmer and Marcos south, before they found signs to indicate that the five riders had moved in the latter direction. Macias, having found nothing of special interest, rejoined them and by dusk, they came upon Pena Oro Lake.

Here, beneath some disturbed earth, they found the remains of a hastily covered campfire, horse and boot-prints that were already familiar to them, the inevitable cigarillo stubs and the smashed glass of a tequila bottle; and this last finding produced unspoken concern among them. Four conscienceless renegades, tequila, and a woman could spell trouble they did not care to discuss or think about.

Macias, on his knees, sifting earth through his fingers like a prospector feeling for gold dust, found the sign that gave them cause for their greatest alarm. Not yet fully dried, some of the earth clung to his fingers. On closer examination, he discovered that the moisture was blood, darkened by exposure to air, but blood nevertheless. Lighting dried branches, they searched in a wide circle and came upon more of it deeper among the trees, a small puddle clotted on the disturbed earth and grass where someone had lain for a while bleeding, then had been helped up, carried to the side of the campfire site where he—or, God forbid, she—had had the wound dressed before moving on. There was a scrap of cloth, blood-stained, covered hastily with dirt. •

But there was no map to tell them what had happened or to whom.

Spurred on by this alarming picture, they continued southward through the bitterly cold night along the only trail that led down from the mountain and eventually descended to the desert floor, now well into Sonora where there was only open country ahead of them to their right and left, the mountain at their backs. There were two well-worn trails, one leading south, the other west, but the night wind had created a sandstorm and every readable track had been obliterated. They dismounted for a discussion and Benito Macias offered the first opinion.

"It is my thought," he said, "that Lizardi would go toward the west. To the south, the nearest village is Andalucia, a good forty miles through open country. To the west, less than fifteen miles, lies Cienguilla. Therefore, it would seem to me that, since Lizardi was born there, as was I, and since there is one among them who is wounded, he would go to the nearest village where he is known and knows others."

"It is a reasonable thought, Benito," Palmer agreed.

"Also," Macias added on this note of encouragement, "Cienguilla lies south of Monte Babiacora and if the rumors we have heard are true, then Lizardi has had frequent dealings with the Apaches in Babiacora with Anaka, now with Bokhari. He knows the land and the mountains well."

Palmer nodded. "Then we go west," Marcos said.

344

"*Señores,* no," Macias said. "A stranger would be noticed long before he reached Cienguilla. Word would be carried to Lizardi and he would disappear. I would be the least to fall under suspicion for I have family and friends there. Thus, if I go alone—"

"While we suck our thumbs here?" Marcos said.

"If we think only what is best for *la patrona,* it will be better if you and Señor Palmer remain close by and suck your thumbs until I bring you word. If she is not the one with the wound, and is still alive, I will return quickly as I can. Otherwise, *señores*—"

"He's right, Marcos," Palmer said quickly. "We will find a place in the foothills and wait for Benito. If we need more men, we can send for them to Tres Flechas."

Christmas Day at Tres Flechas came and passed with a deep solemnity. Even the children found little joy in the gifts of clothing, toys and rare candy, sensing the serious mood reflected in their elders. The headmen of the three range camps rode in to pay their respects to *el patrón* and express sorrow for his—and their—misfortune in what they delicately referred to as "the absence of Señorita Caroline." In the chapel, candles were lighted and prayers recited for her well being and safe return.

Max, Laurie and Loren remained close together, although there was little conversation that passed between them; like mountain climbers roped together for mutual security. On the range, the riders scanned the ground and hills as though some miracle might appear to lead them in a new direction. And at every opportunity out of Laurie's hearing, Loren asked Max more questions than could be answered, offering himself, his gun, anything that might be of help; but there was nothing, Max repeated over and over again, anyone could do until word was sent back by Sam, something significant enough to warrant following.

Laurie went among the women to reassure them that what could be done was being done, unable to tell them exactly what it was that was being done. She had had her differences with Caroline but these were now too small to think about in the face of the magnitude of her disappearance, and its effect on Max and everyone on Tres Flechas. The word had spread to the village in Tubac and old friends and acquaintances came to sympathize, offer to help in whatever way they could.

On Christmas night in Cienguilla, Benito Macias sat at the table of Henrico and Concepcion Macias, who gave special thanks to God that their son had come to visit them. For gifts, Benito gave them silver coins, a sight rare enough these days in this poor village. He had emptied his saddlebags of what food he carried and this, added to the meager fare in the house, became a banquet for three. He listened to the gossip of the village, of the young who had, like himself a long time ago, left to find work in larger villages many miles away; of those who had died, of names no longer remembered or known, who had married, of children born and died, of the Apaches who lived in Monte Babiacora, near enough to look down their throats.

"No others come to visit?" Benito asked.

Henrico shook his gray head sadly. "Why should anyone wish to return once he has left? One leaves because there is nothing to keep him here. He remains away because there is nothing to come back to."

Benito felt the shawl of guilt fall upon his own shoulders. "Ah, it is not easy to travel for pleasure. There is much work to keep one busy, to look after his own family. If I had learned to write—"

"And if we could read," Concepcion said tonelessly.

The two-room *casa* in which he, three sisters and two brothers had been born now seemed smaller and more depressing than he could remember it. The adobe walls were bleak, the dirt floor, recently swept in his honor, already scuffed and its dust upon everything. The homemade tallow candles stank and gave off a dim flickering light, hardly enough to see the lines of age etched into his parents' faces, the veins in their hands.

"Porofiro Caminez, he still lives in Cienguilla?" Benito asked.

"Porofiro. Porofiro." Henrico was running the name through the catalog of his mind. "Ah, yes. Three years ago, I think, he married the widow, Carlota Matanza—"

"Their son is six years old," Concepcion said.

"Ah, then it was seven years ago," Henrico conceded and continued over the interruption. "The widow of Adolfo Matanza, he who owned the *cantina*."

"And Porofiro?"

"Now Porofiro owns it."

"I will go to see him. We were good friends long ago."

"Yes. Yes. He will be happy to see an old friend."

Later, as Concepcion rocked herself into a doze in her, ancient chair that Henrico had made for her with his own hands, and Henrico lay on his straw mat asleep and snoring, Benito blew out the two stubs of candles and went down the dusty, rutted street to the *cantina*. Inside, two men sat at one table, one at another, and one stood at the bar over a drink, talking with Porofiro, who tended the bar. Nearby, Carlota, short and fat, sitting on a stool at the money drawer, bulging out of the V of her dress, the fleshiness of her fingers almost hiding her gold wedding band, stared as Benito entered. Porofiro looked up and eyed him curiously as Benito, smiling, approached the bar.

"Benito? Benito Macias?" Porofiro asked in disbelief.

"Porofiro, old friend!"

Caminez came from behind the bar, himself a near-obese figure, and embraced Benito, exchanging salutations. Benito paid Carlota a compliment, received a stony stare in return, then ordered tequila and invited Porofiro and Carlota to drink with him. Later, the two men sat at a table and talked together.

"What brings you back to this hole in hell, Benito?"

"And what keeps you in this hole of hell, Porofiro?"

They both laughed and Benito said casually, "It is the season for visiting. I came to see my father and mother."

"You are a good son. *Madre mio,* it has been a long time since I have seen a friendly face from the old days."

"Also, I seek information."

"Eh?"

"Of other visitors, Porofiro."

Porofiro sat in stony silence. "You heard me?" Benito asked.

"I heard you."

"So?"

"So, old friend, I have learned to keep my mouth shut about visitors. In this way, I stay in business. And alive."

"For an old friend, Porofiro."

"For old friends, I have good advice: Do not ask questions."

"It is important to me."

"When one seeks information of others, it is always important to the one who asks."

"Porofiro, there have been times when the *rurales* asked questions of me concerning my friend Porofiro

Caminez, who was once suspected of being a *salteador,* one who robbed stages in Arizona—"

"Not so loud, *amigo.* Carlota has big ears."

"Then tell me about Casimiro Lizardi and his three *vagos*—"

"Ah."

"They are here in Cienguilla, no?"

"They came last night."

"With the Anglo girl they kidnapped."

Porofiro nodded.

"She was hurt?"

"No. Campos. Julio Campos was shot. It was the girl who shot him."

"And the girl?"

"She was not harmed."

"Where are they now?"

"In hiding."

"That much I can guess. Where?"

With an expression of pain, Porofiro said, "You will not say who told you?"

"On the sacred souls of my mother and father."

"They were in the stable of the old Lizardi *casa,* but the girl is gone. Lizardi, Vega and Moreno have taken her into Monte Babiacora."

"Monte Babiacora? To the Apaches?"

"To whom, they did not say. To Monte Babiacora, yes."

"When?"

"Before dawn this morning."

"And Campos?"

"He remains in the stable. A woman is with him, one of Casimiro's relations who lives on the old place."

"You have talked with them?"

"Only Casimiro. He trusts me."

"He has told you why he has taken the Anglo girl, why he gives her to the Indios?"

"No. Nor do I ask. Benito, I do this for you as an old friend. Do not—"

"It is as though you have not spoken, *amigo.* Your name will not be mentioned. Also, I can promise that if we find the girl unharmed, you will be rewarded. Her father is *el patrón* of Tres Flechas, for whom I ride."

"*Madre mio!* Lizardi has become a madman."

"He has become too mad to live. Now give me a bottle of tequila. I have a long ride to make."

In a small, dark wickiup at Bokhari's retreat, Caroline Potter lay on the dirt floor, wrists and ankles bound tightly, the gag removed from her mouth, her body stiff and hardly able to move. Outside, she could hear the low mutterings of the two braves who guarded her. The three men who had brought her here had gone into the larger wickiup nearby with the one who, by the deference shown him by all the others, could be no one but Bokhari himself.

Her face was bruised, her body sore, her wrists rubbed raw by the thongs that tied them together. Fortunately, the riding boots she wore prevented the rawhide strips from tearing into the flesh of her ankles.

She wondered, as she had since her capture, what was happening back at Tres Flechas, knowing that by now there must be search parties out looking for her. Max and Sam would be there—and suddenly she remembered that this was Christmas Day, which would begin with an early mass in the chapel, then turn from solemn prayer into a day-long fiesta of gift-giving, feasting, laughter, music and dancing. Or, she thought now, would her absence turn that once happy occasion into one of gloom?

There had been little talk among the three Mexicans and she had no way of knowing what they intended to do with her after she shot Campos. At that moment, she had expected instantaneous death and was surprised that the others had displayed no great degree of anger with her. There had been some mention of her "value" to them, and finally deduced that they were holding her for ransom.

She remembered skirting a village, finally stopping at a small farmhouse while they carried her and Campos into a filthy stable. Ignoring her, a slattern of a woman had tended the wounded man. They rested and ate there and she had slept for a while, only to be awakened in the dark of night, placed upon her horse and led by the three men into the mountains; and seeing Apaches in groups of two and four as they penetrated deeper into the hills, she experienced honest terror and had prayed in fear.

Why, if ransom was their objective, were they handing her over to the Apaches? How much more was she worth to Bokhari than to her father? Old stories of Apache torture and mutilation were reborn in her mind.

349

Slow death by knife. By fire. At best, to be kept in captivity as a slave to serve the chief's wives. But why so great an effort to take one woman?

Outside the large wickiup, Vega and Moreno, unarmed and with some misgivings, sat cross-legged on the cold ground under the eyes of four braves. Inside, Lizardi and Bokhari sat on woven pallets in discussion, the Apache leader showing a measure of disbelief despite the Mexican's assurances that his plan was completely workable. In rapid Spanish, Lizardi sought to convince Bokhari further.

Bokhari said, "A man would give himself up to die for a woman?"

"It is the way among the White Eyes, Great One. A woman is more highly prized than the finest horse or rifle. And this is a very special woman, the daughter of *el patrón* of Tres Flechas. He has no sons, therefore he will give anything he owns to have this one returned unharmed."

"Even the White Eyes, Pom-mer?"

"The man Palmer will himself make the offer when the demand is made."

"How shall the offer be made?"

"You will send one of your people to Tres Flechas carrying a white flag of truce—"

"We do not believe in the white man's flags of truce. They have too often attacked and killed our people under such truces."

"*El patrón* will honor this one. His daughter's life is at stake."

Bokhari's face registered doubt. "No," he said.

"Then send a woman. They will see she can do no harm. She will leave with them your demand; the White Eyes, Palmer, in exchange for the girl. They will parley, then send her back with word. Once she crosses into Sonora, you will have a dozen, two dozen braves waiting to see that no one has followed her."

Bokhari grunted. "I will think upon this carefully. If it is as you say, you will receive your reward when I have Pom-mer. How shall I send you word?"

"I will return to Tucson. In Cienguilla, there is one called Juan Portero. He will know where to find me."

"*Enju.* We will take her to the main camp and I will plan what I will do. Go now."

Benito Macias returned to the home of his parents, made his farewells, then rode east all the rest of that night. When he came to where Sam and Marcos had arranged to meet him, he was surprised that Marcos was not there.

"I sent him back to Tres Flechas to report to *el patrón* what we have found so far," Palmer told him. "It is better that he know we have found the trail. I told Marcos not to mention that we found blood at Pena Oro Lake."

"It is of no importance," Benito replied. "The blood was not that of *la patróna*."

"Then you have news."

"*Sí*. Good and bad."

"Tell me."

"The good news is that it was the *señorita* who shot one of the *bandidos*, Julio Campos. How this came about, I do not know, except that she was unharmed. The others are whom you have suspected. Lizardi, Vega and Moreno."

"Where is she?"

"That is the bad news. Lizardi, Vega and Moreno have taken her to Bokhari in Monte Babiacora. Why, I do not know."

"So. It will be a hard thing to tell *el patrón*."

"*Sí*. So soon after the loss of Señorita Ruth—" And suddenly remembering that Ruth had been Sam's loss as well, "Forgive me, *señor*. I have too loose the tongue."

Sam, lost in his own thought, remained silent. Benito said, "He will come, *el patrón*?"

"He will come. You are tired, Benito. Get some sleep while I keep watch."

That suggestion, after the long night ride, was appealing. "Wake me in two hours, *señor,* and I will take over the watch."

But Sam was in no mood for sleep and Macias did not waken until late in the day when he smelled the frying bacon and boiling coffee. He rolled out of his blanket, folded it and came to the fire to take the cup of coffee Sam held out to him. "How long, *señor*?"

"Not long now," Sam replied.

"You have not slept?"

"I do not need it, Benito. I had many things to think about to keep me awake."

It was not long after they had eaten, the fire covered

351

with earth and the horses fed, that they heard the sound of horses coming up the trail. Palmer slipped out of the woods to check the riders and returned with Max, Marcos, Loren and Atticus. Macias at once built another fire and brought out the coffee pot while Max and Sam sat on the ground to discuss the situation.

"I brought Perry along, Sam. He told me he'd spent some time up in Monte Babiacora as a prisoner."

"I'm glad you did. He'll be helpful." Sam looked at Loren questioningly, squatting beside the fire with Macias.

"I had to bring him along, Sam. He insisted that if I didn't, he'd follow us. He feels beholden, maybe his way of paying back what he thinks he owes us for taking care of Laurie."

"He's a good man, Max, but a little too quick with his gun. We'll find some use for him. I'll get Benito over here. He can tell you better what we know so far."

When Macias had explained to Max what he knew and how he had learned what had taken place, Max asked, "Why Monte Babiacora? If she was taken for ransom, why turn her over to Bokhari? It don't add up to anything with sense to it."

Deceptively calm, Sam said, "It's ransom of another kind, Max."

"What other kind?"

"An exchange, I think. Lizardi has made a deal with Bokhari. He's turned Caroline over to him in exchange for me. When the exchange is made, Lizardi will collect a lot more reward than he could get from you for Caroline. There's no other reason why he'd take so much risk to kidnap her, then turn her over to Bokhari. One thing I'm sure of, they won't harm her in any way. She's too valuable to them for trading purposes."

Max was plunged into gloom as Sam continued. "We won't have to wait long. They'll be sending a message with Bokhari's demand—"

"And what do we do then? Sam, I can't ask you—"

"You don't have to ask anything, Max. This is up to me, so let me work it out in my own way."

"You know what you're talking about, son?"

"Better than anyone else. And I've had time to think about it while you were on your way here. Just be sure of one thing, Max. I won't do anything that will endanger Caroline."

Max stood up and began pacing back and forth. He

turned suddenly to face Sam. "What if we put together every *vaquero* we've got and—"

"You can't do that. The minute you take the *vaqueros* off Tres Flechas, Bokhari will know it and send in his people to attack. If you massed them for a raid on Monte Babiacora, Caroline would be the first to be killed. Remember Rufino Flores—"

Max did not have to be reminded of the morning when Rufino had been staked out within sight of the walls of Tres Flechas. He sat down heavily and wordlessly, stared at his clenched fists, then looked up and said, "What's our next move, Sam?"

"You go back to Tres Flechas in case they send word. Leave Benito, Marcos, Atticus and Loren with me. We'll work something out."

"I'm not asking you to turn yourself in to Bokhari," Max said. "I'll gladly match anything Cochise will pay to get his hands on you—"

"It's too late for that now, Max. Bokhari's got his ace in the hole and he's not going to give that up. We'll have to work it out another way, play it by ear. Why don't you get back to Tres Flechas so we can get started."

CHAPTER III

MACIAS, THE ONLY ONE OF THE FIVE WHO KNEW THE route to Cienguilla, took the lead. Atticus and Loren were directly behind him. Marcos and Sam, allowing fifty yards between them, brought up the rear. As Macias had planned, they reached the outskirts of the village just after night had fallen and turned north off the main road. After about a mile and a half, Macias pulled up inside a grove of trees. Here they dismounted for a conference, eating a cold meal.

While they ate, Macias said, "From here, we move on foot. The farm is but a rifle shot to the west."

Palmer questioned Atticus about Monte Babiacora, where he had been held slave-prisoner by Anaka, later by Bokhari. He described the main camp in meticulous detail, the guarded approaches from the south, north and west.

Macias nodded and said, "Along every trail, there are many eyes that keep watch."

"There are other camps," Atticus said. "Smaller ones. About four or five, like outposts. Some to the north, the others west of the main camp. About twenty braves and their women and children in each camp. They're used for raiding and hunting parties, like the one I was in the time we went to Dos Viudas looking for cattle."

"The question we need answered," Sam said, "is where they're holding Caroline. Until we know that, we can't do any good."

"Well," Atticus said, "there's another place, a private camp where Bokhari goes with his number two wife and sons when he wants to get away from things. I don't know where it is exactly, but it's east of the main camp. Bokhari would send his wife and the two boys there with a few braves a whole day before he'd go. Sometimes they'd be away for two-three days, sometimes as long as a week. If something important came up, they'd send word by a relay of messengers to him."

"I have heard of this place," Macias said. "Long ago, before the Indios came, there was a valley where a clear stream ran. There was good hunting there in those days. I would go with my father. When the Indios came, it was forbidden for the villagers to go there or anywhere else in the mountain."

"How well guarded is this private camp?" Palmer asked.

Macias shrugged. Atticus said, "I don't think there's anybody there unless Bokhari and his family are there. If they are, I'd guess no more than a handful of braves to watch over the wife and sons."

"Would it be reasonable to say that Caroline would be taken there?"

It was a question neither Atticus nor Macias could answer. "It is only a *conjetura, señor*," Macias said. "I would say that whether the *señorita* is there or not, it is the safest way to enter the mountain. From Cienguilla, from the north, south and west, any trail would be dangerous. From the east, there would be little to fear until we were close to the camp."

"There are trails?"

Macias thought for a moment, then said, "For a part of the way, we could ride. The last few miles would not be possible for the horses, through the woods, heavy undergrowth and malpais."

"And then?"

"Then on foot up a mountainside and down into the valley where the stream runs. It has been a long time, *señor*, but I think I could find the way. But if Señorita Caroline is not there, we will have wasted two days."

Marcos spoke up then and said, "All our talk is guesswork. Maybe if we could talk to Campos—"

"Campos won't talk," Sam said.

"Sam," Marcos replied, "you know more about Indians than I, but I think I know more about Mexicans than you. I have seen Lizardi and his *vagos* in my mother's *cantina* many times, and I know Campos. If I could see him, I can make him talk."

"Benito?"

Through pursed lips, Macias said, "It is possible, but I am not sure of what value it will be. I can do this, take Marcos to where Campos lies helpless in the stable. I can see that they are not disturbed, but more than this, I do not know."

Now Loren spoke for the first time. "I think it's worth

355

the gamble. If we can get anything out of him at all, we're that much ahead. If Campos won't talk, we're no worse off than we are now."

"That makes sense," Sam said. "All right, Marcos. You go with Benito. Loren, Atticus and I will wait for you here."

They slipped through the dark woods together, Marcos' left hand gripping Benito's right sleeve until they came to its edge, which was the beginning of the clearing. Benito raised his right arm, directing Marcos' eyes to the outlines of two low structures. "On the left is the *casa*," Benito whispered. "The other is the stable."

Silently, they crept across the stubbled field toward the house, crouching low. A single window was open. They stood beside it for a few moments, heard the muffled sound of snoring. Marcos felt Benito's finger tapping his shoulder and the two men moved off in the direction of the stable. As they approached it, Marcos said, "Go back to the *casa*. If the woman wakens, make sure she does not call out or leave it."

Benito nodded and walked back to the small adobe structure. Marcos went to the stable, circled it and found a shuttered window at the rear, then returned to the double-doored entrance. He tested the doors and found they were not barred from the inside, slowly pushed one inward. It creaked loudly as he stepped inside quickly, at once enveloped in its musty odors of staleness, decay and disuse. He paused, heard the rustle of straw and cloth as Campos stirred and called out, "Rafaela."

Marcos moved toward the sound of Campos' voice in the total darkness, testing each step to avoid tripping over some unseen object.

"Rafaela! It is you?"

Marcos' boot tip touched the straw-filled sack upon which Julio Campos lay. He struck a match, holding it so that Campos could see the revolver in his hand, saw Campos reach his right hand toward a gun belt that lay beside him. Marcos stepped over the reclining figure quickly and kicked the gun belt out of reach.

"*Quién es? Qué pasa?*" Campos called in a shrill voice.

The match went out, but Marcos had another ready. He struck it, found a candle in a metal holder affixed to a wooden post and touched the match to it, but its ray was weak. Marcos raised the candle and held it within two inches of his face, then replaced it in the holder.

"Marcos!"

"It is I, Julio. Do not raise your voice. I would not wish any harm to come to the woman in the *casa.*"

"Qué pasa, Marcos? I am hurt, a gunshot wound."

"So I see." Marcos holstered his revolver and knelt beside Campos. *"La patrona* did well, but not well enough."

"Why are you here in Cienguilla? What—?"

"Let me ask the questions, Julio. Where is she?"

"Who?"

"Julio, do not prolong this with stupid questions, eh?"

"Marcos, I swear to God—"

Marcos withdrew his hunting knife from its sheath and held it so that Campos could see its finely honed edge. "Julio," he said, "within one minute you will witness a miracle, how with two swift moves, I can change you from man to gelding. Even if you do not bleed to death, you will never again know the joys of a woman's body. Then—"

"Marcos, no! You are insane! Lizardi will—"

"What Casimiro will do will rest between Casimiro and me, Julio, but you will not be alive to learn the outcome. Talk now, quickly."

The knife was aimed at Julio's groin, its point barely touching the cloth of his trousers. Whether from terror or reluctance, Julio's mouth dropped open as he shrank backward away from the knife, but no words were forthcoming. With a swift, darting move, Marcos stabbed at the cloth, ripping it, and at the touch of the blade against his flesh, Campos uttered a muffled scream and tried to roll away, but Marcos caught his shoulder and pinned him back against the sacking so that his fear-stricken face was turned upward, reflecting the pain of his gunshot wound.

"Marcos—" he groaned.

"Talk, Julio, your minute is almost up. Next time, you will feel it in truth."

Campos began to talk.

"Where-Fresh-Water-Runs-Between-Moutains," Marcos told Sam, Macias, Atticus and Loren. "That is the name of the camp where Lizardi was to take her."

"That's the one," Atticus said, "Bokhari's private camp."

357

"The question, *señores*," Macias said, "is, can we believe him."

Marcos said, "I think so. There was the fear of death in him, like one who makes a dying confession. They came to the farm where Lizardi's cousin, Rafaela, could care for Campos. Lizardi sent Moreno to Bokhari and returned with instructions to bring Señorita Caroline to the small camp so she would not be seen by too many braves who might wish to kill her in vengeance."

"Benito?"

"If Campos has spoken the truth, we must leave at once. We will need to backtrack eastward, climb into the mountains over the old hunter's trail, then go on foot. We can sleep during the afternoon, which is good, allowing us to arrive in the valley by dark."

"Let's move out," Palmer ordered.

At daybreak, Bokhari emerged from his private wickiup and went to the one occupied by Lo-Kim and his two sons, Malha and Tanzay, Lo-Kim had already prepared Bokhari's meal and was pleased that he was in a much better mood than the day before, although the exact reason for this escaped her. She had watched the three Mexicans ride into camp the day before, bringing the young White Eyes woman. She had expected that the woman would either be killed or become a slave, but Bokhari did not speak of the matter to anyone and the Anglo woman lay tied hand and foot in the smaller wickiup, guarded by two braves. The Mexicans were awake and had eaten. Now they awaited Bokhari's pleasure.

Lo-Kim knew that Bokhari's mind was clear, for he asked to have Malha and Tanzay eat with him, and this was unusual. The two boys sat facing their father across the straw mat while the three ate the food she served them. The boys spoke only when Bokhari addressed them and when he had finished his meal, he stood up and said to Lo-Kim, "I go with the three Mexicans and the woman to the main camp. You will remain here with my two sons and six braves and their women. If all is well, I will return with the next sun."

Lo-Kim accepted his words in silence. Bokhari placed both hands on her bare upper arms for a moment, then lifted and embraced each son and went out. Minutes later, Malha and Tanzay left the wickiup to watch as their father rode off toward the main camp with the Anglo woman and three Mexicans behind him, four armed braves trailing the Mexicans.

Lo-Kim went happily about her chores, putting the wickiup in order. There were two women servants, six braves and the wives of three who had remained behind, but Lo-Kim was young enough, active enough not to require the help of the servants. It pleased her to do what little work was required to keep Bokhari's wickiup in order and look after his two growing sons. It pleased her even more that, unknown to Bokhari, she was now carrying his child, hopefully another son, which she prayed he would refer to as "our son" instead of "my sons" as he always spoke of Malha and Tanzay who had been born to his first wife.

As the sun rose higher and the air became warmer, Lo-Kim prepared a meal of ground beef and corn, to which she added some fat, then formed it into small cakes. These she wrapped in cloth, put on a warm deerskin dress and went outside to find her stepsons, who were engaged in a game with a boy of similar age. As usual, it was a game designed to strengthen their endurance, one which required them to run a distance of two hundred yards and back to their starting point, each boy carrying a sack of stones upon his back and his mouth filled with water. The boy who returned first with the sack still tied to his back and the water unspilled would be declared the winner.

Neither Malha nor Tanzay won this contest and their disappointment was clearly evidenced by the expression on their faces. Lo-Kim called to them and told them to get their bows and arrows and come with her for an exploration trip. This pleased the boys greatly, for they knew that Lo-Kim would tell them stories of Apache heroes of the past. She could read sign, identify birds, flowers and trees by name, sing and teach them to make marks on trees and in the earth that would spell out messages to other Apaches of their Chiricahua tribe. It was schooling of a kind, yet it was more enjoyable with Lo-Kim who was far less rigid than their father, less demanding than their strict mother who never laughed.

When they left the camp, two of the six braves waited until they were out of sight, then picked up their trail and followed. This, Lo-Kim was aware, they would do on Bokhari's strict orders, but would keep out of sight to preserve the fiction that she and the boys were alone and free to enjoy a fine bright day with Mother Nature.

Running ahead of Lo-Kim, Malha and Tanzay flushed out woodcock, ptarmigan, grouse and quail, shrieked delightedly when the bushes literally exploded as small coveys rocketed into the air from their places of concealment. They found the tracks of a kit fox and trailed them to an underground burrow, but failed in their efforts to dig him out of his home below the earth's surface. They each killed a pair of rabbits with unerring accuracy of their small bows and arrows, and Lo-Kim supervised their cleaning and skinning.

Beside the stream that ran through the valley, they built a fire, cooked the rabbit meat on sticks and ate the meat-and-corn cakes with it. Later, sitting on either side of her, the two boys slept with their heads in her lap while Lo-Kim rested with her back against a tree; wondering what her son—and it must be a son!—would be like.

Some five hundred yards above them, in the fringe of the woods overlooking the valley, the two braves, armed with repeating rifles, looked down across the grassy meadow and stood watch over the peaceful sight and the trio.

Marcos and Benito Macias had ridden ahead of Sam, Atticus and Loren, moving swiftly in order to get up into the high country as early as possible since the last few miles would have to be made on foot through the thick woods and undergrowth. If they could come within reasonable distance of Bokhari's retreat camp by dusk, there would be time to eat, scout the area and plan some form of action that would not endanger Caroline. If Campos had not lied. If he had, Marcos was fully determined to ride back to Cienguilla and kill him.

As they moved higher on the eastern slope, the old trail became more difficult where the rocks were loose. Here, they dismounted and led their horses and by mid-afternoon had reached a forest where the old trail became totally obliterated and Macias called a halt.

"From here," he said, "it will take two hours on foot to reach the crest, perhaps shorter, perhaps longer, I cannot remember. We will picket the horses to give them room to graze and each of us will keep the route well in mind in case it becomes necessary to return separately."

Inside the forest, the shadows were deep, but the way was easier and free from the underbrush. Between stands

360

of trees they had to battle through leaves, branches and vines that were often knee-deep, but these stretches, fortunately, were few and the forest provided excellent cover for their passage. Less than two hours later, Macias held up a hand and the others drew up on him.

"We are approaching *el copete*—"

Palmer translated this for Loren. "The crest."

"—and we will be in the open beyond that point. I will go ahead alone, Marcos and Att-ee-cos behind me, and signal back if all is clear. When you advance, bend low and do not permit your heads to appear above the crest line until we know what lies ahead."

Palmer nodded and sent Macias ahead, Marcos behind him, then Atticus. To Loren, "I want you to keep behind me at all times, to protect our rear. In close contact with Apaches, there's no way to anticipate where they are, what they will do, how they will split up. Or if they are already behind us—"

"Don't worry about me, Sam, I'll—"

"I'm not as worried about you as I am for all of us, and that includes Caroline. You'll do what you're told to do, Loren. I know you've had some experience with a gun, but with Apaches, all the rules change and you can't depend on speed alone."

Loren persisted stubbornly, "She's my cousin—"

"Stop it, Loren. You've seen how Macias, Atticus, Marcos and I work together. At this moment, I'm taking orders from Macias because I respect his knowledge of this part of the country. You're still new out here and until you learn more, a lot more, you'll take orders from those who know more than you."

"Mexicans and niggers?"

"I'll put that down to your youthful experience. Any one of our Mexicans and Atticus can run rings around you when it comes to survival tactics." Stiffly now, "Keep your eyes open on the back trail and do as you're told. And keep your gun in your holster."

He could sense Loren's resentment and wished he had not permitted him to come along. Loren turned and looked down the hill they had climbed and said, "In Yuma, they told me if you live too close to Indians or Mexicans you become one of them."

"Now just what does that mean?" Sam snapped with impatience.

"Don't you know, Sam?"

"No, I don't. Your Cousin Max has lived close to Mexicans for over twenty years and—"

"He married one, didn't he?"

"Loren, that attitude will only buy you a bushel of trouble. What the hell is eating at you, anyway?"

"From what I've seen of Mexicans, I don't like them. And what's more, I don't like my sister being too friendly with one of them."

Sam exhaled some pent-up breath. "Loren, if there's anything between Laurie and Marcos, this isn't any time to open a fresh can of worms. Settle it when we get back, but don't underrate Marcos Espuela as a friend and a decent person. Or as an enemy, if you really need one. I've seen you in action with a gun, but I've seen Marcos, too, and I wouldn't want to see you try to test his speed." When Loren began to reply, Sam said, "And that's enough of this kind of talk. We've got more important things to worry over. Stay here. I'm moving up. Watch for my signal."

Palmer turned away abruptly and started up the hill, looking back occasionally to make sure Loren was in sight. Within a hundred yards, he came upon Marcos and Atticus crouched behind a tree, looking toward the crest, which was another 100 feet above them. When he stopped, Macias looked down from just below the crest and signaled him to approach. Palmer sent Atticus and Marcos up the hill, then turned and signaled to Loren. When Loren reached him, Sam said, "Wait here while I move up to the crest with the others."

Sam threaded his way up the incline and knelt between Marcos and Atticus while Macias was whispering to them. "It is well. In the valley below, a woman rests beside the stream with two children. Just beneath this crest, two Indios stand guard, armed with rifles."

Marcos' voice, pitched low, was tense and urgent with excitement. "Two braves to guard a woman and two children can only mean they are important to Bokhari. If—"

"Wait," Sam cut him short. To Macias, "Benito?"

Macias said, "It is known that Bokhari has two sons. If these are his, it is fortunate for us, for nothing could be more important to an Apache leader than his sons. The woman—" Benito shrugged—"but the two guards must be taken first, and quietly. We do not know who else may be nearby. Rifle shots could bring the whole tribe down upon us."

Atticus said, "If I can get close enough, I'll know if they're Bokhari's sons. I've seen them in the main camp many times."

Sam said, "Benito, how far are we from Bokhari's camp?"

"Perhaps three or four miles. In this mountain air, the sound of rifles would carry easily."

"The question is, are these two children and woman as important to us as Caroline is to Bokhari?"

Marcos said, "If these are truly the sons of Bokhari, they would be important in any bargaining, but I think we must first find out where Señorita Caroline is being held before we make any decisions."

"Then let us find out," Benito said. "If Señor Att-ee-cos will make a wide circle to avoid the two braves—"

"In any case," Sam said, "we've got to take the two braves out, and without raising an alarm. We'll do that first. Benito?"

Macias nodded his approval. "It must be done silently so that the woman and two children will not be alarmed."

Sam now signaled Loren to come up and when he joined them, outlined their plan. When they were in agreement, the five crawled up the incline to the crest. Just below the rim, they halted. Sam sat down and began removing his boots. The others followed suit, laying their rifles on the ground beside Loren, but retaining their revolvers. Each took his hunting knife from its leather sheath and carried it in his left hand. To Loren, Sam whispered, "When we slide down over the crest, keep us covered, but don't fire unless it's a matter of life and death. One shot could scare the woman into running back to camp before we could get to her or the children."

Loren nodded. To the others, Sam said, "Let's move out."

Now Loren began to appreciate Sam Palmer's wisdom. He marveled that these four men could move as silently as snakes through the underbrush, scarcely able to hear the movement of leaves as they slithered over the crest and disappeared from his view. He cradled his rifle in both arms and began to crawl as he had seen Sam, Marcos, Atticus and Macias do, finally reached the rim, removed his hat and looked down into the valley.

On the other side, Sam and Marcos were belly crawling toward the two braves from the right side. Atticus and

363

Macias were invisible to his eyes, but he knew they were buried somewhere in the brush on the far left side.

Fifty yards away, where the forest ended and on its farthest fringe, Benito Macias held a finger to his lips and brought Atticus Perry to a halt. He pointed downward and Perry saw the two Apaches and nodded his head. One sat on the ground, his back to a tree, rifle lying across his lap, with a clear view of the valley and the rippling stream below. At that moment, the second Apache stood upright, looking down into the sunlit valley. Both wore the traditional Apache winter wear, a headband of scarlet cloth, deerskin shirt, loose trousers and soft boots that reached above their calves. The standing brave turned and spoke to the seated guard. Macias and Perry froze. The face of the one who stood was daubed with white and red splashes that ran from ear to ear across the flat bridge of his nose. The belt he wore was only too familiar to Atticus; it was a regulation Army cartridge belt, well-filled with shining cartridges. Attached to the belt was a beaded sheath from which the hilt of a knife protruded. And one incongruous touch: an Army emergency medical field kit dangled from the belt, its contents and use probably a great mystery to the Apache who wore it, yet highly prized because of the "U.S." stamped upon it.

From behind trees, Palmer and Marcos waited and watched, not daring to move across the thirty yards that separated them from the braves. Early discovery would give either or both the time needed to bring their rifles into play and fire warning shots. And buried in the undergrowth, Atticus and Macias also waited.

Then the Apache who was on his feet spoke to the other and walked into the thicket of trees, carrying his rifle with him. After taking about ten steps, he halted at a tree, rested the rifle against it and began relieving himself. And at that very moment when few men can think of more than accomplishing that simple, necessary act, Palmer made his move.

In a sudden dash, he ran forward. The preoccupied Apache heard him and turned, but it was too late to defend against the White Eyes who circled his left arm around the lower jaw of the brave to prevent him from calling out, while his right hand drove the long-bladed hunting knife between his ribs. And at that exact moment, Atticus and Macias made their run toward the seated brave, who leaped to his feet and turned in their direction,

364

only to receive the full force of Benito's knife blade into his heart with such force that he fell backward to the ground. Atticus leaped astride him, but the brave was already dead.

Benito came up beside him, removed the knife from the chest of the dead brave and stabbed it into the ground several times to remove the blood, then sheathed it. Sam and Marcos joined them then and the four men dragged the body back into the woods where the other brave lay. Loren came down from the crest, carrying their rifles, and together they walked to the fringe of the forest and looked down into the valley and saw the woman and two boys sitting beside the stream, the heads of the boys in the woman's lap.

Palmer looked inquiringly at Atticus, who shook his head and said, "From up here, I can't make 'em out. The woman looks like Bokhari's younger wife, but I can't be sure about it."

"Benito?"

Macias said, "We can take them now or wait until they start back to camp. If it is not they whom we seek, it would be better to let them pass by and follow them, which will be the easiest way to find the camp. Or, I can go ahead now and see what I can do to find the camp and learn if *la patrona* is kept there. It is for you to say."

Palmer deliberated for a few moments, then replied, "No. We can learn what we need to know from the woman."

"And since when can an Apache woman be trusted?" Marcos asked. "She will lie."

"Not if the lives of the two children are at stake, Marcos."

Macias nodded. "I would say that if *la patrona* can be rescued, Bokhari's sons are of no importance to us. If she is not in the small camp, they become of the greatest value to us. Therefore, let us first take the woman and two children and see what we can learn."

Palmer surveyed the valley carefully. "It is no problem. They would not cross a swift-moving stream, so they will return as they probably came, on this side of it, which means they must come within sixty yards of where we now stand. We will go down to where you see that bend in the footpath, there by the large rocks. Loren, you will wait here as extra insurance."

This time, Loren made no objections.

365

It was nearing four o'clock when the party of three in the valley began climbing the incline to return to their camp. Each of the boys carried a blanket and Lo-Kim had slung the near-emptied food sack over her shoulder. Malha ran ahead while Lo-Kim held Tanzay's hand as they came upward over the grassy slope, Tanzay calling out to Malha, who would stop, turn, and shout a reply. Tanzay tugged at Lo-Kim's hand and for a while they ran to catch up with Malha, who showed no inclination to be caught, laughing at their efforts.

Sam, Atticus, Marcos and Benito, once they had determined their route, had quietly made their way to a group of rocks that would put them at a strategic point of interception. Loren waited above them, his rifle ready in the event of some unforeseen emergency.

Thus, Malha, Lo-Kim and Tanzay came into the outcropping of rocks to find Benito Macias and Marcos Espuela in the center of their path. Malha, who was running ahead, came into Benito's arms and froze in terror. When Lo-Kim and Tanzay rounded the bend, Palmer and Atticus dropped down from the larger rock behind them and cut off any hope of retreat.

Lo-Kim was speechless with fear. Tanzay and Malha clutched at her dress, eyes looking up at her, seeing the appalling fright in her face, staring back at the men who blocked their way; feeling the trembling of their own bodies, wondering at which moment death would come to them. This was their first contact with a dreaded White Eyes or Mexican, or the strange black man, although they had often heard of the evil practices of these Enemy against the People.

In carefully chosen words, spoken softly, Palmer said, "We will not harm you or the children. I speak the truth. We mean you no harm."

Tanzay whimpered and Lo-Kim found that her throat muscles were paralyzed so that she could not reply. She stared open-eyed at the man who had spoken to her, heard him saying in her own tongue, "You will come with us into the woods where we will talk. I say again, no harm will come to you if you will tell us what we wish to know."

Again, Lo-Kim could not answer although she understood the words of the white man, marveling that he spoke her language so clearly.

"Come."

With Malha and Tanzay clutching her deerskin garment, she followed the two men, with the other two behind her. She wondered about the two braves she knew had, as a general practice, followed her; then assumed correctly that they had been killed by these four enemies. And as she walked along, she also wondered if she could come to a bargain of some kind with these men. At this moment, she considered her life to be over. No matter what they did to her, Bokhari would never forgive her for allowing his sons to fall into the hands of the enemy. Even if by some miracle she were released, or managed to escape, she would be banished. Now her concern was mainly for Malha and Tanzay; she no longer mattered. If they wanted her for her body, she would gladly acquiesce and bargain for the release of the two boys.

Stoically, Lo-Kim followed the two men ahead of her, giving what comfort she could to the two boys by her presence, communicating her own courage to them by the touch of her hands. They neither questioned nor cried, but trailed along beside her, climbing uphill and through the underbrush without showing their fear; and for this, Lo-Kim was proud, even drawing her own courage from Bokhari's sons.

Some of her composure evaporated when they reached the small draw on the other side of the mountain crest, and where yet another White Eyes with golden hair awaited them. This new one and the younger of the two Mexicans took the two boys to one side, leaving her with the white leader, the older Mexican and El Negro, whom she vaguely remembered having seen before. The white leader spoke in strange words to El Negro, who answered after staring at her and the two boys carefully.

"Atticus?" Sam asked.

Perry nodded. "She's Bokhari's number two wife. The boys are his sons by the first wife."

Palmer nodded with satisfaction and walked back to Lo-Kim. "Again," he said, "I will tell you no harm will come to you."

While he waited, Lo-Kim spoke her first words to these men, her enemies, the enemies of her people. "Why, then," she asked, "have we been taken?"

At this, Palmer's eyes brightened. "You have been taken because one of our people has been taken by your man, Bokhari. A young woman with eyes the color of the skies in early morning, her hair like the leaves that have begun

367

to turn before winter comes. She is of your height and her value is to us as those of the wife and sons of Bokhari are to him."

"The one you speak of was not taken by our people. She was brought to the Great One by three Mexican men."

"It is the same thing. We want her returned unharmed. Therefore, it was necessary to do this thing we have done. I ask you now, where is this woman? The truth."

"I speak only the truth."

"Then say where she is held."

"Until last night, the woman was in the small camp, Where-Fresh-Water-Runs-Between-Mountains. Early this morning, she was taken to the main camp by the Great One and the three men who brought her to him."

"For what purpose was she taken?"

"This I do not know."

"Do the names Lizardi, Moreno and Vega have meaning for you?"

"The one, Lee-zardi, I have heard before. He is the leader of the three who brought the woman to the Great One."

There was little doubt that Lo-Kim was speaking the truth. There was no guile in her straightforward manner, seemingly unconcerned for herself, only for the safety of the two boys, on whom her eyes were riveted between questions and answers. Atticus exchanged glances with Palmer which indicated his acceptance of her replies. Marcos returned to the group and now leaned over and whispered into Sam's ear.

Palmer addressed Lo-Kim again. "Does the name Van Al-len have meaning for you? Mar-tin Van Al-len."

Lo-Kim frowned and said, "It was he who brought the Mexican, Lee-zardi, to Bokhari many suns ago."

Sam took a few steps backward and began organizing a plan in his mind. Meanwhile, Lo-Kim stood quietly, hands clasped, eyes on Malha and Tanzay who sat apart with the golden-haired Anglo. Sam sat down again and spoke to Lo-Kim. "This is how it will be," he said decisively. "My men and I will leave now. You will be free to return to your camp——"

"The children——" Lo-Kim exclaimed in anticipation of some white evil.

"The children will go with us." He saw Lo-Kim's anguished look and added quickly, "I speak the truth and you will say this to Bokhari. Heed my words well that you will remember them.

"The children will not be harmed. It is a solemn oath I take. They will be kept by us until Bokhari agrees to return the woman to us. You will say that if he refuses, he will never see his sons again. If he harms or kills the woman, the two sons of the Great One will die and be left in the desert for the carrion and reptiles to devour." As Lo-Kim shuddered, he added, "A means of exchange must be arranged. His two sons for the woman. And it must be before four suns have come and gone. You understand my words?"

"I understand."

"Say to Bokhari that his Mexican friends will know we are from *el rancho* Tres Flechas. Say to Bokhari that he is to send word of his agreement to me there at Tres Flechas, where his sons will be held. He will send one brave, carrying a white flag. We will parley with his messenger and send him word how the exchange will be made. You understand?"

"I understand."

"*Enju.* We will leave here first. When we do, you will make your way back to your camp and send word to Bokhari. I say this to you: if any braves are sent after us tonight and they attack us, the first two to die will be Bokhari's sons. It will be the same if they attack Tres Flechas. How are you called?"

"Lo-Kim."

"And the children?"

Pointing, "That one is Malha, the elder. The smaller one is Tanzay."

"Go in peace, Lo-Kim. And remember, the matter of their safety lies in the Great One's hands."

Only at the moment of parting did Malha and Tanzay show their deep distress. Tears welled up in their eyes as Lo-Kim spoke to them, trying to reassure them that all would be well, that this was a new game they were playing, a test of their courage. If they passed the test, she told them, their father would indeed be proud of them.

Riding in front of Benito Macias and Atticus Perry, the two boys looked back until Lo-Kim was out of sight.

CHAPTER IV

AT TRES FLECHAS, MAX POTTER AND LAURIE OLMSTEAD heard Sam Palmer's account of the events that had occurred in Monte Babiacora. The two frightened children, weary beyond any capability of remaining awake, were asleep in the *casa* of Benito Macias, guarded by two armed *vaqueros* who were stationed at the front and rear of the house in order to keep the curious Mexicans from alarming them further. The guards on the walls had been doubled and messengers were on their way to warn the outlying range camps of possible attack of retaliation, in which case, they were to forget the herds and protect their homes and families. Those women and children who could be spared were to be sent back to the *jefetura* for greater safety.

In front of the Macias *casa,* Benito told the gathered men and women of their experience with the Indios and recounted the capture of Malha and Tanzay. Happy to learn that *la patrona* was still alive, there was considerable apprehension over the possibility of a massive attack on the home ranch by Bokhari, but Benito reassured them that the two boys were their greatest insurance against that. Meanwhile, they regarded Atticus Perry, who had been taken under Benito's wing, with mingled curiosity and awe, watched as he consumed a gargantuan meal with relish.

On the front porch beneath the *ramada,* Marcos Espuela sat in a chair smoking a cigar, his rifle leaning against the wall beside him. Loren Olmstead stood at the forward rail looking toward the front gates and ramparts, all cloaked in darkness.

"It will be better if you sleep, *amigo,*" Marcos said in a friendly tone. "The men on guard have eyes like eagles."

Without turning, Loren said coldly, "When I want your advice, I'll ask for it."

"Ah. That is the Anglo in you talking now. Tell me,

señor, what reasons do you have for hating a man you do not even know?"

Now Loren turned slowly to face him. "I don't like you cozying up to my sister. Is that plain enough?"

"The words, yes. The reason, no."

"All right then, I'll make it plainer. You're a Mexican, she's white."

"That, *amigo,* is the intolerance of which only a young, immature Anglo is capable."

"Call it what you want. You asked for a reason and I gave it to you."

"And your cousin Caroline, whose mother was Spanish?"

"They're not the same."

"If you were not so young, Loren Olmstead, and if Laurie were not your sister, you would be dead by now," Marcos said simply and without rancor.

Loren's body was turned toward Marcos, his face in total darkness, but the fury in him was apparent by his stance; legs stiff and slightly apart, arms dangling at his sides, right hand within drawing reach of his revolver. "Watch it, Marcos—"

"Your eyes are not as used to the dark as mine, *amigo.* I have my gun in my hand, aimed at your chest. I am a *mestizo,* so naturally there can be no sense of trust or fair play in me, no?"

Loren took half a step backward, stopped by the porch rail. Marcos laughed lightly and stood up, hands raised chest high, extended outward and empty. "Ah, Loren," he said, "hate is such a waste of time and makes one say and do foolish things." He dropped his hands and picked up his rifle, then started off the porch, past Loren. On the second step he turned and said, *"Amigo,* do not put too much faith in your reputation or speed with a gun. Some day you will force me to prove which of us is faster. I would hate to lose Laurie's friendship because I killed her brother." Without waiting for a reply, Marcos walked toward the kitchen for a cup of strong coffee. Loren spat over the rail, then went inside the house.

When he entered the study, Max was saying, "We could send word to Brett Mitchell, ask for a troop to be sent down until the exchange is made."

"I don't think I'd do that, Max," Sam replied. "I'd guess that Tres Flechas will be under Apache eyes until we come to some agreement with Bokhari and the exchange is made. Let them catch sight of one soldier and it becomes

371

a military thing, and there's no predicting what Bokhari would do then."

Max·sighed. "I guess you're right. We'll have to play it close an' see what his next move will be. I just hope—"

"He wouldn't dare do anything as long as the two children are here, would he, Sam?" Laurie asked.

"That's what we're counting on, Laurie. I'm sure of this much: Caroline is alive, and nobody could be more important to an Apache chief than the only two sons he's got to succeed him some day. He'll deal."

"That's putting a lot of faith in an Indian," Loren said.

"Until you know Indians a lot better than you do," Sam replied, "don't be too quick to pass judgment, Loren. Ask your Cousin Max."

"There have been plenty times when I'd sooner trust the word of an Apache, Coyotero or Mimbreno than some white men I've known in my time," Max said, "an' I go along with Sam on this. All the way."

Later, while Max made his rounds to see that the guards on the wall were alert, and Laurie went to the kitchen to check on the food and coffee for the guards, Sam found Marcos in the bachelor *vaquero* quarters, cleaning and oiling his rifle. They smiled at each other with some sense of satisfaction in having done well thus far. Marcos said, "The children are asleep. Benito and two others guard them well. Lina Macias says she would like to keep them. They are better behaved than her own four."

"For now, they are a novelty to her. It would not be long before they were like the others." Sam took Marcos' cigarillo from his mouth and used it to light one of his own. Handing it back, he said, "The next few days will be long ones."

"When one waits, all days and nights are long. You must be careful, *amigo*. It will be of little satisfaction to me if we gain Señorita Caroline's release and I lose a brother."

Sam smiled bleakly. "I will be careful, Marcos. I'm not that anxious to fall into Bokhari's hands and be turned over to Cochise. I will want you close to me. Keep a close eye on Malha and Tanzay. They are our only hope. Without them we haven't a whisper of a chance."

"Trust me, *amigo*." Then, "When this is finished, I have another venture in mind."

"Lizardi?"

"Lizardi, Moreno and Vega."

"Don't go out of your way to look for trouble, Marcos. It will come soon enough."

Marcos laughed lightly. "This is the Anglo philosophy, no? A mountain lion who preys on a man's cattle may be shot on sight, but a two-legged coyote who kills many soldiers, steals a whole supply train and kidnaps a man's daughter must first be proven guilty, even though we know he is a thief and murderer."

"It is the law, Marcos."

Marcos snorted with contempt. "Anglo law. I prefer Mexican justice."

"A subject we will discuss another time, *amigo*. I'm going up on the wall. *Adios*."

"*Adios, amigo*. Go with God's hand on your shoulder."

Loren, rifle cradled in his arms, walked restlessly around the compound, watching as Laurie led the kitchen help, laden with baskets of food and large pots of coffee, up the steps to the rampart. He went to the kitchen for a cup of coffee to drive the chill away and found Max there.

"Loren," Max greeted, handing him a thick mug. "Help yourself."

Standing together, drinking coffee in the warmth given off by the huge fireplace, Loren said, "Cold night."

"Yeah. Not many gettin' any sleep here tonight. Why don't you turn in, be fresher in the mornin'."

"I don't think I could sleep, either."

Max said, "Somethin' botherin' you, son?"

"Well, Cousin Caroline—"

"That bothers me more'n it does anybody else, but right now, I don't mean Caroline. I mean Marcos an' you. Somethin' wrong between you two?"

For a moment the silence between them hung heavily, then Loren said, "Yes. Laurie."

"Loren," Max said, "I don't want to try to influence your judgment about another man. Everybody makes his own judgments an' lives by 'em. I can tell you this, though; out here we judge people by what they are, not by what they were born. Marcos is a good man—"

"Laurie is my sister, Cousin Max. I don't want her to make a bad mistake."

"You're her brother, true, Loren, but you're not her father or mother. I never knew her before she came to Tres Flechas, but in a short time I've seen a girl grow into a woman. A fine, sensible young woman. Tell you, Loren, most times, I'd a lot rather go by what a smart woman feels an' thinks than a man who's only proved he's fast with a gun. Marcos, he's proved that, too, but he's more'n a gunslinger. He's what we call out here a *macho hombre*. Means a lot of man. You can't get much more of a recommendation from another man."

"He's a Mexican," Loren said with rising heat in his voice.

"Sure. He's half-Mexican. Just like Caroline is half-Spanish. So was Ruth. It didn't bother me even a little bit to marry their mother, nor Sam to marry Ruth."

"Half-Spanish and half-Mexican aren't the same."

"You're just bouncin' words around, son. I'd a hell of a lot rather see a daughter of mine marry a good Mexican than most of the white men I've known in Tucson. Or a son of mine marry a good Mexican girl."

"I don't feel that way."

"Well, first off, you don't have that much say in it. Second, you try to wedge yourself in between Laurie an' the man she picks to marry, you're goin'a lose the only sister you've got. Whatever you think she owes you, Loren, she don't owe you that much."

"What you're saying is, you approve."

"I don't approve or disapprove, but when somethin' looks right to me, I let nature take its course an' don't try to influence it one way or the other."

Loren stared into his coffee cup, then put it down and went outside.

For three days and nights they waited. In the compound, little more than preparing food and taking care of the animals had been done; and on the walls, weary men peered over the rims with tired eyes, hoping to see the lone Apache brave they had been told would appear carrying a white cloth of truce.

As the first rays of dawn broke on the morning of the fourth day, Paco Segura stood and rubbed his eyes in disbelief. No more than fifty yards away, facing the gates, stood a blanketed horse with the small figure of an Apache upon it. Simultaneously, others along the wall saw the lone courier, a branch in his right hand with a square of white cloth dangling from its tip.

The hoarse cry, *"El patrón!"* came from several throats at once. Max, Sam and Venustiano Carras ran up the steps to look out over the wall. Marcos and Atticus came running from the Mexican quarter, Loren from the main house, Laurie on his heels. Within moments, more than fifty men, women and children had gathered before the barred gates, looking up at the ramparts where two dozen men pressed forward around *el patrón*.

Max said, "By God, Sam, by God Almighty—"

"Just you and me, Max," Sam said. "We'll go out to him. He'll be scared to death at the sight of this mob."

"Let's go! Venustiano! Two horses!"

"Ahora mismo, señor!"

"And keep everybody except the guards off the wall."

"Sí, patrón."

Sam and Max rode out of the gates side by side. Clearly, the messenger came in peace, without a rifle or bow and arrow and had come silently in the night to stand and wait until he would be seen from the top of the wall. As they drew up and reined their horses to a stop before the messenger, raising their right hands, palms forward in the Apache sign of peace, Sam threw a startled side glance at Max.

Under his breath, Max muttered, "What the hell—!"

The messenger was Lo-Kim.

Sam said, "We make you welcome to Tres Flechas, Lo-Kim."

She replied, "I come from the Great Chief Bokhari to parley with the White Chief of Tres Flechas." Her words were directed at Palmer, whose face was the only one she recognized. "You have kept your word?"

Sam replied. "You will see with your own eyes that Malha and Tanzay are alive and well. And the daughter of *el patrón?*"

"She lives and is also well. I have ridden a long distance."

"Then follow us where you will dismount and rest. You may eat with your sons. We will parley when you have finished."

Inside the compound, Carras had ordered the crowd to disperse to their homes and duties, but many remained in the open to watch. To one side, Marcos, Macias, Loren and Laurie stood watching as Sam, Max and Lo-Kim rode in and dismounted. Marcos whispered to Laurie, told her that this was Lo-Kim, stepmother of Malha and Tanzay. At once, Laurie uttered her sympathy. "The poor woman. Why did they send her, put her through this?"

"Because the children were in her charge when they

were taken. If it had been anyone but Bokhari's favorite wife, she would be banished or dead by now."

Max and Sam, with Lo-Kim between them, walked to the Macias *casa,* past the armed guards, and entered. The two boys were alone with Atticus, who had been speaking to them in their own tongue. Malha and Tanzay ran to Lo-Kim and she bent to embrace them both. Lina Macias came bearing food and water and the three sat on the dirt floor and ate. Sam signaled everyone else outside.

When two hours had passed, Atticus was sent to tell Lo-Kim that the White Chief was ready to parley. He escorted her and the children to Max's study where Max, Sam and Marcos waited. Atticus remained.

"My daughter, you have told me, is well," Max said.

"She is well."

"Where is she kept?"

"This I am forbidden to tell you, only that I have seen her with these eyes. She is well. She sends greetings to her father."

Max glanced at Sam, who now took over. "You gave Bokhari my message?"

"Yes."

"Is he willing to exchange the daughter of the White Chief for his two sons?"

"Yes. It is a question of where and when. He will not come to this place, nor will he permit you to come to his camp in Monte Babiacora."

"I will tell you what the White Chief has decided. Six hours' ride south of here and north of the Oro Blancas there is a flat piece of land, perhaps four hundred yards in width, which lies in the open between foothills to the north and south. Do you know this place?"

"No. I came from the direction of Dos Viudas."

"I will draw a picture for you to give Bokhari. You will tell him that it is here the exchange must take place."

On a piece of paper, Palmer sketched the peaks of Oro Blanca and its foothills, then the foothills north which faced them. Between them, he indicated the flat area. "Between these foothills, in the exact center—" he marked an "X" on the paper—"we will meet for the exchange. You will say to Bokhari he is to send no more than twenty braves. On our side will be twenty *vaqueros.* When both sides are in place, a white flag will be raised by us. Bokhari will then send a single arrow here, where I have made this mark.

"Two from our side will then begin to cross the open space with Malha and Tanzay. At that moment, two of your people will begin to cross with the daughter of *el patrón.* This is understood?"

Lo-Kim nodded without raising her eyes to Palmer. "*Enju,*" she said.

"Say to Bokhari that if one shot is fired during the exchange, twenty rifles will be aimed at the backs of his sons, as we know that twenty of your rifles will be aimed at the back of the *señorita.* To come so far only to see his sons killed will be foolish."

Lo-Kim nodded, but remained silent.

"You have understood everything I have said to you?"

"I understand and will speak your words to the Great One."

"Then repeat to me what you have been told."

Faultlessly, Lo-Kim repeated Palmer's instructions as to terms and place, her eyes on Malha and Tanzay. When she concluded, she asked, "When?"

"When do you wish to leave here?"

"At once. I will reach Bokhari after moonrise tonight."

"Then let one full day pass and on the next morning, when the sun has risen to its full height, we will meet and make the exchange."

"*Enju.*"

"Then make your farewell to your sons now. Your horse has been rested and fed. He is ready for you."

When Lo-Kim left Tres Flechas, Sam found Laurie, Loren and Marcos waiting for him on the porch of the main house. Quickly, he told them what had transpired in Max's study, that the exchange would be made two days hence.

"Hey!" Marcos exclaimed with high glee. "December 31. A good luck day. All will go well."

"What makes you so sure?"

"It is the day of my birth."

"Has it always been a lucky day for you, Marcos?"

Marcos laughed. "Always. In a country like this, any day when a man reaches his next birthday is a lucky day for him."

"Then let's hope your luck holds this time."

Laurie said, "It will be all right. I know it."

"And I hope your feminine intuition is working."

In the three of them, there was quiet elation, which was not shared by Loren. He glanced at Laurie, then

377

Marcos, turned away and walked toward the corral. Then Emelita and Marguerita came out, each holding the hand of one of Bokhari's sons. Atticus was with them.

Laurie went toward them and followed the foursome to the Macias *casa*, leaving Sam and Marcos together.

"When we have Señorita Caroline back, we return to Tucson?" Marcos asked.

"Maybe a few days after that."

"I think that as soon as she is back, I will go to Tucson at once."

"What's your hurry, *amigo?*"

"I have business there."

"Marcos, let it be. We'll go back together and take care of it."

"No. This can't wait."

"Don't take the law into your own hands."

"The law again. We know who took Caroline to Bokhari, no? Yet you want witnesses to go to court and swear Lizardi, Moreno, Campos and Vega were the men? Who will speak for you, Lo-Kim? Bokhari?"

"You're right, Marcos, but don't try it alone. Three to one are tough odds to beat."

"If I wait for you, will you be on my side this time?"

Fifteen seconds passed before Palmer answered.

"Yes," he said. "This time, yes."

On Monday night, December 30, the rain fell steadily from shortly after supper until eleven o'clock, when it slackened. At midnight, Max, Sam, Marcos, Loren, Atticus and Benito Macias rode out of Tres Flechas at the head of fourteen *vaqueros*, carefully chosen from among the best riders and riflemen on the ranch. They headed due south for almost three hours, then turned slightly toward the east in a direct line to the designated meeting place. Atticus and Macias carried Malha and Tanzay, who were wrapped in blankets and slept most of the way.

They reached the foothills shortly after seven o'clock and moved over the malpais singly, carefully, until they found a site for their encampment. Here, they picketed their horses, fed and watered them, then ate a cold meal in the dark. More than anything else, they longed for hot coffee and their cigarillos, which Max and Sam had forbidden them.

When the meal had been eaten, Malha and Tanzay fed by Atticus apart from the others, Sam led them downward, on foot, behind a rocky barricade where, when the mist and overcast would be burned away by the sun, they would look across the flat land into the opposing foothills of Oro Blanca. Here, the men wrapped themselves and their rifles in serapes and blankets and slept away their saddle weariness. Atticus, Sam, Marcos and Max took turns standing watch. From Oro Blanca came no sound or sign of another presence.

At ten o'clock, the sun broke through the mist weakly and in another half hour, was blazing. The men awoke and removed their coverings and heavy outer coats, checked their rifles, changed the guard and talked or dozed. Now, Sam gave them permission to leave their posts, two at a time, to smoke in concealment and answer nature's call.

At eleven-fifteen, Atticus signaled Palmer and reported some movement in the Oro Blanca foothills. When Sam reached him, there was no sign of human or animal movement. Thirty minutes passed and Macias sent word from his post that the Apaches had arrived. Hidden behind the rocks, Sam and Max crept to his side, looked over the rim and agreed. Malha and Tanzay sat on the ground playing a child's game with stones they had gathered.

At noon, a single column of smoke arose from above the rocks where the Apaches had taken cover. There was a slight break, then the smoke rose again. Suddenly, it was cut off. A moment later, Marcos raised a long branch to which was attached the white signal flag. Almost at once, an arrow came arc-ing high into the air, curved gracefully and buried its head into the earth, equidistant between the two groups of rocks, at the very spot where the exchange had been designated.

Heads popped up on both sides as though both were perfectly willing, even eager, to make their presence known to the other. And now, to Loren's chagrin, Sam chose Marcos to make the trip with Malha and Tanzay. Atticus spoke to the two boys, telling them that their father awaited them; that they were to remain silent, like the young braves they were, and walk erectly, proudly, with their heads held high, their hands held by—pointing to them—Sam and Marcos.

A few moments later, Max, using his brass telescope, called out, "Now, Sam. They're moving."

Sam and Marcos crept over the rock rim and waited while Atticus handed over Tanzay first, then Malha. The young Apaches gave their hands to the two White Eyes without any sign of fear and the downward climb among the rocks began.

Across the stretch of flatland, two braves had leaped over a similar rim of rocks. With his telescope focused on that departure point, Max saw Caroline being lifted and handed over to the two Apache men. Beads of sweat broke out over his face although his hands and body felt cold and clammy. On either side of him, Atticus, Loren and the *vaqueros* watched grimly.

Marcos and Sam reached the sandy floor first and held Tanzay and Malha firmly by their arms until they saw that Caroline and the two braves had reached the bottom on their side. Then, as if on a given signal, both parties began to cross the open stretch toward each other.

"I wonder, *amigo*," Marcos said as they walked, "how many rifles are aimed at our hearts at this moment?"

"If there are twenty, as we agreed, I would say eighteen. As many as our rifles are aimed at those two braves with Caroline."

"She walks well, no?"

"Yes. Thank God they haven't hurt her."

"You will tell her that?"

"Mind your own business and keep your thoughts on what we're about."

"I think if I were you, *amigo,* I would marry her and—"

"Shut up, Marcos."

"Ah, well. It is a pity you are not half-Spanish or half-Mexican. An all-Anglo heart is made of cabbage leaves."

"Like Laurie's?"

"Ah, Laurie. No. All the cabbage leaves went into Loren's heart."

"Quiet now."

They were close enough to see Caroline's face, tense and rigid, head held high. Her hands were tied behind her back, causing her to swing her body from side to side, the soft sand making it difficult for her to walk in high-heeled riding boots. Sam and Marcos had reached the arrow with their small charges. The thirty seconds it took Caroline to reach them seemed interminable. Then she was there, the two braves on either side of her. Sam and Marcos released Malha and Tanzay, who ran toward the two braves joyously and were swept up into their arms.

Marcos whipped out his hunting knife and cut the rawhide thongs which bound Caroline's wrists behind her. When they were free, she opened her arms to Sam.

"Are you all right, Caro?"

"Yes. Yes. Get me away from here. I'm scared."

"So are we. We're going to walk back to those rocks. Don't worry, we're covered and Max is there waiting for you."

"They—they've got new rifles, Sam. They'll start shooting as soon as they think it's safe."

"Not while our rifles are aimed at Bokhari's boys."

Caroline linked her arm inside Sam's and drew it tightly to her side. Without looking at her, he knew she was crying as she said, "Sam, oh, Sam, thank you. I'm so glad you're here."

"It's all right, Caro. You're doing fine. We're almost there. Just a few more yards."

She turned to look back and saw Marcos, who was directly behind her. "Marcos, thank you, too."

"*De nada, señorita,*" Marcos replied. "Look ahead into the rocks. Your papa is there."

"Come up here with us."

"Keep going. I'm fine where I am."

She realized suddenly that he had been using his own body to shield her from a treacherous shot from behind. Then they reached the rocks and Max was there to meet them. He guided her over the rim and into the hollow before he took her into his arms and kissed her as both wept with relief.

"Let's get back to the horses and out of here, Max," Sam urged. "A few hundred yards leaves us still within range."

They clambered over the rocks, keeping low, Caroline helped by Sam and Max, Marcos below her. Willing hands outstretched over the second rim hauled them to safety and within minutes all four were safely behind the rock barricade. A rousing shout went up from the men and after a few more minutes, they were on their way down the trail to where the horses were picketed.

They wasted no time getting out of the area, using the *vaqueros* to form their rear guard, but no attack came. Two hours later, they stopped for a hot meal and coffee, then rode swiftly toward the safety of Tres Flechas.

BOOK V

CHAPTER I

DESPITE A FEELING OF OVERWHELMING GRATITUDE TO-
ward his gods for the safe return of his sons, Bokhari's
inner fury was boundless; yet he remembered well an
important lesson he had learned as a youth squatting beside his father, Heah-Lik.

*To vent one's rage in open view of others is a display
of weakness. A leader must exercise control over himself
before he can control others. Calm, deliberate thoughts
and decisions are the marks of leadership.*

Therefore, he remained openly stoical as he received
Malha and Tanzay from Vicenzo and Kimo, then ordered
the party of twenty braves to ride swiftly toward the main
camp in Monte Babiacora. He felt he had been betrayed
by the Mexican Lizardi, and this was something he would
think about later.

By the next morning he was well aware that many of
his braves—and their women—knew he had listened to
the Mexican and had accepted his word that the White
Eyes, Pom-mer, would willingly give himself up in exchange for the daughter of *el patrón* of Tres Flechas.
Now he felt the sting of defeat as never before; because
the defeat was one in which he alone was marked with
ignominy. It was the most degrading experience in his
entire life, with complete loss of face.

And there was another matter that threatened his personal security and left him with a feeling of further humiliation; he was certain that the quality of his leadership
was being questioned.

With the new repeating rifles and a very substantial
amount of ammunition on hand, each brave had been
equipped and spent every spare moment learning to use his
weapon. Within a week, a group had appeared in Council
to plead that they be put to test. Bokhari, sensing their
earnestness, sent three small raiding parties out to strike
at the more isolated ranches north of the Dos Viudas.
Such was the eagerness of those braves that they returned

within four days to report total success: five ranches had been destroyed, twenty-two White Eyes and Mexicans killed, an even dozen fine horses, ten mules and thirty-two head of cattle brought home with only two braves bearing wounds. Clear enough evidence, they claimed, of the superiority of the rapid-firing rifles and testimony beyond doubt of their ability to attack larger, stronger targets.

Bokhari had delayed his final decision to move out in force and now this weighed heavily upon him, for his own watchers had reported that the rifles taken from the supply train by Lizardi's men had already been replaced, increasing the firepower of the bluecoats at Fort Bandolier. And now, this latest humbling blow to his pride.

He must, he knew, and very soon, plan a major strike. No longer was it a question of *how*, but *where*, and *when*.

Planning required a clear head and calm deliberation, but he had not as yet, and which would be expected of him, punished Lo-Kim. Therefore, he sent for her to appear before his Council of Elders and although it grieved him deeply to do so, ordered Lo-Kim banished from Monte Babiacora. On arrival of the next courier from Cochise's Stronghold, due soon on his monthly trip, Lo-Kim would be sent back with him in disgrace.

This act completed, Bokhari retired to his private wickiup to plan a strike to drive fear into the hearts of all White Eyes, bluecoats and civilians alike. First in his heart's desire lay the plan to strike back at Tres Flechas in burning revenge for his recent shame, but also because it was here that his closest rival, Tan-hay, had failed.

Two days later, he emerged from solitary meditation and called a Council meeting. In a long speech replying to his subleaders, he pointed out the wisdom of a strong attack against an objective he considered equally as formidable, yet more vulnerable, than Fort Bandolier. In proper order, he proposed a full-scale attack on Tres Flechas, then on the town of Mesa Plata, followed by raids on the ranches in the Carancho Valley.

This, he outlined, would force the bluecoated soldiers of Fort Bandolier to send patrols to the southeast, south, southwest and west, thus depleting their numbers inside the Fort. Scattered about in many directions, Bokhari would then sweep in from the north and destroy the Fort.

There were answering speeches from the subleaders, some of whom disagreed and thought their primary target

386

should be the hated Fort. Once destroyed, it was pointed out in rebuttal, there need be no fear of strong military interference, permitting the Apaches to attack their other objectives as they pleased, strengthened by the rifles, ammunition and horses they would gain by the fall of the Fort.

At the close of that night of Council discussions, Bokhari was forced to admit there was great merit to the countersuggestions. He agreed to give them careful consideration and thought. And that night, he slept better than at any time since he had come to Monte Babiacora, although he secretly mourned the loss of Lo-Kim and knew that her banishment would have a strong effect on his sons.

At dawn, however, he was awakened by the arrival of a messenger from Cochise. He greeted the near-exhausted courier, Es-kin-ta, a brave of his own age whom he had known since childhood, and ordered food and drink prepared at once. When Es-kin-ta had eaten and drunk, Bokhari sat cross-legged facing him.

"You have come sooner than I had expected you."

"The Great One was eager that I come now."

"And what news from the Great One?"

"On my last trip, I brought him news of the raid on the Army supply train of the White Eyes, that the new rifles were in your hands. He asks now why you have delayed in striking at the Fort, brother?"

"There have been other matters that have been important. We have made some small raids to test the firepower of the guns. Those raids were successful."

"The Great One sends you this word: 'The Fort must die.' "

Bokhari frowned.

"The Fort must die," Es-kin-ta repeated. "When it is dead, you will seek out Chamuscada in Monte de Lágrimas and take him and his people into your camp. Without the Fort, there is no treaty and he is free to join you. Whereupon, you will arm his braves and attack the silver village of Mesa Plata, destroy the Carancho Valley ranches, then strike with all force at Tres Flechas and remove it forever from his thoughts.

"You will then send what guns, ammunition, horses and cattle you can spare to the Stronghold, which is in need. When this has been done, the Great One plans to attack Fort Lowell from the east while you attack Tucson from the south and west. It will be the end of the White Eyes in Arizona, for the Mimbrenos and Coyoteros will see our success and join us. Then Mexico—"

Thus, Bokhari experienced another personal setback. Having outlined his own plans of attack and strongly defended them in Council, he would, by direct order from Cochise, be forced to reverse himself and accept the suggestions of his subleaders, whose views coincided with those of the Great One.

"Enju," he said reluctantly.

"Without delay," Es-kin-ta said.

"Say to the Great One it shall be as he wishes. When it is done, I will send him word."

"Enju, brother. I will sleep until nightfall, then return to the Stronghold."

"You will take a new rifle to Cochise as a mark of my respect and admiration for him. Also, you will take with you a woman who has been banished from my tribe. I will leave you to sleep now."

Bokhari retired to his wickiup to consider the new plan, plagued by his disappointments.

He had almost lost his most treasured possessions, his sons.

Lo-Kim, who had given him much joy, was gone from him.

The White Eyes, Pom-mer, had slipped through his fingers and was still at large.

Because he had failed to move quickly, the Fort had now been resupplied with the new fast-firing rifles.

Who could be blamed?

Lizardi, the Mexican? Blame the Sun, the Moon, the Winds. But in the end, the responsibility for failure must rest on his own shoulders. *The Leader,* Heah-Lik had taught him, *is always given the lion's share for his successes. Likewise, the blame for failure is his alone.*

Nor was it inconceivable, he thought morosely, that if he failed in his next venture, Cochise would recall him to the Stronghold and send Tan-hay to take his place.

This last possibility danced through his thoughts with unspeakable agony. He removed the amulet Cochise had given him, placed it upon the pallet before him, and muttered a series of prayers taught him by a *shaman* long ago. Calmed now, he began to plan his next strategy as Heah-Lik would have planned it—with a clear mind unmarred by personal or emotional consideration.

As his plan evolved, it occurred to him that he could utilize parts of his early plan; forget the full-scale attacks on Mesa Plata, Carancho Valley, the scattered ranches, yes, but use these as diversions to draw as many patrols out of the Fort as possible and strike hard and fast when its numbers were at its lowest point.

He took up a pointed stick and began drawing designs and symbols in the earth. Here, the Fort; here, Mesa Plata; here—.

Three hours later, he summoned his subleaders into a War Council.

At Fort Bandolier, Colonel Hatfield sat in conference with Major Boyden and Chief Scout Willy Logan. Spread out on the rectangular table before them lay the map that had been taken down from the wall for closer examination. Upon it, Logan was using a red pencil to mark the last of five small "x's" to indicate the ranches which had been burned out during the last four days. Now he began crudely lettering a name beside each "x": RAINEY, SCOTT, WILLIS, DELMAN, COPELY. When this was completed, he looked up at Hatfield.

"Mr. Logan?" Hatfield said.

Willy scratched his cheek with his steel-pronged hand and shifted a wad of tobacco from one side of his mouth to the other.

"Wal, for one thing, Colonel," he said, "if we had any doubts about who got them new repeatin' rifles, shouldn't be none now. What's more, I got a pretty good idea this is on'y the beginin' of our troubles in these parts. These five ranches lay within a thirty-mile circle just north of the Dos Viudas. 'Cordin' to Ira Gorton an' Cato-Joe, who scouted the area, they come out of Monte Babiacora, maybe two-three small parties, hit them ranches hard an' fast, then moved back across the border."

Logan's hand swept across the area of attack. "I got a notion that with them rifles an' all that ammunition, Bokhari's got bigger plans in mind, maybe spread out all over hell an' gone, to give us more of the same. Small groups, same as these, to pull as many troops outa here on patrol as we c'n stand."

"And then come in with a strong force and attack the Fort," Hatfield said.

"That's how it reads to me," Logan replied.

"It makes sense," Major Boyden interjected. "And what

389

makes it worse is that if it happens soon, we'll have most of the Fort families within these walls. Not exactly the kind of homecoming welcome they will be expecting."

"Any suggestions, Major?"

"Yes, sir. At the moment, only the wives and children of the Fort Brennan personnel are in Tucson, three wives and seven children. My own wife is there. Within the next week or ten days, approximately eight more wives and nineteen children will be arriving in Tucson from their homes in the East and mid-West, Mrs. Hatfield and your daughter among them, sir. I think it would be advisable to send word to Fort Lowell to hold up on any plans to transport those women and children here for the time being. They can be quartered temporarily at Lowell until this situation is cleared up."

"Get Captain Greene in here and see to it, Major."

"Also, when the next eastbound stage goes through, which should be this afternoon, word should be sent to T-Y Lines in Tucson of the impending danger and hold up passenger and freight service in both directions."

Captain Greene came in, received the orders and started out to prepare them. "Hold it a moment, Captain," Hatfield said. "I will want one officer and eight men to ride to Mesa Plata. He will warn the town of a possible Apache attack and remain there to organize the miners and ranchers in the Carancho Valley in a program of defense. Send Lieutenant Kennard. When you have done that, sound Officers' Call. Troop officers only, one hour from now. I will have the administrative and technical service officers in later."

"Yes, sir." The note of urgency in Hatfield's voice was enough to send Greene on the run.

"Mr. Logan, I want Mr. Gorton and our Pima scouts—"

"Cato-Joe, Pah-tel, Quana an' Huan-Ti," Logan supplied.

"Yes. I want all scouts to get out into the field to look for any sign of Apache movement, in particular, their numbers and direction of movement. They will operate independently. At the first sign of anything worthwhile, each will return here and report his findings. I want you to remain here to coordinate those movements and evaluate the word they bring back."

"Yes, sir." Logan got up and went out.

"Major, I want a quick, accurate inventory of ordnance, medical and quartermaster supplies on hand. Hold the courier to Tucson until we learn what our shortages are. I'll want every able-bodied man to share guard duty. The only noncombatants in the Fort will be our civilian employees and laundresses."

"Yes, sir. A suggestion, Colonel?"

"What is it?"

"We could send word to Governor Mitchell and apprise him of what we know and what we suspect may be happening. It is very possible he might persuade General Litchfield to send another column of troopers here on a temporary basis."

"Do that, Major, and at once. Spell it out plainly and advise him that a troop of sixty-four men would give us the manpower we need to allow us to send out skeleton patrols without seriously depleting the Fort manpower. The unknown answer is timing; it will take three days to get the word to Tucson. If action is taken immediately, another five or six days before the troop could be outfitted and arrive here. Impress on him the seriousness of the situation if our assumptions are correct. The Fort is the Army's sole defense west of Tucson and south of the Gila. If we fall, every town, village and ranch in the area will be wiped out. At all costs, this Fort must be protected."

"I agree, sir. If I may be excused now."

Within two hours, the two groups of officers had been called in for planning sessions and every man in the Fort was made aware of the possibility, even probability, of a major Apache attack.

Many of the men even looked forward to it.

On the following morning after her release, Caroline slept late. She had had a steaming hot bath the night before, but showed little interest in food with the exception of Emelita's strong coffee. Emelita applied soothing ointments to the bruises on her face, body, and chafed wrists. Laurie remained with Caroline from the moment of her arrival until after she had fallen into a deep sleep.

When she awoke at ten o'clock the next morning with a voracious hunger, she came into the dining room to find Max, Sam, Loren and Laurie there in conversation over coffee. Emelita came running to find out what Caroline wished to eat, then ran to the kitchen to prepare it.

She answered the multiple questions asked about her

well being, then, over the meal, told in greater detail the story of her abduction and those next days of captivity.

"Lizardi, Vega, Moreno and Campos," Max ticked their names off.

"That's right. I'll never forget those names, especially Campos, the one I shot. It was a crazy thing. The moment I pulled the trigger, I expected to be killed then and there."

"They're marked men, Caro," Max said. "We'll see they don't harm anybody else."

"Look, I don't want anybody getting killed over this. They're gunmen, dangerous gunmen."

"Don't fret yourself over it, Caro," Max said. "Question is, we're due back in Tucson. We been waitin' for you to wake up, see if you an' Laurie wouldn't want to come with us for a change of scenery."

Caroline looked at Laurie and saw the eagerness in her face. "Please come, Caroline," Laurie pleaded. "I've never been to Tucson. Max says if you go, I can go, too. We'll be company for each other."

Caroline smiled. "I wasn't too sure you'd want me for company, Laurie."

"Of course I do!" Laurie replied explosively.

"Remember what I—"

"I've forgotten it already. Can I help you get ready?"

"It won't take me long to dress and pack. You go ahead and get your own things together."

"I've been packed for hours."

They left shortly before noon, Max, Sam, Loren, Caroline and Laurie, with Marcos and Atticus riding well ahead, three *vaqueros* on either side and three at the rear. The other *vaqueros* who had come home for the holidays remained behind at the request of Venustiano Carras, in case of an attack of reprisal by the Apaches.

Exercising great caution, they moved slowly and stopped at six o'clock for a meal, not expecting to reach Tucson until eleven or midnight. The January night turned cold and except for the two point riders and four *vaqueros* standing guard, the others huddled close to the fire. When the meat and beans were cooked and the coffee poured, Caroline said to Sam, "Where is Marcos?"

"Up ahead on point, with Atticus."

"Could we ask them to eat with us? They must be cold and starving."

Sam looked around and checked the four *vaqueros* who

were standing guard nearby. "I don't know why not," he replied.

"Will you invite them?"

He studied Caroline's face by firelight and for a moment it was as though Ruth had spoken to him. He said, "They might turn me down. But if you asked them—"

"I will." Caroline stood up and walked north to where Marcos and Atticus waited to be relieved for supper.

Sam turned to Max and Laurie and saw their grinning faces. Loren sat in stony silence. Max said, "Now what the hell ever brought *that* on?"

"She's your daughter, Max. You'd know better than I," Sam replied.

"Shuh. I think my daughter's growed up into a woman in a mighty short time."

"A woman and a very fine lady," Sam said.

"I'm glad you think so."

"I've thought so for a long time, Max. It was only a question of time before it showed through."

"Yeah. Well, let's get us all fed an' on the road. Cold enough to freeze a man's gizzard."

After the meal had been eaten and the fire put out, Sam said, "I'll take the point from here in. Loren, how about riding with me?"

There was no way for Loren to refuse. He mounted up and rode ahead with Palmer. Caroline fell in beside Max, Marcos with Laurie, and Atticus behind with the three *vaqueros.*

They reached Tucson just before midnight, where Max took his usual room, Laurie and Caroline in the room next to it, sandwiched in between the room Loren and Sam occupied. Marcos rode off to Espuela de Oro while Atticus and the nine *vaqueros* bedded down in the bunkhouse at the T-Y Depot.

It was just before the sun went down, when the mountains were splashed with purple and the shadows stretched to their greatest length, that Quana the Pima scout rode into Fort Bandolier. His horse was wet with sweat and Quana, no less damp, beginning to shiver as the air grew colder. When he swung himself from his horse's back, his knees buckled, unable to sustain the full weight of his slight body. Logan and Sergeant Art Petrie helped him to the mess-hall kitchen where he ate some shredded meat which had been mixed with the soft center of a loaf of bread. He welcomed the heat of the coffee which he drank in great gulps, and when he had eaten his fill, Petrie and Logan took him to Major Boyden's quarters where Logan interpreted Quana's words.

"I have ridden hard and long these three days and nights," Quana said.

"Where?" Logan asked.

"First, in the direction of the rising sun, then toward Dos Viudas, as I was told to do by you."

"So?"

"Thus. Early this morning, as I neared Dos Viudas, I had ridden until the sun rose to where—" slanting one arm upward to indicate an approximate ten o'clock—"and when I found no sign, I rode in a wide circle until I came upon their tracks. Apache."

"How many?"

"Many. As many as there are soldiers here."

"You trailed them?"

"Long enough to learn that they later divided themselves into smaller groups, with one large group remaining together."

"What other sign did you read?"

"So. The smaller groups rode thus and thus—" indicating south, southwest and east—"and also toward the setting sun."

"And the large group?"

"They rode—" again indicating north and east of the Fort—"in a line as the hawk flies. I then turned and rode here."

"What else?"

"These were war parties. There were no tracks of travois, thus they carry no women or old men. They ride close together and fast."

"You have done well, Quana. Go and rest now."

"My horse. I have lamed him. He was a good animal."

"The sergeant will get you another one." Logan nodded to Petrie, who took the Pima away.

Logan had repeated Quana's words exactly as they had been spoken. Now, Boyden stopped pacing and reached for his hat. "Stand by, Willy. I'm going over to Colonel Hatfield's quarters. Have the orderly bring some hot coffee to his office."

Hatfield and Boyden returned to their office less than half an hour later. Captain Greene sent an orderly to fetch Captain Ahearn, Lieutenants Vickery and Zimmerman and Sergeant Major Riley.

"Mr. Logan," Hatfield ordered, "repeat for these officers what Scout Quana reported."

When Logan had concluded, Hatfield said, "Gentlemen, it would seem our earliest suspicions are correct. Bokhari's main body is now somewhere east and north of us, between the Fort and Malhado, probably this side of Malhado Pass, and probably north of the main road.

"Smaller bands have broken off and are proceeding south, southwest, east and west. I read their intentions to create diversionary raids among civilian ranches, in Mesa Plata, the Carancho Valley, possibly into Monte de Lágrimas, to persuade or force Chief Chamuscada to join with Bokhari's Chiricahuas in a joint attack upon this Fort.

"Lieutenant Kennard and eight men are in Mesa Plata to help the civilian miners and ranchers organize a defense group. A courier should already be in Tucson to ask for additional assistance from Fort Lowell. It now appears unlikely they can get here in time to help. That is the situation as it stands at this moment. Questions?"

Zimmerman spoke up first. "Sir, according to the figures given us earlier, we can match them in strength with something of a small reserve. Besides, there is the howitzer."

Boyden said, "If we remain behind these walls in order to match Bokhari's people man for man, you are correct, Lieutenant. As for the howitzer, we are in very short supply of ammunition for it. Also, as long as we remain here, those loose bands can hit every ranch in the area without fear of military reprisal."

"Which," Colonel Hatfield added, "puts the problem back into our laps. Reconsidering the situation, gentlemen, it is not a palatable thought to know that those Apaches are going to kill a good number of the people we are here to protect while we concern ourselves only with our own protection and wait for an attack at some day or night or time that will be predetermined by Bokhari."

"Sir—?" It was Ahearn.

"Yes, Captain."

"Sir, I would like to volunteer to lead a troop on a search-and-destroy mission."

"I will take your request under consideration. Meanwhile, I propose that we will send out patrols in small strength, say eight men in number, led by junior officers and senior noncoms, their purpose to cover all ranches within one or two days' distance, attacking bands of Apaches in equal or near equal numbers or, in the case of superior strength, draw them off and lead them toward this Fort. The map, Mr. Logan."

Willy removed the map from the wall and placed it on the colonel's desk. "Here, here and here—" Hatfield pointed out the areas—"we will send out eight-man patrols, each backed up by another eight-man patrol only two hours behind them. Here and here—" again pointing —"two eight-man patrols, both within four hours' ride from the Fort. A total of sixty-four men, plus eight junior officers and senior noncoms in charge. We will necessarily allow Mesa Plata defend itself with the aid of Lieutenant Kennard and his eight men. There are enough well-armed miners and ranchers to fight off a relatively small attack if properly organized by Mr. Kennard."

"And the main strength, Colonel?" Ahearn asked.

For the first time in days, Hatfield allowed himself a flinty smile. "Come closer to the map, gentlemen—"

By morning, Ira Gorton returned to the Fort with word that a band of no more than thirty Apaches was on its way to Mesa Plata. While he reported this to Hatfield, Quana, a fresh horse under him, rode out. An hour later, the first three eight-man patrols left the Fort. Shortly thereafter, the three back-up patrols left, then the two patrols to the southwest went through the gates.

Scout Cato-Joe was next to appear, then Pah-tel. Quickly, their reports were made to Logan, who translated to Hatfield and Boyden. This information, as well as that furnished by Ira Gorton, was marked upon the map and bore out some of Quana's original report.

With seventy-two troopers, five senior noncoms and four officers on patrol and in Mesa Plata, and Corporal Zentz on his way to Tucson as courier, the total strength of the Fort had been reduced from 331 to 249. Bokhari's strength was generally believed to be in the neighborhood between 250 and 300 braves. According to information supplied by the four scouts, approximately sixty were involved in sporadic raiding, leaving the main body with from 190 to 240.

As Colonel Hatfield would have put it so succinctly, Satisfactory.

However, of the Fort's 249 officers and men, twenty-two were in the hospital and approximately sixty were technically classified as noncombatants: clerks, messengers, orderlies, medical attendants, warehouse and supply men, others assigned to such duties as stablemen, carpenters, masonry work, blacksmith, farrier and general maintenance work.

Of the remaining 167, a little more than half were trained cavalrymen, the balance designated as infantrymen, yet all were able to ride if the horses were available. There were 150 horses for the entire command and now only sixty-eight remained in the two corrals and stables.

Officers' Call was sounded and eleven responded; all but the O.D., Lieutenant Russell Isaacs, Captain Morris Lapham (Ord.-QM), and Captain Breed (Med.). Present with Colonel Hatfield, Major Boyden and Captain Greene were Captain Ahearn, Lieutenants Zimmerman, Carpenter, Mason-Field, Albee, Lynch, Vickery, Benjamin, Tennant and Farmer. While Hatfield outlined his orders of preparation and disposition, Riley held a briefing for First Sergeants Mike Tyler, Dan Cicero, Quint Patrick and Sergeant Art Petrie.

When the two briefings were concluded, all normal work routine had been suspended.

Ordnance and Quartermaster details issued bandoliered ammunition, checked individual medical aid pouches and equipment. Inspections were held to determine additional clothing needs. Cold weather outer coats, gloves, warm socks and extra blankets were issued to all administrative personnel, who would begin to stand day and night watches on the ramparts.

In checking personnel records, Boyden discovered that Lieutenant Laurence Benjamin was a qualified artillery officer. He was at once assigned to take charge of the twelve-lb. howitzer and select and train a crew to man it.

Civilian cooks were set to preparing large kettles of soup and prepare sandwiches to be carried to the guards on duty on the walls. Carpenters bored holes through the logs at shoulder height for use by infantrymen on the ground.

From the huge water storage tank, barrels and kegs were filled and distributed around the Fort for use in putting out fires created by burning arrows. Beams, planks, roof tiles and sheets of corrugated iron were carried to the center of the Fort where barricades were erected in the event the Apaches were successful in breaking through to the inside.

Noncombatant personnel were armed with rifles and stationed on the roof of every structure, where one or two barrels of water were placed for fire-fighting purposes.

Lieutenants Tennant and Farmer were assigned the task of giving intensive rifle drills to all noncombatants whenever they could be spared from other assignments, although this amounted to "snapping-in"; that is, going through the motions of loading, aiming and firing without the use of live ammunition.

The howitzer was placed about forty yards from the Main Gate, its muzzle trained and zeroed in at a point-blank range, to commence firing at the first sign of a breakthrough. A detail was organized to sweep through the Fort to gather up every small piece of scrap metal to be used when the single case of eight shells had run out. So zealous were these scavengers that door hinges, locks, knobs, spurs, bits, horseshoes, metal stirrups, nails and even small tools began disappearing at an alarming rate.

Troop Officers Zimmerman, Vickery, Carpenter and Mason-Field held infantry drills for cavalrymen and riflemen alike, while Lieutenants Albee and Lynch gave outdoor blackboard talks for clerks and warehousemen who had been away from the field longer than six months. And everywhere, the attitudes of the men changed overnight. They marched straighter, walked more erect, talked bolder and spent what spare time was left to them on the ramparts, acting as extra lookouts.

Sergeant Major Riley was everywhere, checking behind Tyler, Cicero and Patrick, looking in on every inspection, checking each guard station at night independently of the O.D. and Sergeant of the Guard. He was on hand for every drill exercise, every roll call, every meal formation and colors ceremony, seeking out the occasional malingerers lining up for sick call. And woe unto any man who, after close scrutiny by Captain Breed, was declared to be in excellent health and fit for duty, for Riley, in the presence of the others, forced such a malingerer to swallow a generous amount of castor oil. But these were few. In the face of impending action, morale was very high, the men in good spirits.

Yet, few slept the entire night through. Some had written letters and talked soberly among themselves. Some spoke rashly, overly bold, boastfully of previous encounters with Arapahoes, Sioux, Comanches, Navajos and Apaches. And others roamed through the Fort silently, looked after their horses or climbed the ramparts to look out into the blackened desert, standing beside those whose duty it was to maintain their four-hour vigil.

Quana found them.

He came across their sign shortly after noon and carefully studied the marks of their passage. They had moved north into the foothills of the Sauceda Mountains and he dared not go closer on his horse. The count was not too clear and he knew the first questions Chief Scout Logan would ask him. *Where? How many?*

Quana hobbled his horse and moved northward on foot. A few miles farther on, the band had halted for a rest. Meticulously, he surveyed the area and found where the braves had relieved themselves, where they had squatted on the ground to eat, where the horses had grazed. He counted hoofprints and moccasin tracks and when he had made a fair determination of their numbers, he ran quickly to where he had left his horse, mounted and rode swiftly toward the Fort, arriving at dusk.

For Logan, he made marks and symbols in the earth with his fingers to tell of their numbers and when questioned as to his accuracy, pointed insistently at the earth. Logan seemed satisfied.

"I make it close to 175 braves, Colonel," Logan said.

"He is sure?"

"He's sure. Spent two hours just fixin' the number in his mind."

"I'll accept his count. Tell him to eat and rest," Hatfield ordered, "and send Captain Ahearn to me." To Boyden, "Well, Major?"

"With the count we have on the other groups, there are about 235 Apaches on the loose, but our primary concern are those 175 up in the Saucedas. If they hit us alone—"

"I doubt if they'll do that," Hatfield said. "Chances are they'll wait to see if we move more men out of the Fort when those roving raiders make their strikes. They'll expect us to move out when the word reaches us. Then those smaller bands will double back, link up with the main body and hit us with their full strength."

Logan said, "That's about as close as I can read it myself."

"What," Boyden asked, "if we could make the decision for them, force them to attack before the other sixty or so join them?"

"How do you propose to do that, Major?"

"Let us suppose that Captain Ahearn were to lead a full patrol of fifty men out of here around dawn, heading east. I'm sure Bokhari will have scouts in the area keeping watch, and will get the news within an hour. Then, if I were to take a second patrol of about forty men out and head west, I'm just as sure that this would also be noted and passed on to Bokhari. With ninety men out, I'm fairly certain the temptation to strike at the Fort would be too great for him to pass up, knowing that our strength here would be down to less than one hundred. After three hours, Ahearn would turn and ride back as fast as possible. I would do the same from the west.

"If Bokhari falls for the bait and attacks, Ahearn's troop and mine could do some effective damage from the outside while those remaining here fight them from the walls."

"And if he doesn't take the bait?"

"Then ninety men and four officers and scouts will have had a few hours of good exercise."

"Let me think about it, Major."

The courier to Tucson got only as far as Malhado Pass. Riding swiftly, his mount showed signs of tiring as they came within three miles of the canyon mouth. Having pressed too hard, Corporal Mannie Zentz dismounted, cursed himself and the animal heartily, and began walking slowly to allow his horse to recover. When they were within a mile of the mouth of the Pass, four Apaches rode out of it, almost as surprised to see Zentz as Zentz was to see them.

He looked around for cover and found none; not a rock or tree large enough to hide behind, standing exposed as the Apaches heeled their horses to pick up speed as they unlimbered their rifles. Zentz, a lover of horses, and this one his own during the past fourteen months, did what he had to do. He shot the animal through the head and fell flat on the ground, taking cover between its legs, leveling his rifle over its corpse, placing his revolver beside him.

The Apaches came on at full speed, shouting into the wind, at one another, and at Zentz, who was drawing a careful bead on the lead man. In the act of firing at a stationary target, the nearest Apache died with a bullet through his chest. The three others swung out and formed a wide circle. The second Apache was shot through the head and was dead before he hit the ground.

Two more, Zentz thought. Jesus, be with me and I'm home free with a good Indian pony under me.

The two remaining Apaches came at him from opposite sides, firing their rifles, levering fresh cartridges into the chambers, but firing from moving horses did little for their accuracy and although they came uncomfortably close to hitting their target, close was hardly enough to cut down a man lying behind the bulk of a dead horse.

As they crossed each other's path only thirty yards from their target, the third Apache was hit and flew over the head of his horse and lay still on the ground. Seeing the broad back of the last Apache retreating from him, Corporal Zentz made his only, and fatal, mistake. He stood up to fire at this fine target.

But in that instant, the Apache wheeled his horse around and started his return run. Zentz remained standing, firing as the horse thundered toward him, now hoping to hit the horse, then the Apache when he would be thrown. But the Indian lay low along the animal's neck, right arm outstretched, aiming his rifle at the standing figure. This time, he caught Zentz in the abdomen. Zentz fell across his dead horse, both hands covering the area where he had been hit. The Apache howled as he rode past him, turned and came back slowly. Then he stopped, dismounted and took out his scalping knife.

It was Corporal Mannie Zentz's dying regret that he had not been killed instantly.

CHAPTER II

THE MEXICAN SECTION OF TUCSON, WHICH WAS THE original township laid down in the days of the Spanish invaders, was a city within a city (if it could be called city at all), and was generally referred to by Anglos as The Quarter. Where it touched the growing commercial area, its stores, shops, *cantinas,* restaurants and one or two small hotels were occasionally patronized by Anglo drifters, miners, soldiers on liberty and transients who were lured by a sense of something foreign and different from more familiar cultures they had known elsewhere. Also, the drinks were cheaper and there were women available.

Easterners expressed the opinion that The Quarter was far more impressive than the small villages they had passed through in New Mexico; that the Mexicans they had seen in Texas were more servile and dependent upon Anglos. By comparison, although Tucson was not a city of particular charm or beauty, and was in fact crowded and dirty, it hummed and bustled with activity and gave off an aura of frontier adventure.

Few Anglos ventured into the core, or heart, of The Quarter. When such a trip or visit was necessary, as in the case of a rancher or storekeeper seeking laborers, he seldom went alone or unarmed, never entered a house, generally remained in his saddle or on the wagon seat, and this only by day. Hardly ever was a white man seen deep within The Quarter at night or on foot unless he were drunk or lost, in which case his body, stripped of boots, money and any other valuables, would be found in an open ditch on the road leading west or south at some later date.

From The Quarter, Casimiro Lizardi drew the men he frequently used when he needed more manpower for larger-scale operations, as in the case of his skillfully planned raid on the Army supply train; hard, grim, lean, tough men who sought such opportunities to line their pockets with gold, refusing to become laborers in the fields of the enterprising Anglo ranchers whom they despised.

For their last venture, they had gambled with Lizardi for riches, but Lizardi had come with explanations that the Apaches had refused to pay the high price he asked for the rifles, ammunition, horses and mules they had made off with and therefore, each share must be cut to five ounces of gold per man. And although five ounces of gold was far more than most Mexicans saw in an entire year, it was far below what had been promised them at the outset.

There was angry talk among the men of The Quarter that Casimiro Lizardi was not to be trusted, a *ladrón* who, like the Anglos, preyed upon Mexicans and Indians alike and walked hand in hand with the Anglo *ladrón*, Martin Van Allen. It was common knowledge that Lizardi and his three *tenientes*, Moreno, Vega and Campos, were fat with gold, food, tequila and women while others must be satisfied with their lean leavings. And what of the families of those who had been killed on the road, buried out in the desert wastelands where they could not be grieved and prayed over by their wives, sons and daughters, they who had received nothing for the lives they had given up?

In the *casa* of his woman, Ema Arboleya, the word of such discontent among the people was not long in coming. Casimiro became aware of the strong feelings against him. Julio Campos, upon whom he once relied strongly, was no more, dead of infection in Cienguilla. Moreno and Vega were silent, but showed their nervousness in every movement, every dark look, occasionally rising from their chairs to pace back and forth across the small room, scuffing the earth, kicking clouds of dust up, drinking too frequently from their bottles of tequila.

The word had come from Ema, from Campos' woman, Maria Elena Duarte, from Inez Espuela herself on the very night the three had returned to Tucson from Monte Babiacora. Not only had the news of the abduction of *el patrón's* daughter reached Tucson, but immediate suspicion pointed to Lizardi and his three aides, who had been absent from Tucson at the time.

By the silence and darting glances of the patrons in Espuela de Oro, Lizardi at once recognized that he had been tried and convicted by his own. Their fear, he knew, was that the Anglos would descend upon The Quarter and

403

burn it down in retaliation. In the privacy of her rooms, Inez was more explicit.

"You have committed a foolish crime, Casimiro," she said. "You and your *compañeros* are marked men. Señor Van Allen has sent word that when you return he wishes to see you at once."

"An *inferno* on Señor Van Allen," Lizardi retorted.

"You are so big now you can say this to his face?"

"I am Lizardi," Casimiro shouted, banging a fist on the table. "If Martin Van Allen wishes to see me, let him come to The Quarter."

"Ah, Casimiro, I think your time grows short. If you send him angry words, he will not come alone, but with others. You have seen angry Anglos before, what they do when they seek a wanted man. They kill him, burn and destroy what is all around him, like the Apaches. You cannot remain here. I will not allow it. Leave Tucson. Go to Sonora, Sinalao, anywhere else, but do not stay here."

"Tú perra! I have paid you well for many years and now you tell me, Casimiro Lizardi, to go? Like a dog in the streets?"

"If you are a dog, it is not my doing, but yours!"

"We are of the same blood, by the same mother and father!"

"Brother, that too was no fault of mine. You have given me gold, yes, but I have given you refuge here, the only home you have known since you left Cienguilla, provided you told no one we are brother and sister, or that you are the uncle of my son. Go now, before others learn you are here. And take your *piojo* with you."

"I cannot leave Tucson now. I wait for a message from Juan Portero—"

"I care not who you wait for. Find a place elsewhere in The Quarter, among those whom you have paid so liberally for their services. If your messenger comes here, I will send him to you."

Lizardi gulped down half a tumbler of tequila. *"Puta!"* he raged. "The whore of an Anglo who looks down on all Mexicans!"

"Casimiro, go now before I call for men to throw you out."

Lizardi stared at Inez in smoldering fury. "I will go, *hermana mia.* The messenger will come from Cienguilla. Send him to the *casa* of Ema Arboleya."

"Yes. And when you leave Tucson, take Ema with you. She will no longer work here."

"*Adios.* Give your lover my blessing and tell him I no longer need him. Soon, I will have more gold than he has ever dreamed of. And to my nephew, tell him he is my sworn enemy. When I see him, I will kill him on sight as a special tribute to his mother."

Inez drew her lips into a grim, tight line and said nothing. But as Casimiro left, she sat down and wept. Marcos must be told. For the first time, he would know that Lizardi was his mother's blood brother, his uncle, and must be on guard against him.

On the night he returned to Tucson with the party from Tres Flechas, Marcos felt the soft warm glow of love. For hours, as he rode beside Laurie, they had talked of many things never touched on before; her life in Fort Leavenworth, growing up with Loren, of Aaron and Libby whom she missed more than ever. Marcos had spoken little of his youth, more about his ambition to become something more than those he had known most of his life; of his admiration, almost love, for Sam Palmer; his respect for Max Potter; to some day live on land that was his own, to raise and break horses, breed cattle.

"And T-Y Lines?" Laurie asked.

"That, too. I want to be a part of T-Y, but one can do that and own a ranch as well, a home where his wife and children can live and grow, look out and know that all the land they can see belongs to them. Someone to come home to."

"It sounds wonderful, Marcos. One day you will have it."

"With the woman one loves, it is everything. Without her, it is nothing."

"Marcos—"

"What, Laurie?"

"We will have it together."

Marcos did not answer, but his head turned in the direction ahead where Loren and Sam were riding ahead on point.

Knowing what lay like a stone in his heart, Laurie said, "When we get to Tucson, I will talk to Loren. It will be all right. You will see."

"Yes," Marcos replied, but the word was heavy with doubt.

At the Congress Hotel, Marcos said, *"Hasta mañana,"* and led Atticus and the nine *vaqueros* toward the T-Y Depot where they were to spend the night.

But sleep did not come easily to Marcos this night. For a while, he lay on his cot in the darkness, fully clothed, then arose and pulled his boots on. In the cot next to his, Atticus rose up on one elbow. "You going out, Marcos?"

"I think so. I am restless."

"I can't fall asleep, either. Got too much on my mind, I guess."

"Then we have the same problem. Come with me to Espuela de Oro where you will meet my mama, who will feed us like kings, eh? Maybe that is what we need."

"You think it will be all right?"

"Because of your color?" Marcos laughed. "Atticus, among my people a man is a man because of what he is and nothing more or less. You are *macho hombre*. You will be welcome."

Atticus drew on his boots and both men pulled on their outer coats, buckled gun belts around their waists, put on hats and tiptoed out past the sleeping *vaqueros*. Outside, Marcos spoke with the two armed guards in front of the Depot and he and Atticus hunched forward against the cold wind as they walked toward Espuela de Oro.

At the bar, Paco Mendirez, who had tended that station for Inez as long as Marcos could remember, had little to do at this late hour. There were less than a dozen people at the tables and only two men standing at the bar engaged in a dice-rolling game for drinks. Only four of the eight bar girls and waitresses were present, sitting at a table drinking coffee or sipping tequila.

"Paco amigo, cómo está usted?" Marcos greeted the bartender.

"Bueno, Marcos. Y tú?"

"Muy bueno. My friend and I have had a long ride and we are thirsty."

Paco was already pouring two glasses of tequila. Marcos asked, "Where is my mother?"

"In her room. She has a visitor. She longs to see you."

"I will wait."

Paco, the two men at the bar, several of the patrons at the tables and the bar girls were staring at the large Negro with curiosity. Negroes were not entirely strange to Tucson since the end of the Civil War. A number had come to stay and work, others had passed through with wagon trains en route to California. Few, because of the strong white Southern antagonism, had remained. Some had moved on west to California, a good number headed south into Mexico, some east to Texas, and others had returned to wherever they had emigrated from, desperately homesick for the comfort of sharing their misery with their own.

Maria Elena Duarte, who was Campos' woman, left the other three girls and came to the bar, her eyes on Atticus. She greeted Marcos coolly and Marcos responded with a smile that showed little warmth.

"A drink for me, Marcos?" she said.

"Of course. Paco, a drink for Señorita Duarte."

"That one?" Paco replied. "Look into her eyes, Marcos. She has already drunk enough to drown in."

"Old man," Maria Elena snapped angrily, "do as you are told and keep your dirty tongue and thoughts to yourself."

"Give her the drink, Paco," Marcos said. "She is the good friend of my good friend Julio Campos, who lies wounded in a stable in Cienguilla."

As she took the drink, aware that the large Negro was staring at her, Maria Elena's hand shook. "Then you have not heard?" she asked.

"Heard what?"

"That Julio is dead. The word came this afternoon." She sipped at the drink. "Was it you who wounded him?"

Marcos grinned. *"Muchacha,"* he said, "if I had shot him he would not have lingered so long. No, he was shot by a woman, the daughter of *el patrón of* Tres Flechas, whom Julio, Hector Moreno, Orlando Vega and that *macho hombre,* Casimiro Lizardi, kidnapped and turned over to Bokhari for ransom."

"You lie, Marcos," Maria Elena said with a rising voice. "No woman shot Julio. Casimiro told me—"

"Then Casimiro was here tonight, here in Tucson?"

Paco nodded. "With those two fine *caballeros,* Vega and Moreno." Paco spat on the floor behind the bar to indicate his contempt.

Marcos said to Maria Elena, "Take your drink back to your table." When she turned and left them, he asked Paco, "You know where they are, those three?"

Paco nodded. "Vega and Moreno have gone. Lizardi is in the back. He is your mother's visitor."

Marcos and Atticus exchanged swift glances. Marcos said, "Wait here for me, *amigo*."

"I think I'd better go with you, Marcos."

"No. This is something I have promised myself to do alone. I want him that way. Alone."

Marcos went to the back of the room and through the door. Paco said to Atticus, "If Marcos is your friend, *señor,* go with him. I have seen Lizardi at work before."

Atticus went to the doorway and stood just inside the hallway, watching Marcos as he walked toward the last door on the right. Before Marcos reached it, the door was thrown open. Lizardi stepped into the hall and slammed the door shut with an angry curse. His back was toward Marcos, who called out, "Lizardi!"

Lizardi wheeled to face Marcos, his right hand reaching for his gun. When he saw Marcos, he dropped his hand at his side and smiled evilly. "So, *muchacho,* it is you."

"It is I."

"The dutiful son comes to visit his mama, eh?"

"*Si.* Also to talk with the great Lizardi, the brave one who bushwhacks supply trains, murders men for money, trades with the Indios and abducts young girls to hand over to the Apaches for money."

Lizardi's face froze. "You talk foolishness."

"And your *compañero,* Campos, talked sense. Also, I will tell you this, *amigo.* The girl is no longer in Bokhari's hands. She is safe with *el patrón* and Sam Palmer. Your reward will be an arrow or a bullet, if you are lucky."

"Marcos, you have a long tongue."

"I was there, Lizardi. Palmer was there. We witnessed Bokhari's shame when he returned Señorita Caroline in exchange for his two sons at Tres Flechas yesterday. Where will you go now to sell your stolen guns, eh?"

At that moment, Lizardi's hand moved upward, but when his gun was a little more than halfway out of his holster, the bullet from Marcos' gun struck him in the abdomen. Lizardi, eyes wide open, glazed as if in astonishment at witnessing a miracle, buckled and fell to his knees, then forward.

Marcos walked toward him and kicked his gun to one side. "Now you know, Lizardi," he said as the door burst open and Inez came out, ran to Marcos and embraced him, trembling with terror.

Atticus turned back to the bar. Paco poured a glass of

tequila, spilling some on the bar. In the *cantina*, everyone was standing on his feet staring at the open doorway which led into the hall.

"Drink up, everybody," Atticus called out in Spanish. "The king is dead. Long live the king."

By early morning, the word was out. Marcos Espuela had outdrawn Casimiro Lizardi and killed him. Marshal Yarborough accepted Atticus Perry's word for it, then went to Espuela de Oro to talk with Inez who, once assured that Marcos was safe, told Yarborough she had not seen the actual shooting. But from Paco the marshal elicited much information about Lizardi and his companions, including the news that Hector Moreno and Orlando Vega were hiding in the *casa* of Maria Elena Duarte. Yarborough went to the house, picked up the two men and lodged them in his jail on suspicion of having been implicated in the raid on the Army supply train, following which, Max Potter appeared and charged them with having participated in the kidnapping of Caroline.

"Well, *amigo*," Sam said to Marcos at T-Y, "you said you would do it and you did."

"It was a fair fight, Sam. Atticus saw it. Lizardi drew first."

"You and Loren. The two fast-draw kids. Some day somebody's going to try to make you prove just how good you are. I hope it won't be Loren."

Marcos shook his head. "Sam, I never killed a man I didn't have to."

"You mean like Loren, with Harry Penn and Dutch Macklin?"

"I don't mean anything except what I said."

"All right, Marcos. I don't know of anybody needed killing more than Lizardi. You saved Max or me the job. Just do me one favor."

"What?"

"Don't give Loren any excuse to draw on you."

"I pray every night he won't find one for himself."

Max came in then and was all business again, wanting to bring the talk of Lizardi's death to an end.

"We got a stage an' freight line to run," he said. "First stage out for Yuma is loading an' ready to go. We're shorthanded because of the men we left at Tres Flechas, so we've got to scratch an' scrape."

"I'll take it," Marcos offered.

409

Max said, "Maybe it's a good idea to get you out of town for a while 'til this hubbub dies down."

"I'll go along, too," Sam said. "We'll need all the hands we've got to handle the freight run day after tomorrow. They'll be carrying full loads with all the stuff been piling up these last ten days."

"There's nothing for me to do around here," Loren put in. "I'd like to go to Yuma and see how Sheriff Kinnick is getting along."

"All right," Max said. "Take Perry along to break him in on the run. That makes four of you. Pick up two *vaqueros* and start moving."

"Any news on the mail franchise?" Sam asked.

"It came in yesterday. I'm goin' over to see Brett Mitchell and pick it up this mornin'. Also, I've got half a dozen people to meet at the bank with Boyd Kiner at noon. Investors, son, just droolin' at the mouth to put their dollars in our laps for pieces of T-Y."

"You're letting them buy in?" Loren asked.

"We sure are, ain't we, Sam?" To Loren, "They're all merchants who need T-Y to bring goods in and ship out. We let 'em in an' get all our original money back, keep control, an' pick up all their business. That puts us in for free."

Sam, Marcos and Atticus had left the office to get the two *vaqueros* and their horses. In front of the Depot, passengers had begun loading into the stage.

"Cousin Max," Loren said, "could I take my share out of the Line?"

Max's head turned sharply toward him, his forehead wrinkled into a puzzled expression. "Sure, if you want it. I don't know why, though, particularly now." He paused and asked, "You talkin' for Laurie, too?"

"No, only for myself. Only my share of it. I want to move on after this trip. California, where I was heading when I left Fort Leavenworth."

"You talk to Laurie about this?"

"Not yet. When I get back from Yuma I'll explain it to her."

"All right, son. You go ahead. We'll talk about it when you get back."

Minutes later, Max stood at the window and watched as the first post-holiday stage for Yuma pulled out.

At Encantado, the stage for Yuma met the eastbound

410

stage for Tucson. The driver and guard sought Sam out as soon as they pulled into the relay station, surprise written across their faces. "What in the name of God you doin' here?" the driver asked.

"Same thing you are, Jess, except heading in a different direction. What's up?"

"Didn't you get the word?"

"What word?"

"Man, all hell's broke loose, or about to. Colonel Hatfield sent a man to Tucson two days ago, askin' for a relief column. Bokhari's broke out of Monte Babiacora an' the talk is they're headin' for the Fort to wipe it out."

"No word reached Tucson, Jess. You see anything on the way in?"

"No, but just about every scout at the Fort's been readin' sign like it was a newspaper. We got out fast as we could early yesterday mornin'. You better turn that stage aroun' an' make for Tucson."

The passengers on the eastbound stage, meanwhile, had been talking to those on the westbound stage. Sam and Marcos went to where they were gathered in a large knot.

"What about it, Mist' Palmer?" John Ferris, a Yuma merchant who was heading home, asked.

"Well, you know as much about it as I do," Sam replied. "We've got three men and three women passengers, driver, guard, and six others of us. I'm going to put it to you passengers to vote yes or no. If you say no, the stage goes back to Tucson."

The vote took a matter of seconds, five noes and one yes from Ferris. Sam ordered the driver to follow the eastbound stage to Tucson. The driver was told to pass the word to Max Potter for relay to Governor Mitchell.

"And we, *amigo?*" Marcos asked, already knowing Palmer's decision for himself.

"I'm going on to Fort Bandolier, Marcos."

"You are still the soldier, eh?"

"Well, I owe the Army a lot, *amigo*. They need every rifleman they can find. Also, any fight against Bokhari is in the interests of T-Y Lines."

"We can get through?"

"I think—*we?*"

"I owe the Army nothing, *amigo,* but I work for T-Y, too. Also, I cannot let you go alone."

"Thanks, Marcos. I think we can make it. They wouldn't be on the main road."

"And the *vaqueros?*"

"I'm sending them back with the stage. They work and fight for T-Y Lines and Tres Flechas. I can't ask them to do this for the Army."

"Atticus?"

"He'll go with us, I'm sure."

"And Loren?"

"I'll put it to him, but I hope he'll go back to Tucson."

"Don't ask him, *amigo*. Tell him. Laurie has already had two losses too many in her life."

Sam studied him with a slow grin. "You really love her that much, don't you, Marcos?"

"So much that I want to spare her more pain."

"Then—good luck with her, *amigo*. I'll talk to Loren."

But Loren, which surprised neither Sam nor Marcos too much, elected to ride west to Fort Bandolier with them.

The order to the stages given, Sam, Marcos, Atticus and Loren rode westward.

It was, as Sam told Max later, a nervous trip. They rode somewhat apart from each other in order not to give the Apaches, should any be lying in ambush, a bunched target, rifles held ready for instant use across their laps.

At Malhado, they stopped to rest, eat, care for their horses and sleep for four hours. The relay-station people, alerted by the eastbound stage, wore revolvers and carried rifles as they went about their duties. They had no word whatever about Apaches on the move.

Early next morning, they rode through the treacherous pass, eyes scanning the rims above them, and were relieved when they finally broke out into the flatlands on the west side. Careful not to overtax their mounts, they rode steadily, warily, allowing the animals to set their own pace. In mid-afternoon, after a brief rest, they continued on. Once, in the distance to the north of the road, they spotted an Apache lookout, who disappeared behind a hill at once. During the last few miles, they applied pressure to their horses and reached the Fort at sunset, just as the colors were being lowered.

Colonel Hatfield and Major Boyden received the news with cold calm. Somewhere along the way, their Tucson courier had been intercepted and was presumed to be dead. However, there was some satisfaction that by now the two stages should be in Tucson and the word passed on to the Governor and Fort Lowell. How long it would take to get a relief column started on their way was a matter that lay between red tape and conjecture.

"But," Colonel Hatfield added, "I appreciate what you four men have done. It is an act of—oh, hell, Sam, thank you." To Boyden and Greene, "Kane, Marc, see that these men are fed and quartered and turn them loose under Mr. Palmer's care."

The reception of the men of the Fort toward Palmer came as no surprise to him, but he watched with delight as they greeted Atticus warmly as a comrade in arms, including Marcos and Loren in their hospitable welcome. Any addition of rifles, no matter how few, was like a gift from the gods.

In Riley's quarters, Sam had the complete story capsulized for him. "You come in at the right time, Sam. Colonel's about to start movin' things aroun' an' try to suck Bokhari in before his other boys c'n meet up with him."

"Where is he now?"

"North of here, as best we know, up in the Saucedas."

"That's a lot better than having them loose in Monte de Lágrimas. What's the plan?"

"Come mornin', Major Boyden an' Captain Ahearn—"

In the morning, the Fort awoke for reveille roll call and breakfast as usual. Colors formation was held, the old guard relieved. At eight o'clock, the first patrol, Captain Ahearn and Lieutenant Vickery at its head, rode out heading in an easterly direction. At eight-twenty, Major Boyden and Lieutenant Carpenter led the second patrol out, heading westward.

Sam, Marcos, Atticus and Loren went up on the ramparts to add four pairs of eyes to the many that looked out from every point of the compass. Below them, they could see the preparations for the expected attack; sentries on rooftops, water barrels, internal barricades, the howitzer crew going through their loading and firing dry runs under Lieutenant Benjamin's critical eyes. Sandwiches and coffee were passed up to the men manning the walls, and off-duty men sat on their barracks porches running ramrods and cleaning rags through the muzzles of their rifles, crossed bandoliers of ammunition weighing heavily on their shoulders. Others were sharpening bayo-

413

nets and hunting knives while several practiced knife-throwing at targets nailed to the walls.

The Fort, Sam concluded, was as ready as it would ever be.

The question remained, For what?

In a grassy valley in the foothills of the Saucedas, they waited with growing impatience. Late yesterday, a watcher had come in with word that four men, not soldiers, had ridden toward the Fort from the east.

Bokhari sent the watcher back to his lookout post with crisp, angry words. It was not the word for which he waited, but news that patrols were leaving the Fort.

Two days ago, an eastbound stage had passed the main road and Vicenzo had pleaded to be allowed to overtake and destroy it. Again, Bokhari became angered and raised his voice to all, shaming Vicenzo for his overeagerness to give their location away for such small reward. Yesterday, several small patrols had left the Fort and the hubbub to move in for the kill had commenced again, and once again Bokhari had grown angry and chastened his braves harshly.

Now they still waited.

Bokhari had no way of knowing that the small bands he had sent out to draw the soldiers from the Fort were meeting with some little success and greater failures. Several ranches had been burned out, but not before the Apaches had taken serious losses. At Mesa Plata, which they had expected to find unprepared, thirty Apaches came riding in swiftly at first light, only to be welcomed by a veritable army of miners, ranchers and a few soldiers who were hidden between buildings and fired from many rooftops. In the heavy exchange that followed, the Apaches were driven off. Trying again, they suffered more losses, and no matter from which point they tried to attack, the White Eyes were waiting for them. In trying to move east again to rejoin Bokhari, they were cut off in that direction by another force of miners and ranchers and were, at this moment, being chased southward toward the Mexican border, their force cut almost in half with casualties.

When the sun had risen to the halfway mark to noon, which would be nine o'clock by the white man's reckoning, the word came. A patrol of fifty men, riding eastward, had left the Fort. A half hour later, a second rider streaked in to report a patrol of about forty men was riding to the west.

Ninety men. Almost half the known strength of the Fort.

The time had come.

Bokhari raised his arm in the signal for all to assemble. "Listen, brothers, and hear me well. Today is our day of victory and the hour is at hand. We are greater in numbers, we are stronger in heart. Each of you knows how important is his task. Say to yourselves, 'The Great One watches and sees me. He knows that our cause is just and right. He knows we will destroy the Fort and every White Eyes in it before night falls.'

"We go into our first major battle together as brothers. Let each of us return with honor."

He turned and a path was made for him to ride through the circle, and as he rode slowly to lead them, he could see and feel their strength, eagerness and grim determination. It was a day they had long awaited; and he knew that his entire life of work and study had been aimed like a flying arrow toward this one day of all days.

He broke through the circle, raised his rifle in his left hand and heeled his horse into a gallop. Behind him, the braves formed up into an irregular column and spurred their horses forward.

Today the Fort would die.

"Here they come!"

On the ramparts facing the north, a nervous finger squeezed a trigger and the first shot shattered the quiet.

"Hold your fire, you knucklehead!" Riley's voice boomed out from below.

The Fort moved into action.

Men poured off the barracks porches and out of their quarters. Officers leaped to their battle stations and the Mexican civilians scurried into their quarters and other buildings to safety. From the sutler's store, its windows boarded up, Fred Wheeler emerged with rifle and revolver, his coat pockets sagging with extra ammunition.

Colonel Hatfield mounted the north steps carrying a pair of service binoculars. Captain Greene, a rifle gripped in his hands, was hard on his heels. Lieutenant Mason-Field, also with binoculars, was on the wall over the Main Gate, looking toward the east, where Ahearn's patrol had ridden earlier, then west, where Major Boyden had taken his decoy patrol.

"Hold your fire!"

The word was passed as every man on the walls, crowded now with others who had come on the run at the first word, faced northward from whence the first shout had come.

Hatfield, binoculars to his eyes, saw only a huge cloud of rising dust in the distance. Feeling no stirring of air, he knew, as the first man had surmised, that this was dust being raised by the hooves of many horses. As yet, no sounds reached them. Beside him, he felt the restlessness of the men, heard their words of self-assurance mingled with prayers and curses.

"Steady there."

He spoke calmly, coldly, and the murmuring dropped off, but eyes were riveted on the cloud lying close to the ground, coming closer, like an ocean wave rolling into a shore. Thus far, no human or animal form was discernible.

Then, as if by an act of nature, the wave parted in its center and moved to right and left, forming two half circles as though they would envelop the Fort from east and west.

"They'll come in from both sides and ride in two circles, clockwise and counter-clockwise," Sam Palmer said to Marcos.

Marcos, his rifle still at his side, looked on with an expression of contempt. "They are fools to think they can take a Fort like this from the open."

"Fools? Marcos, they've been fighting that way since the beginning of time, and they're still around. A lot of Spaniards who thought the Apaches were stupid primitive fighters aren't here any more."

Marcos raised his rifle and rested its barrel in the notch between two log uprights. "When?" he asked.

"Not until the colonel gives the word."

"And when he does?"

"It's every man for himself. Watch for Ahearn and Boyden to come back. The Apaches'll be forced to come in closer to us for a while. That's when we'll really go to work."

"Well, *amigo,* good hunting."

"Buena fortuna, amigo."

"And to you, my brother." It was said soberly and with meaning and Palmer knew for certain now the depth of feeling that lay between them. He gripped Marcos' shoulder with one hand, then moved off toward where Loren and Atticus stood side by side. Loren turned and Sam was astonished by the radiance in his eyes; his complete and total absorption in the task ahead. The look, he thought, of a killer who enjoys his work.

"Take it easy, Loren."

"I'll be all right." Loren's voice was a rasping whisper. "Keep your head behind a post except when you're firing."

"I know how to do it. Don't worry about me."

"You're tense. Loosen up."

"I know—"

"This is different. It's not one for one. There's close to two hundred of them coming at less than a hundred of us. It can come to you from any angle."

"I know," Loren repeated like an automaton. "Don't worry about me."

Atticus said, "I'll keep an eye on him."

Loren turned toward Atticus in a cold rage. "I don't need you or anybody else to look out for me. I'm a man and I'll look out for myself, you hear."

Atticus turned away without replying. Sam walked away, saddened by Loren's reaction to the kindest of all motives.

Then they began to appear as individuals, as men with faces, contorted with rage, howling defiantly, rifles held forward at arm's length, coming from two directions simultaneously. As they came within range, they began firing erratically. And still no reply from the Fort, which seemed to enrage the Apaches even more. Bullets thudded into the log walls and whistled overhead. In long single lines, they continued in two wide circles around the Fort, then the inner, clockwise circle moved in closer, forcing the outer circle closer to the Fort.

Colonel Hatfield turned and gave the order.

"Fire at will!"

In every direction outside the Fort, Apaches fell from their horses. The near circle moved back and poured intense fire toward the ramparts. Here and there, men fell and other men carried the wounded below where Captain Breed and his medical aides separated the wounded from the dead and began to give first aid.

From the outer circle of Apaches came a hail of arrows, and once having found the range, these were followed by flaming arrows that *tunk*-ed into the dry logs that formed the wall. Others flew overhead and buried themselves into wooden roofs and building walls. From the ramparts, men dipped buckets into water barrels and tried to douse the flames, and some were killed in the act by rifle bullets. On the roof of the mess hall and headquarters building men threw water and dragged wet blankets over the flames and were more successful.

Below on the ground, riflemen aimed and fired their weapons through the holes that had been bored into the logs, but were restricted because they could not lead their targets and only fire straight ahead as a target passed by.

Loren Olmstead was in his moment of high glory. He had four sure hits to his credit and the right side of his face was bleeding from a wooden splinter chipped from the upright next to him and of which, in his excitement, he was unaware, leading his next target, cursing when he missed, exulting when he hit.

"Five," he counted to himself.

Marcos, standing beside Sam Palmer, was silent and cool. About four feet below them, the outer logs were aflame. Other fires had started in various parts of the wall and were burning freely, throwing up clouds of blinding smoke. Around the platform lay more dead and wounded awaiting the overworked medical aides.

Suddenly, the Apaches withdrew out of range and the "Cease fire!" order was given.

"Captain Greene!"

"Yes, sir!"

"Get me an accurate count of dead and wounded. Get some hot coffee to the men up here. And start the water details moving. Use extra men from below."

"Yes, sir."

Lieutenant Benjamin's howitzer team, commandeered for extra water details, mounted the stairs to the ramparts and were greeted by hoots and catcalls.

"Hey, water boy!"

"Drinks over here, boy!"

"Hey! Bring some over here an' lemme soak my feet!"

The replies they received in return were cordial and hostile obscenities, enjoyed by all within hearing. Below, the less seriously wounded were patched up and returned to duty; the more serious cases lined up outside the surgery awaiting attention from Captain Breed, the dead covered with blankets.

Greene came back with his report for Hatfield, who accepted the count and a cup of hot coffee.

"Any sign of Captain Ahearn or Major Boyden, sir?" Greene asked needlessly.

Hatfield pulled out his gold watch and checked the time. "Another half hour, give or take a few minutes," he replied.

Now they came in again. Two waves. The first, a smaller group, drove in hard to the base of the wall while the second poured intense fire up at the defenders who were hanging over the rim trying to get to the Apaches directly below them. At the base, fires were being set. In protecting the arsonists while they placed burning brush at the base of the outer walls, the outer ring of Apaches were forced to stand still in order to produce an accurate curtain of covering fire, thus becoming targets themselves, sustaining heavier losses than those they inflicted. Yet, they stood their ground heroically and returned volley for volley.

Inside the Fort, flames in some sections began to burn through from the outside. Water became the most precious commodity as barrel after barrel was rushed to each critical area to prevent gaps from opening into the wall. Twelve feet west of the Main Gate, flames broke through and raced upward toward the platform. At once, four teams of two men each rushed in behind one another and four barrels of water were flung into the flames. The fire was put out, leaving an open gap through which a man could enter.

An Apache leaped through the hole and was instantly killed by a shot from Sergeant Petrie's revolver. Another came through, shot by Lieutenant Lynch. A third leaped in and shot Lynch and was in turn killed by a water tender's bayonet. Four more Apaches raced through the hole, fell flat on the ground and shot three soldiers before they were themselves shot, stabbed and clubbed to death.

From outside, there came a signal hooting and the attack was broken off again. On the platform above the Main Gate, Colonel Hatfield, damp with sweat, yet outwardly cool, checked the time again. He looked up into Captain Greene's solemn face.

"Six minutes to go, Marc," he said.

"We're hurting, Colonel," Greene replied.

"There's never been a battle without bleeding, hurting and dying. Look out there."

On the desert floor lay the Apache dead. Not all, Hatfield knew, were dead. There were wounded among them, trying their stoical utmost to remain still and be counted for dead by the White Eyes enemy. Each knew that he would be left where he had fallen and only when a battle was won could he expect to be carried off to have his wounds treated. If the battle were lost, he could count himself lost as well.

Again, the Apaches had drawn back out of range. They dismounted and squatted on the ground, eyes on the symbol of their hatred. The Fort. Cochise had sent word that the Fort must die. The word *must* was the key in the message. Interpreted, it meant, *the Fort must die or you must die in the effort.*

This was the battle they had asked for, pleaded and argued for. This was their day of glory. The gods had smiled upon them by sending two strong patrols away from the Fort this very morning. Let the White Eyes behind the wall believe they could stand off a superior force of braves, but before the day was over, they would be inside and the Fort would lie in ruins and the cowards forced to fight in the open. Then—then their sworn promise to the Great One would be fulfilled.

Bokhari, astride his white pony, signaled Vicenzo to his side.

"This time, brother, open a gap in the rear of the Fort in the same way. Their strength is failing. We will keep them busy on this side so they must divide their forces. Six braves to place the fire, the others to fire at the White Eyes overhead."

"*Enju.*"

The six chosen began to gather bundles of dry brush while sixty more formed up behind them. The signal given, a burning brand was passed from man to man and the brush ignited. Now, the run for the rear of the Fort. With sixty rifles firing overhead to give them cover. Suddenly, the six turned off, three to the right, three to the left, each trio followed by thirty braves.

On the ramparts the word was passed quickly. "The back! They're heading around to the back!"

Atticus Perry followed the sound of the calls, running along the platform, leaping over men who were resting, wounded or dead. On his heels was Loren Olmstead, unwilling to miss a moment of the action. When they reached the rear wall, the six Apaches were already at the base,

420

setting their fire. The dried logs caught almost at once and the flames of the six bunches of burning brush leaped toward one another, licking upward. Water tenders carried their barrels to the spot and dumped them over the sides, but the water missed by several feet.

Two of the water bearers were hit, one wounded, the other killed. Perry leaned over the wall and shot one of the six as he remounted to ride off. Loren caught a second, then a third. Others shot the other three off their horses while still others sighted in on the Apaches who were stationary targets and had been furnishing the covering fire. The troopers continued a sporadic return fire, taking casualties as they sighted between the uprights.

The supply of water in the central storage tank was gone. Water from the two wells was now being drawn up in single buckets, a slow and tedious process, while the water bearers waited impatiently for their empty barrels to be filled. Along the back walls, flames had broken through the old sun-dried logs where a group of troopers slapped at the roaring blaze with wetted blankets. From the outside, Apaches were using lances to punch holes through the weakened area, then began firing into the opening.

Trumpeter Galt, acting as lookout on the east side of the wall, came running toward Colonel Hatfield, binoculars dangling from their neck loop. "Sir," he announced, "I think I see them. Captain Ahearn's troop, about four miles away."

"Get back to your post. When they are within five hundred yards, sound the charge."

"Yes, sir!"

"Captain Greene!"

"Yes, sir!"

"Check the lookout on the west side for any sighting of Major Boyden's troop."

"Yes, sir!"

At that moment, Lieutenant Frank Tennant came on the run from that direction. "Colonel, Major Boyden's troop approaching from the west. About five or six miles."

"Good. Pass the word. When both troops approach within one hundred yards of us, cease firing except at sure, isolated targets. Sergeant Major!"

"Yes, sir!"

"Do you have a count of our able-bodied men?"

"Yes, sir. Fifty-one, sir, plus the four civilians from Tucson. Twenty-six dead and wounded, sir."

"Pick the best twenty-five marksmen among them to remain on the ramparts and keep an eye on those two entry holes. I want the other thirty to mount up. Have two men stand by the gates."

"Yes, sir!"

As he ran down the steps to the ground level, the men Riley chose to follow him were close on his heels, heading for the corral where their saddled horses waited nervously. Without being asked or told, Atticus had joined them.

On the ramparts, Sam Palmer turned when Marcos tugged at his sleeve. "We ride, *amigo?*"

"No, Marcos. We can do more good up here. Let's stay and improve our shooting practice. Where is Loren?"

"Look below. The corral. He is there, beside Atticus." Loren was mounting a horse, milling around with the others, waiting for Colonel Hatfield, who was standing beside the howitzer crew talking with Lieutenant Benjamin. Lieutenant Zimmerman, already mounted, led Hatfield's horse out to him. The colonel mounted and took a position about twenty yards behind the howitzer.

"Lieutenant Zimmerman, have the troopers form up behind me."

"Yes, sir." He wheeled toward the corral to give the order.

The Apaches, still standing off and firing rifles and flaming arrows toward the Fort, had obviously seen nothing to indicate danger from an outside source. Being close to the ground, their view obstructed by high-growing saguaro and other winter-blooming cacti, the advantage was with the soldiers on the ramparts, some twenty feet above the ground. Now Bokhari raised his war lance in signal for another attack and his subleaders relayed the word to their braves by a series of shrill cries.

From Post Number One came the warning shout, "They're movin' in!"

Hatfield's voice boomed out the order. "Open the gates and take cover! Howitzer detail! Fire when clear!"

The locking bar across the main gates was raised and thrown to one side. The two massive doors swung inward and the two troopers raced to either side for safety.

"Fire!"

The howitzer belched flame and caught the lead Apaches head-on. For one moment, they were on the verge of entering the gates and at the next, they had virtually disintegrated, horses and braves alike. Behind them, the attackers broke to either side in milling confusion.

There was no longer a target for the howitzer and Hatfield raised his saber and shouted the order. "Forward gallop! *Charge!*"

Up on the ramparts, Trumpeter Galt heard the command, raised his bugle to his lips and blew the Charge.

Out through the gates rode the column of thirty troopers with Hatfield and Zimmerman at its head, driving into the milling Apaches who were retreating to where Bokhari and a group of resting Apaches stood out of rifle range, waiting. Troopers and Apaches commingled, bumped and fell to the ground. Rifles and revolvers exploded at point-blank range as horses reared, neighed and screamed their fear. Men were trampled as they fought on the ground, flattened as horses fell and rolled over on them.

Again, from somewhere behind them in the Fort, they heard the *Charge!* sounded, and then once again. Hardly anyone had taken notice that Captain Ahearn's troop had joined the battle from the east, then the patrol of Major Boyden came upon the scene of turmoil.

The air was foul with acrid gunpowder, churned sand, sweat and blood. From the rampart wall, the scene was a panorama of total confusion, so that all firing had ceased for fear of hitting their own men.

A hundred yards to the south, Bokhari had sent his reserves into the fray and sat with a half dozen aides and message bearers as he watched the battle from astride his white horse, unable to see clearly through the smoke and clouds of dust who was victor and who the victims; but he knew without question that he was the loser in the battle of strategy. He had been taken in by a clever ruse, drawn in when led to believe his strength was far greater than it was.

He looked from side to side at his two aides and four message bearers, then raised his war lance and moved it forward. If there was to be a victory won here, it must be his. If a defeat, he must die in battle here with his own braves.

The Fort must die.
Or you must die in the effort.

The battle raged on in hand-to-hand combat. Here and
423

there an Apache would pound his way out of the arena, a bluecoat on his heels. A trooper wheeled and tried to make it back to the safety of the Fort and was cut down from behind. Apaches and troopers fell from their horses and became locked in battle afoot. Rifles became clubs, and hunting knives, to some, were the preferred weapon. Riley shot a brave from his horse and was clubbed from his own by a rifle butt. Kneeling, he drew his revolver and began firing while praying that he not be trampled to death by a horse. A trooper rose before him, knife in bloodied hand, screaming, "I'll kill every goddamned son-ofabitchin' Apache in Arizona—" and fell dead across his victim's body in his own agonizing death.

At the entrance to the Fort gates, Lieutenant Russell Isaacs, who was O.D., turned inside and shouted, "Form up on me, everybody! It's a ground battle! Let's move out!"

The riflemen came down the rampart steps, clerks, ordnance and quartermaster men, all huddling around the lieutenant. Marcos and Sam were among them. Captain Greene joined them, shouting, "Let's get out there and put an end to it!"

And so all but the medical officer, Captain Breed, and his small corps of medical aides, ran toward the struggle across two hundred yards of loose sand and the desert garden of tangled cactus and brush, passing the dead and dying men and animals to reach those locked in a struggle for the ultimate survival.

"Keep an eye out for Loren," Palmer shouted to Marcos, but Marcos was too intent on his purpose to hear the words across the ten yards of space that separated them. Within another ninety seconds, he was too involved to think of anything but keeping alive.

And, finally, it was over.

All but the burials and prayers.

Some thirty Apaches straggled southward in retreat and escape. A party of troopers began to mount up to give chase, but were called back by Trumpeter Galt's bugle on orders from Colonel Hatfield.

Captain Ahearn was dead. Lieutenant Vickery was so badly wounded it was unlikely he would live to reach the Fort. Sergeant Art Petrie was dead. And more. Bokhari had fallen, but Vicenzo had escaped and would no doubt return some day at the head of another band determined to kill the Fort. Private Cleary, Corporal Hudson, Private Salton were dead. And still more.

The troopers began carrying their own wounded, assisting the walking casualties back to the Fort. Mounted troopers rode afield to bring in the riderless horses of both sides, herding them toward the Fort. A detail was set to gather up all rifles and ammunition that lay strewn over the area. Canteens. Other gear. Three of the Fort's flatbed wagons came out to help with the wounded. Later, the dead would be gathered, graves dug, services read for them as they were buried; but for now, the time was for the living.

Palmer caught a horse and began riding around the arena of battle, guiding his mount carefully between the dead troopers and Apaches. Marcos saw him, but remained on foot, checking the bodies. Atticus, holding a bleeding arm, followed Marcos. Sam rode out toward them, dismounted and cut a strip from a dead man's shirt to bind Atticus' arm.

"You have seen him, Sam?" Marcos asked.

"Yes. He's dead."

"Ah," Marcos sighed. "Poor Laurie." Then, "He was a *gitano* at heart, but he should never have learned to handle a gun."

Marcos walked out in the direction Sam Palmer pointed. He came upon Loren's body, lying face up, staring into the sun without seeing. Marcos bent over and lifted him, thinking, he is no heavier than a girl.

And so, as he had lived during this brief and violent period of his young life, Loren Olmstead died.

They brought Loren back to Tucson on the next T-Y freight wagon that came through from Yuma two days later. On the same wagon was another coffin containing the bodies of Ruth and Sam Palmer, Jr. An Army courier who had been sent to Tucson to report the results of the battle to Governor Mitchell and General Litchfield, later rode into the T-Y Depot to bring the news of Loren's death to Max Potter. He saddled up at once and rode west to meet the train at Celeste.

"Have you told Laurie and Caroline?" Sam asked.

"They know. They're together at the hotel."

"How is she holding up?"

Max shrugged. "Not too well at first, but she'll come through this the way she came through the other."

425

For a while they rode in silence together, then Sam said, "Max, I brought Ruth and little Sam in with us."

"I'm glad, Sam. I'll feel better knowing she's home again."

"I want a wagon to take them to Tres Flechas as soon as we get in. I don't want Caro and Laurie riding behind them all the way to Tres Flechas."

"Sure, Sam. We'll start them for home tonight. We'll ride down with the girls tomorrow. The four of us."

"Five, Max. I'll want Marcos to go along. He can help make it easier for Laurie."

In Tucson, they were stopped all along the way by people who wanted to hear about the battle at Fort Bandolier, but Max brushed them aside. "Courier's got the report for the governor an' General Litchfield. It'll be in the *Star* tomorrow, better'n we can tell it."

"What happened to the relief column from Fort Lowell?" someone called out.

"It got there a day late," Sam replied. "They're staying on to help clean things up. Let us through, please."

And at the Congress Hotel, Caroline and Laurie waited to hear the news from Sam's lips. Laurie, tearful and pale, listened to the bare details, then said, "Poor Loren. It had to happen. I had that awful feeling it would happen. Where is he now, Sam?"

"On his way to Tres Flechas with Ruth and our son."

As he said it, he looked at Caroline and saw in her the same compassion he felt in himself for Laurie. "If you're both up to it, we'll ride down together tomorrow. The four of us and Marcos."

"Where is Marcos?" Laurie asked. "Why didn't he come with you?"

"He's taken Atticus to the doctor, then he's going to see his mother. After that, he'll come back here."

At Espuela de Oro, Marcos sat at the table in Inez's room, a meal before him that he had little taste for. Inez sat opposite him, pouring a glass of tequila.

"And now, Marcos? Who do you kill next before you are brought home to me to bury?"

"Mama," Marcos said, "a pretty woman should not carry ugly thoughts such as those in her head."

"Always, you find a way not to answer a question."

"And always, you ask questions I have no answers for."

"Where do you go now?"

"I need to see a man."

"What man?"

"Martin Van Allen."

"Why?"

"To tell him that if he does not stop selling guns to the Indios, if he and that *culebra*, the Indian Agent Rodman, do not stop poisoning the Apaches—"

But Inez was shaking her head from side to side. "Your Señor Potter did not tell you?"

"What?"

"You are too late, Marcos."

"Someone has already killed them?"

"Always you think in those Anglo terms. No. When Vega and Moreno were arrested, they talked to the Anglo marshal, then were taken to the governor and two Army generals. Martin was ordered to leave Arizona and never return. The agent Rodman is under arrest in the Fort Lowell prison and will be sent to Washington for trial."

"Then, Mama, I can answer your question about where I go next and what I will do. In the morning, I ride to Tres Flechas to attend the funeral of the wife and son of my friend Sam Palmer. Also, the funeral of the brother of the girl I will marry when this new sadness has left her."

"I have heard of this girl. You will bring her to see me?"

"No, Mama. Not as long as you are *la patrona* of Espuela de Oro."

"Ah, I am saddened."

"Then sell it, Mama. You have money. You will have more when you sell this place. Buy a house and live like a lady who has a businessman son and a fine lady for a daughter-in-law, a *nuera*."

"Marcos—"

"Sell it, Mama."

"I will. Marcos—"

"What?"

"I have a letter for you. From your papa. He left it with me to give to you."

"I need no letters from him."

"In it, he gives you his *rancho*. It says he won it in a poker game many years before you were born and therefore, it is an honest *legado*, you understand?"

"A legacy, yes."

"You will take it?"

He hesitated for a few moments, then said, "If my wife wants it, yes."

"Por qué, niño? Among Anglos, a man brings a dowry to his wife?"

"Mama, she brings me a dowry far greater than any I can bring her. She brings me a purpose for living, the first time in my life I have had this. She brings me love—"

Inez smiled. "It is more than a fair exchange. *Vaya con Dios, hijo.* When you are married, I will sell the *cantina* and not dishonor you. I will wish to play with my *nietos.*"

"You will have grandchildren to play with, Mama. This I promise you."

CHAPTER III

THE SERVICES WERE HELD IN THE FILLED CHAPEL, THEN the two caskets, one with mother and infant son, the newer one containing the body of Loren Olmstead, were carried in solemn procession to the Tres Flechas cemetery. One grave had been opened beside that of Doña Ysabel, a second beside that of Libby and Aaron Olmstead. The graveside services were said by Father Paz and then it was over.

Sam walked back to the main house behind Max and Caroline, while Laurie and Marcos remained in the tree-shaded cemetery. The *vaqueros* and their families returned to their *casas* and those who had only necessary duties to perform went quietly about their work.

When Max and Caroline entered the house, Sam paused on the porch, removed his hat and sat in a rocking chair looking out on the compound. All was quiet in the on-coming dusk. Even the animals, somehow sensing the solemnity of the day, were still. At this moment, no one feared an attack, yet a dozen *vaqueros* had mounted the platform on the wall and stood looking out over pasture land and the mountains that formed a cathedral-like background. It was difficult to believe that such peace and serenity could exist in a land that had seen so much brutal violence, and would very likely see more in the future.

"Sam—"

He looked toward the doorway and saw Caroline, still wearing the dress she had put on for the funeral. He started to rise, but she came toward him quickly and said, "Do you mind if I sit here with you?"

"Mind? No, of course not. I'd like it very much." He stood then and pulled the other rocker closer to his and she sat in it.

"These two rockers," she said, "came from my grandfather's home in Sonora, given to my mother because she was the eldest daughter. They were handmade to last a thousand years, Papa used to tell us. He said that when you and Ruth came back here to live, he would give them to her, to be handed down to her eldest daughter."

"They'll belong to you now, Caro," Sam said.

"Yes, I suppose so. Will you be going back to Tucson right away?"

"In the morning, I'd guess. We've still got a business to look after up there. As soon as they all get in, we've got the Fort families to transport, tons of freight piling up, the mail to carry."

"I know. I told Papa I want to go back when you and he do. If he's going to spend so much time there, I want him to build a house in Tucson where we can live decently."

"It's a rough town, Caro."

"It won't always be. Don't say no, Sam. Laurie will be moving to Tucson, too."

Sam smiled. "I guess it's all settled with her and Marcos."

"Yes. She told me last night."

"You've changed your mind about Marcos?"

"I've changed my mind about a lot of things. I've been so wrong—"

"About me, too?"

"About that, too. I've been so shortsighted about almost everything. It took Laurie and Bokhari to make me realize that people have to live with what they are, with how things are, not how they would like them to be. I've been living on Tres Flechas all my life, too far removed from reality."

"Caro, you've become a very wise woman in a short time."

"I don't know about that, only how I feel about life and people now. I feel closer to everyone than I've ever felt before."

"You've never been that far apart from anyone, Caro. It was only a matter of time before you learned that for yourself."

"I felt so far apart from you."

"You weren't, no matter what you felt."

"Do you—do you think it was because we were really so close, and not apart at all?"

He smiled slowly. "We've never been apart, Caro, not from the start."

"Is it because I remind you of Ruth?"

He turned toward her, reached over and took her hand

430

into his own. "In some ways, Caro, yes, and I wouldn't want that to stop, but I see you now as your own woman, with everything any man could ever want."

"A man like Sam Palmer?"

"Particularly a man like Sam Palmer. Caro, there's no Ruth except deep in our fond memories of her. If she could see and know, I'm sure she would want us to be together."

"I think she would, too."

He pressed her hand tighter. "We'll wait a while, Caro, then I'll talk it over with Max."

Caroline smiled and said, "I think I can give you his answer right now."

THE EXPLOSIVE NEW BLOCKBUSTER BY
THE AUTHOR OF FLETCH AND
CONFESS FLETCH

FLYNN

He's a tough-talking Boston cop, a family man whose daughter
just got a ruby pin from a guy named Fletch, and whose son
was just fleeced of a violin.

FLYNN

And there they are, talking about rubies and violins when a
plane explodes overhead. Burning bodies fall out of the sky—
118 of them!

FLYNN

Aboard the plane were a Federal judge, a British actor, a mid-
dleweight champ, an Arab potentate—and, wouldn't you know
it, a case for the formidable Flynn.

FLYNN

"Flynn is one of the smartest, gentlest, most sarcastic cops
you'll ever meet."
The New York Times

FLYNN

BY GREGORY MCDONALD
TWICE WINNER OF THE
EDGAR AWARD FOR MYSTERY

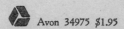 Avon 34975 $1.95